Degree of Normal

A Woman's Journey Out of Childhood Abuse

By

Barbara Harken

Robert D. Reed Publishers • Bandon, Oregon

Robert D. Reed Publishers
P.O. Box 1992
Bandon, OR 97411
Phone: 541-347-9882; Fax: -9883
E-mail: 4bobreed@msn.com
Website: www.rdrpublishers.com

Editor: Cleone Reed
Cover Designer: Cleone Reed
Zentangle Art by Cleone Reed © 2016
Book Designer: Susan Leonard

Soft-cover ISBN: 978-1-944297-10-7
eBook ISBN: 978-1-944297-11-4

Library of Congress Control Number: 2016958148

Designed and Formatted in the United States of America

This book is for my husband Bob
who has learned to be my safe place,
and for all of you out there who are
still searching for yours.

ACKNOWLEDGMENTS

A few years ago, my son Rob suggested that I write my manifesto. Only lately have I approached a topic that has dominated my life—surviving childhood trauma. So this book is my platform. Thanks, Rob, for the idea.

Of course, setting said manifesto as a goal is one thing, writing it quite another. Here is where I have to thank my cousin Paula for her hard work and insight. I could never have done this without her.

Here is what she has to say to you readers:

> "While this is a work of fiction, Barb and I worked hard to incorporate a realistic and truthful depiction of what dissociative identity disorder and PTSD is like from the point of view of the survivor. Situations for individual survivors of childhood trauma may differ, but the emotions and the internal "discussions" in the story are consistent for those of us with DID. As you might assess from following the character of Paula, the journey begins only when the grueling, continuous path of masking the pain becomes more burdensome than facing the agony of healing."
>
> ~ The "Real" Paula

And from the "Real" Deb:

> "For those with intense and long and prolonged trauma as a child, they may develop dissociative identity disorder which serves them well during the trauma but becomes ineffective as an adult.
> May all survivors find their own voice, their strength, and their pathway to healing."

And finally, thanks to Marcia, Vi, Elaine, Karen, Lisa and Julie—the team.

CHAPTER 1

Late August...

D amn, it was hot. Not even noon yet, 92 degrees and counting. Alex Stumme raised his arm and took a quick sniff. Ripe. Bad ripe. The kind that left his boxers limp and moldering—not to mention his balls. Right now they felt like a cheese grater was scrapping away. Thank you, Chicago. Its weather never failed to lash out with one last try at frying its citizens just as the school year was about to start.

Alex stepped into the campus Starbucks to dry out his body as much as drink an iced coffee before he headed to the campus bookstore. While he stood in line for a house special, he scoped out the place. A couple of professor types at the closest table were drinking tea and eating scones. Several students chomped on goodies and the best in summer gossip, lolling at the mid tables in the full splendor of their own coolness, their legs wrapped around their chairs, arms folded across their chests or supporting their heads at the edge. As if on cue, they let titters of laughter erupt to let the world know their status. Of course, the world dared not intervene in their glory; just observe.

But then there was that one customer. The one sitting near the window. She was sitting all by herself, caught up in her own universe, drawing on a sketch pad, every now and then lifting her pen to stab at little lines in the air before she went back to the project. *Cute girl, looks quirky, bet she has some feist in her.* Not like the rest of the girls on campus who either wanted to get laid by some steroid-spouting jock or pair up with a sugar daddy. He watched the artist, index finger and thumb pressed on that pen, the whole world of Starbucks floating by while she worked the air. This was someone he needed to meet.

7

Coffee in hand, he approached her just as she stabbed out another air pattern, her pursed lips making popping noises while she wacked away at nothing.

"Art major or a procrastinator who likes to doodle," he said, setting his cup down on her table and leaning in.

She'd looked up at him, frowned, and answered, "Concerned citizen or stalker between victims?" She held her pen against the tip of her chin. Nice brown eyes. Too bad right now they were less than friendly.

Alex held up his hands in surrender. "Neither. Just a guy back on campus for another year, trying to be friendly."

She tapped the pen against her chin, once, twice. "Okay, I'll bite. I don't have a real major and this isn't doodling. It's zentangle. Sit down before you fall over."

He obeyed, lucky guy. "Zentangle?"

"Yeah, I know, sounds like hippies at an orgy."

"So the stabbing in the air, that a social thing?"

"Nope, this is all about patterns. I'm kind of obsessed with patterns. Need them to coordinate my life. Make things clear. Stabbing the air grounds me."

Alex reached out his hand. "Mind if I take a look?"

When she pushed her sketch pad over to him, he was pretty much stunned. The page was filled with zombies' faces, their decay scrawls of fine lines and squiggles, flowering flourishes and circles, every one black and tiny, a technique that might be on an M C Escher sketch but here added up to irrefutable gore.

"You doodle zombies?"

"Zentangle."

"Whatever. This is awesome." He studied the work, turning it left and right to check out the flow. "Why zombies?"

"Why not? *Dead* is the only show that's real. Buddy, the Apocalypse is now. *The Bachelor,* maybe *Celebrity Wife Swap* might be in the running for a picture of what we've become; but nobody's decomposed enough, shuffling through life looking for a tasty bite. Hands down, *Walking Dead* mimics reality. I'm just an artist historian keeping track."

A girl who stabs at forms in the air for clarification. One who sees *Walking Dead* as a reality show. She was his kind of girl.

He held out his hand. "Alex Stumme, professed non-stalker and fellow Walkers fan."

Leaning back, the girl looked at him, popped her pen against the table twice before she laughed and said, "Jocelyn Quint. Nice to meet you, but I never shake hands on the first meeting."

"Works for me. So what's your favorite episode?"

"Any one except for when Sophia dies."

"Yeah, that was a tough one, even for a steel-pated guy like me."

Jocelyn pursed her lips while she looked at him and shook her head. "No problem with the kid. She was toast the minute she separated from the group.

Alex leaned in. "So. . ."

"The mother. Carol. Way too much flipping out. You gotta know when to let go. Gotta be ready for that great chicken in the sky to float over you and decide to dump. Otherwise, there's an awful lot of shit with your name on it."

Sitting back in his chair, Alex took in the statement. This girl was definitely not typical. Good looking, you bet. Typical? Not on a dime.

This was a girl worth his time.

CHAPTER 2

A few weeks later. . .

Jocelyn Quint stood in the Starwarski Funeral Home looking down at
her mother's coffin. Evelyn Quint had been laid out in full display at the
front of the visitation room, heavy satin curtains draping the wall behind
the coffin, soft lighting surrounding the departed in a shroud of honor.
Even in death, her mother worked the crowd, looking like Sleeping Beauty
lying there waiting for her prince—the one who would never come, the one
who did not even exist.

The guests had left, all twelve of them. Fellow waitresses, her boss,
one lady who tearfully related how she had tried to persuade poor Evelyn
to come to Jesus. These few strangers—customers perhaps—had simply
shaken Jocelyn's hand and left. In the lobby, Virgil and Steve Starwarski
waited to escort Jocelyn to the limo for their trek to the cemetery, a funeral
parade of one before the cemetery workers swung the vault toward the final
resting place. She felt the grind of her teeth. Only in Chicago, in her life,
would the daughter watch the mother in this final dance. Why didn't they
have the vault in place like everywhere else?

It's Evie, silly. Nothing she did was typical. Even in death.

Jocelyn glanced to the right. Virgil had eyes glued to his watch, his
foot tapping. This was Tuesday, a slow day for the dead. Still, time was
money.

Too bad for Virgil. He was on Jocelyn's dime, one of her few. *Few*
was vastly approaching *nil*. Three days ago, a phone call had dropped
Jocelyn into this scene at Starwarski's. "Jocelyn, this is Harry Mack, your
mother's boss. Evie's had a heart attack. They're working on her now at
Presbyterian Memorial." She had hung up the phone, grabbed her purse,
and hurried out. By the time she made it to the hospital, Evelyn Quint was

no more—just this thin shell of a woman worn by choices and disillusion.

How pathetic Evie had looked in the ER room, head lolling, mouth agape. The Starwarski's might work their magic for the visitation, but standing in the ER, Jocelyn saw her mother as no more than a husk, her face empty and dusty pale. Now she was the same husk, cleaned up a bit, polished and rouged, but nonetheless dead in that coffin, remnant of the maternal nonentity Evelyn Quint had been most of Jocelyn's life—polished and rouged on the outside, dead to the slightest whim of maternal instinct. A daughter should be able to see her mother for who she was. That had never been a problem for Jocelyn. Even now.

A small spasm in her jaw argued with her assessment. She gritted her teeth to will it away, walked toward the side of the chapel as if looking at the drapes were something important. Reaching out, she let a finger trace a worn trail in the cheap velvet.

Time to say those final farewells. Jocelyn drew back her hand, walked to the coffin, and steadied herself against the hardness of it, palms down, fingertips smashed against the cheap satin.

Evie's red hair was stiff. Not much different from her style in life. The mother had been a living testimony to hair spray. Jocelyn studied the embalming job. Grooves around Evie's lips from smoking. Too bad. Guess embalming fluid didn't plump you up after all. White, white skin. *Stay out of the sun, Jocelyn. You'll ruin your face.* Guess that didn't matter any more.

But the gestalt of Evie-in-the-coffin didn't match Jocelyn's memories. Evie the corpse had this tight-lipped smile, as if she had a secret. The lips of Evie the woman, numb from alcohol and remorse, looked like they were melting wax. No secret there. She had been a lush, always looking like an apology waiting to happen.

But Evie-in-the-coffin, dead Evie, even with her eyelids sewed shut, looked upward in knowing.

No one will ever have the impact on you I had. You may think I am gone. Such a silly goose.

The energy of that message snaked its way through Jocelyn. No freakin' way. Her entire body started at the thought. Jocelyn had left the influence of her mother years ago, that weak, pathetic woman. Now the mother had left her for good.

So why did her mother, decked out in embalmed elegance and lying on satin, seem to laugh at her?

Jocelyn left the coffin area and sat in the front row of folding chairs, head forward, hands on her knees. How did this daughter feel about letting her mother go? Was that sense of Evie mockery Jocelyn's own guilt pushing against her? She shook her head in acknowledgment to a moment that no one could anticipate, one that now battled in her mind in this Chicago place that tried to hide death's finality. How did one say goodbye to a mother who made promise after promise and then let those promises float away as afterthoughts not worth the energy to consider? As daughter, Jocelyn had learned to numb herself. Was that what Jocelyn was feeling—a numbness?

No. Numb meant absence of feeling. She had never had feelings that could be absent. Feelings came from attachment. Attachments take time and caring. Evie cared about her men friends. She cared about her bottle. Her daughter? Not so much.

At this exact moment, saying goodbye to Evelyn Quint was like saying goodbye to a cigarette that had burned down. Except that for the cigarette there was at least ash.

While Jocelyn rubbed her palms against the metal of the chairs, she searched through the cubbyholes of her brain like a winged phantom checking out the alleys of a city. Surely there had been mothering—at some time in Jocelyn's childhood. The memories filed past quickly; they had to so that they could not conjure up pain. Evie's endless love of cheap vodka and foul men, the string of live-in boyfriends who came and went. Jocelyn had learned to sleep with a baseball bat. Just in case, her mind had told her. She had learned to do a lot of things. Ply on Goth make-up. Hook on a studded dog collar—caress the razor that tried to slice away her pain.

She leaned back in the chair, head against the backing, and closed her eyes. Start with a happy memory, she told herself. Surely a memorial for a mother demanded a happy memory. There had to be one somewhere. A picture of her birthday at age five shot up—along with Jocelyn's head as she responded to the nudge long forgotten. Birthday candles stuck in a frozen pizza Evie had heated up. They both were laughing at the candles—five of them—wedged in pieces of gum stuck on top of the pepperoni. That was

12

back when Jocelyn had birthdays, the days before the men and the screaming and all what she would not remember. Jocelyn discarded the memory into the litter on the floor of her mind, bent over and rubbed her neck and upper shoulders. What was the point? Her childhood defied definition—lying like dust under pictures of what had been.

Sit up right now, young lady, her mind chided. *She was your mother. This is her funeral. Cry, for God's sake. Don't be petulant.* Automaton that she was, her body obeyed. The fresh posture gathered its own anger. *Petulant.* Fancy word for little bitch.

Jocelyn spit the word out like a well-gnawed chaw. Evie had called her that often enough. They both knew the mother meant something much more crass, but the sound of *petulant* hurling at a knobby-kneed child with matted hair and broken barrettes leveled an adult-level shame.

What would Jocelyn call herself today as she looked back at the years? A character in Jocelyn's favorite book called herself *mean.* Much better than a pussy word like *petulant.* Jocelyn liked the word, let the pressure of it settle on her lip. *Mean* went straight to the bone, nothing fancy there.

Hey world, Jocelyn thought. She had earned her attitude. Five lousy candles in a lousy birthday pizza didn't count for squat. There was one hell of a gap between them and the miracle when she was fifteen and a new kid yet again in a new school, chip firmly embedded on her shoulder. Two teachers had stepped in, helped Jocelyn emancipate herself. Evie was scared of DHS, more scared of them than the dickwad who slapped her around. So she signed off to let Jocelyn live by herself. Mother and daughter saw each other once a week. Evie as a snack rather than a full meal was doable even if most meetings were tear-studded "How could you leave your *mother*?"

Now, thanks to Amber Helm and Marti Butler, Jocelyn was a junior in college supported by scholarship and the fourth year of a waitress job.

And thanks to her mother's weak heart and weaker sense of self-control, Jocelyn was an orphan. What the hell. She had felt like an orphan for years now.

"Goodbye Mom." Simple. What else could she say when her only emotion was a wishing for regret, at least a flitter of grief. She reached into a pocket and pulled out a piece of paper. A coupon. Half-price pizza at Dahl's. She left her chair and walked forward, reached into the coffin, placed the paper in her mother's hands. Go out with a good memory. She could do that much for the woman.

Her mother's hands. They were rock. Cold. She swallowed a shudder and stuffed the coupon in the cave that was her mother's folded hands. The paper edged out between the thumbs and index fingers like a tag at a sale.

Something grabbed in her chest, the kind of small tightening that could promise reaction out of almost nothing. She felt it as it turned into a knot, spread its force upward until it rested in her throat and tugged. Tears begged for a little recognition. But they died like water vapor in a drought.

So much for homage to the dead. Jocelyn gripped the edges of the coffin, her fingernails pitted against the edge.

She turned away. A woman stood in the doorway to the visitation room, probably in her fifties, small, like Jocelyn. The daughter approached the visitor, certainly the last if Vern had his way. Midway to the door, the woman's features came into focus. With each step, Jocelyn realized the woman looked like her. The same brown hair and slender nose, the same full eyes with a slight tilt, the same full mouth that Jocelyn and Evie shared. Her hair, however, was bedraggled by the rain of early November. She had on a well-worn overcoat and clutched her purse against her chest. The woman looked like a waif looking for a home, lost before anyone passed judgment.

Jocelyn put on the smile of a dutiful daughter and walked toward her. As she drew closer, she noticed even more how life showed on the woman's face, crevices around her mouth, gray eyes ridged with shadows. Eyes the same color as her own. "Excuse me," she said. "Did you know my mother?"

The stranger let her purse drop and simply hung onto the handles, her eyes steadfast on the tableau of that which was Evelyn. Then she turned, tilted her head and took in a deep breath while she studied Jocelyn's face. She nodded slightly.

"Yes, I knew Evie Quint. I'm her sister."

Damn you, Evelyn Quint. You *would* have the last word.

Hours later, Jocelyn walked across the parking lot littered with fast-food bags and broken bottles, the only landscaping outside her cheap apartment complex. The day had ended bone cold, the kind of chill that

14

Chicago sucked up from the lake. Inside apartment 2C, she wound up sitting at her kitchen table, a blue light special even for a thrift store, chipped and yellow with age. A daughter freshly orphaned should have been looking at pictures, mother and daughter moments. Too bad Evie never had a camera, not to mention the slightest intent to capture a moment on film. Jocelyn felt the pitch of abandonment. She swatted it away. Silly girl. Someone had to be wanted in the first place in order to feel abandoned.

No pictures for sure. Instead, a pile of post funeral business to dig into. She started at the top, the death certificate, neatly officious, life and death boiled down to fill-in-the-blank on government-issue paper. As Jocelyn focused on a detail, a change came over her face—a look of speculation as if she were seeing truth for the first time even though she had known it all along. Her mother's date of birth. Evie was dead at forty-three. Forty-three. Jocelyn had never paid attention to dates of birth. Her childhood remained in her mind as a series of images lurching along between spaces of forgetfulness. Why remember what couldn't have counted? But here was a family tie staring her in her face. Right here, right now, Jocelyn was twenty-one. She'd have a birthday this winter, turn twenty-two. She would be the same age as Evie, the new mother, come February. She pictured her mother waddling down an unknown Chicago sidewalk, hands pressing against the whale in her belly, alone, no hovering father-to-be by her side.

No way in hell would Jocelyn have a kid at twenty-two, especially a kid she didn't want. And how dumb was her mother? Hadn't she known about birth control?

Asking how dumb was her mother was like asking *why do we need oxygen?* It is what it is. Or in Evie's case—was. Jocelyn set aside the document and turned her attention to the bill for the funeral—$8,789.99 minus a couple of hundred from Social Security. Starwarski Brothers owned her. Her boss had loaned her $700 and promised her overtime. In front of her, a few cards lay on the table. Her new-found aunt had left one with a hundred-dollar bill in it and her business card. $343 from donors. She had $867.42 in her checking account. Tuition was covered for the semester from her scholarship, rent paid. But it was early in the month.

No matter. The pressure—her old enemy—built from deep within her, beat against her skin like the force of waves beating against cliff walls. Only she hadn't the strength of the rocks. Only skin.

15

Jocelyn fingered the funeral bill, slipping her thumb against the edges and longed for her old friend, the releaser. Her fingertips begged. *Please, please, please.* One little paper cut; that's all she needed. Just enough to draw blood. The red would pool quickly, let her embrace the relief. It could flow across her hand until the warmth settled in. Quick pain; then the love.

Or she could slice. Just the thought of the blood flow, the blood catching on the hair of her arms and soaking them, just that thought sent a beautiful pressure through her, that ache that preceded the cutting. She felt the jab and looked down. Her thumb was beating against the edge of the envelope. She dropped it like it was etched in acid.

Standing up, she eyed the sink and headed toward it, put on a pot of coffee for distraction. The drip of the water running over the grounds made her yearn all over again, her arms once again beg for attention. She yanked open a drawer and grabbed a metal nail file, imagined a razor's edge along the surface of the file.

She couldn't cut. Wouldn't. No slices. No squares. No circles. She'd promised those who had reached out. She owed it to her saviors. They would tell her she owed it to herself. Whatever, it was a commitment.

So, she compromised, stood at the counter, feet rooted into the linoleum, file slanted on its side; she ran it on the diagonal across her left arm, pressing in on the hardness of the edge, lapping up the pressure, her breath in and out, the tension in her neck, her shoulders, her gut subsiding. Cutting masturbation. She was one screwed-up orphan.

"Oh Momma, I'm in fear for my life." She sang the words that had come from nowhere. The Styx lyrics made her press harder as she stroked back and forth.

That night she dressed in her trolling clothes and headed for the bar down the street. She'd find some guy who saw her worth as a hottie and tell her she was pretty. If he texted her in the morning, she could delete it. If not—as was usually the case—nothing lost. What else could she expect?

Toward morning, back in her own bed, in her own place, she dreamed of her mother. Evie was in her coffin, sitting straight up, looking at her wayward daughter. "Time's a wasting, child. You're almost twenty-two. Put away the games. Who do you have that loves you? Who's gonna keep you warm at night? I had all sorts of beaus by that age. And one of them was your daddy. Too bad he left because of you." Evie's mouth had turned hard, her teeth brown and sharp. She raised one stone-hard cold arm, looked at her watch.

"Tick tock, little girl. Time's a wasting. So many things to do, memories to gather. Can't ignore what must be. Busy days ahead. Get a move-on.

The corpse mother lay down in the coffin, arms straight at her side, head perfectly propped by the satin pillow.

The corpse turned her head and looked at the daughter. A husky voice, cracked with death sang out, "Nothing to fear, child. Remember, Mommy loves her little girl and can't wait to see her grow up just like her."

Tick tock.

CHAPTER 3

The following Thursday night, daughterly duties set to rest—at least the ones she could check off her list—Jocelyn sat across from her study partner in one of the city college library's study rooms. The far side of the room was lined with students seated in club chairs busily wearing out their fingers texting. At one table, a young woman bent over a sketchpad, her blonde hair tipped with pink, a Celtic tattoo on her neck more pronounced as she worked away. Jocelyn studied her. Modern child-woman, born of the city, she thought. *Take away the blonde, and that could be you in days gone by, kiddo.* She stared at the girl as if the pink-tipped blonde were a work in progress. *Watch yourself, girlie. Don't let the ink turn into fangs.*

"Earth to Jocelyn." Alex Stumme threw a wadded up piece of paper at Jocelyn's fisted hands. It bounced off the knuckles of one, and she turned her head toward him, startled out of her people-watching mode. Cute guy, that Alex. Strong chin. Dimples. Dark brows above brown eyes. He loved to arch one brow at her—his personal signal that something was amiss. Right now, Alex was watching her with that crooked smile that said she should pay attention but not take him too seriously. That smile was about to fade, one eyebrow about to pop up, she thought, when he found out she had done zip, zero, nada on their project during the past four days. Goofy Alex turned into focused Alex when it came to school. Nary a bit of humor over goals not completed. She felt the stir of grief for a relationship of weirdly connected souls now about to split.

Gripping her pen, she started drawing boxes in the margin of her legal pad, her fingers thrust into a grind of drawing. Box after box, all connected. As in what surrounded her, those boxes that squared up and squeezed. The din of Alex's voice banged against them. He was no doubt lamenting his decision to be her partner.

Give it a break, a part of her said. *You've been a bit preoccupied with the daughter bit.* He's your friend as well as your project partner.

Tell that to the part of him who has to present with you, the rest of her replied. *He'll toddle his trusting sweet ass right out of the project. He's your buddy only because he doesn't know what a loser you are.*

The two sides of her mind held a dark caucus while Jocelyn struggled to find something to say. She let her mind open to his words and breathed inside herself. All was hidden from the outside world, however, just as always.

"Here," Alex said as he slid a pile of writing out of a binder. "I've got the background on the crash, statements from Geithner, and analysis from *Congressional Quarterly* all fact checked. What did you find?"

Nothing. She had found nothing. Time to take the beating. Her muscles knew their job. Rigid, they gathered their tension like sentinels arming against the slings of the moment while her inside hid itself from the moment. She could feign attention and still protect. She had practiced the ritual often enough.

"Joce?" Alex's voice had an edge to it.

She looked up, bit at her upper lip, and took in a breath. She was ready. "I don't have anything since we met last Tuesday."

Loser.

Alex sat back in his chair. For sure, no smile now. "Joce. We're up in a week. We should be ready to edit the first draft. Twenty pages. Twenty pages of critical analysis backed up by research. Thirty percent of our grade." His voice had moved from surprise to condemnation. "What in God's name was so important you risked thirty percent of our grades?"

Here goes. Even though this was Alex, she stood armed against the humiliation her betrayal deserved. It wasn't as if she were in the throes of grief, just the clutch of lots of post mortem aftershocks, shut down by impending debtor's prison, a tradition they'd bring back just for her so she could nose-nuzzle with some tattooed gang moll. If she'd been throttled by grief, that was one thing. She was just whittled down by life.

Her mind bitch slapped her.

She had no excuse.

"My mother died." Her voice was flippant, the tension in her body hidden by a skewed mouth and a glib tone.

Alex laughed a derisive laugh. "Yeah, and the dog ate my homework." He shot her a look, drummed his pen on the table for emphasis. "Never mind the lameness, madam jokester. We've got to get this done." A sense of anger grew in both his voice and face. "Joce, you're a powerhouse of ideas, but that power fizzles if I'm not on your ass. What the hell happened that you ignored this? We took this class together for a reason. We have to be editing the draft by tomorrow."

Jocelyn leaned in, tried to steady herself into truth—the guy was her friend after all—but the mindset of detached survivor that had served her so well over the years slid into place and took hold. She looked at her study partner, her friend, the guy who teased her, hung out with her, thought she was smart and fun, the one who was a budding best friend since they met in August. What if he walked out on her? No more *Walking Dead* marathons. No more who's the scarier zombie, Church Lady with pearls or napalmed zombies half melted in a parking lot in Atlanta?

What would he do if he knew the truth about her, that she was the poser who couldn't even find a couple of hours to do a little research?

That she couldn't conjure up a smattering of grief and cry at a funeral?

There was a reason she lived by herself. She'd get her own walking dead papers—bam, you're on your own, sucker.

The words spilled out like so much garbage. "Sorry about that. It was such a bitch, getting Mommie hauled off from the hospital, arrange a funeral that, by the way, I can't pay for, and come up with at least one plant for the place in case no one sent flowers which, by the way, is exactly what happened . . . " She shot Alex a smile that should have had fangs. "Anyway, couldn't do the homework, pal. Somebody had to bury Evie."

Jocelyn saw the tightness cement in Alex's face. Watched the poor guy grope for something to say.

"Yeah, the guys at Starwarski's took care of most of it, but . . . "

"You're not kidding." The realization was clear on his face, clear in the shocked tone of his voice. He should have cut her to shreds. Instead, he reached across the table and grabbed her hand. It was so warm against the cold of her own. "Your mom died? Really?"

The slick nasty left, replaced by a reaction Jocelyn hated. At least sarcastic girl had balls. Her lower lip trembled and hot tears stung at the back of her eyes. Sniveling baby. Get a grip. Cold, shut down. Do it or die.

She jerked her hand away.

"I'll get it done."

"Joce, Professor Huntsman will understand. She'll rearrange and give us some time." The smile was back, this time sweet, laced with tenderness. He tried for her hand again. "You've just lost your mother . . . "

Jocelyn jerked back her hand and shot him a look that usually withered.

"I'm going to research every second I'm not slinging hash." Her jaw trembled. Alex was Jocelyn's fall-to guy, the one place of safety that she felt comfortable enough to snarl at. He had this way of making her feel on iron ground while she slipped through her life. And he had no clue that she needed him; hell, he'd probably run if he sensed even a squeak of need. The thought of losing him through her own inadequacy panicked her. She held that look as if her life depended on it. At that moment, it did.

"Jocelyn Monique Quint."

Jocelyn didn't have a middle name. Alex had given her one—called her Mony when he was especially into teasing. He stretched out the three names, sounding like a mother about to scold a child, assuming the role of disciplinarian but in awe of what said child had done. She knew in the outer reaches of her logical mind that détente was imminent, but the sense of panic gnawed away. Her eyes softened in spite of that jaw that stayed locked. The rest of her, evidently, did not accept safety. She looked away.

"Joce, look at me."

She sighed, sat back in her chair and faced him. He wore his smart-ass smile but she sensed the lecture. Alex never preached. He mocked. He had to. It was the only way she'd listen. "So let me get this right. It's your fault that we're not ready to go just because of a little glitch in your life? After all, mothers die every day and we carry on without a blip."

Jocelyn shot him her stony look.

Alex was on a roll. "You always beat yourself up. I suppose if a meteor had landed on the library, that would be your fault, too?" Now his right eyebrow was cocked. No use in fighting the guy.

Her voice was only slightly sarcastic. "Yes, partner of mine, we will plead our case to Dr. Huntsman. I will get the work done and Earth will be safe from pesky meteors. Is that about it?"

"No."

"What do you mean, 'no'?" Her defenses flipped up again, ready from a lifetime of practice. She readied herself for a hammering.

He leaned in. "Before we even begin to figure out school, you're going to tell me what happened. I didn't even know your mom was sick." He grimaced. "I mean, I know that you two have been . . . well, apart doesn't quite cover it, but . . . I mean, she died?"

Jocelyn sucked in a retort.

"And you didn't call me?" The last part of his statement was laced with hurt.

C'mon, universe, don't dump on me now, even if I deserve it. Here was a guy she had basically just screwed over and he's only pissed about a phone call, or lack thereof. That sounded ominously close to caring.

Sometimes you have to take a chance. Jocelyn heard Marti's voice from four years ago. That's what the guidance counselor had said, words from someone who had cared and proved it. That wall of defense wanted to stay up; it really, really did. She was so well practiced with her walls. But the tension melted like morning fog. A speck of panic hit her gut as she felt the wall dissolve, more subliminal than conscious.

Easy sweetie, you can do it. Look at what's happening from outside your hurt. Jocelyn should have had a pillow inscribed with the words as often as she heard them. Alex's reaction was not the hammering of her childhood. It was a slap with a feather. Who could fight a feather? Alex she could let in.

Jocelyn let the pen drop. "Go and get us a couple of coffees from the Starbucks next door. By the time you get back, I'll be ready to tell you all about it."

Two coffees and three giant chocolate chip cookies later, Jocelyn had filled Alex in. The words came out in lumps. Evie's sudden heart attack at the age of forty-nine. Being too late to see her alive. The apartment cleaning and decisions, the hapless Starwarski brothers conducting a burial ceremony with one attendant. The *three of them had stood beside the blue funeral van as a crane hauled Evie's vault toward the burial site, swinging in the air like a wrecking ball.* But as she relayed her tale, her voice paced faster, her eyes rolled, and she felt the burden of the past three days lift. Sisyphus could finally put down her rock, at least for the moment. By the time she talked about the visitation, she was the old Jocelyn, at least Alex's old Jocelyn, the one her friend thought was real.

"I'm telling you, Alex, I stood there like I was the corpse, all gaping mouth and drool, not a brain cell snapping." Jocelyn stuffed her hands in her hair and drew her eyes wide. "I mean, my mother had a sister. I have an aunt."

Jocelyn banged her head down on top of folded arms. "I have an aunt. I have an *aunt*." The words spun into each other like spools of liquid glass. She slowly raised herself up, squared her shoulders and looked at Alex. "Hey Alex, guess what. I have an aunt." Then she lifted her shoulders and gave a snicker, the laugh of an innocent who had just heard her first naughty joke.

Alex started to laugh, in turn, but stopped short. Before he could even answer her bit of drama, his Joce was gone, replaced by a Jocelyn whose eyes held a far-away glaze. Not the eyes of a woman exclaiming surprise but more the eyes of a child staring at a party where all the guests have left and only empty tissue and dead balloons remained. His Jocelyn would have cracked—"Just what I need. Another relative with stupid in her blood." This Jocelyn looked used up and sat quiet.

"What are you gonna' do?"

Jocelyn leaned back in her chair, stretched out her arms, fingers of both hands entwined, shoulders hunched. She looked up and spoke to the ceiling.

"I'm going to get another cookie, thank you very much. " She scrunched her lips. "I'll get you one, too, but I'll make you choke on it if you give me any crap."

An hour later, he was snarfing down the last of his cookies while he drove home. Red lights every block, it seemed. Stopping without even getting started. Sort of like his day with Jocelyn. At one of the lights, somewhere between Halstead and Harlem Avenue, he killed time checking out a mural next to a Sweet Philly Steak joint.

A wall of patterns swirling upward; below them the word, *Friend*. That stuff that Joce did when she was stressed. Something tangles. She'd been doing them the day he met her. Did them whenever things stressed her out. Bet she had done a shit-pot of them this week.

He pictured her on a ladder there, finishing up the last of the mural, probably an art deco middle finger to the sky. "Take that, Stumme," she'd be muttering. "You're going to be stopped at a light right here; look over, and there will be a message screaming at you to pay attention. My message, courtesy of Madame Fate." She'd swirl her brush in the air. "So, listen! I don't decorate these things for nothing." By then her voice would be a snarl, followed by a laugh.

That was the point. He *was* paying attention. He reached for his phone and dialed. No answer. A horn blared behind him. Green light. Means go, jackass. He kept his voice steady while he left the message, even as he pulled the car forward in the endless traffic of Chicago. "Joce, it's all about being a friend. Just want you to know that."

The streets blurred by, and then he was home. He sat in his car in the alley, holding his phone, willing it to ring. Nothing. What did he expect? Joce never did anything expectedly.

She was smart, funny—and yes, more full of feistiness than he could dream about. And she was good for him, put him in perspective. "Stumme, for a wacko guy, you're too uptight. Sit and relax before you split your britches with worry."

But today, worry had ridden her. Today, the Jocelyn he had seen was like a flickering light behind a metal screen. Her mom had died, and she acted like it was a bump in the road that had made her late. Why hadn't she called him? And why the flips? He stared at the back of the triplex in front of him, at the busted gate and peeling garage, the weeds overtaking the yard, the endless rows of backstairs zigzagging on the rentals around the neighborhood. They had nothing to offer but the sameness of blight.

His thumb rubbed against the plastic of the phone. Jocelyn. What can you do with a girl like that?

The answer was pretty simple even for a blockhead like him.

CHAPTER 4

Sal's Family Restaurant bragged of free French toast with the Big Man's omelet and a kid-friendly atmosphere sure to please. The red vinyl seats of booths and table chairs were tear-free, a boon for the buttocks of families and omelet eaters alike; and kids could count on fresh crayons for their fantasy maps and coloring pages, and the place made its own version of Chicago Famous chocolate turtles. What was not to love?

This morning, however, twenty minutes before the breakfast crowd was due to arrive, something was askew in Sal's. One of the waitresses, a college sophomore trying to balance the need for food and rent with the cost of tuition, a daughter trying to find enough money to pay for burying her mother, sat at a corner table, head in hands. Her mind said, *I cannot fucking believe this.* Her sense of self-preservation knew better than to voice the words.

The owner, George—not Sal—sat next to her, smelling of bacon and old coffee and regret. He reached out to pat her on the shoulder but drew back. A good man giving bad news. "It's not you. You're great, Jocelyn. But Connie's been with me for fifteen years, and JoElla has two kids to support all by herself."

Jocelyn looked up at him. The poor guy's eyes begged for understanding. It was evident he was upset.

Tough. So was she.

"Mr. Stravicacous, I have to eat, too. I need this job." Her hand reached up and grabbed at her hair. Jocelyn had been fired. No matter that she worked long hours for four years, covering any shift that didn't interfere with her class schedule. Weekends? What were those except an opportunity to scrape up a few bucks and keep back the chaos?

And now this. The economy. And some bullshit about his niece needing a part-time job. She needed the money. She needed her degree.

George Stravicacous extended a carrot. "I'm sure I can get you a few hours over the holidays." He reached for his wallet. "And I can throw in a couple of hundred to get you by while you're looking for something else." He sounded so hopeful, like rent and gas and food only needed a couple of hundred dollars. Hell, that would barely cover toilet paper until she had a chance to grab some hours in December. And how could she even begin to pay for the funeral. *Nice going, Evie. Fucked me over again.*

Her mean voice teased, *Don't blame your mother. That's like blaming yourself.*

She wadded up the napkin in her hand and stood up, thrust her hands in her apron pockets. "Whatever," she mumbled, her head averted. No way would she ever be her mother. "I've got to get ready for customers. At least I have a job until *Stephanie* gets here." She said the girl's name like a second-grader might say *butt face.*

After she washed off her face in the bathroom sink, she surveyed the damage. Brown eyes—supposedly her best feature—were a swamp of red, and her sliver of a nose, which had leaked enough to soak through the napkin she had grabbed, still spewed like an oil rig spill. That square face, normally pale, was splotched with red. She gave herself a salute. "Jocelyn Quint, about-to-be-unemployed waitress, reporting for duty."

She had actually trusted this man, the one who bragged about having smarts in his restaurant, who cajoled her, "Hey college girl, we'd have to throw this bread out. And take some roast beef to go with it. You know how you love my roast beef." She was such a baby believing her boss cared, that he wanted to help her out, go the extra mile for solid work. And now he had made her cry. She beat her fists on the edges of the sink and pressed her head against the mirror.

Those tears, all that snot, had been birthed in a place she usually plugged tight. The boss had yanked out that plug with the firing. "Oh-gee, I'm so sorry; it's not your fault," he had whined. Right. A shit sandwich is still shit even if the bread's buttered. Jocelyn had taken a big bite and let the crap flow. What an idiot. An unemployed idiot. She flicked her middle finger against the mirror and pulled back, stared at the mirror as if somehow the damn thing would change the picture and she'd be back in the world of the employed, a world where everything was all right.

26

No such luck. She reached out and grabbed at a paper towel. Stood up and squared her shoulders. *Do not blame yourself, Jocelyn Quint.* She managed a good five seconds of confidence, looked up and checked herself out again in the mirror. Who could she blame, the freakin' universe?

Same shit. Different day. Love it when the cynics are right.

She rinsed her face again. Good thing the job didn't require make-up. Grease and Cover Girl didn't mix. She blew her nose clean, heaved in a heavy smell of the bathroom's air freshener, and went out to face day.

The hours, the minutes, fell one onto another. This was a Tuesday, a full day of work. At 7:00, after a full twelve-hour shift, she counted her tips. Forty-seven dollars and eleven cents. The change came from a cheap old man who stank of Braunschweiger and onions and the seven refills of coffee he demanded. Oh yeah, and she had a piece of Big Red gum from some kid who said she looked pretty. Tomorrow she had class, and a meeting with Alex. Goodie. They could wrap up the presentation on the bail-out. Their presentation. You go Timothy Geithner. Too bad she wasn't a bank, too big to fail.

Back in her apartment, Jocelyn sat on the edge of the couch, hair pulled back in a scrunchie, one of Evie's cotton night gowns thin against her white skin, staring at the card her newfound aunt had slipped into her hand at the visitation.

Staring at the card meant not staring at the dark and cold. She rubbed her arms for warmth and then twisted on them, thumbs and fingers digging in until she could feel the pain. Pain made the cold not quite so cold. "Action," she whispered like a mantra. "Action." She dug her nails into her skin hoping for blood.

"Call me," Aunt Paula had said, like a social worker cajoling a child to narc on a parent. Fat chance, she had said to herself at the time. When you're in a can of worms and a new can presents itself, it's better stay in the can you know.

She grabbed at the card and sprang up, paced back and forth across the room shaking her arms. No job. She had no job. No food, no shelter, no hope. She stopped mid-pace and read the card again. "Luna's," the card said.

"Art and Wine." The address was in Logan Square, artsy up-and-coming neighborhood on the North side. Beat the hell out of her neighborhood. Logan Square had an obelisk on a grassy boulevard. Her neighborhood had street after street of pissed off Southies flipping the bird.

Logan Square, huh? What the hell? She might get a job. Or at least a free glass of wine.

She worked her thumbs against the tightness in her neck, breathing in deeply to keep herself from scoring the flesh. Tomorrow she would play student, and on Thursday she would meet Auntie Paula.

She sat back down, grabbed the book for her lit class and read about a pond that was the ocean for creation and a boy who had to grow a heart.

Serendipity has such a great time. While Jocelyn was reading, Jocelyn's new-found aunt was across town sitting in a club chair in her Logan Square apartment. She loved the chair, the way she could sink into the cushions and let the curve of the chair envelop her in safety.

Three days. Three days since she had met her niece. *My, she looks like me, at least the me I see now when I look in the mirror and see Paula.* She picked up the journal she had been working on, the one for her therapist Deb to read during their next session. She usually had pages written by now.

Right now the voices inside her were quiet. Probably shock. Or hiding in their rooms. They all had agreed to her sister's visitation, every one of her alters. A sister deserved respect. A dead sister posed no problem. But the niece, what a surprise to look at history in one girl's face. Paula shook her head and told the children to relax. She would read to them as soon as she finished writing in her journal. She wouldn't see her psychiatrist for three days.

Maybe she would call Deb in the morning for a special phone session. Skype? Virtual analysis. Gotta love the technology age. She set the thought aside and began to write.

A niece. I have a niece. A piece of my blood. Poor child. She looked so pale, so frazzled. But then, she had just lost her mother. My sister. My lone sibling. My enemy. One of the many.

Evelyn was so young when she left. So needy. So pregnant, a belly carried by a child. I can see her sitting on her bed, pouting. I was the prettiest girl in my class and now I'm ugly, ugly, ugly. *Of course she ran away. Once the fantasy castle you've built in the air begins to crumble . . .*

Paula laid the journal down on the black lacquered end table, but held onto the pen, twisting it while she laid her head back and felt the cush of the club chair. Talk about the proverbial pot mocking the kettle. She was a walking universe of fantasy. Bet her niece doesn't need to dig through the debris of her life to find a way to talk to her selves.

Silencer spoke out inside her. He was such a nuisance, always prattling about impending doom. "You'd better listen to me, woman. Don't even think about telling her about us. If you tell, the world will end. Where will that niece of yours be then?"

Paula grabbed her journal, hugged it to her, and rocked.

CHAPTER 5

From the journal of Paula Ross

No one had raped our mother when Evie had been conceived. Not just a rape, mind you. A real family affair. My sister Evie was merely an inconvenience. I, on the other hand, was a curse. Not such a surprise, really. Evie's daddy was off on a business trip when his daddy, as folks used to say, 'had his way' with Evie's mother, the soon-to-be Paula's mother. Vern's 'way' had included a half bottle of Jim Beam, a lot of screaming, and more than a few bruises, bruises on my mother's body and in her soul.

Oh yes. And some sperm driving their way with great gusto toward a penetration that would lead to misery. Me.

Funny, how no one ever talked about the incident. They didn't even talk around it like some folk do. Well, you know, old Vern had a real connection to his family in so many ways. Or that family tree has its own vine twirling around on it. But then, I missed so much of that time. The Littles took care of me. Must have been a heavy burden; there are so many of those babies who don't even have names. Just Littles. Bless you babies for what you've endured. I only know one of their stories. They only told me one.

Mother said they couldn't afford two cribs. Evie was three by then. Could have had her own bed. But no, the sisters had to share. Sometimes I think I can feel the gauzy scratch of the sheet, but it's more of a weightless sense than a memory. Mother fed me my bottle while I was in the crib with Evie. She propped the bottle in my tiny hands and left the room. I was too insignificant to feed.

No one could figure out why I was so puny as a baby. Failure to thrive, the report said. The doctor couldn't believe I was fed regularly. And yes I was. Mother never lied. No, she put that bottle in the crib with great regularity.

I just stayed underweight while Evie pudged out. Who would think a three-year-old would still want a bottle? Who would think she would steal from her sister?

I can't even remember the hunger. The Littles help with that but even they are confused. Deb laughs when I talk about confusion. "Paula," she says, "there's so much in your life that's knotted and frayed; I'd be surprised if you remembered more. Even at this point."

Note to Paula. Give that woman two hugs at your next appointment. Then have her make you laugh.

When I was thirteen, I snuck into Vern's shed out back while we were visiting for some stupid family holiday. It was a shambled old sot of a building ready to collapse onto itself, grimy and faded with grease and neglect, smelling of oil and dirt. Dirt-caked windows hung over an old work table littered with tools. On each side of the window, so that old Vern could see no matter which side of the table he was putzing at, the old man had plastered magazine pictures.

I was used to Highlights for Kids and a Ladies Home Journal or two that belonged to my mom. These were for neither kids nor ladies. Penises plundered every kind of female orifice imaginable, some on women, others on little girls, a few on animals. As Paula, I had never seen a penis—that was Charlie's jurisdiction; in fact, as Paula, I had to study a couple of the images before I figured out what the thing was, but slowly my head began to buzz with understanding; and even as I flinched, a warm vagueness tugged at me. Charlie could keep secrets, but some times that task wore too hard on the child.

Some time went by. I have no clue how long, but my mother told me I had been missing twenty minutes and she had been yelling her head off. When I heard her calling, I jolted. My hand was down my shorts, inside my underpants and I was rubbing myself while I chewed the insides of my mouth.

I froze, flinched once or twice, and pulled out my hand. I could hardly snap my shorts shut, I was shaking so hard. The flesh above my teeth pulsed with rawness, and I dropped to the floor, pulled my hands over my head and wailed.

When they found me, I had been running away from the yard toward Wrightwood Avenue. She tssked at me, slathering me with layers of guilt for ruining the day. Mother always fed on criticism, and I was a tasty meal.

When I got home, I took a scissors to my panties and shorts, cut them into tatters and shoved the remnants under my bed. St least that's what they told me when the accusations flowed. I couldn't remember—that is for years until I could at least let it flit into my consciousness in dreams once I connected with Charlie.

Sometimes I picture the scraps of cloth rolled into a ball, dust balls filtered through them like pixie dust. They sing of a fairy tale any old Grimm brother couldn't even imagine.

CHAPTER 6

Jocelyn pulled on her best pair of jeans, the one without grease stains and droopy ass, while she eyed her tee-shirts lying there on the bed for perusal. *Heisenberg is blue*? Nope. Just her luck, Auntie would be a *Breaking Bad* critic. Or some kind of hissy prude. *Einstein gives smart head?* Definitely a no. She chose a Klimt flower garden tee. Lots of pastels against dark green. Looked pretty and spoke of a sensitivity that Jocelyn lacked. Her sullen side must have been napping when she grabbed up that one at the farmer's market in Woodstock.

On Jocelyn's way out, the pissy old lady who lived across the hall turned to look at her and gave a grudging nod. Normally the old gal kept her lips tight in case she gave in to a smile. Good luck sign? Jocelyn pocketed the hope of an omen along with a gloss stick—both just in case. She needed a job, and now. Alex had told her not to worry, that aunts were made to come through. Good for Alex. He lived in a world of normal relatives.

Just as she pulled up to her aunt's business in Logan Square, a morning wind reared up and swept yellow leaves across the grass. A gust grabbed at the door as Jocelyn was getting out of her car. She jerked at the door handle with a curse. Great start, she thought. Even Mother Nature doesn't like me. Holding tight to the business card her aunt had given her, Jocelyn walked the half block until she reached the corner address and stopped to check out her aunt's business.

Luna's the sign said. *Art and Wine and Refreshment.* The place was one of those cool flat-iron three-story brick buildings where the first floor stretched across the vee of the sidewalk like a smile above a pointed chin, the upper floors curving at the corner where two city streets met. Architects in old Logan Square had played with a sense of geometry. Jocelyn loved the pattern. On each side of the red front door sat two black boxes filled with ivy and Queen Anne's Lace, the last remnants of the summer now tousled by the Chicago wind.

Nice digs, Auntie Paula. Her former employer had his place on a corner all right; an eatery plopped there with well-worn siding and fading green-striped awnings. The only thing out front at George's that might catch a customer's eye was the bench riders sat on while they waited for the bus, and that was decorated with a hodge-podge of advertisements for real estate, ambulance-chasing lawyers, and a tattoo parlor or two. Just because a job is a job doesn't mean it can't come with a few perks. Maybe Chicago had sent her that wind to let her know the past few days were swept away and better ones were ahead.

Right. Like Mother *Nature roots for you all the time.* Remember, check out the exits as soon as you walk in. Lollygag and they may clamp shut. Don't forget your life slogan: *Be ready; that bird above your head needs to drop a delivery.*

Jocelyn opened that red door to what might become her new life. Inside Luna's, the weather was calm, but the place had a movement all its own. Wooden window seats stretched across the front on both sides of the door, art growing there in a well-planned tumbling. Wrought iron easels displayed pieces, sculpture of all sizes, vintage metal signs, and enough handcrafted jewelry to create a single sense of craftsmanship. No plastic wind chimes here. She had definitely left the home neighborhood.

Why hadn't her mother ever talked about a sister who could own a place like this? Wait. Evie was velvet Elvis and bobble-heads. This was class.

But this was also her mother's sister. Blood could very well trump taste, even if the first glance looked enticing. She'd check the place out for an exit strategy just in case.

Jocelyn opened the red door and walked in with her aunt's card clutched in her hand and a ménage of emotions scuttling in her brain. Anxiety. Confusion. Anticipation. Cross the threshold and you can't go back. She rubbed the card with her thumb and forged ahead; then she stared in awe. She couldn't help herself. No Elvis in this house, velvet or otherwise. The place was amazing; kind of Pottery Barn meets Edvard Munch.

Don't get suckered in quite yet, child. Just like in the Munch painting, you could be the guy in the road screaming.

Hey, but in this place, it would be with class and a damn fine wine glass.

She moved to just inside the doorway, her purse pressed to her side and looked up. The copper tin ceiling had to be eighteen feet high. Squares, long lines, only a little flowing. At the back, twin antique paneled doors led to what—the kitchen?

High-top tables had matching copper tops and thick, curved cherry legs. Nice. Lots of symmetry. The swivel stools had black leather seats, their backs wrapped in off-white linen. Good touch. Neutral. Simple. Paintings lined the dark gray wall to her right, some in a collage of small pieces; others, giants slashed mostly with red and black or gray, a few bits of sepia. The back wall handled the mixed media. Even from the distance Jocelyn could make out a child's doll, split and mounted on canvas, its mouth duct taped and a hangman's noose around its neck. Whoa. Nothing simple and neutral there. Maybe she should have worn her Heisenberg shirt after all.

"Can I help you?" The invitation came from behind the bar to Jocelyn's left. She stepped toward the voice's origin. A bartender stood behind a bar that stretched thirty feet, a dark-haired young guy dressed in the requisite black silk shirt. He was good looking, all right, but the bar was the real attraction. Wine corks set in a herringbone pattern under glass stretched the entire length; four huge chunks of cherry wood rose four or five feet upward supporting an etched glass top. Carved into each column was a woman's face, the same woman, but each column told a different story based on her emotion. One column was a study in sullen, another a picture of delight, still another one of contemplation. And that one on the end . . . Jocelyn stepped forward to get a better look. Was that . . .

"Yep," the bartender—Cole, his name tag said—answered. "The sculptor's wife was the most sexually satisfied woman on Earth according to the artist. Must be true, given the look on her face." Jocelyn couldn't help herself. She hooted. Hadn't had a laugh that good since that snotty bitch that sat in front of her in Western Civ had slipped on a dead bird on the way across the quad.

"So, gathering from your reaction, you're a lady who likes her wine rich and red." His face and voice were even. He might as well have been at the grocery store. "Paper or plastic?"

Jocelyn's curiosity had been piqued at the red door. It was on full thrust now. She pulled herself up onto a bar stool. "Red. Definitely red. And rich as you can pour."

She took the wine with her as she walked along the paintings wall. They were stunning. Not the kind of *Gee, I'm in the Art Institute* stunning. No, these works stunned the viewer, made Jocelyn want to reach into the images and grasp the story. In one of them, a wall of barbed wire ran across the canvas, men and women gaunt, strung up on the wire like flotsam tossed by the wind, arms and legs stretched and broken. Their faces, petrified in their terror, were stark skulls covered with the thinnest of stretched skin. The whole piece was done in charcoal except for thick drops of blood squeezed from the bodies and running down the wire. A ray of light stretched down from the top of the painting, nothing of a blessing here, more like exposure. At least that's what Jocelyn sensed.

Jocelyn let her fingers air brush the forms, called to them to share with her. Her jaw locked and she felt a shudder. She couldn't stop the dance of her fingertips so close to the canvas. They felt the hum of the story.

She looked for a signature. It wasn't signed. Only had a white card that gave the price.

Jocelyn took a sip of wine while she watched the blood. Same color. Sisters, she thought. She turned and called out to the bartender, "Who did this one?"

Cole answered, "I think that one's Charlie's."

I think? If these were for sale, shouldn't they know who had done what?

Jocelyn put on her smart ass. "And Charlie is . . . ?"

A voice interrupted. "Me."

Jocelyn turned around to see the artist. There stood her Aunt Paula.

What the hell? Paula painted under a pseudonym?

Not much of a stretch, actually. *Charlie* sounded better for a piece like that than *Paula*.

The aunt stepped toward the bar, held out her glass for a wine. Cole poured something white. She turned to Jocelyn. "Welcome to Luna's my

36

dear." She gave the picture a dismissive wave. "Forget about who signed what pictures."

To Cole, she said, "This is Jocelyn, my new-found niece. Put her drink on my tab."

Cole nodded his head. "As well, I welcome you to Luna's. And congratulations on having a great lady as your aunt."

Paula put on a stern face even as she laughed. "Not going to remind you again. You only get to flirt with the young ones." She took Jocelyn's hand and pulled at her gently. "Let's share our wine and get to know each other."

Jocelyn stepped back into the world and took another sip of wine, hopped up onto the bar stool and faced her aunt, a smile haphazard on her face. She couldn't help the smile even as her mind told her to beware. Paula now sat across from her on her own bar stool, equally smiling.

Here we are, Jocelyn thought, aunt and niece in a classy bar where tortured dolls are the décor du' jour and the aunt is also an artist named Charlie.

Perfect.

"Let's move to the back where we can have some privacy." Even as Paula spoke, Jocelyn noticed the slight nod of the bartender's head. Hmm. Blessing or warning? Whichever, the day would prove interesting—and hopefully profitable.

So the two women, talking for the first time—if no one counted that moment at the funeral home—sat across from each other at the appointed table where Tapas style yummies waited for the munching. Prosciutto-wrapped asparagus, Gorgonzola with apple and walnut, seared tuna. Jocelyn had only heard of these dishes. Now she was about to lap them up.

Jocelyn rubbed her finger along the rime of her wine glass. *Earth to Jocelyn. You're noshing with an aunt you've never heard of. The sister to your wacko mother. The bartender might like her, but she pays the bills. Be wary. This could be Hansel and Gretel redux.*

While Jocelyn steadied herself, Paula began the conversation, voice hesitant, eyes hopeful. "It's not every day a woman loses a sister and gains a niece." Then she picked up a stem of asparagus and held it halfway to her mouth while she eyed Jocelyn.

Jocelyn stared at the appetizer—the crisp green of the vegetable, the thin wrapping of the meat. Symbol? What was at the center of what wrapped around the two of them? She gave a wry smile. "Not all that surprising. It wasn't the first secret Evie kept from me."

Paula took a bite of the appetizer. "You call your mother *Evie?* Not *Mom.*" Statement, not question. It could have been innocuous. Then she finished the bite, wiped her finger with the cloth napkin.

Slow down. Keep it in check. You know better. Remember, a sisterly tie here can be more curse than connection.

Jocelyn made her answer sound dismissive. "Must be an adult thing. Big girl now, put away the mommy talk."

Paula looked at Jocelyn above the rim of her glass as she took in a slow drink of wine.

Jocelyn's mind still held high alert. What did this woman know?

Paula returned to the ordinary. "And you're going to college? I have to admit, you're not like your mother. The only studying she found interesting was of the opposite sex . . . and herself." The tone scoffed even more than the words.

The sisters and their relationship. Evie kept Paula a secret. Paula didn't seem to be a big fan of Evie's. Important point to know.

A question nudged at Jocelyn. How did Paula know she was in college? That wasn't in the obituary. "Yes, I'm a junior at St. Thomas on the south side. I have an apartment about a mile away. I can walk to campus on most good days."

Enough about me, Jocelyn warned herself. Time to schmooze the potential boss. She leaned forward. "I've never been to Logan Square before. Never get much past 71st and Cicero. Logan Square is foreign travel. Totally exotic." Jocelyn turned toward the center of Luna's and gestured with her wine glass. "And this place—this place is so overwhelming. Art on the South Side is graffiti and falling piles of bricks. Lots of AstroTurf on front steps for those who have made it. This place is so . . . so not the South Side. I mean, there's a darkness—and I don't mean that as a slam in any way—it's so from the soul."

Jocelyn's chest tightened. Whoa. This was rapidly moving away from controlled buttering up to real conversation. First she had talked about her mother, and then she opened up about the feel of the Luna's. Such admissions are blue-light specials at Kmart for potential sociopaths. *Soul* comes from the heart. Too personal. *Soul* means vulnerability; vulnerability equals danger. Time to protect. Do it, her mind demanded, the ritual that had protected her all these years.

Jocelyn went to work, felt her walls—those imaginary sheets of metal—start to creep down, the walls that kept her safe. In that empty space inside the walls, the place of *me*, no one could hurt her. She could live in the emptiness while the world attacked. She did not know this woman, sister of her mother, blood of her mother as enticing as the lady seemed. An aunt she was talking to for the first time? Not scary. An aunt who depicted people as skulls strung to barbed wire? Had to be a bond with weird there somewhere.

That's it, girl. Stuff down the feelings. Bring up the walls, all the anger and fear of your life coalescing, frozen into steel, impenetrable. Come on muscles, come on mind, do your jobs. It was the unsung mantra as much a part of her as sinew and blood. But in this moment, this place, the stuff of the walls hung above her, impermanent and unsure whether to lower or ebb away while waiting for a stronger signal.

Her body tightened. Then the walls found substance, slid into place. Her psyche felt the jolt, the slickness and strength of the steel that protected her.

Outer Jocelyn was safe. Inner Jocelyn was safe. No feeling, just numb safety. Back to the interview. And Aunt Paula was buying the wine. Whatever she said, inner Jocelyn was safe. The walls held a guarantee. She would not need to feel the blade's edge if they held her safe. This newfound aunt of hers—she could explain a lot. Just keep those walls in place and let the conversation roll. Nothing can hurt you. You're protected. Work it, girlfriend.

Wine glass still in hand, she turned back to face her aunt and leaned back in her chair. That patter she knew. "I'm not sure what I expected coming here, not any neon—that was for sure—I figured that out when I met you. You'd have a few potted plants, maybe little Tiffany lamps on the table." She took a sip of wine. "But this place. Wow."

Could have been the ambiance. Probably was the start of a second glass of wine. Whatever, as newly found niece and aunt chatted, the conversation not only rolled, it tumbled out with ease. Such a foreign moment, as if she might have entered a place that she already knew. Granted, Jocelyn's walls were still there, but they were on the very edge of becoming porous. Jocelyn was in survival mode, milking the moment, but right now it felt so good. The girl her mother's boyfriend called "more squirrely than shit" was sitting with someone who got her.

Where did the act end and the girl begin?

She found herself blathering and didn't care. She hadn't done that in years, not since she and Marti had sat in the guidance office and laughed at the world. Paula had brought up the topic of creative meandering. Jocelyn jumped in. She could be a regular font of discussion as long as she was safe. "I had a great imagination as a little kid. I'd sit on the bus for hours, just riding to who knows where, and make up stories about the people who rode. You can go a long way if you figure out how to make the most of a transfer. Moms ran away from abusive husbands. Preps were undercover for a Satanic cult. I'd picture stringing up rude adults with fishing line and hanging them outside of the bus so they'd bump against the side and cough up exhaust."

Paula leaned back and tssked, but her face had a naughty Santa look to it. "And what did your mother think about that?"

Jocelyn snorted. "Evie? She was either at the bar pouring drinks or sloshing them down herself. Never noticed I was gone."

Paula shook her head and laughed. "Jocelyn, my dear, I am not one bit surprised." She reached out and patted Jocelyn's hand. "I am so sorry about you losing that job. " She smiled in a quick pause. "And so happy that you came here. Can you start work tomorrow night?"

Careful. This place could more than grow on you; it could tear open . . . The thought stopped dead before it could finish. What would tear open? Jocelyn closed her eyes for just a second, then opened them and pursed her lips. It wasn't all weird slasher art. There were some nice photographs of Millennium Park and local Logan Square architecture. The jewelry looked pretty safe. Safe. What a pleasant word.

Bottom line. She needed a job. If things went south, she could quit.

"Aunt Paula, if you need me, I can start right now."

"Oh no you don't, young lady. I just found you and I intend to spend some time getting to know my niece." She turned and called to Cole while

40

she patted the seat beside her. "Two more glasses for the family, please."

Jocelyn took another glance at an art wall and breathed in deeply. Family. What had she stepped into? The walls squeezed tighter just in case.

Jocelyn lay in bed listening to the sounds of the neighborhood. Two dogs on the next block vied for the loudest barking award. Even after midnight, the cars sped past on their way to wherever, a few drivers squealing tires just because they could. In the safety of her apartment, Jocelyn laid the pieces of the day out in her mind like a puzzle. Paula was so nice. So smart. So giving. So strange.

Granted, Evie had never talked that much about her own childhood, dismissing it with a haughty "You don't even want to hear," followed by that tight-lipped clenching that Jocelyn had inherited from her mother. Bits and pieces had slipped out on occasion. A boyfriend who had slipped her a first shot of liquor when she was only fourteen. The YMCA where the cool kids went for dances. A special dress of yellow eyelet that had hugged her tiny waist and flared out forever. She had talked about her favorite doll, one with red curls that matched her own and made the neighbors marvel at the collective beauty.

Jocelyn finally fell asleep and slipped into dreaming. She was about five and playing with worn-out Lincoln Logs and a knock-off Cabbage Patch kid with one eye. And she had plenty more to worry about than going to dances. During the night, a dream monster, a big dark shape, had crawled into her bed and pinned her against the wall. It was gone when she woke up, but she had been so scared. She thought she'd throw up her Cheerios at breakfast.

The doll gave Jocelyn a sly smile. "I have a sister," the doll mocked. "But you don't know anything. Secrets, Jocelyn. It's all about the secrets.

"You have no idea the number of secrets that can dance inside you. They twirl and twirl and stomp—until they pull you down and smother you. No matter how much you fight, the secrets win, you know."

The dream flashed into a whole new scene as dreams do. Now she was a teenager on a bus that travelled the streets of Chicago while Evie's body banged away on the side of the vehicle. Evie was dressed in a yellow gown and tied up with fish line bumping along the side of the bus. Inside the bus, dolls with delicate faces chugged whiskey. One looked at her, perfect eyelashes attached to eyes that opened and closed in perfect rhythm.

When the whiskey was gone, they all sang, "The wheels on the bus go round and round."

Tick Tock.

CHAPTER 7

From the journal of Paula Ross

*S*o much of childhood is a secret. They act, then whisper, "Don't tell." I stiffen and let the secrets fall onto my child body. They pile there atop me like rocks on an innocent of Salem, one who wonders what has led the mob to call her witch. All I have are the smells. These odors—now they sift through my days, the stuff of memories, olfactory ghosts haunting my gray matter, observing inward, then reaching out to beg attendance. They demand attention. When I first began to write, the memories flicked like sensory snapshots moving at warp speed. The trauma of them allowed less than a peek, only that flick—that millisecond to stamp itself once again in my gut.

Now I can take them out, hold them in my mind's hand while I seek healing from the abuse.

I never saw myself as a writer. Now I know I must write. To record is to vanquish.

Lily-of-the-Valley. The scent of her talc, cloying sweet and vile. Whenever Mother beat me with her hairbrush, the trace of its perfume on the vanity reached out to draw me into the horror while I took the swats and bled out her need for redemption.

Cigarettes. His stark cologne, edged on his clothes, his hands, his hair, suffocating while he played man of the house. The burning of liver and onions on the stove, its message pure. You will eat them. If you puke, you'll scoop it up and eat them again. I can stir my fear with my spoon.

Motor oil. In his garage, the smell of him, that cloying smell, sweat and grit and what I must not think about.

Even the absence of smells leave their mark. Birthday cakes never baked, candles never lit. I knew their smell from the realms of other children, celebrations for children who had purpose. Fresh pillow covers scented with sun and goodnight kisses never imagined by a daughter who lay in fear.

In my own woman's mind, we've come to know these smells not as a universe but as part of the duty of each of us. Not that we had much of a choice. We are a community, not a cacophony. We find a peace in that.

CHAPTER 8

The scent of lemon filled Paula's apartment. She loved its freshness when she took herself back through her journal. At first she had used the scent to cloak the odors that still wafted from the words. Lemon was clean even when life was not. But then she learned to welcome the scent; lemon meant facing the past and not being eaten alive.

Today, the lemon held a promise. Not only did she have a niece, she had one who worked for her, one whom she would see every week, who would speak to her and laugh with her and share. The joy of the news played through her

Paula looked down at her journal paper. She had been drawing again. So much of what she said there were pictures, usually scratching and scribbles from the children. These were scribbles, all right, but in no way childish. These were her circles of desperation, arcs and ovals that formed a maze only the shrinks could love, knotted and crazed. Mazes told her she was hurling forward too fast. *Be still*, they said. *Wait*. Let your present unfold as it should. Paula set the journal and pen aside and went to the kitchen to pour more tea. She found peace in the stirring, in the gentle sipping as warmth fell down her throat. Yes, she promised herself. Yes, she would be still; let Jocelyn come to her.

Her hand stilled as a foreign thought poked through. Jocelyn was Evie's child. Jocelyn was twenty-one, far too young. What had happened to the other child, the one who drove Evie away from the hell they called home when Evie was seventeen? Evie was too pregnant to miscarry when she left. Had she done something? Ridded herself of that burden like she did everything else. Or had she given birth?

Jocelyn was twenty-one; she had said so herself. The timeline didn't fit.

So if Jocelyn wasn't the baby, who was? And where was the child?

CHAPTER 9

The first week working at Luna's was busy, but uneventful as a whole. Lots of regulars with names to learn. Lots of tips. A couple of teenagers came in on a Tuesday, off day for serving food, to stare at the art work. Jocelyn couldn't tell whether they were high or just scary horny. She kept an eye on them just in case.

She needed tippers, not tweekers. Her stash was building. Slinging hash at Cal's barely paid for food. Tippers at Luna's started with twenties. Starwarski Brothers would get off her ass this month. Paula had offered to pay for the entire funeral, but offering Jocelyn this job smacked of nepotism as it was. Besides, the whole scenario of working for an aunt who wanted nothing more than to dote was a boat still bobbing in waters that might only look still. In Jocelyn's life, too many times had looked upward and then went south.

On Friday night, after closing, Paula, Cole, Alex, and Jocelyn sat at the bar, the last four bodies in what had been a packed place only an hour ago. Paula was figuring receipts, Cole was putzing with the last of the bar glasses, and Jocelyn gnawed on a toothpick and wished for a masseuse.

Luna's owner shut down her calculator with a flourish—she used a calculator, for God 's sake, one with two-inch numbers so "an old lady could *see* all the money she was making—and piped up to Cole, "Drinks around, Barkeep. This was a good night."

Alex hollered out, "Hey Psych Guy, how about another Boulevard Wheat?" For some reason, Alex found the name he had pinned on Cole amusing. Whatever. Jocelyn said, "Make it two." Paula stuck her finger up and said "Pinot for me," and the party was on.

While Cole uncorked a bottle of Pinot to add to the two bottles on the bar, he asked, "How good, boss lady?"

"Good enough that I'm taking my niece shopping tomorrow."

Jocelyn started to choke on her beer, the bones of her upper back cracking either in protest or thanks, most likely a bit of both. "Shopping? Whoa." She was still reconciling this budding relationship with the woman who was both boss and family. Boss lady who bought drinks after a shift, no problem. Shopping buddy? Not quite ready for that. Girlfriends shop. Mothers and daughters shop.

No wonder Jocelyn had nothing to use as a yardstick here.

"I see that look on your face, young lady." Paula's tease brought a flicker of emotion. Jocelyn had heard those words enough times in her life, usually right before, "You should be thankful you have a roof over your head and food on the table."

A warm hand patted Jocelyn's knee. "I'm kidding." Paula winked at her. "Part of the job description is keeping the boss happy. And Jocelyn Quint, tomorrow you are going to make me one happy aunt. I've always wanted someone to spoil—and you're it, by default if nothing else." She sounded like a camp director high on wood smoke, but the words took the sting out of the flicker.

Cole took a swig of wine and inserted, "Sometimes, if you let someone do something for you, you're doing the giving." Typical Cole statement, the smart ass. No wonder Alex's tag. He was Cole Heiple, psych grad student checking out the universe in the microcosm of a bar while he attended grad school.

Fine, she'd go.

Paula grabbed at Jocelyn's arm, flashing that camp director's smile, all perfect white teeth. "C'mon. It'll be fun. A whole afternoon, lunch out, browsing through Logan Square boutiques and thrift stores."

Fine. She'd have fun.

Jocelyn pictured herself preening in that flowing thirties dress at Cotilla's or a pair of leather jeans at 1021. She was used to TJ Maxx and Kmart. The closest she had been to this neighborhood's stores had been window shopping. And every time she peered into one of those stores, she felt like the unfortunate step-sister needing to shake the ashes from her apron. Get over yourself, Cinderella, and climb onto that carriage.

Of course, Jocelyn's inner voice had to step in. *Repeat after me. There is no fairy mother. There is no fairy mother.*

Spoil sport.

Practical Jocelyn told her to relax. So what if it really is nothing more than a pumpkin?

You still have the dress and the shoes.

The next morning, when Jocelyn left for Luna's, she held herself in check. For the first few stoplights, she focused on her driving. Keep to the speed limit. Watch out for lights changes. Chicago drivers too often took red as a suggestion. But as she headed into North Side territory, she felt the itch, not so much desire as curiosity. Hitting the mall with friends was one thing; boutiques with the boss who also happened to be your aunt quite another.

When horns blared, she flipped the bird, but she smiled. Reggae music set her shoulders matching the beat. By the time she hit Milwaukee Avenue, she was full out ready, palms tingling, smile permanent.

Luna's was pretty quiet, but then Saturday morning was not exactly rush time. When Jocelyn pushed open the big red door, there were three customers slurping coffee and eating croissants and a strange woman at the bar with Paula. She approached carefully. Don't interrupt, but hey, show me the stuff. The bar itself was strewn with jewelry—wire wrapped gemstone necklaces. Jocelyn ached for a blue one wrapped in copper. Funky key necklaces. Vintage crafted silver that reminded her of zentangle. And bracelets, earrings, toe rings . . . think jewelry and it was there.

Paula was holding up a necklace made from thin silver shells. "Gorgeous," she commented. "This one for sure."

"I want that copper piece." Jocelyn needed to announce herself. Early shopping worked.

Paula started, then turned around and smiled. "Jocelyn. Perfect timing. I want you to meet my friend, Sonia. We've known each other for what—eight years now?"

The woman next to Paula, Sonia, nodded her head while Paula filled in Jocelyn.

"Sonia hand makes these beautiful pieces of jewelry for our place. You've probably noticed them in the window. We sell them on consignment, quickly I might add. The work of this talented lady turns over in a snap."

Sonia extended her hand. "I try to bring in beautiful things. Paula deals in barbed wire. I try for more gentle decorations."

Paula rolled her eyes and tapped her fist at Sonia's shoulder.

"So nice to meet you, Jocelyn. I'm trying to sell my wares to your aunt, here, but her heart's set on taking off with you."

Nice lady, Jocelyn thought. Pretty in a delicate, ash-blonde way. Classy, just like Aunt Paula. Wonder what their story is. Whatever, that merchandise is awesome.

"No problem," Jocelyn answered. "I'll just grab a cup of coffee and mess with my phone while you two take care of business."

"Good," her aunt answered. Then she turned back toward the collection and made her pile—pretty much whatever Sonia had brought in.

As soon as Sonia left, Paula said to a waitress, "Sally, please take these back to my office. My niece and I have plans." To Jocelyn, she said, "Sonia has more talent than I'll ever have. What she can do with found objects and wire is a miracle."

" I guess I'll have to take a look. 'Found object' seems right up my alley."

Paula laughed and hooked her arm through Jocelyn's. "Silly girl. But in this case, 'found' means 'precious.'"

Jocelyn looked down and checked her phone for messages.

The shops in Logan Square were a hoot. Vintage. Campy. Unique. Jocelyn let her senses have a field trip. Each place had its own tang, its own feel. She couldn't help herself. Her fingers tingled.

Clarabell's meant the first purchase. "Of course you can have a clown hanging. What's more comic than the two of us? Here, feel this," Paula cooed as she handed over her choice. "Imagine, the softness of vintage fabric on a hanging of Howdy Doody's buddy." Jocelyn rubbed the fabric against her face and laughed. "Well, Auntie, if you insist." Never had her bedroom walls had such texture.

"And look here. This orange is an exact match." Paula held up an oblong form with puffs of orange and sprigs of orange fringe.

"Paula, what an eye you have." Jocelyn couldn't help herself. She smiled like a kid at Christmas. "Love it!"

When they left Clarabell's the haul needed three bags. At Cotilla's, they nixed the dress. Made her look like an orphan. No point in pursuing the obvious. But the Miss Me jeans. Paula told her if she didn't get them right on the spot, she'd double Jocelyn's shift and give her them for Christmas anyway. Six stores later, they were bag ladies all right. Happy bag ladies.

Back at Luna's, they sat at a back table surrounded by their loot. "I think this calls for a bottle of Simi," Paula said. "We can lick the cork in celebration."

Jocelyn took in the ambiance of the loot. Not a broken doll in the midst of this. A quirky purple pig lamp and a pair of ET earrings, but no busted toys. "I'm going to fix up my bedroom first," she said. "Girls are supposed to love pink, but I am definitely an orange girl myself." Her eyes misted as she looked at her aunt. A lump formed in her throat. Guilt, she thought as she felt it. Her throat had to be stuffed with guilt. Walls she could handle. This made her want to cry. Mean girls don't cry. They sneer.

Shut the hell up and have some fun.

"Aunt Paula, I can't begin to say thank you enough. I've never. . . "

Paula shook her head at her niece. "Nonsense." The word came out as a dismissal, friendly, but dismissive nonetheless. A smile shifted the tone of her face. "I'm the one who should thank you. Thank you for the 'girl time.'"

Paula waved her hand. "My husband left me enough money to shop until we drop every day and not even begin to spend it all. What else should I do with it?" She pointed to a wall. "If you're worried about my investments, I'll sell a couple of paintings and you can feel vindicated."

Paula picked up the wine list and said, "Now, what's the best wine to go with shopping spree."

Cole had them sipping wine and swapping shopping stories in no time. "You saw Christine Olsen looking for leather pants? No judgment intended, but I can't see that lady in leather." He may have said, "No judgment." His expression told the truth.

"Hey, the lady may be eighty-four, but she likes to have fun." Paula was protective of her regulars.

Cole held up his hands, "Far be it from me to tell the wizened Ms. Olsen what to wear." He paused and furrowed his brow. "Red? Really?"

"She told me they went with her Christmas sweater and she would be wearing them to our party this year."

Jocelyn chimed in, "Hey, I have a purple pig. Christine gets to have a red leather ass. This is America after all."

Cole held up the bottle of wine. "Ready?"

That night, Paula sat in her apartment curled up in her favorite chair. The day had been glorious. Just as she reached for her journal, the parts started in; her head felt like the inside of a restaurant packed with customers, impatient and noisy.

The *Children* wailed, "Not fair. She got all the stuff."

The others started harping. Hadn't she vowed to wait, to let life unfold? Just look at her. She couldn't keep a promise to herself for more than one day.

Protector scolded her, "You're rushing her. Deb warned you. Don't rush. But then, if you won't listen to your psychiatrist, you probably won't listen to us." *Protector* stomped off.

Jen laughed at Paula. "You're such a stupid cunt. Can't ever do anything right. Shame on you again. When will you ever learn? Never, that's when."

Paula bowed her head, crossed her arms and rocked. The last of the daylight left the Chicago skyline and still she rocked, her lips clenched in sorrow, her jaw trembling. Only later would she write in her journal.

I have created a beautiful mansion for my alters where they each have their own rooms fashioned for their needs. They are safe. But where can I go when they attack me?

Even the journal had no answer for her.

The next morning, an hour before leaving for class, Jocelyn played decorator while the purple pig lamp cast a good morning glow in a bedroom facing an alley. She'd never cared much about what the place looked like. So what if the only landscaping outside her bedroom window was dumpsters and litter. For her shabby was shabby, nothing chic about it.

51

A poster of Darryl Dixon and his crossbow, ready to split a biter, was the closest item she might call décor and even that had a ripped corner.

But someone had turned a switch on in her body. Granted, she only had a few purchases, but they were a jumble of new toys for a child with just one doll. Barney the pig glowed next to her bed. The clown, newly hanging next to the window, laughed at the outside, Barney's buddy in denying the dowdiness of the neighborhood. And the orange pillow plopped on that threadbare chair added some class. Now if she could get some kind of a throw to hide the rips on that chair . . .

Jocelyn laughed at herself. Holy Martha freaking Stewart. What was she thinking?

What was she thinking, indeed. She was thinking that she could have some fun in her life, that the dump she lived in didn't have to be quite so miserable. The chair, in all its threadbare glory, whispered to her. *Don't get so high and mighty, Lady Jane.* Funny how the chair sounded just like sober Evie. No problem Sober Evie was an anomaly. Just wait it out and it will go away.

Regardless, Jocelyn walked over to the chair, picked up the pillow and hit that critic right in the arm. Then she carefully set the pillow back, gave its center a swat to plump it just so, and went to find her purse. She could take a picture of her new bedroom look and show it to her aunt. Suddenly, the thought of two hours in the library and four hours of lecture didn't seem as much of a trial as she had thought when she woke up. It was, after all, a good day. Wait until she told Alex that the clown had taken Daryl's place on her wall. He'd give her shit and then bet the clown was a psychopath turned zombie killer.

A nagging voice from deep within scolded her. *You are so damn trusting. You watched your mother trust all those years. Trust is another word for stupid. Didn't you learn anything?*

Or maybe you do want to be a good girl and grow up to be just like your mommy. She'd trust a hole in the wall. What else can a daughter expect?

Tick tock.

While Jocelyn drove to her class, Paula struggled downstairs behind the bar. All night long, the alters had pounded at her. Why wouldn't they? They were right. She stood in front of the coffee machine in a dance of anxiety, taking a new filter out and putting in another fresh one, turning toward the water dispenser, carafe in hand, then turning back to the coffee machine without a drop of water. Cole was sitting at the bar, coat still on, thumbing his fingers on his gloves. She finally noticed him after three unsuccessful tries at brewing.

"You're early today," she muttered.

"And you need to talk."

"Take off your coat while I make the coffee." She set the carafe on the back bar and stared at it. "At least I'll make it if I can get my head pulled out." By her tone, she was directing her words to herself. Then Paula was silent. She was silent as she measured the grounds and poured the water into the coffee maker. She was silent as she watched the coffee sputter into the carafe, the machine hissing and groaning as it gave birth to the brown liquid. She was silent as she brought the steaming liquid to her mouth. Silent sucked, got her nowhere.

"It's that bad, huh?"

She barely heard Cole, but obviously, he was on to her. A lunkhead Paula was a Paula in crisis. That boy was going to make a hell of a shrink some day. No need for grad school. He got to practice with her, no doubt more than he wanted.

As Paula carried two white cups across the bar for them, she raised one side of her mouth and lifted her eyebrows in the universal sign of cynicism. "Cole, remind me what you said about taking on too much too fast."

He kept both tone and posture firm but neutral, a loving kind of neutral in its own way. "Okay boss lady. As long as you remind yourself that you're a woman who has come far from so sorry a place. As trite as it sounds, life is a journey." He shook his head and breathed in. "And your journey would have made the ancient Greeks stand up and take notice." He blew on the coffee and took several sips, his eyes all the time focused on her.

She couldn't help the bitterness in her voice. "Kids shouldn't have to watch out for bogeymen on every corner." Her throat felt her sigh. "Especially the ones that devour their young." She joined him in those quiet sips, and then set her cup down, her hands wrapped around it for warmth. "Enough of that. I have a niece. I want to know my niece, envelop her into my life without eating her alive. I want to know if the sister I knew was capable of treating a child—any child, much less that wonderful girl—the way a child deserves to be treated. I watch Jocelyn, looking for signs of the stuffing and masking that drove my survival.

"When she's not aware, I can see shadows. I can't openly say, 'Jocelyn, pray tell, any problems to tell me about?' She'd hightail it out of here faster than I could say 'crazy lady.'"

Cole leaned forward and smiled. "Move slowly, boss lady. Slowly. Truth has a way of announcing itself, given time.' "

"I know, I know, I know." The words blurred into a curse. "She is the daughter of an alcoholic. She's never had an ounce of normal in her life. She wouldn't know trust if it sat down next to her and asked to share a cup of tea." Paula set her elbows on top of the bar and rested her head on her folded hands.

Cole reached out his hand to touch her and pulled back. He knew better than to touch at a time like this. "You sound like you know what to do. Now you just have to take it in, internalize it."

Paula slapped a wave at him, woman in dismissal, then another, but didn't bring up her head.

"You're right." She lifted up her head and snarled with her lip. "You're always right."

Cole went behind the bar and stood before her, offer of a hug clearly visible. She thought, *give him another few years and he might be as good as Joe.* So, she hugged into him, and gave him two solid pats. "Thank God I've got you. You're my sounding board in all this."

Cole returned the thanks. "No, thank you. You're my thesis."

"We are all here to serve." She stood up, bent across the bar, and gave Cole a kiss on the cheek.

CHAPTER 10

Chicago hot dogs. Nothing like them. Must be the pickle relish. Jocelyn licked the green stuff off her bun like it was ambrosia. It was. She and Alex were poking around the Chicago Ridge shopping mall munching on dogs and sodas, sort of a south-side happy hour a few hours early. The place was packed. Teenagers dressed in the best of tatters and low slung pants. Mothers carting babies and snotty toddlers. A few elderly stragglers, one pushing her walker, her face a mask of terror every time one of the teens jostled by. The air screamed with the din of a thousand shoppers, some spouting English, some Spanish, some languages neither of the couple could recognize. Every now and then, a "Get over here or I'll swat your ass" called out. Probably a harried mother. Maybe a girl friend. Gotta get to Charlotte Russe for those eight-inch heels, lover boy. Don't make me late.

When she had been a teen, a mall was the place to be. Hustle a few guys and dump them, then start all over again. Smoke a little pot in dark corners or walk around with vodka-laced seven-up if you needed to feel light. She had let a guy feel her up for the first time behind the palm trees right by the kiddy land. No big deal. She got a Dairy Queen for her acquiescence. Now she and Alex wandered the halls and laid bets on who would be the first to go if the zombie apocalypse hit this particular mall. So much for growing up.

"My bet is on the mothers. They'd be trying to herd the kids. Four-for-one sale for a Walker."

"I'm thinking the glitzy girls. They all ready look like the undead but they still smell human. Sort of."

A trio of girls ambled by. One of them had *Juicy* on her rear and swung her butt cheeks to offer possibilities. Jocelyn pointed. "I wonder if there are *Depends* that say that. Gives a whole new meaning to the message."

They stopped outside of Hot Topics. Usual awesome tees in the window and bobble heads of the Governor and Rick Grimes. They still needed Daryl, but commercial zombie land hadn't yet made him available. Then she saw it in the display window. Walking Dead string lights. Now that says Halloween. She could string them over her clown hanging. Daryl would surely forgive her for the displacement.

Arm in arm, they sauntered into the store, crazy kids whiling away a Saturday afternoon. No test or papers approaching. Halloween season was about to break loose. She had enough money to buy two things, as long as one was on sale. While they prowled inside, she could tell Alex about shopping with her aunt. "Lucky girl," he'd tell her. And he'd be right. She was free to add to her cache of goodies. Free to celebrate a known friendship and one that was blossoming. Something inside her melted, one of those clogs of pissy that had jammed itself inside her. Amazing. She felt so light.

Maybe there wasn't so much crap clogging her up after all.

From the speakers inside the store came the sounds of organ music, campy chords followed by a few shrieks and then the exhale of more chords. Jocelyn grabbed Alex's arm. "Oh dear, whatever shall we do?" Alex did his lifting one eyebrow thing while he led her toward a plastic crossbow. "Don't worry, Babe. Whatever the Apocalypse sends our way, we can handle it—as long as we have each other."

They burst into laughter and went looking for the lights.

CHAPTER 11

Halloween night. All right, not Halloween exactly. Just Logan Square's take on a reason to throw a costume party and treat the holiday as a season instead of a night. Second Saturday in October. The Ides of October. As close as you could get to the real day and still not have to get up the next morning. Shops advertised "killer deals." Bars promised a pub crawl with "Best brains in town" and a zombie beauty pageant at Psycho Suzi's as the last stop.

At Luna's, Jocelyn first checked herself in the employees' bathroom mirror one last time before officially starting work. Gotta have the image on such an auspicious night. Not too much blood and gore; simply blackened eyes and some gluey pink stuff on her lids. Art was a matter of simplicity. Retro zombie housewife. Black polka-dotted dress complete with pink apron and crinolines and—oh yes, plenty of rips and blood. Ethyl and Lucy meet the Apocalypse. She peeped out of Evie's old rhinestone studded chrome glasses, thank you Momma very much. Of course there was that little drip of red tissue hanging from the frame. Went so well with the ear necklace Alex had found on line. She'd thought about sticking one of Paula's dolls in her apron pocket, but she didn't have room. No problem. She had one for later. If she couldn't scare them, one of those dolls certainly would. She'd have to put some ketchup on her ticket pad before she started work. Only then did she venture out to check in with the bar crowd before she put her polka-dot persona to work.

Cole had on a phony white goatee and glasses and a tweed coat. His name tag said, "My name is Sigmund. How is your Id today?" No surprise there. Elsa, the new girl, was bride of Frankenstein. Must take her name seriously. Even Sonia was there, decked out in her own creation, multiple strands of skulls, snakes, and wire-twisted wraith. She had come to wrap Paula up in gossamer fabric wings. A satin sash of brushes and pods of paint hung around her waist. Again, thin wire and jewels throughout. Jocelyn needed to get to know Sonia better.

8:00. Time to check in. Only three hours of work and then the pub crawl. Jocelyn checked the gore glued to her shoes, patted her gelled hair, and rubbed a new piece of sculpture near her station for luck. Glass drops of blood spilling from a daisy lined with eyes.

By 9:00, Jocelyn was sure her shoes had blood for real. Everyone within a ten-mile radius had crowded into the place. Murmurs and growls, an occasional shriek, one werewolf howl every ninety seconds—ah, the ambiance of Luna's. And everyone wanted a drink—now. Jocelyn pressed herself next to the bar to avoid two vampires who nibbled strings of red licorice off of each other's necks. Get a room, people, or maybe a crypt.

Cole lined up three blue drinks steaming from only who knew what, wiped a rag off the bar, and ducked candy corn flying across the bar. That boy could do anything and still keep his good mood. She could use a nip or two of good mood right now. "Hey Joce," he said, pointing to the drinks. "Table twenty-four. The guy dressed like a top hat will pay."

Who the hell dresses up like a top hat?

By 10:30 most of the crazies had left. Luna's would close in a half hour. Only three couples and a party of four left from the frenzy. One couple was fighting, the top-hat guy and his date. The party of four was slithering lower and lower down their chairs as the line of shot glasses grew. Cabs for them for sure.

One lone twosome, nestled in the back corner, had to be in their seventies and dressed to the nines, he in a suit from the sixties, she in a sheath and pill box hat posed just so on her permed hair. Bet those hadn't always been costumes for them. They had been party-watching all night, feeding each other snacks and beer when they weren't oohing over the entertainment. Jocelyn wasn't sure whether she wanted to hug them or feed them rat poison.

She hadn't heard the footsteps behind her, never felt the fingertips until they jabbed her sides. While she jerked around, fists ready to swing, a voice called out, "Happy Pseudo-Halloween!"

"Alex, you idiot. Good thing I don't have a tray. I'd be jerking it out of your neck right now."

58

"Love you, too." Her buddy backed up and did a turn-around. "Like the look?" He was dressed as a clown, red nose and mouth, white of face. Lime green hair stuck out from above his ears to the bald top of his head. "Look on and love. I know. It's a lot to take in." He pointed to Paula and waved. "Your aunt likes it."

"Of course she does. Have you noticed her art?"

Yep, his head was typical clown. That is, except for the knife sticking out from the bald spot and the streaks of blood that snaked their way down his face. He sported a huge blue polka-dotted tie slathered with some gelatin substance. Jocelyn scanned his torso. More blood and goop. A rubber sword hung from a scabbard tied to a purple belt at his waist.

"See? A hybrid," he said, triumph on what she could see of his face. "I'm your wall. Clown meets Zombie hunter. I wanted Daryl's crossbow, but that'd be too wieldy in the bars tonight. I settled for a sword." He frowned. Too bad. "If I had the crossbow in the first place, that walker wouldn't have stabbed me."

Jocelyn made a face, one that tried to look peeved, and pointed to the bar. "Go sit down while I make the rounds. Freud there will take care of you. I'm still working until midnight." Thank the good Lord Luna's wasn't on the pub crawl list. Paula knew better. She'd have to man the place by herself if she kept it open. She even promised the help they could leave at eleven and she'd clean up.

Forty-five minutes later, Alex and Jocelyn were ready to go. Cole waved them over, turned his attention to Alex. "Before you take off, I got something to show you. He took off his jacket and turned around. There, on the back of his black tee, in glorious bright fluorescent green were the words, "Psych Guy." Cole beamed while the others laughed.

Alex jibbed, "Thought you were supposed to dress up like someone else. The way I see it, you're just you a few years later."

"Well, I could certainly say the same about you. Figured you found your inner self, especially the clown part—nah, the hatchet in the head."

Alex turned up his lip. "Funny, Dude."

Cole, arms folded, shook his head. "I must be right because I am (he flexed both biceps) 'Psych Guy'!" He snapped his towel. "Now you two children take off and have fun.

Alex grabbed Jocelyn's arm and shouted "Whatever," but he was laughing while he did it. The two of them were shoved out the door. Paula the artist fairy waved her magic wand at them and told them to have fun. "Hurry up or I'll spray-paint you pink."

Lucky Fulci's had once been a cold storage building. Nothing was cold about it tonight. Wildly garbed patrons pushed in and out of the entrance full of raucous laughter and spitty sounds. Jocelyn and Alex barely missed being rolled over by someone dressed like an eyeball. Inside, two girls collected cover charges, one dressed top to bottom in gray, complete with writhing gray dreads and face paint, the other in green. Green girl had razor-like teeth and bloody eyeballs. From her back rose five snake-like monsters, two on the left and three on the right. Jocelyn said to the gray creature, "I'd guess Christian Gray, but you only have a couple of shades."

Alex piped in, "Let's play mythology. Scylla and Charybdis. Hot monsters." He raised his eyebrows. "Odysseus never had it so good."

Snake girl did a campy hiss. "Pretty good. Most people think we're some kind of zoo." She held out her stamp and Gray girl said, "Got a ticket?"

Both Jocelyn and Alex held out their hands just as the sounds of Obituary celebrated with "Kill them all. Let them rot." Nothing like undead metal to start the night rocking.

Lucky's was amazing, really. Thirty-foot ceilings, walls lined with hooks and kill tools from Chicago's stockyard days. Impressive. Who did he have to bribe to get away with that in a public place? Tonight, in honor of the season, the owner had added what Jocelyn didn't even want to imagine, red and dripping, to the tools. In a back corner, a dry ice machine cranked out atmosphere while dancers writhed and stomped. A disco ball hung from the center of the ceiling cast dizzying swaths of light from wall to wall, engulfing the dancers in even more weirdness, their bodies shape-shifting under the light.

The two of them headed to the bar three steps down from the entry. "Can't even imagine what kind of drinks tonight."

Alex nudged her. "Bet that won't keep you from finding out, though."

Jocelyn paused on one of the steps. "Then I'm going to have to depend on my own special clown hero and his trusty sword. That is, if you can get it out of your head in time to save me."

Grabbing her hand, Alex leaped down the last two steps. "C'mon, Lucy, stick with me and we won't have to find out."

Three Voodoo-punches later, Jocelyn was on the dance floor, arms up, hips celebrating the night, Alex all elbows and shoulders across from her. She leaned forward to shout something to him and felt a heaviness behind her, pushing at her. A pair of large hands grabbed at her hips. In a wisp, the noise, the lights, all the sensory deluging the bar was gone, replaced by a darkness. Her throat tightened. She looked toward Alex. He was busy gyrating, oblivious to her. The form pushed against her, a man's form, legs and groin and hardness. Her polka dots and crinolines were no bridge against this invasion.

She was no cheap piece of ass to be groped in a bar with meat hooks and blood and swirling whatever. At least that's what her mind told her. That is before it screamed, *move, bitch*. It was an order right out of fight or flight. Trouble was, the rest of her body soaked itself in stiffness. She couldn't breathe. She was going to choke to death. Her left hand held the doll that mimicked the one from Luna's; she forced her right hand to form a fist. She swerved and turned around. The form, garbed in black, was moving, white teeth in a smile the only color on his body. He was a shadow. A huge, broad-shouldered shadow leering at her, his arms now up, hands clasped, waiting. She froze, nothing but a statue standing in the middle of the dance floor while sound and sweat bounded around her.

"Jocelyn!" Alex grabbed her just as she was about to pass out. She managed two deep breaths, regained her balance, and braced her feet against the floor to know she could feel the hardness beneath her. Then she fled, bumping into shoulders and hips as she ran through the bar and out to the street.

When Alex grabbed her outside, she screamed silently. No noise could make it out of her throat. She was still trembling.

"My, Joce, what's wrong? What happened?"

Her knees gave out. Once again, Alex held her so that she wouldn't fall. "I have to go; I have to go; I have to go." She steadied herself enough to stand. "I'll explain tomorrow. I have to go." Her voice was a rasp as she ran toward her car two blocks away, her hands digging into her apron pocket for her keys. Horns blared when she darted across the street. She left her best friend standing on the sidewalk, mouth agape, watching the girl he thought he knew run for her life.

She might have worried about cops out that night, but the shaking, the tears cut through any hope of rational thought. *Stupid, stupid, stupid,* she told herself. No matter. Street lights were a blur, steering a challenge, even holding onto the wheel.

She lay in bed that night, every light in her apartment on, holding on to a doll with a duct-taped mouth. She was her very own gruesome piece of art.

The next morning, the world still felt skewed. Jocelyn pushed herself awake at ten, but only because her phone was ringing. Aunt Paula. Bet she wanted to know if she had fun last night.

Fun? Sure. Some douche-bag tried to grab me on the dance floor, and instead of clobbering him, I turned into a freak. Oh yeah, and my best bud thinks I'm a loon. I turned hysteria into aerobic exercise, but what-the-hell. We had a blast.

"Yeah, I had a great time. Have a bit of a hang over. Need some sleep, though. You know how it is."

Did she? How many pervs had grabbed at Aunt Paula?

"Too much bar boogie, huh. I'll let you go. See you next week."

When Paula hung up, Jocelyn sat there with the phone in her hand, squeezing it. She rubbed the phone against her arms, up and down her legs. Not enough pressure, worthless thing. A ball point pen lay on her bed stand. Could she force a tiny rip, just one to draw attention away from the panic? She fell back against the pillow, phone still in hand.

She should call Alex.

What would she say? *Hi, it's your good friend Jocelyn, the one who thinks most survivors of the Apocalypse are pusses. Of course, I run from a stupid costume for no reason at all except to prove I'm an idiot. Oh yeah, and I want to rip my skin and watch the blood flow.* Might as well drown the worthless pile she called Jocelyn in the bathtub.

Even as she poured contempt upon herself, a separate darkness bubbled inside of her. The walls she had built so wisely buckled within her.

What was her problem? A guy grabs your ass in a bar; that's a Friday night. A faceless figure that grabs said ass conjures up images that slapped against those walls, images that smelled of sewage, black and oily and deep, images that had sent her on a night of helpless weeping. She shook even thinking about them.

Get yourself together, woman.

No way would Alex put up with last night's Jocelyn. She needed to shake this off. The walls would hold. They had for two decades against crap worse than this.

They better. Because if they folded, she would too.

Good advice, self. So why did the feel of panic knotting in her gut pummel her?

He should have a headache. They'd had enough to drink to score at least the start of a burner. Alex sat up in his bed, his feet on the floor, head face down held by his hands and elbows on his knees. He tipped his head up, glanced to the right. His green wig lay on the floor next to the scalp cover with the knife still in it. Above the leftovers from last night, on the wood box that served as a nightstand, more leftovers. A half-empty bottle of Captain's and a fully emptied glass.

He shook himself into awareness. The place was a mess. Clothes piled on top of towels, books sprawled and stacked. Pretty much his style. But not the rum bottle and glass. He wasn't a bedroom drinker. Or hadn't been until last night.

Ides of Halloween. Supposed to be fun. Celebration. Reverie. They were bathing themselves in gruesome, a couple of gore geeks burning off the stress of working students.

Then she'd run away. No reason given. No *something's wrong, I'm sick, my knees are dying*, whatever. She'd just flipped out and run.

She exhausted him. He'd promised himself he'd hang on. Be there for her. The old through thick and thin. The trip, though, was leaving him scarred.

Get over yourself, Stumme. Was that his idea or her words? No matter. The advice was right on. Jocelyn was his friend. His Dead-Head buddy. When she had run last night, she was no retro zombie. No, she was frozen panic, a girl hopped up on adrenaline in full flight mode gurgling nonsense.

He wanted to reach out to her, to comfort her, to wrap her in safety and promise her the ghouls would never get her.

He was her friend, after all. And he had promised her buddies-for-life.

He reached toward the floor to scoop up his phone, scrolled down the contacts list and stopped just short of pressing the button. What would he say?

He could tease. *Zombie girls are tough. They don't go running.* That would get him a click. And an ex-friend.

Hey, want me to go find Shadow Man and stomp on him? I could beat him with my rubber sword. Jocelyn fought her own battles. She'd more likely save him in a fix.

Again, a click.

So, what do you say to a best friend, the essence of tough, the one who had flipped out in front of you?

He texted *Call me,* dropped the phone, leaned back and sprawled onto the bed, flung his arm across his forehead and waited.

CHAPTER 12

From the journal of Paula Ross

I love cemeteries. Lots of people say they do, that the meander of the road and the peace of the setting are so comforting. I can see their point. But what I love are the patterns. The wrought iron fence, each perfectly uniform bar keeping out the chaos of the living. The great old trees marching through the acres. The old stones from centuries ago worn smooth by weathering. The obelisks, the cherubs, mother's hands, even a hunting dog, rows and rows of remembrances to plead with decay not to win. They march in rows, each its own entity and yet, in this place of death, so much the same. One stone says, brother, son, friend. Why brother *first*? Was this a sacrifice of a mother to comfort a stricken sibling? It has its own story among the stories of them all.

Yes. When I walk through a cemetery, I want to know the stories, even if they come from my imagination. These stories, they too, are patterns. What patterns do they form? The patterns of my own life are splintered and etched in pain. Many I know now. Many still lie hidden.

So I walk and speculate. The child buried beneath the angel. Was he an imp, given to tantrums and a mother's futile wish in miracles? Or was he an angel, too young to know how life beats on the living? That modern stone with the couple's picture. Technology is amazing. Put the photo there for all time while the pair rots beneath. But the picture shows them arm in arm. Perhaps a happy life. I found my love and lost him. Perhaps the stone lovers still hold on for eternity.

My family is buried close to Logan Square, except for my sister. She I visit. Here.

I come here every week to see Evie. Her silence is a gift, her grave a test. No stone. Nothing but a metal marker with Quint in brass. Ah, if the dead, indeed, can turn in their graves, my sister is rolling. Demanding attention *in life; ignored in death. I honored her at the visitation by showing up and gained a treasure. Jocelyn. Can she break our curse and be whole? The girl had to sleep with a baseball bat to be safe, she told me. When she spoke, she wore the words like a shield. What was her danger?*

When I wander through the sections, I'll ask the dead. They know as much as anyone.

CHAPTER 13

Jocelyn parked her car in Row 117 of the Franklin Cemetery and got out. She hadn't been here since Evie's internment last September, disrespectful daughter that she was. Starwarski Brothers had left a burnished metal marker stamped with *Quint,* part of their package. The grave was new, covered in dulled green sod in need of watering, not yet part of the carpet that went on forever. She walked forward to lay some plastic-wrapped flowers she'd picked up at the Jewel at the head of her mother's grave.

Why was she here? That question had wormed at her the entire way here. Not grief. If she grieved, the loss was pain from someone she couldn't access. Not accessing her mother was a relief. Not guilt, at least right now—though there probably would be plenty of that to dredge up once she had a mind to. All she felt was a free-floating anxiety that made her want to start chain-smoking.

She backed away and stood at the foot of the grave. "So Mom, things are a little crazy with me right now. Yeah, I'm still in school, no worry about that. Made the honor roll even. You always were proud of my grades. Not me, of course, just the grades, something you could brag about while you poured for your customers. Oh, and I met your sister. Thanks for telling me about her while I was growing up. Nothing like finding the family at a social setting.

"I should have known. Why have a family? That meant completeness. Nothing was complete in our house, nothing ever a set. Not the dishes, not the sheets, not the boyfriends you carted home." Jocelyn had to pause. Otherwise, she'd choke on the words. She kicked at a branch.

"The thing I want to ask you, though, now that we have a moment together, is 'Why am I such a fucking loon?' I survived crappy apartments, crappy boyfriends—the ones who acted like I was part of the deal were especially fun—crappy everything and I did fine. And now that the crap is over, I feel like a lunatic."

A soft voice behind her gave an answer. "You're not a lunatic."

Jocelyn's gasp surged through her before it left her throat. She almost choked on it before she turned around to see her Aunt Paula standing there. Paula's arms were folded across her chest, her mouth tightened into a whip cord.

"You are not a lunatic!" Paula's voice held that fifth-grade teacher tone that said, *"And that's final."*

Jocelyn hunched over, her hands splayed across her mouth. The vision of a red-haired ghost was still stamped on her mind, probably would be for eternity, a ghost that hovered and waited for something her daughter could not give her—tears and forgiveness. "You scared the crap out of me!" She looked at the ground and rocked back and forth, toe to heel.

Paula bent forward and placed her hands on Jocelyn shoulders. "I'm so sorry. I didn't mean to frighten you."

A couple two graves down watched the scene, bodies turned forward in case they needed to help, but then went back to plucking grass the trimmer had missed around the grave.

Jocelyn stood up and swiped at imaginary dirt on her coat, then gave Paula a limp hug before she stood back and asked, "What are you doing here?"

"I come here occasionally, when I'm not stomping in other graveyards. Weird hobby of mine. I like to think where it's quiet, and there's not much going on in a cemetery. Since your mother died, I mostly come here. It was my favorite cemetery, anyway." Paula held out her arm. "Here, let's take a walk and you can tell me why in the world you would think you're a lunatic when you've obviously survived my sister. You have every right to be a lunatic, of course, but you're as sane as any of . . . well, you're sane."

Jocelyn stuck her hands into her coat pocket, pulled one out and ran it through her hair. "Thanks for the assurance and the offer. If it's all right with you, let's find a bench and sit down. My heart needs to find its way back into my chest. Right now it's in my stomach."

"Bench it is, then. There's one right over in the next row." She patted Jocelyn's hand. "We'll get your heart back in place, and then you can tell your Aunt Paula why you're here, and why you think such a ridiculous thing about yourself."

Five minutes later, they were seated. The bench felt cold beneath Jocelyn's jeans, so she unwrapped her scarf and sat on it. Two pots of geraniums on each side of the iron bench had survived the fall so far. They gave off a bit of hope to a college girl who wanted more to cut her wrists than face what she was sure she was becoming, a slobbering baby who ran from shadows, pathetic nut case. She sat back on the bench, face tilted toward the sky—as if that would give her answers. Several beats later, she pulled her head back down and looked outward, toward her mother's grave.

Paula sat quietly next to her, hands folded.

"You have to understand," Jocelyn began. "I am the poster child for surviving. Mom was such a spineless twit . . . " Jocelyn grimaced and drew in her shoulders. Nothing like talking ill of the dead right in front of her.

Paula took Jocelyn's hands in hers. The warmth soothed Jocelyn's shaking. "I think 'spineless twit' pretty much covers it, as I recall."

Jocelyn felt the squeeze of her aunt's hand as she talked. She lost the shaking and now felt resentment rise in her even as she continued to look at the ground. "As soon as I found even the promise of a friend, we moved. Each apartment was crappier than the other. Some kids had lawns. We had oil-stained alleys and cardboard blown onto cracked sidewalks. Mom didn't care—as long as she had someone warm and a cool bottle of vodka.

"When I was twelve, she'd get so drunk, she didn't even notice the guys who took a turn toward my bedroom before I kicked them out." Jocelyn's chest, her throat, turned to stone. She had to stop talking and make herself breathe.

"I was a walking, talking autobot. It's how I survived." Jocelyn turned to face Paula, keeping her hands warmed inside the leather gloves. "Then things started to go right. I got out. Made friends. Earned my way. Forgot all that crap. Life wasn't great, but it was okay."

Paula shook her head. "We don't forget the crap. We just don't let it run our lives." She pulled Jocelyn up by her hands. When Jocelyn was on her feet, Paula put her arm around her and stepped them forward. "Let's walk. It's so much easier to talk it out when you're moving."

The first few steps were awkward, but the two women were quickly side by side. Paula began. "Tell me more about how you earned your way. That seems like the Jocelyn I know. Then we'll try to figure out the rest."

Her life spilled out. All the years of cheap apartments and broken promises. Days were a constant maybe. Have a program at school, a conference, anything. Momma may show up. She may not. She always promised. She always cried afterward and made more promises she wouldn't keep.

Nights alone while Evie wasted herself downstairs—those were a for sure. They usually found a place to live over a bar; that way her mom could wait on tables and pick up strays while she stayed upstairs and did her homework. Jocelyn learned to sleep through the sounds of two a.m. She learned to sleep through all sorts of things. And she learned to swallow the anger until it became a dull weight in the bottom of her gut. Jocelyn told her story all right, didn't hold a thing back. When she finished, she hunched over, set her clenched hands on top of her head, held her elbows tightly against the side of her head.

Paula did not touch her. She simply talked, low and calmly. "If I tell you that this is a good sign, you'll think I'm the one who's nuts. But sweetie, a good sign it is. You did what you had to do in order to survive; did a damn fine job of it. Now it's time to let the pain settle so you can let it go."

Jocelyn stood up and looked at her aunt. "Are you telling me this is a good thing?" Her voice laced with sarcasm. "If this is so good, why, I bet a full-out fall into lunacy would be a blessing."

"No way it should be full out. Baby steps, my child. Baby steps. You've worked so hard to cope with the bad that you haven't had the time or strength to work on the healing. All that hard work stuffing down the pain and trauma. It's the storm before the calm. You don't just get over it any more than the cow can jump over the moon. The thing is—you need to find out who you are, not simply what has happened, even if what happens to us in part defines us."

Jocelyn kicked at an imaginary rock, her head down so she didn't have to keep eye contact. "The thing that scares the hell out of me isn't just not knowing who I am or even being some kind of lunatic. It's becoming my mother." She wrapped her arms around her. "I'd rather be in a straightjacket than living the life of that woman. What if it's *like mother, like daughter?*"

Paula leaned forward. "Let me tell you a secret. Your chance of being your mother is about as likely as my chance of being the first broad on Mars. Won't be happening, Kid."

Jocelyn shoved her hands in her coat pockets. "Thanks for the confidence. I've walked away from any guy dumb enough to want to be 'my thing,' more out of fear of baggage than anything else. A little hooking up? No problem. But talk of romance sounded like the warning rattle of a snake before it bites."

Paula folded her arms and smiled. "And some day you'll be able to separate the snakes from the good guys. When that day comes, you'll know."

Jocelyn smiled back, but inside she thought, *Momma thought they were all good guys.* Look where that got her.

A short time later, Jocelyn, calmed and freshly hugged, had left, a promise to take care still in the air as Paula walked back to the bench to have a seat and think. Their meeting had been anything but expected, but in Paula's mind proof that coincidence was design in disguise. The two women had formed a bond. But a bond had to be based on truth. She knew that in her blood. Jocelyn needed the truth about her aunt. All of it.

"Don't rush it." Cole's words came back to her. "I'm not rushing, my friend." The words tumbled onto the cold pavement. "I'm just going to give our relationship a little push." And she knew exactly how she would do it.

Today was Tuesday, slow day for business even on a sunny day, much less a day of gray mist. For Jocelyn, it was a day of no scheduled classes and relief that midterms were over. Here at Luna's, a temp bartender with enough tats on her upper body to count as a work of art sat on a bar stool watching television. Cole was off on a four-day trip to Door County. And no boss. Again. This week, Paula had come down from her upstairs apartment a couple of times, but mostly either holed up in her second floor studio or spent time at unnamed appointments with someone named Deb.

Jocelyn missed her. The feeling was strange. Jocelyn didn't often miss anyone. Marti and Amber, sure. But they were part of a life long gone. Alex? She saw him too often to miss him. But this dystopic fairy mother that patted her hand and told her she was wanted, Jocelyn missed her. Even the tortured dolls were growing on her. What the hell. Jocelyn congratulated herself on being Lunaized and walked behind the bar to clean glasses.

Around 2:00, the FedEx man tooled in with a delivery—large narrow pieces that probably were canvasses and eight other boxes. After Jocelyn signed for them, she glanced around, wondering where to place them until her aunt returned.

"Oh, Joce, I almost forgot." Tattoo girl—was her name Elsa—spoke up. "Paula left a key to her studio. She wants you to take the delivery stuff up there and set it on the big painter's table."

No problem. Nothing heavy. No more than three trips up stairs. Ten minutes later, Jocelyn had the boxes parked on the landing outside the studio door. She tucked one of the papered canvases under her arm and unlocked the door. When she used her elbow to flip on the light switch, she faced away from the chaos that was Paula's art studio, so when she turned and entered, her first thought was *National Treasure,* the part when Nicolas Cage looks at the unfolding labyrinth of artifacts. Okay, that wasn't a fair comparison, but this place was a trove, at least forty feet long, cavernous yet stuffed with all things that spelled out *artist*. Baskets, tables, rows of canvases both painted and fresh, industrial shelving, a six-foot round clock made out of rusted tin, furniture plugged into the chaos.

Jocelyn took it in like a tourist in awe. Wooden floors beaten into submission by decades of feet stretched the length of the room, broken up by a couple of paint-stained tarps. The ceilings, held by beams, weathered and formidable, made *cathedral* an understatement. Chicago nightlife carried on outside a wall of windows to her left. At the back, a lifetime of supplies was housed in ten-foot tall shelves. To her right, against an exposed brick wall, ancient doors and windows were stacked, with artwork of all sizes leaning against them. One canvas, fastened to the wall, had to be at least ten feet tall, a mural of muted shapes and colors as a background, its central image a barren tree reaching clear to the top of the canvas and continuing for several feet above, its branches a part of the wall.

How the hell had she done that? Two sofas faced each other toward the back, centered by a rug and table. So artists had down time. Cool.

Jocelyn carried the first canvas into the room and set it down while she searched for the painter's table. Okay. Where was the painter's table? She kept up her scanning, this time to her right. Had she been facing the other side of the room before she set it down, she might have dropped the canvas, probably on her toe. As it was, she gripped it until her hands turned white and she shrieked at a five-foot high portrait of a little girl propped up on a low easel in front of the painter's table, the single piece of art not against a wall or a shelf.

The child swept into life on that canvas couldn't have been more than six or seven. She wore only her underpants, Granny Annies her friends would call them, cotton whites that stretched above her waistline. Very 1950's. The child had no arms. It wasn't a Venus di Milo thing, not by a long shot. The little girl's arms had been ripped off, the skin flaps folded over near her armpits, unwieldy stitches of black x's marching across the flaps.

Disgusting.

The girl's legs were centered with knobby knees splashed with freckles. From the end of her underpants words fell, smears and tatters of red and blue and brown, tumbling like worn Tinkertoys from a box. Each word, no matter the color, no matter the quality, was the same. *Shame.*

Scary.

But the clinker, the cherry on the sundae, the star on the crown, was the girl's face. The face was innocent, freckles here dotting the girl's nose and cheekbones, a sweet little mouth rosebud lovely. The face was void of expression, eyes dull with a sadness, a grief no child should know.

The face belonged to her Aunt Paula.

When Paula came home, reached the second floor landing on her way to her apartment, all the pieces of her delivery had been neatly tucked inside the studio. The landing was empty. Except for Jocelyn who sat on the floor, legs stretched out in front of her, arms folded across her chest. The key to the studio was in her pocket. A good niece would not take a chance on losing her aunt's key. Family is so important, after all.

"Why Jocelyn, dear, whatever are you doing here? Elsa locked up an hour ago." Aunt Paula's voice sounded so sincere, so concerned. Jocelyn certainly needed to answer.

Answer she did. Not with her voice, however. She answered with her eyes, hard circles that held the question, the cement of her shoulders, the rigidity of her body as she rose.

"Who are you?" She spit out the words. Her body cried it out along with her voice. It was an accusation, not a question.

Jocelyn Quint turned toward the stairs and walked out. Her back ached. A knot had taken possession of her stomach. And her heart? Numb as a boxer battered beyond pain. She stood up and turned toward the stairway. She could have been a model, so erect was her frame, so well held was her head. She walked that way until she came to her car, sat in it and gripped the steering wheel, fingers in a death grip and shoulders shaking. Images, black and white, flashed through her mind so quickly she could not even identify them. But she felt them. They were fearsome. She wanted to vomit.

Minutes or hours later—who knew—Jocelyn raced up the steps to her own apartment and thrust in the key to her door, hands shaking, mind demanding her to hurry, sure that the boogieman was female and about to strike. Once inside, she slammed the door shut, locked it and turned, her back braced against the door. Then she let her body slide to the floor until she sat there, head down and knees up, arms wrapped tight, clutching her purse. Damn, she was so stupid. When would she ever learn? Idiot.

Trust. Her body was laughing at her. She had trusted. Stupid, stupid girl. Trust is an illusion. A joke. It's like Santa Claus, real until it's not; and the truth of that kicks you in the gut, the pain a lesson in never believing. She rocked, banging against the wall, the force against the hardness a staccato of her anguish.

Going to bed was out of the question. Monsters weren't just under the bed; they were everywhere, so lying in bed just invited them to swoop in. She stood up, threw her purse onto the sofa bed and stalked to the bathroom.

She looked in the mirror. A white face stared back, eyes huge and rimmed with red. Her body hummed with need. No way. She would not cut. Darkness. Cold. They sang their siren song to her. She grasped the edges of the cabinet mirror until the edges cut into her fingers. She leaned in with an aahh, and then let go as if her fingers were burning.

She could call Marti. She should call Marti.

What the hell could Marti do, you fool?

She moved her hands down to the sink, grabbed the porcelain edges, wrapped her fingers tight to find control even as she rocked against the thing. Her words came out. They had to be spoken as if sound would give her stability. "You are stronger than this. You are stronger than shame. You are stronger than pain." The words coursed out of her at the mirror. She stormed out of the bathroom and sat at her kitchen table. No way should she be in complete dark after what she had seen, but she needed the darkness. The bathroom light would protect her while she took in the darkness.

She couldn't quit her job. Out of the question. A realization seeped in. Her first instinct was to beat against it. But it stayed and demanded of her. What about Paula? Could she quit her aunt? The woman had welcomed her, hugged her, listened to her. The woman cared.

Are you out of your mind? Her past screamed the question. Have you learned nothing? They all care. They all hug. Frank hugged Evie too. When he wanted something. Just before he hit her.

Your aunt is a whack job. Just like the rest of the family.

Just like you.

Tick tock, stupid girl.

"Shut up! Shut the fuck up!" Her fists pounded the table, and she wept, her tears globs of pain, pulling at her until her throat ached and her head knotted. Too bad. It wasn't like the tears were an option. They just were. Just like her life.

She woke with a start. It was light out. How long had she slept?

She sat up. Her head hurt. She noticed that first. Then she felt the stiffness of her back, the rest of her body following. Some parts throbbed. Some parts ached with a dullness.

She stared out the kitchen window at the brick wall of the next apartment. A small welling started in her belly, more energy than substance, so light, just a flitting. She felt another nip in her shoulders, the nape of her neck. Feelings, just babies. Feelings that could comfort.

Give it time, the feelings told her. *It's more than a crazy lady and her paintings.*

Easy for you to say, she answered. You're not living in a kaleidoscope.

Kaleidoscope for sure, that tumbling—she knew it, that tumbling, felt the freak-show of rawness when trust turned on the dupe who trusted. She wanted to believe in trust, had clutched at the hope of it in abject hunger as a child. Over and over, it had kicked at her, pounded at her belly. But

75

then she met Paula. Paula had awakened something in her that had been knotted for so long from all the letdowns.

Way to go, Auntie Paula. Way to make me hope again and then stomp on me for the fool I am. You are one with the Evster. She'd line up the sweet words when she needed her daughter to behave. So often the woman with a motive.

"Yes, you're my baby girl. Let me brush your hair and make you pretty."

"Here's a burrito and a couple of Ho Ho's. Stay in your room, Jocelyn, and for God's sake be quiet."

"Be nice to the gentleman, Jocelyn; he's my new friend."

"You're my baby girl; of course you're my baby. Now just be quiet and go away."

Might as well slit your throat and bleed out as lay your heart open and trust.

She looked out the window at the bricks in the building next door. No guidance there. Big surprise. Must be easy, being a brick.

CHAPTER 14

From the journal of Paula Ross

A *fool. I am such a fool. Cole told me to wait, not to rush. Jocelyn cried out, "Who are you?" It was a curse, not a question.*

How could the girl know that "Who are you?" is plural? We are Paula. All of us. The children. They're still hiding, terrified. A closet is safer for them right now than a relationship with me. Jocelyn's face in that hallway, contorted and full of contempt, those great dark eyes of hers rounded and terrible. The face terrified them. What did they think? That they were getting a new sister?

Jen curses. Mother *comforts. It's what she does, no matter the sin. How can she comfort a fool?*

What a pissing contest between the two, Jen *and* Mother. *They've been at war for hours. My bet's on* Jen. *She's hyped when I binge. Doritoes. Cheese curls. Muffins and brownies. Everything I could sweep up at the 7–11, it sits like cement. Stuff it in, the body demanded. But cheese curls? I hate cheese curls.*

I've centered myself as much as I can. Breathe in, one, two, three, four, breathe out for seven. Shoulders are still cement. Legs numb. But my arms work. I can write.

What can I say? I blew it.

CHAPTER 15

Two weeks after THE INCIDENT, as the days crawled by, Jocelyn drove her clunker to Luna's, today for the seventh time since her discovery in Paula's studio. Just as every other of the six trips, her mind was playing ping-pong.

She had to work. No brainer. Food and gas were not luxuries. No brainer. Mocking her was the other side. Jocelyn's aunt had scared the crap out of her. Her arms still felt empty, numb inside. Practical side hit back. Like you haven't put up with crazy your whole life? Deal and take home the check. Besides, she didn't have to sit and chat with the boss. She couldn't. At least not yet.

That's where aunt and niece were now, not quite a Cold War between them, but a chill nonetheless. Her aunt kept her space. Even Cole held in his usual teasing. Good thing.

So, eggshells being what they are, the walk at work today was tough. Customers enjoyed her quick service and equally quick wit. They didn't know they were in a play being acted out while they noshed. She smiled. She doted. She wore her mask like a real trooper. But her body needed cracking in places she had forgotten had bones. Her teeth set a record for gritting when she wasn't consciously working her attitude for the job. And now, detente was rearing its ugly head.

The whole time she worked, Jocelyn had kept a note folded in her apron, one that had been left for her at her station when she walked in last week. The penmanship was art in and of itself etched on parchment. Paula Quint Ross knew her stationary skills.

Whenever you're ready . . . Paula had written. Which, Jocelyn wondered every time she fingered the folded sheet, was more important—*whenever* or *ready*?

The first days after she had run, *Screw you* had been embedded on her tongue. Slowly, the two words lost their edge. Now they just rolled around in her mouth unable to form anything of sense.

Welcome to my world, little words. No sense at all. On a break, Jocelyn ripped a sheet off her order forms and scrawled a note. "I guess it's *whenever*. Talk to you after my shift." She folded it until it was a tiny triangle, slipped it into a paper clip, and dropped it off at the bar to Cole. He nodded, just a hint of relief in his eyes telling her his stand.

For the rest of her shift, Jocelyn watched Paula work her job as welcoming committee. The woman had style; that was for sure. As far as Jocelyn could tell, Paula had not slipped so much as a peek at her niece. But then, Paula probably had her own mask, even if it was an old one she had to pull out in an emergency.

Finally, the closed sign turned outward at the front window and all hands took on the tedium of closing up. When all was ready for the next day, Paula walked toward the steps to the upper floors, grabbed the rail, and said, "I'll be upstairs, gang." Cole whispered to Jocelyn, "*Gang* means you and me, and I'm betting the boss doesn't need to see my mug."

Jocelyn rolled her eyes. "Gotcha." She walked slowly across to the stairs and took them slowly as if she were heading toward a haunted house, fearful of that first ghost yet determined to ferret out its secrets.

And sure as hell, that ghost had better not piss her off. Fool me once, shame on you and all that rot.

As she maneuvered the stairs, Paula took in the sound of Jocelyn's steps. Yep, the second and fifth steps creaked and gave a climber away any time. Now they sounded hope. Oh please let them sound hope—or at least a second chance. The door to the art studio was closed. She had locked it herself the minute she read Jocelyn's note; double locked it just in case. Paula stood on the second floor landing facing the last of the steps up to her apartment, hands folded like a kindergarten teacher waiting for her charges. When she spoke, her voice held stilted humor. "Don't worry, upstairs is safe. That . . . " She gestured back to the art room. "That contains the horror. Just keep climbing." With her back still to the girl behind her, she waved her hand with a flourish. "You'll love the place upstairs." *Upstairs* had a definite emphasis.

Time to face the music, the older woman thought. Hopefully there was a song worth singing.

Paula was right. Well, sort of. The apartment was cool. Not what you'd think a crazy person should have at all. Nobody armless and covered in "shame" here. Nice fireplace. A while back, her aunt had told her that her fireplace mantle had been rescued from a mansion torn down just a few blocks over. So Aunt Paula liked to rescue things and make them pretty. The furniture was gorgeous. A taupe sofa—the piece could never be called a *couch*, that meant ratty like her duct-taped special—tufted and regal next to chairs that duly promised luxurious seating.

How about a niece, maybe? Would she love the luxury? The thought gripped her, called for the walls. She stepped forward, one foot, then another. Was there glass under her feet?

The kitchen was gorgeous. Wide plank wood floors buffed yet artfully marred enough to let the guest know they were expensive. Gas stove. Two ovens. White cupboards with glass doors. Jocelyn should get a few of those, she thought. That way she could display her Ramen Noodles. Say, can you bake Ramen noodles? Two stoves could cut your cooking time in half.

You're babbling, her mind told her. *And no one can hear you.*

She took a seat at the round dining table across from her aunt. Each woman had a glass of wine in front of her. Paula was drinking hers.

Jocelyn kept her face stoic and ran her hand along the fabric of the chair seat. Linen. In her own apartment, Jocelyn's chair was a plastic reclaim from the thrift store, part of the duct tape collection. Back to business. Jocelyn folded her hands in her lap and waited, facing her aunt directly. This was Paula's gig.

Paula put down her wine glass and looked at Jocelyn. The aunt's face was blank. So different from the child's face from the art studio, the face on the self-portrait.

"You threw out, 'Who am I?'" Paula's voice was as neutral as her face. "Do you really want to know?" She rubbed her hands across her face once. "It's not simple."

Jocelyn knew full well that was an understatement. Did she want to know? The night she walked in the art studio, the answer was simple. Hell, no! Tonight was far less simple.

Paula the aunt with a funky bar and art collection on the first floor was one thing, Paula the second floor artist quite another. Million dollar question. So Neo, blue pill or red? Yes, Alice, how 'bout that mushroom?

Jocelyn was dancing on bones. A job was a job, and this was a good one, but what happens when the boss holds the keys to the asylum?

Right. Like you were Anne of Green Gables. Jocelyn of slimy trash alley was more like it. Even as she poised herself in stoicism, she pictured her teenage self, a study in black and piercings, all angst and snap and decisions of the too stupid to live. A memory whispered to her from somewhere deep. "Why not go out on a limb? That's where the fruit is." It was one of those posters up on Marti's office wall. Some guy named Frank Scully. Jocelyn had always laughed at it, pictured the limb in her life, pretty sure that another Frank, boyfriend du jour, would have grabbed the limb and smacked her.

Yep, Marti. Easy for you to say. You're back at school saving kids. I'm here drinking wine with an artist who sees herself without arms.

Fruit, sweetie. It will be sweet. The woman has *taken you shopping.*

Grrr.

Jocelyn picked up her wine and took a sip. Holding the glass between her hands, she rolled her eyes at Paula and said, "Okay, Auntie Paula. Let her rip."

Paula exhaled. Her face softened. Jocelyn let herself study her aunt. Why hadn't she noticed how pale the woman had been? And her eyes, they were watering. Not the sign of a sociopath.

Of course, sociopaths could dress in drag. At least when it would work for them.

Paula reached forward and started to stretch out her hand, then crept it back, held onto the edge of the table. "Yes, I wanted you to find the art work. Had the whole thing set up." She sat back, held her hands in her lap while she looked Jocelyn in the eye. "I couldn't think of another way to tell you. And I couldn't just give you the guided tour, announce my 'issues' like they were a hang nail." Paula let out a smile. "Niece, you would have run like hell itself was chasing you." She stopped and gave a grim grin. "In fact, you did."

All right, Jocelyn conceded to herself. Fair enough. Fleeing had been the reaction du jour, damn straight—but flight was what it was, a mechanism for survival. What was so horrible that Paula had to register it in oils?

Paula tapped her fingers—those manicured nails of hers had been a wonder to Jocelyn before the roof fell in. Now they made a clicking, the only sound in the room. Jocelyn waited for her aunt's words. When they came, they were right to the heart.

"My therapist said that I had to choose not to stay a victim. I had to face the abuse, tell the story. The child in the portrait that sent you tearing off was my story." Paula stopped speaking.

Was she collecting her thoughts? No surprise there. What in _____'s name would make a child see herself with severed arms? Even the pitiful children in television ads, the ones starving to death, had arms. Jocelyn studied her aunt in the woman's silence—Paula's face one of sorrow, of defeat. What, she wondered again, had reduced this woman to a tumbling of the word "shame" in an endless tattoo?

Her aunt began to speak and Jocelyn listened for answers. "I used to paint more than horror, back when I held the filth inside. Lovely scenes of Chicago grandeur, landscapes, portraits. Had a good client base for the mundane. But then I needed to tell the story. The horror itself was too graphic. But I knew of symbols. Find the symbol; let it swaddle what cannot be said."

Jocelyn took in the words slowly. Symbols. Raw stitches where slender arms should be, a kid with no arms, a kid that was her aunt. And that condemnation in glorious dripping color. The painting was indelibly stamped in her mind forever. *Shame.* There it was again, settling in Jocelyn's mouth, bitter and familiar. The word grated at her insides and gave her a sick kind of understanding. Shame, Jocelyn could understand. She had danced in its arms often enough.

As the night wore on, Paula's explanation began its spill, seasoned with clinical attachment and a touch of self-deprecation. Dissociation. Alters. Multiples. Coping mechanisms of the abused and abashed. When she was finished, she sat like stone, her arms wrapped around her. Only her eyes showed any form of life, and they showed . . . what? Terror? A plea for understanding?

The shock of the woman's life hit Jocelyn. Her aunt was freakin' Sybil. Welcome to the world of crazy. Flashes of the art studio night hit her, the terror, the tears that sent her over the edge. She had run right out of the apartment, into the streets and back to her own place. Even now, her feet gripped the floor even thinking about that night.

It's not a picture of you. Why the big to-do?

Because my aunt painted herself without arms, idiot. Wrote shame all over her. The kid dripped with it.

And you've never taken a swing at yourself with a knife? Perchance thou protests too much.

Jocelyn shut that thought down with a slam. This was about Paula, the aunt who never was until Evie had died. The aunt that added a twist to the story of Jocelyn's life, that the whole bunch of what loosely could be called *family* were no more than a collage of genetic clusterfucks. Evie was bad. Paula et al was a cauldron of bad. Dammit. She was done with bad. That's what her mind hammered at her. She lowered her eyes. She couldn't face her aunt's stolid anguish.

The woman's pain, it seeped into her. She thought of the day at the cemetery, her aunt's warm hand and warm words. The shopping. The space that this woman had granted her even as Jocelyn had walked by her in silence these past days.

There, sitting across from one who both terrified her and gave her hope. She had dreamed of being wrapped in the silk of a mother's love only to have that slosh into oblivion, the dream and the trust it implied. Evie always promised a lie, a fantasy of what they never could have. At least this woman laid the truth about herself out before Jocelyn, a horrible truth instilling fear and possible rejection, but truth nonetheless.

Paula stood up and walked to the kitchen. Jocelyn could hear the sound of water running. The sluice of the water—the water running, heading down to the basin was the only sound in the room.

Running. The word hit her in a twist—wasn't that what she wanted to do—take off in a full-out panicked run once again? Wasn't she the one who fantasized a hunting knife big enough to lay her open at the sternum and let the hurt pour out? Who was she to judge this woman?

And another thought toyed with her. *If you learn to know your aunt, maybe you can learn to know yourself. Can you handle that?* The other side of the family issue. The question jolted her at the same time she felt this umbilical cord reaching from her under the table and attach itself to the woman in the kitchen. Jocelyn Quint, the smart ass who prided herself on sarcasm sharp enough to slice any ego, felt an urging of family, of connection that shocked and scared her. Jocelyn Quint, the crackpot who ran away in her own mind, now the one who might have found a home at last, was contemplating staying. The thought nipped at her, gave her a sense of warmth.

Twenty-one years old and here she was, sitting in a kitchen with her aunt. Norman Rockwell, eat your heart out. So, maybe not Norman. Maybe Dali or Picasso on a bad day.

Damn it. She had taken care of herself, done all right, survived high school, survived . . . don't' go there. She didn't need, didn't want to dredge up the past. It lay like a rock deep inside her.

This wasn't the past. This was her future, a possible future if she had the courage to grab onto it. If she had the courage to seek it.

And the poor woman in the next room, the one reduced to liquid in her confession. What of her? Jocelyn just wanted to cradle this woman who had popped into her life, this woman whose mission seemed to be saving Jocelyn. Jocelyn wanted to save the savior, cradle her. She wanted to make her aunt laugh. Laughter made everything better. Her face, earlier so etched with pain and distrust, softened into the smooth cream she wore when life was serene, a color as rare as its absence was telling.

Funny how this was working out. They'd laugh, all right. As soon as the world stopped tilting.

Jocelyn stood up and joined Paula in the kitchen. The woman was leaned against the sink, drinking the glass of water. She was as still as she had been in the living room; only her hand and arm moved, bringing the water to her mouth.

Where to begin? While Paula the robot drank her water, Jocelyn rocked back and forth on her heels while she opened up. "So you're telling me *Charlie* the artist is you? That *Charlie* painted all . . . everything?" She searched for something to say. "Guess that's pretty cool since the piece is so good. It'd suck to be you and not have at least one of your parts have some talent."

Great, Jocelyn. Way to take control.

84

Paula set her glass aside, movement in her body returned. Some of the color had returned to her face. But she still faced the sink rather than turn to her niece. "*Charlie* and several more members of the family. We're quite the community, in fact. Oh yes. We come in all sizes, shapes, even genders. One of us even speaks French. For the life of me, I can't figure out why." Paula's voice was edged in an emotion turned inward. "Who I am—or was—depends on the trauma."

Trauma. There was a word Jocelyn could understand. The weight of that word held a toxicity that defined her youth. Children should spend their mornings eating Cheerios, not picking up empty booze bottles and avoiding the leers of nameless men. She felt her breath leave her nose, felt the inhale as she took in air again. But she had survived intact—hadn't she? She swatted the question away. Her life was not the point here.

She watched her aunt at the side of the sink busying herself moving around the hand sanitizer and a glass jar of wine corks. So. Her aunt had said *trauma*. What kind of trauma? Battering? Words slung at a tender ego? How much? Jocelyn clutched the wine glass that she held, let the cool settle into her hands, and reflected on of the word *trauma*. What could send a child into splitting? She pictured a little girl, sweet, with freckles and pig-tails, suddenly cleaved in two, each side falling in perfect symmetry. She shuddered. The image was too much like the art work that had sent Jocelyn running in the first place.

Paula turned toward Jocelyn. Hopeful move there. Finally, her aunt spoke, her voice raspy. "The parts are banging around in there. Let me take a break here and have a talk with them." She stood up and walked to the hallway off the kitchen, her back toward Jocelyn, while Jocelyn sat there allowing the artwork a place in her mind. She looked for answers—if not answers, at least the start of the right questions. What did artist *Charlie's* blood, her swatches of gray and black, skulls twisted in wire have to say? Jocelyn studied the piece of art in her head, but it hung there still as the dead.

Paula broke in. When had she returned to the kitchen? "A few of the *protectors* tell me it's okay to talk to you. Some are busy settling down the others. I'm afraid many of them are hiding. They don't like strangers." Paula had returned, was standing in back of Jocelyn. When had that happened?

Paula reached for Jocelyn's wine glass and then took another one fresh from the wine rack. She filled both, tilted her head toward the living room. "Let's go back in there and sit down. Craziness is so much easier to take when you're comfortable."

And like the obedient girl she had never been, Jocelyn followed and reseated herself exactly where she had been when Alice had explained Wonderland.

Jocelyn's face was tight with dark wonder; Paula's was open when she resumed talking. "Not too many times a woman gets to tell the truth and not have the listener running for the hills."

Jocelyn bit at her upper lip, rolled her head and shoulders, felt the cracking. She bent forward to take up her glass and leaned back against the sofa pillows. "Aunt Paula, you could have told me the moon was made of hummus, and I couldn't be more surprised." She watched her aunt's face, a wary face, a face trying to arrange hope and fear and who knew what else? Jocelyn reached across the table, wine glass in her left hand, and put the other on Paula's. The hand was so cold. She smiled as she said, "And in this weird—I can't figure out for the life of me—way, I'm not surprised at all. It makes sense."

Paula's sense of self was in shambles. A few of the parts stirred within her as Paula watched Jocelyn's reaction, only mildly mistrustful. Some were out and still terrified, a few angry. *The girl was laughing at them. Mother* shushed them. Sharing the truth was a blessing, yes, she told them. Even knowing the truth. This girl, the niece, had a joyful laugh, a warm hand. A special bond was in the making. But oh the courage and the pain that paved the way. One of the parts, *Annie*, whispered among them. She was a teenager and recognized what others did not. Did Jocelyn have a journey to make? Was that why she was so accepting?

Jen scoffed. Cunt. What was the point of trusting? They couldn't trust Paula to do anything right. Why trust a stranger?

Paula listened to her alters, took in the fears and let them ride. All of us, she told them have trusted strangers. Deb. Cole. Paula's husband Joe. Pastor Sara. Pretty short list of those who could listen without a flinch. But they stepped up and stayed. Now we have one more. Jocelyn is ready to love us, all, even mean-girl *Jen*.

86

Mother smiled and gathered as many who would come. Yes. We can trust her because her life knows so much that we have endured. She will bond.

Joey raised his hand. "And if she trusts, then can we help her too?"

Many of them nodded. Paula could feel the communion as *Mother* spoke. "In due time. In due time. For now, just rest."

CHAPTER 16

Alex and Jocelyn cozied up in the front corner of Delilah's Confectionaires. They had planned to hit Millennium Park like a couple of tourists, but mugging under The Bean with a cold lake wind blowing gave way to killing time back in Logan Square before she had to walk next door and go to work. Presently, Jocelyn was scarfing down a triple chocolate fudge. She needed it. Understanding Paula was one thing. Explaining Paula to Alex would be another thing entirely.

Right now, he was on a roll, his skeptic voice clearly defined, eyebrow lifted in derision as he faced his friend. "So let me get this straight. Your aunt, the one you never heard of until your mother died, the one who expresses herself with images of dripping words and blood, this aunt has people running around inside her." That eyebrow of his lifted even higher.

"No, goofball. Not people." Jocelyn gave him a jab. "Think of the headache she'd get from all those feet stomping."

"Knock off the smart ass. I'm serious."

"I know." She shoved a clump of chocolate into her mouth and gulped coffee to wash it down. Then she took a couple of sips. Slowly. Much easier to stall that way. She was still processing the events of the evening and now she was going to explain this to Alex? Definitely slipping across ground that was iced over. Lose focus and you're on your ass. Jocelyn had only begun to accept, much less understand all that Paula had unburdened—too much to talk over right now. She looked around, as if the walls could give her something to say.

While the two friends sat looking at each other in impasse, a couple walked in and ordered hot chocolate. They were both dressed fresh from J Crew. He had his hair neatly moussed despite the fall wind. She had on a snappy raspberry cloche hat complete with rhinestone broach. He rubbed her hands for warmth while they waited.

"Guess what," Jocelyn said, leaning in, her eyes rolled to her right. Alex just looked at her.

"That guy at the counter, the doting lover, he's going on a business trip to Cleveland next week. The first night, after too many Macallans with the boys, he's going to get a bright idea. Send a postcard to his wife and one to his girlfriend."

"Right." Alex knew better than to interrupt.

Jocelyn was wiggling in her seat now as the story progressed. "Trouble is, he'll address the one to his wife with the girlfriend's address and the one to his girlfriend with his home address. When he gets home . . . " She left the rest off and smirked, her head shaking back and forth ear to ear.

Alex shook his head. "Nobody sends postcards. They text."

Jocelyn folded her arms and sat back. "Now you know why."

"You can do all the avoidance ritual you want, my friend. Back to the question at hand."

Jocelyn picked up another piece of fudge. Good thing she had a pile. "Want one?"

"What I want is to get back to talking about your night with auntie."

"Just so you know, Aunt Paula says I'm supposed to take some time to wrap my mind around all she told me. It's kind of hard to wrap when you're scowling at me."

"Fine. I'll can the scowl." He gave her a contrived smile, all tight lips and cheekbones.

Jocelyn sneered. "I think I like the scowl better. You look like Alfred E. Neuman on crack."

Alex kept the smile. "Talk."

Jocelyn sighed. "She doesn't have *people* running around inside her." Her voiced softened, and she felt the muscles of her face relax. "The poor woman's been through so much—she only gave me a glimpse of what she's endured—but I can imagine so much more given the paintings." Jocelyn leaned in and set her elbows on the table, her chin on her folded hands. "This morning, before I met you here, I studied the one with the barbed wire."

"*Charlie's* painting. It's really hers." Alex had no sense of question in his voice.

Jocelyn's eyes looked upward, visualizing. "The blood red, all the gray and black of charcoal in smears, pools." She screwed up her mouth and gave her head a shake. "That barbed wire piercing, spits of blood pooling, the start of all the red. The heads of all the victims, they're stripped bare. There's just these skulls and skin stretched tight, all this shock and pain. The skulls look so ancient, like they're made of stone. And the red. The paint's piled up, like the blood's angry." A heaviness rose in her chest, blocked her breath. Her voice was the merest of whispers. "What do stony skulls and blood have to say about her life?"

"Fine. Her life's been hell. But why start a party? She's an adult. Why can't she put the past behind her."

Good question. Tough answer. Jocelyn thought about her own childhood. Frank, the last of Evie's live-in's, had laughed at her when she locked herself in the bathroom. "Go ahead, hide. I can get you any time I want." She still shuddered at the ice of his laughter even as she was able to face it in the light of day. Swirls of deeper memories never acknowledged did their bump-in-the-night bit within her. The past did not go gentle into that good night.

Jocelyn's voice was firm. "The way she explained it made perfect sense—at least at the time. Everyone spaces out. Haven't you ever been driving in the middle of nowhere and all of a sudden, you're at your destination and you didn't even realize the last few miles had flown by?"

Alex shrugged. "Sure, everybody's done that."

"So who did the driving?"

"Duh. I did."

"Absolutely. But which you? Not the one normally observing the road." Jocelyn watched her question settle into her friend.

"Okay, I get that. But that just means I'm in the zone. I did the driving."

"Sure, but you weren't aware of you doing the driving. When some kids are traumatized, so traumatized they can't take the horror, they let someone else do the driving. When it happens over and over, that *driver* sticks around. Complete with name and identity."

Alex uttered no words, but his body spoke, his eyes narrowing, mouth tightening. Jocelyn waited, took a slug of coffee, then another, her eyes connecting to his over the cup. A cup to her lips beat a foot in her mouth. She knew to wait.

When his words came, they came hesitantly. "So somebody's doing the driving. Where is the original kid?"

Jocelyn held the cup halfway between her mouth and the table, elbows supporting her arms. "Hiding."

"Permanently?"

"No. Just as long as there's danger."

"So when the danger's over, where's the driver?"

"Waiting in the wings for the next gig."

"Why doesn't the driver leave? She's done."

"Not as far as the child is concerned. The same abuse happens over and over. Never know when you need to call up a friend."

"How come there has to be more than one driver?"

Jocelyn set down her coffee cup. "Kids who need a driver start needing them early." Her gut ached as she said the words. "And they need them for years. Same day, different shit kind of thing. For some of them, one driver can't handle the abuse."

Now it was Alex's time to drink. While he took in the liquid, his eyes stayed on Jocelyn. The wheels must be turning, she thought.

"Here's how Paula explained it. Not all of the parts are individuals. It kind of depends on when they were born. There are groups like the *Littles*. They're the babies and toddlers who are more fragments than personalities. The youngest whole part is *Joey*. He's eight."

"He." *Charlie*. Now *Joey*. Androgynous Aunt Paula. "So *Charlie's* not the only boy?"

Jocelyn breathed in fast, felt her teeth tighten, her jaw stiff. She bent forward, pressed her elbow to the table and ran her fingers up and down her forehead. "*Charlie* isn't a boy. She just hates being a girl." A silence hung between them, and then she shook her head and sighed. "Poor *Charlie*. She's got an awful burden."

Alex took in her words, and then when the meaning struck, his eyes widened and he shrank back.

"Yep," Jocelyn said, "*Charlie's* driving a real nasty car."

91

While he finished off his coffee, Alex faced Jocelyn, his focus more on the window behind her. Shoppers meandered by, a dog walker or two. Did they have monsters in their closets? What squeezed on them; drew blood? Were they normal? And what the hell was normal anyway? Wasn't it all degrees?

He looked at his friend. Her face was a study in passive. He knew better. He reached over and touched her arm. "Joce, I'm glad that you get it. I wish I did. I hear you and the words just roll around. They make sense to you, but they scare the hell out of me. We can both celebrate your aunt coming out to you, but you're my friend. My priority is you. And friend, this much I know. Tread carefully. The muck factor here is lethal." He paused for a second. "It hasn't been that long since you ran from the dude in black. You say you're cool, now; but I saw you that night, and cool was the last word I would have used to describe you."

Jocelyn bit her lower lip and nodded, the slightest of nods, one that spoke volumes. Yet that tug she had felt last night, the one still fresh and unknown, that tug nudged her on levels she could neither understand nor explain. Red pill or blue pill, indeed.

On his way back to his place, Alex Stumme flipped to a country music station while he drove back to his apartment. Something about red trucks, good ole' boys, and the assurance of an American flag—maybe that would ground him. He gripped the wheel, a solid move amid the comfort of the sardine-can world of Chicago traffic. No way in hell he would space off while driving. After his talk with Jocelyn, he'd probably never space off again. He resolved to settle in to the world of Jocelyn—she was his friend, his best friend, one of the few people who got him. He'd do his research before going to bed tonight—what was the name of the book Joce gave him? United something. It was on the seat next to him. *United We Stand*. The cover had kids, adults, men and women all hanging out inside the graphic of a head. Freaky. Short sucker. He'd read it tonight before he went to bed, wrest some sense out of all of this.

He'd better. He'd never get to sleep if he didn't.

As the traffic picked up enough to move a block, Luke Bryan twanged, "Girl, I know I don't know you." No shit. Thank you universe. That was the problem. Who could ever know Jocelyn? And her aunt—did he have to meet everyone running around inside her? And sorry to say, but Aunt Paula, too bad for you. Your niece is my concern, all that bravado that she slings when she's David up against a Goliath. He knew Jocelyn , knew how fragile she was.

When the song lyrics hit, "You're rockin' in my truck," Alex laughed. Double no shit. Okay Joce, we are in for a ride, no matter what.

What the hell, Stumme. Looks like you'll be hanging at Luna's on occasion. Good beer. Funny bartender. How bad could it be?

CHAPTER 17

From the journal of Paula Ross

*M*y need for the sensory patterns my day. Rocking. Pushing on walls. Chewing the whole pack of lemon gum at one time. Deb says it's because of neurological disruption in my childhood. I say I need to touch in order to prove I'm alive. That's one reason why the art is so important. The feel of the brush against my hand, the swirl of the hairs brushing against my skin before I press form and color, the hardness of the handle as I begin my work. The touch of my fingers against the canvas. I rub the color in. I feel. I slip my fingers over the dried mass from my pallet knife. So sensual. My husband used to say that was a gift passed on to him, the brushing of my fingertips to find meaning. Even now I laugh, "Sure sweetie, that's what you loved—my art.*

He was the only man I ever trusted. He knew that was a gift.

I watch Jocelyn watch my work, her eyes searching, lips tight in concentration. That is a comfort. She can look and not run screaming. But that is her first step. She only sees the chaos and the pain. She does not see the road out of them. The swirls, the splotches. They are the space between me and the pain. I rise on that road.

When will she see her need for a road? Will she understand that spreading the color is work, but keeping the canvas blank is work as well?

Have I learned? Can I stand back and wait? How can I not gather her in and force the healing that is not mine to give.

CHAPTER 18

Jocelyn woke with a start. Sweat had collected between her breasts. Her chest was heavy, her throat dry; she hated dreams. Her mother had been seated on a large rock somewhere on a deserted Lake Michigan beach, her legs crossed, yoga style, her sister Paula's prone body in front of her. From Paula's body, children leaped and scampered toward the waiter's edge. Evie was counting them like sheep. When she was to twenty, she turned and announced to a sleeping Jocelyn, "It doesn't matter, you know. They're all sheep. They'll all drown." She turned back to the forms huddling on the cold sand. "If only you had loved me. Hurry up, little sheep. The water's waiting."

She threw off the covers and leaped from the bed as if under attack from alien bed bugs. In the bathroom, she washed her face, scrubbing it until it turned red. Teeth were next. Her toothbrush attacked her teeth while she watched. She pictured them as hard skulls, her gums red with blood.

Jeez, she was a total flake. She stood silent, leaning forward and looking into the mirror. Her face looked normal. Same dark eyes, same fine nose, same line of lips that often used a grimace as a defense mechanism. She had a zit on her forehead. When had that hit? She threw her toothbrush into the plastic glass that kept such daily accouterments.

Normal. She needed normal, something to stall that sense of alarm that gripped her, this gathering of broken promises, slivers that piled and groped their way to slice at her life. Why was she such a freaking baby? Look at her Aunt Paula.

There was a woman who could act normal. She peered into the mirror again, narrowed her eyes at the reflection that looked back and laughed at it. Understanding her aunt, accepting her aunt was one thing. Looking at her aunt as the model of normal? No wonder her body was having a fit.

A mere two minutes later she was on the phone taking care of business. "Hey Alex," she said. "How about some study time?" Man, she wanted some fudge.

Her work shift had started that night at 7:00. It was 11:00, bewitching hour coming right up. Too bad her feet weren't bewitched. She sat at the bar, rubbing her sore calves. Bartender Cole plunked a Blueberry Beer Lager onto the bar. "Have a little fruit to celebrate your hard work." He grinned. "Uncle Sam Adams told me you deserve this."

Jocelyn sat up, scrunched up her shoulders, leaned her head back and pulled her hands through her hair. She enjoyed the feel of her laugh as well as the stretch. "Tell Uncle Sam I appreciate the offer." She took a sip, letting the flavor nip at her tongue, then indulged in a full out swig. Her throat welcomed the slide of the wet while her taste buds investigated the mix of the known and the new. Blueberries and beer. Who would have figured?

"Cole," she said, "you are a man of adventure and wonder. Love this stuff. What a great way to get my fruit."

"I always figured you more for a car-bomb gal myself." Jocelyn turned around at the sound of a familiar voice. Alex. Twice in one day. Cool. He was here, all six feet of him.

Jocelyn leaped off her chair and gave him a hug. He leaned into her and hugged back while she asked, "What are you doing here? Need more notes?"

He stepped back, hugged her into him again before he let her go and took a seat at the bar, his eyes still on her. "This morning was all about studying. Tonight? Well . . . it's Friday Eve."

Jocelyn let the feel of her study pal wash over her, slip in and suck away the ache and tiredness of a hard day. It was late on one of those crappy early November nights; the ache of cold city rain had iced the ache from carrying trays. Now she was warm and off duty. Cole and Amelia could take care of the trays and the rest of the customers, all four of them. Luna's was a neighborhood bar, but on this Thursday night, midnight seemed to be two hours past bedtime.

"How about we get some of those chocolate brownie things?" As Alex asked the question, his eyes swept past the form of his friend, looking for the owner. The talk at Delilah's was under the rug, or in the case of Luna's, under the cement, but his guard was still up until further notice. For now.

This morning, Jocelyn had told him to keep an open mind. He was, after all, an avid *Walking Dead* fan, so he had embraced Paula's gore as an art form. Why not life? But this place. What had been a place of funk had new meaning now that he knew more about the artist. Dolls and little kids. It wasn't some weird dude painting clocks on the moon. The guy who dreamed up the Governor and snapping zombie skulls would either have an orgasm or pick up his inking pen and go home in defeat.

Jocelyn slid her arm around Alex's shoulders and nudged him forward. "Let's start with the some hummus. Then we can tackle the chocolate."

"You're a hard mistress. One good-for-you and two desserts."

"Deal."

He gave a glance back toward the portrait of a large screaming mouth laden with toys and insects spilling out. "If I didn't want to drink when I came in, I sure do now." As they moved to the back, he stopped and looked closely at the art work he had taken for granted. "I always wondered how a funny, nice lady like your aunt could come up with this stuff. I figured she just knew what sold, and I should only worry about the buyers."

"I warned you. Art is art, for whatever reason. And we have our avant-guarde customers, but you'd be surprised by the normal folk who buy here." She scanned the room. "Of course, every now and then I want to lace a Pinot Grigio with some valium, but that's only for the skinny bitches."

Alex nodded toward the painting next to him. "Don't go scamming me." His face reeked with indecision. "There are roaches pouring out of a kid's mouth here. I always thought it was pretty sick, but now I'm more concerned about the artist."

Jocelyn crossed her arms and stared down her friend. But her ears caught the bruise of his worry. "Stumme. Nobody's putting bugs in my mouth, but if anyone tries, I'll run to you first." She chuckled. She couldn't help herself. "Of course, I'd have to take the bugs out. You don't like bugs."

"Promise me, Joce. Promise me if anything goes weird, I'm your guy."
She held up her little finger. "Pink swear, big guy."

"Good. Let's eat." He changed direction and pulled her along behind him. "I want to sit near the front. Faster service."

No problem. Jocelyn knew when to placate.

As if fate had a director's wand in her hand, the door opened to two customers, a woman in her thirties—the very epitome of said skinny bitch that Jocelyn had just derided—walked in with a guy some years younger. She was clad in Eileen Fisher and an air of entitlement, her blonde hair perfectly highlighted and protected by a red umbrella. He had on a hoodie that said Northwestern and a grudging smile that said he was here but not by choice.

Her voice carried as she folded her umbrella and shook her mane. "Douglas, be a dutiful brother and help me pick out some pieces for the apartment. I know I promised to be out of your hair by 10:30, but you're not going to believe this place."

Douglas obviously was in agreement with the *out of your hair* part of her statement. As he surveyed Luna's, his expression evolved from surprise to disdain. "Sis, this place is sick. And I don't mean that as a compliment." Then he saw Jocelyn walking toward the bar, led by Alex. His face softened and he kept his gaze on her laughing form. When Jocelyn and Alex settled in at the bar and ordered, brother Douglas led his sister to the table nearest the two and took the menu from the swirl of silver that held it.

"Hey," he said loud enough for Jocelyn to hear. "If a brother can't help out his sis, then the Apocalypse is surely upon us."

All of this was lost on the two friends who ordered some hummus and a couple of beers. They were in their own zone. At least three times, Alex leaned in when he asked about Jocelyn's aunt, his face a blur of concern. Dog with a bone, that was her Alex. At least three times, Jocelyn laughed at him and finally rumpled his hair and told him to chill.

"Sad. Sad. Sad, good buddy. Give it up." She watched his face change—just a twist. He's so cute, and so open, she thought. If he weren't my friend, I'd want him for a favorite cousin.

98

She reached forward to give him a playful jab. "I take it back. Not you. You're not sad." While she leaned back, she pulled up the side of her mouth. "Well not *really* sad." She looked toward the bar and turned back to him. "I love this place. The customers are great. This is the part of Logan Square that houses all the preps I mocked in high school. They turned into bankers and lawyers and desses of white collar heaven—but if they're not angelic, they're at least pretty nice. Always someone saying hello complete with my name, smiles, and darn good tips."

"I figured you were doing well here." Alex dipped his pita bread into the hummus. "Those holey shirts you favor have been replaced with *couture;* one does not usually find at consignment stores or on sale on the internet because no one else would buy them. Are we up to Macy's now?"

"H & M, sucker. Still cheap, but more locale appropriate. And sometimes I wear my *Surrender Dorothy* tee under the new stuff just to maintain my roots."

Jocelyn held out her pita chip for a hummus toast. "Here's to life changes without selling out."

Alex attacked her chip with a swing. "Talk all you want. This is not the Jocelyn I know and love. Where's your disdain, your biting quips . . . your nose ring?"

"The ring's in my pocket at all times just for grounding. My disdain? Don't worry, pal; it's ready and willing at all times." She let out a half-laugh. "It's all good."

And while she said it, she caught herself believing it. She caught herself in a flash of the other night, balled up against the door, and then realized she had let it go. A life with Evie had prepared her for letting go of the crap only to wait for more. This time, there was no *until next time* looming.

Who could have thought? Jocelyn Quint, kid with scarred knees and perpetually ragged hair, Goth teen embracing the color black and dog collars as a way of life—that Jocelyn Quint had found a connection, and in the weirdest of all possible places. Crazy does as crazy is.

While she shook her head at the guy across from her, she gave her own self a bit of a shake. "Alex, don't turn culture-of-stupid on me. My Aunt Paula is pretty much normal. At least now. She can even lay out her clothes at night."

There went Alex's eyebrow. Jocelyn laughed. "It's a true sign of progress. Before, she had to wait until the morning. At night, she never knew who she'd be in the morning." Jocelyn's voice found its sarcasm. "Such is progress for wackos like us," she told me. "But then, we're talking baby steps."

"You two sure are getting to know one another fast. Only a few days ago, you wanted to run out of her place kicking and screaming."

Jocelyn gave her head a short shake. "It's ultimately pretty simple. Not too hard to put much trust in the only living relative you have. I can't even dig up a fourth cousin anywhere. Besides, after my mother, Paula's a piece of cake—many flavors—but a piece of cake nonetheless."

Alex lifted his arms. "Sorry. You won't have to kick my ass for insensitivity. I just did it myself."

"We laugh about things like playing surprise when you get up in the morning. I like it when she flips off on herself. Self-deprecation is a high form of humor, you know." Jocelyn paused and looked inward even as she kept speaking. "If she can laugh about life, then maybe I can, too."

At the table next to them, a brother may have looked like he was listening to his sister, but his ear was bent more to catch the snippets of conversation coming from the girl at the next table.

CHAPTER 19

They were going shopping again. Paula insisted everyone needed a little distraction. The *children* wanted to look at toys, Paula told her niece, and how could they say no to the *children*. Jocelyn knew better. She put her arm around Paula and teased, "Don't get too smug now. Kids, my rear-end. This is about clawing through the goodies."

"You caught me. It's really about the two of us. The little rascals want to look at toys, indeed, but I said not today. They've stomped off and are pouting. The nay-sayers are off in their own rooms, naying away. That leaves the more grown-up alters ready and willing to share us with you."

The day was a study for Jocelyn. Now safe, the parts allowed themselves to enjoy the trip openly. In one store, Paula rolled her eyes like a mother when Jocelyn reached for a pair of glitter jeans. Ten minutes later, no longer the mother figure, she reached for a Juicy top and held it up, those same eyes now a teenager's looking for approval. "Bet this looks better on me than it would on you. And you're pretty hot." The kids' selves had a hey-day in the toy store. Rocks that contained geodes just begging for a hammer. Princess make-up. A piggy bank that oinked every time a coin fell through the slot into its belly.

Jocelyn took it all in. Nothing about Paula was threatening. Weird, sure. But not threatening. Kind of like having your own traveling carnival family. She stayed behind once Paula left to take on the shop next door and bought the pig. As far as she was concerned, the *kids* were cousins. Imagine that. All these years she had never fit it. Now she did—with people who didn't exist except inside the mind of a crazy woman, one who was one of the sanest people she had ever met.

And it was fun. Still, questions nagged at her. How had Paula's world happened? Would she share?

CHAPTER 20

From the journal of Paula Ross

I catch myself searching my face when I smile and tell her that her Alex is a treasure. That we all have treasures to cherish.

I met mine, my Joe, the night I hit a tree. Big, old behemoth of a tree, knotted and skeletal and beautiful right there on the curve, waiting to snatch me up and take me home. I loved it for its promise before I ploughed into it. Mother would probably have shaken her head and said, "Why make the tree suffer?" but then she only saw the rain where there was a rainbow. Lucky she wasn't the one to have found me.

Fate must have been laughing her ass off. Who meets the love of her life during a botched suicide attempt?

Suicide. Dumb word for escape. The idea of escape had touched my thoughts, played with them—not to mention the tips of my fingers whenever I ran a finger over the rim of a bottle of booze or the keen plastic of a pill bottle for months back then—but until that perfect curve outside of Crystal Lake, I had never embraced action. But the tree. It smiled at me. Stretched those gnarled limbs to embrace me. I'll take you, sweetie. It can all be over. Was it the tree who said that or one of the alters?

At the time, it didn't matter. As soon as I saw my escape looming in the distance, I begged for the crash, the relief after a little physical pain. A broken rib or two, glass slicing my face? Hell, I'd known pain that went on for hours, the hurt that crawled under my skin and settled into meat and bone, the pain I called my life. What was a crash, a slam through a window, maybe the first crack of bones breaking, a lung, a heart, a head begging for seconds before it gave up. It couldn't be all that bad.

And I could at last rest.

I undid my seat belt, screeched toward that tree, foot on gas pedal, waited to fly into its arms, my body tight with the mingle of fear and anticipation. Then I hit the embankment and jolted to the right. I had my hands locked on that steering wheel. Fat lot of good that did. I landed hard. The car door flew open and I sailed out and landed harder, rolled onto piles of brush and grass. Missed the glass and rocks. Probably saved my life.

Only I could fuck up a suicide attempt. For years, Joe said the same thing, only he laughed when he said it, squeezed my hand, and added, "Thanks." Joe was always into divine intervention.

He was right behind me. Called 911. Waited with me for the ambulance. Told me to hang on while he held my hand. I swear my hand still has the memory of his touch that night in the boonies of Northern Illinois. I remember it just as much as I remember the solid sound of the crash and the washes of pain. So much for quick release. Now I see the pain as a sacrifice to earn my Joe for the time I had him.

He followed the ambulance to the hospital, came each day to visit—on his way home, he said, as if Arlington Heights were right next door.

When I opened my eyes in the hospital, there he was. None of us had a clue. Of course. All the alters get clobbered when the head stops working. I saw those incredible eyes, all dark and focused and drenched with worry. I looked at him and thought, Don't have a clue, but that guy looks fretted. *Here I was, a thirty-year-old klutz wrapped like a mummy, plastic tubes sticking out of her, drip lines dripping, and I'm fixated on a stranger's facial language. Joe always told me that was the artist in me. I always told him I knew a hottie when I saw him. When he took my hand, I was in a world of safe. His hands. Big. Callused. The hands of a lumberjack, not a lawyer. They made me safe. Maybe there was something divine about that night after all.*

The love of my life, that man.

I'd get into a rotten snit, and he'd say, "Fate brought you to me. Do not suggest fate is ever wrong. She gets really bitchy when you do." He'd wrap me in his arms with those big hands until the rotten bubbled up and turned to vapor. He'd paint my toe nails. Ridiculous picture. Burly hands with a tiny brush and Cuban Pink at the tips.

Heaven

Jen was so jealous. She, like me, knew sex appeal when she saw it. She'd come out and try to seduce him. "Get back in there, missy, he'd say. "It's against the law to mess with someone seventeen for a reason. Why don't we have a soda and you can tell me what's wrong."

In my heart, *Joe wasn't a lawyer, not even a psychiatrist. He was a god. A big cuddly god with a smile that melted my heart.*

I miss him too much to even voice. But the man gave me safety like nothing else. I heal because of him, that stranger who took a chance out on a lonely road in the middle of nowhere.

CHAPTER 21

C ole picked up a wine bottle and flexed his fingers around the neck like one of the Manning brothers ready to throw a fifty-yard pass. He flicked his wrist, a smooth cock and release, and the bottle sailed upward. Jocelyn watched it flip and looked at Cole as he caught it by the neck and winked at her. Smart ass.

"Bet the gals line up to see that. The ones with glitter on their eyelids."

"Yep. I'm a magnet all right." He grinned. "And all that glitters is not told." He made a zipping motion across his lips and winked again.

"With all due respect, stud muffin, just don't drop the bottle." She slid off her bar stool and sauntered away, her hips swaying, her voice straight from the play yard. "My name is Cole. I am a player." The taunt was laced with laughter.

Cole called out, "No fair giving away all my secrets to the customers." Two girls at the end of the bar giggled. One said, "I'll have a little of that," pointing at Cole.

Lucky Cole. Lucky girls. Cole was definitely munchable. Too bad he was like the brother she never had. *Like you have any time for a liaison lasting more than thirty seconds*, she reminded herself.

Jocelyn heard Cole's voice as she headed toward her customers. He had lowered it to impress his audience. "Can't turn down a mellow taste. Of course, I mean the wine." His voice was smooth, the line not so much.

Maybe her lack of a love life wasn't so bad after all. So much easier just to hit a bar, find a guy, and scratch an itch when she needed to.

Right. Tell that to yourself while you're driving home alone. Again.

While Jocelyn was busy taking an order, a customer came in and sat at a table near the front. This was his second time in Luna's, the first time by himself. He had lucked out on a parking space across the street for his Range Rover and figured his luck was on for the night. He read through the wine and beer list, but his eyes were on the waitress heading for the bar with an order.

Jocelyn had hurried up to the bar. "I need a bottle of Simi and a Guinness." She looked in the direction of Cole's fans and mouthed, "Yes, he's hot." Nothing like helping out a friend. She turned toward the newest customer. "Be with you in a sec, sir."

Doug Lassiter smiled and nodded. He looked at his phone; urban millennial in a Logan Square bar seemingly no different from the twenty or so other patrons chatting, eating, or texting. How many of them had an agenda, he wondered. He smiled at the thought that not everything with a sweet taste could be bought in this place. Some things had to be wooed. He looked straight at the girl with the tray, the waitress who owned the room, the joy of her an aura.

"Good evening and welcome to Luna's." That's what Jocelyn said. What she thought was, good evening and can I take you home? At least that was the thought that popped into her mind before she gave herself a mental slap.

Never mind the hormones, she told herself even as she had to drag her head away from watching him. She had work to do and bills to pay.

But man, this guy was hot. Tall and lanky. Shoulders for forever. And that face. Chiseled. Cleft in his chin. She loved guys with cleft chins. And that hair . . . Jocelyn's rational piped up. Weakly. *Focus, woman.* Her libido gave a growl and rational Jocelyn left the conversation as she looked at him. He had to have played football. In high school, she'd always had a thing for football jocks even as she had mocked them. Something about their swagger and all those hormones rippling. At this moment, snarky girl or not, she had no antidote for testosterone. This guy must have showered with it.

"Is there a problem, miss?"

Jocelyn gave a startled jump, tiny but full of announcement that she had been somewhere else.

Somewhere else all right. And it had nothing to do with domestic beer lists.

Laughing, she boinked her head with her pen. "Earth to Jocelyn time. Sorry about that."

He returned the laugh. "No problem. Jocelyn. Pretty name for a pretty girl."

She felt a shiver. *Pretty girl. He called me pretty.*

Rational Jocelyn kept pounding for attention, but the guy's voice was so deep and full of promise—rational Jocelyn didn't have a prayer. Rational Jocelyn just waited to give the *be careful what you wish for* while the hunk made an order for Honker's Ale sound sexy.

"A Goose guy. Ever been to the Brewery?" She watched him more than listened. North Face quilted jacket. Cashmere scarf. Definitely a crafted beer guy. *My, that jacket fills out well.* She wanted to slide her hands down the front and check out what was under that satiny texture. Damn. There went that heat to her face again. She was blushing. She hadn't blushed since—she hadn't ever blushed, at least that she remembered.

Hunk guy carried on. "The one on Clybourne? Sure. Been doing Honker's ever since."

"What?" Back in the conversation, woman. This is a customer. She gave herself an internal slap. "Love that place. When I grow up, I want those goose handle pourers in my kitchen." *Yep. You could come over and handle my handles any time.* She groaned at herself. She was starting to sound like Cole. Focus. Again, the word was a command.

"For sink faucets? Just so you can turn things on and off?" He was teasing. He wanted her attention. Her job was to make the customer feel at home. Banter was back. What a responsible hostess she was.

Jocelyn groaned inside once again at the possibilities of the two of them in her kitchen turning on, all right. *Get a grip. Jumping a guy's bones is not on the menu.*

"No. But good idea. I'd have them lined up on my wall as art statements."

He reached and grabbed a pretzel from the glass bowl on the table, bit down and chewed, keeping his eyes on Jocelyn. Rational Jocelyn muttered something, but playful Jocelyn swatted it away. This guy has great eyes, kind of green, kind of gray set against a tanned face—eyes on her. And that mouth. Big lips. *Munch on me*

"Art." He turned to scan the room. "So you're part and parcel of the milieu in here."

"Not really. I don't do barbed wire and doll heads. Just geese on a wall. Maybe a clown or two. That's as scary as I get." She shrugged and gave her signature half grin. "Probably why I drink Green Line instead of Honker's. Just a pale ale kind of gal. Nothing too stout for me."

"Somehow I don't believe that." His words came through like a caress.

When Jocelyn went to place his order, her saunter was back, this time governed by a tease not intended to mock the bartender.

Several beers and plenty of laughter later, when he reached out his hand for the check, Jocelyn noticed his hands. Strong. Long fingers. Working hands, roughened but not calloused. Hands on kind of guy, but nothing extreme.

What would those hands feel like against her skin? She took his credit card with a firm handshake and an even firmer sense that something delightful could be done with those hands.

"Doug Lassiter." He smiled as he stood up. A beautiful smile. Even his teeth were sexy. "Hope I'll be seeing you again."

All Jocelyn could do was smile like a middle school urchin with a first crush. The possibilities were too yummy.

Before he headed out the red door at the front, he stopped at the bar to talk to Cole. Cole glanced at Jocelyn, stone faced, shook his head once and then, after a moment of hesitation, slid back the cash Doug had placed there. What was with Cole? Since when did that guy refuse a tip?

After Mr. Hottie left, Jocelyn headed straight to Cole.

"So when did you start turning down money?"

Cole leaned closer to Jocelyn over the bar. His voice was low, but it held concern. "He wasn't tipping me. He was asking for information about you."

"He was?"

"Yeah."

"Cool. Maybe I'll beat you in bar conquests yet."

"Jocelyn. He offered me money for information. That does not fall under flirt. That falls under creepy."

Jocelyn smirked at him. "Somebody's jealous. You can't have all the fans here."

"Fine. I'm wrong, and you are the undisputed winner of the conquest challenge."

She turned around to check on customers. His words followed her. "Just be careful."

Silly Cole. She'd never had a brother, always wanted one, the big brother who would protect her. If this was how big brothers acted, she was better off without him.

Whew. 2:30 a.m. and all was well. Another night on the job, another ride home to boredom. Jocelyn walked out of Luna's. The early morning air hit her, certainly the cold of November, but more refreshing than annoying, certainly a step up from earlier in the night. Off to her left, someone was playing *Take Me to Church*. She turned toward the apartment window. Sad song. Every time she heard it, she pictured the pain of the video. She also wanted to punch somebody.

Across the street, someone was leaning against his car door, waiting—a familiar someone. The hot dude from tonight, Doug Lassiter. Her feet dug into the cement. Her stomach tightened, the breath in her lungs caught, and the pulse in her neck started to throb. She felt all those and a tingling, as if her insides had flipped the on switch and expected her to take action. Good thing for the body. The question was, what action? Was this danger or a possibility?

Doug gave a grin and held up a package. "I went over to the brewery and picked up a few things. How about a picnic?"

"Picnic? At two o'clock in the morning?"

Why not? Jocelyn walked across the empty street. Doug held out the package and said, "Your place or mine?" Before Jocelyn could even give in to a start, he added, "I mean, you want to eat in front of my car or in front of Luna's?

"Car's good. Just remember, I can hit you with my purse if you turn into a dirty old man."

He dug into the bag and pulled out a sack of French fries. "Or you can wallop me with one of these."

They munched on fries and beer, leaning against the black Range Rover and chatting about beers and bars and the best places to have fun. Doug was an architect just starting out and lucky enough to have a father in the building business. He had been delighted by her sense of fun and also knew how much her feet probably hurt and how hungry she would be at closing time. He was a brother-in-arms, former college student who had earned money busting tables and waiting on hopefully top-notch tippers.

Jocelyn thought about Cole's fit over Doug's offer of payment. See, jerk-face, she said in her mind, the guy appreciates working stiffs like us. He's been there.

They ate, they drank, they laughed; then the goodies were gone and Jocelyn was yawning.

Doug laughed at her. "We've had too much fun for you to be bored. Must be time to send you home."

Her body had to agree even though her mind could have stayed. He walked her to her car, gave a smile and a "Good Night." He even waited until she was safe inside before he walked away.

Jocelyn leaned back against the headrest and thanked whatever was in charge of sending that hot guy into her life. When she dreamt that night, it certainly was not about her mother's scorn or scary art.

CHAPTER 22

The next day, Jocelyn walked through her shift, body waiting on customers, mind elsewhere. She stifled a yawn, and then realized—with a start—that she wasn't all that tired. The yawn had snuck in from somewhere not entirely caught up in after-hour picnics. The *date* had lasted well past three a.m. Hence the yawns. But parts of her were down-right jazzed. No problem. Her serotonin levels, still jacked up, would serve double duty—keep her awake and keep her blissful. Even washing bar glasses, she let herself shoot back to early morning, cataloging their conversation. Doug liked the art in Luna's—imperfect symmetry that spoke of splintering pain. He rode across Iowa on his bike the last week of July with his buddies. They wore kilts. He wanted to take her on the architectural river tour, show her the wonders of Chicago buildings.

Doug. The man was soaked in interesting. And hotness.

He wanted to see her Saturday. Take her to dinner. Wisps of brain chemicals held her floating in happy. The hum in her ears must have been from them shuttling back and forth in Doug thoughts.

Of course, reality had to hit her and spoil all the fun.

Get back to work, woman, the non-soaked part of her brain demanded. *Lust on your own time. You'll have more in hot water than those hands.* She listened even as the besotted part of her whined *C'mon.*

She did have a customer, a shopper from the looks of the bags piled beside her. The woman was slender, a millennial with perfectly tousled hair that had no doubt set her back a couple of hundred dollars. Damned nice purse. Maybe it had a good tip in it.

Good thing the lady drank wine. Cole was off at an appointment and Paula was no where to be found. Beer and wine she could do. A little Bacardi rum and diet, no problem. Anything fancier and she was in foreign territory. Daydreaming and ignorance. Bad duo.

She sloshed the last glass from the suds sink into the rinse, her hands pink from the heat of the water. Ten more minutes and she would have lobster claws. Where the hell was Cole? He said two hours and it was close to three.

"Excuse me," shopping lady beckoned.

Jocelyn lifted her head. Some customers liked to drink alone. Most expected camaraderie. Jocelyn wiped her hands and bumped up her happy face to just short of offering a hug. "Thank the Lord I'm done with the toiling. May I get you another?"

"No thanks." The woman finished off the glass with a healthy swig. "Actually, I'm looking for this place my friend told me about. A candy shop." She grabbed for her purse, started rummaging around. "I can never find what I want. I'm looking for the name of this awesome candy place."

"Delilah's."

The woman looked up. "What?"

"I bet you want Delilah's Confectionary. Fudge to die for. Take a right out the door. Two blocks down. Your mouth will water automatically when you're ten feet away. Candy vibrations."

The bell at the front door rang. Both women looked up.

Cole. He strode toward the bar while taking off his coat. "Sorry. Late date with my advisor." He gave the customer a Cole grin that stopped her midway through paying. She sat down. "Maybe I can have one more."

No wonder Paula kept him around. Enough female customers stayed for *one more* that often turned into several. This guy was worth his weight in SVEDKA. Behind the bar, Jocelyn bowed, hands folded, "Oh my liege, your kingdom behind the bar awaits your beckoning."

Cole grinned at the customer who was now running a thumb against her wine glass. "Don't give away my secrets, wench Jocelyn. And don't forget your place in the castle." He pointed to the cash register at the back of the restaurant, his face still in contact with the woman clearly now *his* customer. "Or should we allow the maiden to remain?"

"Oh, of course. Whatever the Lord may say." The blonde pointed to Jocelyn. "Poor child, have a seat here . . . " She looked at Cole, Delilah's clearly postponed. "As soon as you pour me another wine."

The *you* clearly did not mean the pink-handed Jocelyn.

Cole was clearly back as master of the realm. Wine lady was busy reapplying lipstick, while Jocelyn sat at the edge of the bar. Yeah. She could return to sappy girl, caught up in picturing the two of them last night, Jocelyn and Doug, sitting against his car wrapped up in coats and blankets, sipping beers and noshing fries, a couple of rebels caught up in free-flowing banter.

She pictured Doug in his kilt, legs spread on that bicycle.

"Earth to Jocelyn."

She looked up. The bar was empty of customers; wine lady on her way, no doubt, to a sugar high at Delilah's. At some point Paula had come in. Both she and Cole were staring at Jocelyn right now, matching smirks across their faces. They each wore their expressions like a comfortable tee.

"What's up, little girl?" Cole said the words, but apparently the need to know came from both of them.

Jocelyn peered at him from lowered eyes. "What makes you think anything's 'up'?"

"Oh, I don't know. Maybe the shit-eating grin on your face when you're looking at the wall. I mean, it's the same wall as always. Must be a not-same Jocelyn."

Paula jumped in. "Last night, I woke up about three. Hate that hot flash in the night thing. When I looked out the window, you were sitting with someone, definitely a male, someone whose name is most certainly not Alex.

"Very interesting. Three in the morning and you're out having a picnic." She looked at Cole. "Chilly last night. Didn't seem to bother either one of them."

Great. Tag-team smart-asses.

Jocelyn folded her arms. "A girl has a right to have friends."

"At three in the morning? Wrapped in blankets on a cold city street?" Paula turned to Cole. "We should have such friends."

Cole tagged in. "Is that a blush I detect on yon maiden's face? Jocelyn? Blushing?" He turned to Paula in mock surprise. "Whatever has her all a titter?"

"I think 'whatever' is a whomever." Paula leaned forward. "Give it up, niece. What's his name?"

113

Then the game started. Name that boyfriend. *John. Ian. Percy.* That, of course, came from Cole.

Jocelyn stiffened on her bar stool, tightened the grip from her folded hands until her right hand had marks, her face a mask of indignity. Cole sauntered forward, sputtering name after name while he hovered around her. When *Doug* came up, Jocelyn's face cracked.

Paula ran around in tiny circles waving her arms. "Doug! His name is Doug!" Cole stood behind Jocelyn, pointing a finger down at her. Both inquisitors crackled with glee. Jocelyn's leg was jittering up and down in syncopation to their antics.

"Good lord, don't you two have a life?"

Cole spoke. "Protest is futile, my child. The great all-seeing duo of Cole and Paula sees all, wants to know all."

Jocelyn jumped off the stool and headed away from them. "I'm going to the back room. You two try to gain some composure. We will be having customers, after all. No one wants to see such nonsense."

Paula called out after her. "Does Doug have a friend? Maybe we could double-date!" She looked at Cole. "Want to go out with an old lady?"

Enough. Jocelyn turned around. "Doug has plenty of friends. You can't meet them. But you can meet Doug. He's picking me up here Saturday night for dinner." She pointed at Paula. "You've been trying to get me to stay with you for a month. Now you get your wish."

She shook her head at the now quieted couple. "Try to grow up between now and then. I don't want to be embarrassed by my family."

Cole put his arm around Paula. "Aahh. Auntie Paula, now I'm family."

Paula patted his hand. "Good thing. Because I'm not big enough to kick anyone's ass. But you are." She cast Jocelyn a solid *Auntie* look. "No messing around with my niece, thank you very much."

Jocelyn rolled her eyes. "I'm staying with you. Be a good girl. No Gestapo tactics." She put on the look she gave to whiners. "No questions. Information as it comes."

Jocelyn shook her head and turned around. Enough that she had to dress like a girl for the upcoming date. Now she had to hope the Tweedle-Dee and Tweedle-Dumber didn't embarrass her. Good. She was going out fancy. She prayed she didn't embarrass herself.

114

CHAPTER 23

The Gold Coast. Tiara on Chicago's Magnificent Mile. And she, Jocelyn Quint, was here, on North State Parkway, in all its coastal splendor, about to dine in the freakin' Pump Room of the Public Chicago Hotel. Doug was taking her to a place she had only heard of, where America's royalty hung out. *Her.* Little Jocelyn Quint, formerly of Goth-clad loserdom.

He was off parking his car while she waited inside. The entrance literally danced with awesome. Gleaming white staircase, white floors, walls of white wood and mirrors, pillars and open spaces of Art Deco wonder. She raised her head and let herself soak it all in. A cool hotel might have a chandelier. This one had a whole ceiling of chandeliers, each connected to the other as if the crystals and gold were a dance troupe in perfect formation.

Jocelyn hated girls who gawked and said "Oh my." So she lowered her gaze, kept her eyes forward and her comment silent. Her lips wanted to move—they begged for mercy—but no girlie gushing would reduce her to some gum-chomping hair-brain who had never seen a piece of crystal. She'd maintain discipline even while she wanted to yank on her dress to make sure it still hugged her like it had at the apartment. The black jersey clung to her—good thing; with just a thin strap holding up the shoulder-less fabric, she'd be lucky to keep the thing up through appetizers, much less keep her ass from hanging. Definitely the shortest thing she'd ever worn. A wall of mirrors glittered at the end of the foyer. Did she have time for a peek to make sure she didn't have a rash on her neck?

Steady, woman. She looked down the steps leading to the lower floor. A wall of black and white portraits lined up in precision. This place was a study in history. Movie stars, political figures, magnates. They had all come through this foyer. And now here was little Jocelyn Quint. Here at Public Chicago on a Tuesday night with a drop-dead gorgeous guy in a drop-dead gorgeous place.

Please, Lord, don't let there be a rash.

One of the hotel staff hustled by—a guy with perfect teeth, perfect moussed hair, and a fine ass, thank you very much, probably on his way to take care of someone who dressed like her Aunt Paula on a daily basis.

"Good evening, Miss." *Miss.* Holy shit. She tugged on her dress once more.

"So what do you think?" Doug's voice and the hand on her back were warm. Any other time, she might have jumped. But one did not jump here. It simply wasn't done.

She leaned into him. "Oh my!" She couldn't help herself.

"Yeah, it's pretty spectacular." He pointed to the ceiling. "They took all of the chandeliers out of the Pump room when they redecorated. Pretty cool how they worked them into this ceiling of light."

"Good news for here. How about the Pump Room? Does it miss them?"

Doug laughed while he guided her forward. "Baby, you haven't seen anything yet."

And she hadn't. By the time they were seated, Jocelyn decided that she needed to change her major to public thievery so she could afford all the luxe of this place. Doug had managed the only booth not redone in the room, one at the very back, a very private booth, a huge leather semi-circle reminiscent of large cars of the era when its sole proprietor had used it. Frank Sinatra's booth, complete with a picture of old Blue Eyes on the wall next to them.

Jocelyn knew she had a sappy smile plastered on her face. Self-discipline can only go so far. She sat there, mesmerized by the scheme of lights acting as its own Deco art.

Her date obviously had noticed. "Look around. There's five hundred resin globes of light in this room. Every one of them just points out how spectacular you look tonight." Fine. Sappy line. Went well with her sappy smile. Who was she to judge? Might as well just sit back and enjoy. This was a long way from 7-Eleven land.

And don't forget, he thinks you're spectacular.

They ordered the Tuesday special. Surprise. No meat loaf. Not for them. Tuna Tartare and Crab Crostinit. Angel hair pasta with asparagus and shitake mushrooms. Jocelyn barely could interpret the menu. Angel-hair pasta maybe, And tartare meant raw. But shitake mushrooms? She'd just have to trust. At least she knew which fork to use. Old Frank would have to be her guardian angel and convince her not to sweat.

Midway through the appetizers, Jocelyn noticed the couple closest to them. A middle-aged man with a very bad toupee and a loud voice was on his phone. His date, much younger and actually quite stunning, picked at her meal while he talked. Jocelyn leaned in to pick at her own plate just so she could listen. There had to be a story there. One that played out in hotel restaurants around the globe.

"Yeah," he said. "I'm here with my friend Tatiana at the Pump Room. I'll give you a call later." When he finished the call, he turned back to his *friend* who listened intently to his prattle and knew when to smile.

Bingo. Jocelyn was on Earth after all. Johns and escorts were more a part of her south-side reality. There was certainly plenty of class here, but the glamour dust didn't hide the whoosh of the dark side of city life complete with fake charm. Jocelyn shifted in her seat toward the tufted back of the booth. She could survive quite well now that she knew she hadn't landed on a different planet. She might even be able to enjoy herself. She was in a distractingly glamorous restaurant with a distractingly hunky date with a reality show at the next table. What was not to enjoy?

Doug's finger was stroking her cheek. "Come on back to me. I miss you already."

Smarmy line number two. Best hors d'oeuvre ever.

She turned to him, laid her hand on his leg. "Sorry about that," she said, the picture of total innocence. "I was intent on the couple next to us." With a wicked grin, she bent closer and fake whispered, "The lady's name is Tatiana. I think she's a special date, especially since someone that gorgeous is so fully enraptured by a guy who looks like he normally specializes in Budweiser."

Doug nodded and returned her tone. "That's the thing about the Gold Coast. Everything glitters more here and you have to pay for it." He took on Jocelyn's tone. "But don't make screw of our Tatiana. This is the land of free capitalism after all."

Jocelyn sat up, spoke with lightness in her tone. "But what of the upstanding values of the community? Surely they would be shocked to know that decadence had reared its ugly head in their neighborhood." By now Jocelyn had her right hand against her throat and her face in full mocking shock. But that other hand of hers, the left one, was still on Doug's thigh. Her palm enjoyed the hardness beneath the smooth feel of his pant leg.

Doug chuckled, placed his hand over the one on his thigh and rubbed his thumb across the back of her hand, continued as if no game had begun. "Be well warned, my dear, that decadence knows no economic boundary. When Hugh Hefner opened the Playboy Mansion a few blocks away, gentlemen visitors used a series of tunnels to enter the premises unknown to the public. Hugh was a big believer in the right to a good life."

While he bantered about the 1960's, that thumb of his slid back and forth in a motion so slow and warm, Jocelyn felt her finger tips swell with pleasure.

All right, my sexy friend. I'll play. She set her right arm on the table, elbow bent, and propped her chin with her thumb and index finger. The left hand? She sat there and let the pleasure ride while the two of them bantered.

"Well, that's crass for sure. Hope no one hit his head and had to explain stitches to an angry wife."

Doug stilled his thumb but kept his hand on hers, his voice laced with tone of this dance. "That's hardly salacious. In 1926, when this was the Ambassador East, a tunnel was built to connect the hotel to the Ambassador West." Then he slid his hand away, grabbed his wine glass and took a sip, laughter in his eyes. "A few decades later, Marilyn Monroe stayed here. She'd slip through the tunnel and meet JFK at his hotel."

Jocelyn's mouth said, "And oh, if walls could talk, they would be singing 'Happy birthday, Mr. President." Her body begged for that hand back on hers and her head pictured her with Doug in that tunnel, swanky dress pulled up to her waist, her back against cold, hard stone supporting their mutual need to thrust. With an internal grimace, Jocelyn held her wine glass with both hands and took in the delightful burn of the fantasy.

118

Doug leaned back against the padded seating and raised his glass. "Here's to the architecture of Chicago and the people who know how to use it."

Grrr. This guy was smooth. Bet he never had to phone a Tatiana to come and play for pay. She clinked her glass against his and took a long draw.

And then the pasta arrived.

Damn.

The waiter had to give a subtle cough to announce his presence before he began to serve. She settled into the moment, turned her attention from the man beside her to the business of eating. Or at least she tried. While she was twirling the angel hair, she watched him, a bite of pasta held in front of his mouth, his lips ready to receive, take communion with the delicious.

Oh to be a bit of that forkful and smooth her way past those lips. She watched him take in the food; pull the fork out of that mouth. No man should have a mouth like that, full lipped and ready to break into a smile. If a gust of wind would wind its way into the Pump Room at that moment, pick her up in her wine-imposed weightlessness and exhale her to the street, she would ride it with the picture of that man's mouth taking in such pleasure.

He pulled the fork from his mouth slowly, put down the fork, and bent toward her, one side of his face pulled into a smile, his eyes intent. He reached out a finger and touched the edge of Jocelyn's mouth with its tip, took in her slight shudder. "Just a drop of wine here needing attention." He brought his finger back to his mouth, gave the tip a lick. "Tastes good." He brought back the crooked smile. "So does the wine."

Sensation coursed through her. Fine, she told the part of her that set out alarms. The guy is good, no doubt because he's had so much practice. But she would just settle in and enjoy. Sip on her wine. Feel the residual warmth in her hand. Tomorrow she could be sensible.

The guy had brought her French fries after work, and now she was with him in Sinatra's booth. Thank you, sweet Lord, for the blessing.

Doug wanted *her*.

The goodnight kiss was anticlimactic. Full of pleasure, for sure, but Jocelyn had been on an erotic ride of sensation for most of the night. When

Doug kissed her good night and she felt the strength of his erection, she felt it as much in her gut as between her legs. The others—they vanished in a poof as soon as the sound of their leaving faded. With this one, she took in the air as if she could hold on to him moments longer.

She leaned against the door to Luna's and watched the Range Rover pull away, already a sense of loss filling her. The street lights acted as luminaries, growing smaller as Doug drove farther away as tall brick row houses were silent, sad, mere sentinels guarding the neighborhood. Had anyone else here had such a night, so sensory, so . . . yummy.

Some guy down the block was walking his dog, a corgi, no doubt praying it did its duty. Who had to poop at this hour of the morning? Too bad, mister dog guy. You're out here bored and cold. Me? I'm hugging myself I'm so caught up in delicious.

She turned around, put the key in the door and opened it slowly. Yes, her aunt couldn't hear her from here, but just in case. Once she slipped upstairs to the apartment, a note greeted her. "J—I'm in bed. Pinkie swear I won't ply you with questions. Everything's on the sofa ready for you. Hope the night was wonderful."

She fell asleep in the arms of serenity, a state of peace, the antidote to dreams of mothers and dolls and all the uglies that haunted so many of her nights. She rode on the wings of that serenity to a place of quiet rest.

One night like this was pay back plenty for so many that stung. And, she mused as she fell asleep, there would be more to come. It was a promise.

Jocelyn woke up on the sofa, a cashmere comforter thrown over her. What time was it? Why wasn't she in her bed instead of on this thing? Light poured in, too much light for the tiny windows in her apartment. She pulled up the covering, let it caress her with its softness, felt a sneeze work its way through her head.

Wait. She wasn't in her apartment. She was at her aunt's. She had stayed here to avoid the long haul home.

She had stayed here to avoid the tacky of her neighborhood.

"Good morning." Jocelyn sat up, stretched and turned toward the voice. Her aunt sat at the dining table, her head outlined by the morning light coming in.

Jocelyn yawned and stretched more, an aroma breaking through the fog of sleep. "I smell coffee. What time is it?"

"Late enough that I can insist you come tell me all about it—or as much as you're willing to share. I promised no pressure. Anyway, it's all ready. Come grab a cup and join me."

At the table, Jocelyn smeared a croissant with raspberry jam while she inhaled the tang of the coffee's smell. The fog of sleep was definitely gone, replaced now by a grumble in her stomach.

She looked at her aunt sitting across from her, eyes straight, face with nary a crack of emotion. Poor Aunt Paula. Jocelyn took a bite of the roll, closed her eyes, and murmured her pleasure.

"Well?" Auntie Paula was no longer the stoic.

"Well, what?" This was such fun.

Paula put her hands in her lap and sat up straight, elongating her neck toward her niece. "Did Doug like the dress?"

"Loved it. Said I was classy."

Paula nodded, self-satisfied. "Of course you are. You're my niece." She let out a small smile, childlike. "*Chloe* has excellent taste. I could always count on her to make me look special. And she's forever twenty-one. Just like the store department name. Glad the dress worked for you. Way too young for me."

Jocelyn sat back in the chair, relishing the rest of the croissant. She meant to tease her aunt, but the richness of the treat rolled down her throat in promise of a sugar jolt. Perfect. It could merge with the rest of the sweetness that purred in her body, a benediction from the night before.

Paula watched her niece, at first with delight but then with a fluttering of concern. She had seen that expression before. Many times. On her sister.

Oh sweet girl, don't go there.

CHAPTER 24

Stars. It was like the stars had come down to touch the city, bless those who ventured out on a December night. Jocelyn had no idea how much time had passed since she and Doug had left Luna's for their Christmas season walk downtown. Of course it was dark; this was December when dark snatched away the day before it had barely begun, but the Christmas season in Chicago knew how to slap the dark right out of the streets and fill them, instead, with wonder. Bring on the bare trees. Bring on the black skies. Christmas season was a battle the dark could not win.

A light snow was falling, perfect way to end hours of touring Chicago's December extravaganza. The lights were a thing of rapture, all those tiny bits of sparkle, millions of them collectively lighting the sky. And the store windows. Such movement, such colors, such texture. All around them, children tugged at parents. "Mommie, come see! Look at the snow queen ballerina. Hey, those toy soldiers have real swords!" In the streets, horses pulled carriages of tourists and Chicagoans alike, the clomp of hooves steady amid all the music that was this night.

Jocelyn and Doug huddled against each other, watching the displays. She felt her world invite her in as Santa's, elves, trains, tinsel, snow fairies, the collective mythos of Christmas beckoned to buyers. She felt the invitation when she leaned in to Doug's body to keep warm. Grab on to this moment, she thought, and bottle it, take it out and ride its pleasure. A display tree bowed to her, shook with presents and crystal and glitz.

A memory stirred within her, a ghost of Christmas past. She must have been about five. A flocked tree some barfly gave Evie, strangest tip ever. That year the two of them cut out paper ornaments and chains to hang on the woe-begotten thing, spilled clumps of white on their stained carpet as they added the decorations. A cloud of cigarette smoke would hang in their apartment, but that damn thing stood protected, miniature lights fighting through the haze, a blessing—perhaps a glimmer of hope that maybe things would be different.

They never were.

The next year, one of the revolving door boyfriends got pissed about some slight and yanked the tree from the corner, threw the thing across the room. The poor tree shattered into a pile of ripped paper and deflocked flocking.

They never put up a tree again.

The image left her cold, much colder than any Chicago wind could stir, a cold deep and pressing. Jocelyn snuggled against Doug. His body heat soaked through her, first her arms and back, then the rest of her as she gave into the comfort. In the moment, she felt the season sift through her, the promise of happiness that only a story land could give. This was Christmas, a time of light and laughter—if Alex had his way, Walking Dead bobble-heads for tree ornaments. Even the bizarre shared the season. For now, however, it was Jocelyn, Doug, and a window full of velvet-clad models, lifeless and permanently thin, sipping champagne surrounded by antiques and mercury glass, holly and evergreen boughs. Too beautiful to even make her jealous of their plastic perfection.

A gust of wind sluiced up from the lake-seized Michigan Avenue, whirling snow and cold at the storefront gazers, and assaulting Jocelyn's face with its sting. The street was suddenly lonely, even with Doug's arms around her. She shivered once, and then turned her face toward him, snuggling against his chest. She still felt the cold fight its way until she began quaking. If she just fell into him, he would bring back the warmth.

"Hey," he said. "Are you okay?" He took off his gloves and felt the ice of her face. "Let's wrap this up for tonight. Hard to have a merry Christmas when you're in the hospital with pneumonia." The two of them chased back to Doug's car, heated seats more of an agenda than storefronts. Inside the car, when Jocelyn finally felt the warmth seep into her, they were out of the parking garage and on their way. She gave one more glance at displays, this time one on a corner restaurant. In the window, rosy-cheeked children, pint-sized mannequins, reached their plastic hands up to decorate a flocked Christmas tree. Each munchkin was armed with tinsel and paper ornaments.

Jocelyn felt a shudder grip her chest that had nothing to do with the weather. "How about a drink?" She rubbed her hands together. "I can't seem to shake the cold." Even as she offered the idea, she felt the pulses of that shudder, blamed the wind for its lingering even in the warmth of the car. Damn the wind. It couldn't spoil their evening. She wouldn't let it.

"Great idea. I know just the place. Just let me make one phone call." While he phoned someone named Andre, Jocelyn kept her gaze outside, still in love with all the city had to offer but weirded out by the lingering image of that damn tree.

Let it go. You've got a hot guy in a hot car with heated leather. This is the now you've been waiting for all your life. Grab on, baby, and enjoy the ride.

She felt Doug's hand on her leg. "We're going to meet up with a couple of friends at Abbey's. You'll love them."

A couple of miles and light years away from that damned window, Doug pulled into a parking lot. They were almost to Evanston on Clark Street. Jocelyn wasn't sure what she expected—something Irish maybe—but not a shamrock or leprechaun was in sight. Just lots of brick and window. No neon. No flash. Inside, the place was devoted to Northwestern. All the accouterments hung on the walls, the beer mugs, posters, jerseys of the Big Ten school.

She plunked down at a high top while Doug got them a couple of beers. Just as he was setting them down, a couple assaulted Doug. The guy was beefy, thick-necked, probably a red-head judging from the flushing of his face under his purple ball cap. He had his arms around Doug and was grunting something about brothers. Jocelyn could make out a few words she commonly used when snits hit her, but "rat-fucker" was a little much even for her. The girl couldn't be more than five foot, ninety pounds dripping wet. She had jumped on his back and was calling him *Cowboy*. Cowboy, my ass, thought Jocelyn. You're not riding him. He's mine.

Once Doug had regained control and introduced the pair—Austin and Emily—as his former roommates and major couple, Jocelyn let her teeth unclench. When Emily started French kissing Austin right in front of everyone, Jocelyn figured, what the hell, looks like a party.

"Knock it off, you two. You can hump like rabbits when you get back to your apartment. For now, behave and meet my lady."

My lady. My Lady? Was that what she was? Sounded good to her. Jocelyn lifted her glass and started a toast. "Here's to the French. Who knows how much good tongue sucking we would have missed had they not taught us how to kiss."

Emily beamed as she raised her glass. Austin took a big slug and lifted his. Doug already had his in the air. "Hear. Hear." As soon as they had taken a collective drink, Emily reached out and touched Jocelyn's jaw. "You know, you're very photogenic. Have you done any modeling?"

The flat surface of her hand making contact knocked her off balance.

Doug leaned toward Jocelyn and put his arm on her shoulder just as Emily drew back. "Emily's a photographer. A damn good one. Has a great eye."

Jocelyn wanted to cringe but steadied herself. "So, why is a bar devoted to Northwestern called Abbey's?"

Public humiliation averted. Thank the Lord. Austin pointed to the purple banner emboldened with 1924 and together the three told Jocelyn about Wallace Abbey's column calling the Northwestern "Purple" football players "Wildcats" when they almost defeated the University of Chicago. Good thing the name had stuck. What lineman wants to be called a "Purple"?

On the way back to Jocelyn's car, Doug tried an apology. "Sorry about those two. They're great once you get to know them. They just have their own unique style."

"That *style* is called lack of filter." Before Doug could reply, Jocelyn tapped his shoulder with her fist, laughing. "Not to worry. Lack of filter has been my style of choice most of my life."

"That's one of the things I like best about you. Filters are way overrated. Take out all the fun. I like my women unfiltered."

Later, when he kissed her good night, when the force of his mouth on hers bent her body into the metal of her car door, Jocelyn thought about filters. Her lips ached with the want of him, a want that pulsed between her thighs and spread to her gut. She grabbed at his head, her mouth, her tongue, her teeth moving in delight.

Filters, my ass, she thought.

Back at Luna's, in the back corner behind the bar, Cole put his hands on his boss's shoulders and spoke low words of warning. "If you scowl at another customer or bang down one more glass, your customers are going to wonder if you're trying out for a Grinch pageant."

Paula hung her head. "I know, I know." She let a growl. "That Doug guy is as phony as the breasts on a Barbie. Would you give me one good reason why Jocelyn hangs on him?"

"I can give you plenty of bad reasons, but that's not the point. We step in now and she runs faster—toward the dirtball."

"There has to be something we can do. Here she has that sweet boy Alex—granted, he's a little weird, but he's at least real—and Jocelyn goes ape over that glorified frat boy."

Cole had his best grown-up voice on. "There's nothing we can do about it. She's in a fantasy right now. Why wouldn't she be? She's never had anything but fantasy as a frame of reference as a child."

"That's the problem." By now Paula's voice was a plea. She turned toward the tables to see if anyone was listening. Thank the Lord they were all caught up in their own chatter.

"We're here for her." Cole's voice was confident. "She's come miles. She'll come more. If we jump on her, she'll just see it as her making another mistake, or worse, being betrayed."

Paula picked up a bar towel and swatted at the counter. "We may not be able to jump right in, but I bet I can come up with something that skirts around the problem enough to at least dent it a little."

"Patience, boss lady. Patience. One step at a time."

CHAPTER 25

From the journal of Paula Ross

I'm worried about my niece. She's happy. Too happy. She's gone from feistiness on a stick to someone I can't recognize. Cole says not to push her. How can I not?

A normal day for Jocelyn begins with "Karma woke up today and figured, 'Why not stampede on Jocelyn just for practice?'" Today she waltzed in singing Sugar Pie Honey Bunch—*how does she even know that song—and slapped me on the rear. That is not my niece. Jocelyn celebrates sarcasm and PMS; she does not celebrate sappy love songs.*

She's manic one minute, dewy-eyed the next.

She's Evie.

Slap yourself for saying that, Paula Ross, right now, but that's the -awful truth. My spitfire jewel of a girl is acting like her mother. All she's missing are the hickeys. That slut would sneak into the house, lips swollen, hair tousled, neck lit up like an inkblot had hit it, full of demented yapping about love. When I saw her like that, her face a mixture of lust, satisfaction, and dewy-eyed fantasy building, I wanted to slap her, this sister of mine reduced to the town whore building love castles in the sky and truly believing she would move in.

Of course, we had no role models for relationships. Daddy's idea of a compliment was not sneering and you never knew when Momma grabbed you if she was going to give a kiss or smack you. Usually it was a smack. Disappointment lived in our house like a malevolent phantom. It breathed on us early in the morning to wake us up, and tucked us in at night.

"I love you, child. Now go away."

"I love you child. Why do you shame me so?"

"Of course we will do that. Trust your parents." Fat chance.

It took me months to trust Joe. How can you trust when you have no idea what trust looks like?

That sister of mine wouldn't have known a healthy relationship if it sat in her lap—and I bet she sat in plenty of laps to try them out. Boys. If they breathed and knew her name, they were "delicious". Some role model.

Now Jocelyn has that look to her. When I came upstairs tonight, she was staring at a wine glass, sitting with her legs up on the table, leaning back watching an empty glass, twirling it in her fingers, a goofy grin on her face. Her mother all over again.

Do I approach her? Ask her about that Doug guy? Do I bring up her mother? Fairyland Evie she knows about. "Why don't they love me?" She whined it enough to her daughter. At least that's what the girl said. No surprise. She whined her way through life while she lived with us.

So why would Jocelyn choose to be like her mother?

Is it even a choice?

I rushed before and almost lost her. I dare not push too much.

But then, what is too much?

CHAPTER 26

She didn't park in the visitor section. Going to Doug's place meant walking out the jitters. She turned left at the corner past the apartment building and found a parking place next to the park. The day had already given up any light. People were out walking their dogs. Had to get that done now that they were home from work. Most of the pooches had on little wool coats; a black poodle even had on galoshes.

No problem with prying eyes. Dog owners who dressed their dogs could care less about a single gal striding toward her evening. The jitters were easy to figure out, but they were lined with an anticipation Jocelyn hadn't felt for a very long time. Even her teeth had a special zing. She pulled her purse closer to her and strode on.

She reached his building. Security door, of course. To Jocelyn, it looked like a glass and steel chastity belt. What would Cole have to say about that?

Ha. Going to the apartment of a guy hot enough to make your palms sweat was more than a big deal. It was a freaking promise. Calling up on the intercom said, "Invite me in. Let's get it on."

And there's a problem with that?

A couple laughing at each other opened the door, and she hurried through the doorway. Problem solved. She pulled back her shoulders and marched to the elevator, pressed 16. The whole way up, she felt her skin tingling against her body, her nipples tight against her clothing.

The elevator door opened. Jocelyn stepped across the threshold and moved along. Tiled floor. All the doors the same, gray steel, same as the walls. Not much for an architect, but no one had put him in charge of the halls. What would his place look like?

She pushed the buzzer. Normal buzzer sound. Nothing kinky there.

Doug opened the door, his face rugged and welcoming. "There's my beautiful girl." He bent over and gave her a quick kiss before, stupid grin plastered across her face, she ducked around him and walked into the loft onto concrete floors, polished yet proud of their history, the world of Doug introduced to Jocelyn, the novice. Ahead of her and to her right, a thick concrete pillar stretched to a monster of a beam reaching clear across the space. The wall opposite her was mostly windows that stretched up for forever. And that ceiling. Had to be twenty feet high, wood, loaded with pipes and beams. This wasn't a loft. It was an industrial cathedral.

She scanned the room ahead and to her left. Brick walls. Lots of them. Gee, the third little pig must live here, she thought to herself. Dumb humor. Never failed when she was stunned.

The living area was a shit pot of leather, old and weathered by the decorations. Big ass area rug. Drink wine near it at your own peril. Her apartment had a couch from the thrift store with an afghan hiding the worn spots. Her area rug had been on clearance and looked it, a four-foot poly with catsup stains. She didn't have a chair. This guy had two, the same aged beaten leather that screamed money. Aunt Paula had an apartment that welcomed in upscale taste. This one demanded awe.

A telescope in the corner pointed out toward the building across the street. *Dougie, you naughty boy. Are you a peeper?* Somehow the comment, meant to be sarcastic, sounded hollow within her. Power hung in the air like a subtle humidity. And she knew it.

"Here. Have some wine." Jocelyn flinched and then turned toward his voice. Before she could shift, he was moving from the kitchen bar past the glass dining table to the seating area. He had been watching her the whole time. When had he moved? Bet he thought she was a little girl ogling candy through the window. What the hell. She was. This place was candy.

The last of the afternoon sun sliced through the window, sending shards of shadow and light across the space. Surrounded by the aura of leather and sun, Doug smiled, lifting the corner of his eyes. He had that look about him, the one that whispered money and power. He deserved this place. He deserved her. That thought was in his mind. She knew it.

130

"So what do you think?" His words were a purr.

Nice kitty.

She walked over and sank into the sofa, leaned back and sighed. "What do I think? I think my whole apartment isn't as big as this seating area. I think in your spare time you rob banks to afford this." She turned toward him and smiled. "I think this is the coolest place I've ever seen."

"Well, my architecture major self thanks you. Dad's in real estate. He bought this building as an investment when the neighborhood was transitioning and turned me loose. That was two years ago. You should have seen this place. Cramped walls and mouse turds."

Jocelyn was stunned. "You did this? I mean, I figured you made the place yours, but you designed the space, too?"

Doug held out his hand. "Yep. C'mon. I'll give you the tour." He pulled her up, whisked off her coat like a pro and had it hung up before she could take a breath. While they walked through the loft, Doug talked about support beams and creative use of space. And textures. The guy loved texture. Smooth glass and granite. Rough wood. Piling of tiers of leather and materials that fell through her hands. The bathroom had a tiled shower big enough for a dinner party, its glass door next to a wall of slabs of old metal. Above the sink hung another slab of metal. At the bottom, someone had etched, "You look fine." Open the slab and there was the mirror if you really needed it. That did it. The guy had her sense of humor. Jocelyn elbowed his side and asked, "Can I be you when I grow up?"

Doug laughed. "That's the point. You don't need to grow up. Then you lose the edge."

The bedroom blew her mind. Concrete walls. Floating shelves. Steel girders on a wooden platform that rose to make a canopy. Right above the pillows, Doug had set in weathered wood between the girders to create a loft. A loft within a loft. Cool. The platform extended from the bed clear to the bedroom door below the floating shelves. Recessed lighting bathed the bed area in soft light. A basketball hoop hung from the ceiling above the foot of the bed.

"Please don't tell me you shoot baskets in bed." Before Doug could answer, Jocelyn groaned. "And please don't tell me that's some sick artistic expression for scoring."

"Neither. Cross my heart."

Why did that sound like a challenge?

Jocelyn had had good wine, thanks to Aunt Paula, but this was *good* wine. It caressed her throat as it went down and warmed her insides. The second glass was as good as the first. She was nestled next to Doug who felt increasingly homey as the wine flowed.

"How about a movie?" A behemoth of a television set on the wall across from the sofa. Before she could answer, shades of amber and the sound of light jazz played in front of them. Strange. No titles. Just movie. Doug pulled her closer as the images began to come together. A man was drizzling drops of liquid down a naked body. Yep. He was bare chested, too. He ran his tongue down the hollows of another body's naked skin. No dialogue here. Just movie.

Holy *Fifty Shades of Grey*! Jocelyn grabbed her wine glass and thought about sitting up. She really did. At least that's what she told herself later. But good old Doug was doing something really nifty with his fingers and tongue on her neck. Glass still in hand, she settled in for the ride.

Now the wine glistened on a nipple, a hard very erect nipple obviously welcoming the attention. A tongue flicked around the tip and then lips sucked and teeth nibbled. Jocelyn felt a warmth build in her lower abdomen, play on the inside of her thighs. She leaned forward and watched, let the warmth grow into something more substantial. Doug sat up and, still working her neck, whispered, "How do you like my taste in movies?"

The warning bell in her mind was clanging full bore. She ignored it. Then turning toward him, she pushed him back against the sofa and moved onto him. "I think you're a dangerous guy. And I bet you'll taste as good as the wine."

Jocelyn was right, at least about the wine.

Later, Doug wrapped the two of them in the afghan and his arms. "We never got to watch the rest of the movie."

Jocelyn snuggled into him. "Play it again, big guy. I didn't get past the daisies and the second girl's breasts."

Doug laughed while he reached for the remote. "I have to admit, I've never seen a girl into porn like you."

132

"Porn? Are you kidding? My mother's old boyfriends always loved porn, the porn where cheerleaders played with gigantic penises like favorite Christmas toys. Porn is about slurps and grunts. This is art."

The movie raised its colors once again. Doug started kissing her neck, nipping at the softness. Jocelyn settled into the scene, pure anticipation.

CHAPTER 27

"Oh good Lord, that poor horse."

At two in the afternoon, a Sunday binge of *Walking Dead* reruns was underway in Paula's apartment. Paula held her hand over her mouth as she watched the horde of decaying walkers attack Sheriff Rick's horse, but her words came out plain enough, that and a tone of misgiving, fear, and excitement wrenched together. She blinked her eyes and sniffled at the dying keen of the poor animal.

"You laughed when the walker was gnawing on a leg, but you're going to cry over a horse?" Alex held a piece of pizza midway to his mouth, his face composed in contemplation as he nodded his head. "The Apocalypse is for all of us creatures." He was obviously amused.

Jocelyn slapped at him. "Don't be a jerk." She bent forward from the sofa toward her aunt, who was sitting in her favorite chair, dark eyes accusing. "I promise you, Aunt Paula, no more dead horses, no slaughtered dogs and kitties. Just humans."

"Well thank the good Lord for that. I'm prepared for people, but not pets."

Jocelyn held one hand behind her back, fingers crossed. So Auntie, maybe feeding the chickens to the walkers in the barn won't flip you out. For them, it's dinner. After all, zombies have to eat. How cute was it, she thought, to have an aunt entertain her and her best buddy by watching guts and gore. Jocelyn knew, darn well, that this was all a ruse to get Jocelyn and Alex to hang out. The woman had asked about Alex and why he hadn't been around enough, but it was all so cute. She grabbed for her pop and watched Rick whack off a head.

Paula maintained the shocked-at-carnage face while she took in the living room scene. If she couldn't pull off a fake scare for a couple of kids, all those years of juggling alters hadn't taught her a thing. Here they were, the three of them—aunt, niece, niece's recently ignored but still best friend—all happily ensconced in her living room ready to rekindle, at least for Jocelyn and Alex, a relationship that had been all but splintered by work schedules, school, and—Paula gritted her teeth at the thought—that slimy new boyfriend, what's-his-name. Doug. That was it. Rhymed with rug, as in dirt catcher.

"You've got it, Auntie Paula." Jen had her snark tone. Jen was hanging around a lot inside her. Probably a sign that deep down, Paula was onto something about the boyfriend. Nothing subtle about Jen now. "I'm in here for a reason. I know slime when I see it dripping from a guy's mouth to his hands and down to his dick, which is the thing old Dougie is doing in spite of his schmooze."

"I know, dear. I know. Why do you think I'm sitting here watching all this gore and folly?" Paula took a look at the pizza. Meat Lovers, they had ordered. Greasy clumps of sausage swollen atop circles of red pepperoni. All that sauce, thick with grease. She shuddered. The refreshments bore a much too equal appearance to the subject matter of what was flashing before her on the screen. Still . . .

"Aunt Paula. Watch this."

At Jocelyn's command, Paula focused on the screen. Poor Sheriff Rick was under a car, the arms of the dead reaching for him, their faces contorted with rage and want and all things deadly. What a wonderful shot for a painting, she thought. She'd have to keep the DVD for a closer look.

"Well, I certainly will never want to visit Atlanta after *this* evening."

Toward the end of Season 2, when Carol cradled her dead daughter Sofia, cut down now that the child had turned, Paula pushed pause and demanded, "That's it. I'm done." Her shoulders slumped. "Oh that poor little girl. How can the writers do that?" She turned to Alex and Jocelyn. "They will take out that scum bucket Shane, won't they?"

"Not to worry." Jocelyn's voice was sincere. "He gets his by the end of the season."

"Good. We can watch some more." She stood up and drew in a breath. "As soon as I make myself a stiff drink and help Carol mourn her loss." She headed toward the kitchen for the liquor cabinet muttering something about "damn writers."

By the time the walker horde had driven the survivors from Hershel's farm, Paula's face wore sorrow etched with excitement. Gone was the singular plotting manipulator. She was hooked. Two birds with one stone. A new show to watch and an even better one live in front of her. Ah, the bliss of a little manipulation.

Jocelyn and Alex were on the sofa stuffing pizza and arguing with their mouths full.

"Let's push forward to the Governor." Jocelyn loved the Governor, Paula recalled.

"Are you nuts? Let's watch them kill the convicts in the prison. We can run it backward."

"Stumme, you are such a tool."

"Glad you love me. I love you, too."

Paula smiled at the two of them, at their back and forth. Oh you two children, if you only knew. Multiply by thirty times and you could know what goes on in my head when things get bad.

But things were not bad now. Jen even murmured an approval. She loved subterfuge, that girl did. Paula decided to fix herself another drink. Just one. Didn't need Mother getting all over her about family genes and the terror they spewed.

Too late. "Paula, Jocelyn told you about her mother—your sister—don't you remember? She never *meant* to get drunk. It was always, 'Just one to relax, honey, that's all I need.' Before long, she'd be on the floor drooling, her words ashes in her daughter's mouth."

Paula gave Mother a gentle internal pat. "I know, dear. That's why I never have more than three."

Jen jumped in. "Stop your gabbing and get back to the party. These guys are a good time."

So Paula did. But the memory of what Jocelyn had told her, the words Mother had used to nudge her, they stayed with her.

CHAPTER 28

From the journal of Paula Ross

*M*eltdowns suck. No other way to put it. Bitches they are. The triggers pop up out of nowhere like a toddler jumping out from behind a tree and yelling 'Boo!' First, the constriction of the throat. They always start there. Then the trembling. Once that jaw starts in, it's all over. Walk away, run if you have to, don't let anyone see the crazy. Five minutes. Ten minutes. That's all the time you have. The first hour is the hardest. Look to the future. Two or three days and it will be over.

Once I was at a workshop for laying on color and some prissy bitch whined about my self-importance. Self-importance? Are you nuts? It took me three hours to work up the courage to even attend. The leader liked my work. I liked my work.

It didn't matter. One snark and I was gone. I made it out of the class-room with a smattering of dignity. Never let them see you sweat. Then I ran.

I hid in the supply room, back in the corner. Corners are best. You can sit on the floor and feel the wall. By Then, the tears were flowing and I knew better than to fight it.

When class was over, the teacher came back. I expected questioning. A little criticism for sure. Instead, she sat on the floor and talked about my paint-ing. Loved the way I attacked color with a palette knife. Could I work with her with another class she was helping?

So I'd cry for a while. Blow my nose. Cry some more. She didn't care, didn't even seem to notice. Just talked technique.

Blew my mind. Let me reduce the jag to only two hours instead of two days. Three weeks later, I was her assistant for the day. She never mentioned *the crying. Not even when we attended art shows together or I helped her out with classes.*

The meltdown is all about perception. Self-perception. Attack.

Two mornings after the *Walking Dead* binge, just before 11:00, Jocelyn walked through the door at Luna's ready for action—no classes ever on Tuesday and Paula promised treats. No brainer. Sure enough, her aunt had a pile of Tasty Kremes and mugs of Cappuccino already set on the bar. They were the only two in the whole place; but as Jocelyn scanned the area, she crossed her arms and felt a flinch. The bar had a haunted quality to it; all the chairs stacked were on top of the tables, only the stools at the bar right side up. No Cole to crack jokes, just the artwork looking out at them, lonely and ignored.

The drive in had been a chore—early December rain and wind—so Jocelyn wasn't the happiest camper just in from the cold and wet. Probably the reason for the Debbie Downer. She took in a breath to shake off her attitude, let the promise of warmth and sugar settle her, and then rubbed her hands together before she took off her coat and put it and her purse down onto the side of a chair on a near-by table before she joined her aunt at the bar. Paula was already drinking her coffee, but the pile of Tasty Kremes sat undisturbed and waiting.

"Good morning, Dear. Not such a great day to be driving in to see me."

Jocelyn shuddered a couple of times, flexed her shoulders, and then walked over to the seat next to her aunt and sat down. "Sugar and coffee, come to me, Baby." Her aunt reached over and patted those cold hands.

"The weatherman was right," Paula said. "The temperature's started to fall already. We'll be in all kinds of nasty before noon."

As if to prove her point, outside, sleet pushed against the window. Some poor guy walked past, head down, raising his collar against the moisture. A woman a few feet behind him struggled with an umbrella that wouldn't open soon enough to save her from icy hair.

"Not a bad idea you're closed for lunch today. No one would be stupid enough to come out in this stuff." Jocelyn looked out the window. "Except for those two schmucks out there and this orphan of the storm."

138

Jocelyn grabbed at the nearest Tasty Kreme. "Aunt Paula, you sure know how to get volunteers even if the weather does suck. I'll even do dishes if you have these available."

Paula took a doughnut, sat back, and took a bite "Well, I'm certainly glad you made it here safely. I may be a little bit selfish, but it's nice to have company while I work." She adjusted herself once, twice on the barstool before she said, "What a time we had with those shows. Your Alex is such an amusing young man." The choice of topic was obvious, but hopefully not annoyingly so.

Jocelyn gave a half grin. "Yeah, if by amusing you mean talking with his mouthful and rating zombie women on hotness."

"Oh that's just part of his charm." Paula nodded and then sat back. "I couldn't have enjoyed it more." She made it sound like a wish.

Jocelyn was midway through a slurp of custard filling. She snorted and licked her lips while she sat down and answered. "Fun? Are you kidding me? You looked like a four-year-old at a haunted house, scared to death but just as scared of being called a sissy."

Paula swatted at the air, her lips stretched in farcical smugness. "I like to think of the experience as physical fitness. Got my heart rate up."

"Right, and the pizza had tomatoes and green peppers, so it was salad." Jocelyn took a big gulp of her drink. "C'mon, spill. You didn't ask me to come in this morning to unload glasses that don't need unloading and dust bottles that don't need dusting. I figured something was up. If you're trying to set me up with Alex, forget it. He's a brother, not a boyfriend."

Jocelyn paused. "And if you haven't noticed, I already have a boyfriend." An *ahem* carried in her tone.

Paula fiddled with her cup and then took a sip. She let the sweetness of the sugar linger in her mouth. "No, no. I wouldn't dream of interfering in your love life."

That was more than a fib. She almost choked out of guilt.

"I wanted to talk to you about something you had said to me last week, about your mother." Lord, this was hard. There was a smattering of confectioner's sugar on the bar next to the treats plate. She rubbed her finger on it. Certainly a mote of sugar needed her immediate attention. If she were lucky, a few more specks might appear, and she could swipe at them as well. She bent forward to meet the slack. "Sunday night. I couldn't help notice you looking at me while I brought in that second drink. I mean, you and Alex were drinking your pop, and here I was slurping Bacardi . . . "

Paula sat still as a nun in prayer, hands now in her lap. Jocelyn watched her aunt study Jocelyn's face, a tightness around Paula's mouth working her, the sheen of tears in her eyes.

"You have every right to drink in your own apartment. I'm not the booze police."

Paula gathered herself up, sat taller in her bar stool. "I just can't help but think about what you said about Evie, how she never meant to get drunk, how she always meant to only have one drink, but then she would wind up sprawled on the floor before the night was over." She set both elbows on the bar—body turned from Jocelyn. When she turned back to Jocelyn, she shook her head. "I promise you, I am not like Evie, not in the least." Paula's shudder emphasized the point.

The idea of Paula looking like her mother? No way. That was funny. Then the picture of Evie drunk on her ass, melting into the kitchen linoleum slipped through, sucking all the air out of the picture. Nothing like Mommy drunkard to take all the fun out of funny. This was slippery territory. Time for her to swivel and look at the back of the bar. Talking to a wall was easier than talking to a human, even if that human was wonderful.

"I've never seen you drunk. I only saw you tipsy once, and that was the first day we met here—the thought of you in any way, shape, or form, resembling my booze-ridden mother is . . . ludicrous at the very least."

Jocelyn took a deep breath, let it out, but her focus remained on that neutral wall. "I'd laugh at the thought, but nothing about my mother is funny. When Evie was drunk, she was in her own world, hell, her own universe. All conversation, if there was any, centered on her and the present woes of her world." Jocelyn's voice picked up steam, the anger in her giving it a life. "Walk on egg shells. Stomp around. Didn't matter. No truth, no lying. I could say anything I wanted, dance naked with a rose in my teeth. She wouldn't notice. Just Evie, the bottle, and whatever cluster-fuck she was immersed in at the time.

"Yeah. And she didn't give a shit if she crashed on me." Jocelyn's face contorted as she slammed both hands on the bar surface, saw from the corner of her eye that Paula jumped, her aunt's shoulders cringing as Jocelyn's next words spit out. The anger was palpable; but within her, Jocelyn felt that sadness, so automatic over the years. If she sat there long enough, she could melt in that sadness.

"Life with my mother was like a rerun you've watched so many times, but it's the only choice and you have to watch TV."

Paula turned Jocelyn's barstool to face her, took her hands. How dare she chide herself, give two seconds of concern for herself when her niece had been so betrayed. "Oh sweet girl, how awful for you. If it's any consolation, Evie ignored everyone, and when I knew her, she was sober. I think the booze just sent her crashing."

Jocelyn leaned forward into the grace of those hands. The sadness seeped through her as always, but a gentleness nudged some of it away. It was another one of those moments, so few in her life, but so precious, when hope came to visit it and she allowed it to stay.

Outside, a truck backfired and gears screeched in protest. Both women startled and turned toward the sound, a noise so rude in this moment of connection. Paula's instinct startled with the significance of that jolt as omen—talk, woman, it's what you need to do, but guard what you say. Guard what you do. Take control. Do not fold.

But there was no such rescue. The trembling beneath began. Damn those triggers. They assaulted her out of nowhere. She could feel her face take on the visage of her internal struggle, the caring woman who wanted to continue soothing but now had her own battle to wage. She struggled to keep her looks neutral. Some of the alters muttered, a few panicked—she could feel their fear in the din. Not now. Please, not now. She looked at the table while she tried to stabilize herself. Amazing how sprinkles could litter a counter.

Jocelyn waited, still, her upper body pulled ever so slightly back. Had she noticed?

Paula felt the fear rise in her. What if she flipped out? What if the world ended, at least the world she had built with her niece? More breathing. Surely Jocelyn wouldn't notice the strong, rhythmic breaths.

Why the hell had that truck backfired? Why now? Why in this moment of grace?

Paula reached for her spoon, picked it up, ran her free finger around the rim of the bowl, her face focused on that stupid spoon. Jocelyn took in the tightness of Paula's finger against the rim as the woman shook her head. "Ugly." Then Paula turned her head to look out the window. Her face was pale. "Ugly," she repeated. So much in this instant of detachment from the world around her. Sure, Jocelyn had spat out an invective against her mother, but hell, Paula knew full well what Evie was like. She had lived with her almost as long as Jocelyn had.

Maybe that was the problem.

Jocelyn watched Paula breathe in and breathe out, as if the breath itself was her own universe. The woman's eyes were not looking at her, not looking at anything in the room. Paula was someplace else.

The moments passed. Paula continued to breathe, kind of a rote ritual, in and out in a tight rhythm while her shoulders started to shake, her throat to tremble. Her aunt's lips tightened even as she took in a breath and exhaled more purposefully. It didn't take a brain surgeon to realize that the woman was reliving something nasty.

"Paula. I'm so sorry." She gently tugged the spoon from Paula's hands, took those hands in her own. "Talk to me."

Paula looked at Jocelyn and squeezed her hands. She breathed in once again and spoke, her voice no more than a whisper, her attention somewhere within. "I'll be all right. I'll be all right." She breathed out the words.

Holy shit, thought Jocelyn. We started out talking about one too many glasses of wine, slipped into an Evie moment, and now . . . now, I don't have a clue. She sat there dumbfounded as Paula pushed herself from the chair and strode through the bar toward the kitchen. She slammed through the swinging door with both hands and disappeared.

Jocelyn followed slowly, concern and fear driving her toward the kitchen. What was happening? What could she do? She felt the need to grab her aunt; whether to shake her or hug her, she had no clue. This was a woman who had crawled back into sanity. This was a woman who had been nothing but loving to a niece she barely knew. What the hell was going on? Jocelyn did know one thing; this was a woman who needed her.

A little voice inside her pleaded, Goo*d, don't let anybody walk in right now.* A louder voice said, *Other people's the last thing you need to worry about. Hurry your ass.*

Just short of the kitchen door, Jocelyn could hear her aunt sobbing. A second later, the sight of Paula in that kitchen tore at Jocelyn's heart. The woman stood over one of the aluminum sinks, surrounded by pots and pans, the scene an entire spread of silver. Her hands gripped the edge, gripped them while her body, rigid in form yet shaking, moved back and forth against the metal as if she were hysterical and doing push-ups.

Jocelyn felt a surge of dizziness take over, felt frozen in the moment. Was this what it looked like to have a nervous breakdown? What should she do? Should she hug her? Turn around and leave?

Paula made the choice, hands still against the metal, shoulders trembling only a bit less. She turned to face Jocelyn, moving her hands to fan back the hanks of her hair. Her eyes had lost their color, so swollen were her lids. Her face was bone white. Snot dripped from her nose. With one arm, she wiped and sniffed.

"Not my best moment, I should say. Bet you want to run screaming out into the sleet. It'd probably be safer."

Guilt reared its odious head. Hell yes, she wanted to run. But she knew that wasn't an option, that she should walk instead, walk slowly, extend her arms, and take the wretch in front of her into her arms—which is exactly what she did.

Paula both fell into that embrace and stood rock solid. She settled her head into the crook of Jocelyn's neck and put her arms around her niece's waist.

"Joe would hold me just like this when I'd flip out in front of him. It's almost worth it to feel the love."

Joe. Paula's husband. The guy Cole said was Paula's own personal savior. The guy Paula never talked about to her. Yeah, that Joe.

Jocelyn felt the blessing of Paula's comment. She put her hand to Paula's head and stroked her. Funny, she thought even as the wetness of Paula's tears seeped against her shirt. Now I'm the mother.

Paula was the one to break the embrace. She took Jocelyn's hands in her. My Lord, Jocelyn thought, she's still crying. Paula was, indeed. A wave of tears slipped from Paula's eyes, and her body trembled. Yes, that was weird, weird but expected. Equally weird, but most definitely unexpected was the laughter. Paula was laughing. She laughed while she used her palms to wipe at her tears. She laughed as she grabbed for a paper towel to blow her nose, by now chapped red against the whiteness of her face.

She laughed as she said to Jocelyn, "And you thought *you* were the loon. Think about that day at the cemetery. Me giving you advice." The aunt who had just been the child took the hands of the girl who had just been the mother. "I've got to sit down or I'll fall over." Paula looked toward the door. "But we have to sit in here while I recover." The tears stopped their flow. Paula gave one huge sob. Then, hand in hand Paula led Jocelyn to a pair of folding chairs a few feet away.

"I suppose it would be an understatement to say that you wonder what the hell is going on." Paula managed a small sob, but she was grinning when it ebbed.

"That would be correct." Jocelyn wasn't about to say anything else.

"What you're seeing is post-traumatic-stress-disorder. PTSD."

CHAPTER 29

"PTSD? Isn't that what soldiers have? What they have just before they blew off heads in bars?" As Jocelyn stood ready to sit down, she stopped and words tumbled out before Jocelyn's thought process took hold. "Sorry," she added. "It's just that those words were the last thing I was expecting." Only then did she sit.

Paula sat next to her, ran one hand down Jocelyn's cheek. A pipe clinked, its thud an exclamation point. "No, I'm not going to blow your head off. Mine neither. But PTSD is not just for war victims. Victims of trauma come from all sorts of situations. But they share the reaction, the hold of PTSD."

Jocelyn flinched at Paula's words. The woman had been a mass of hysteria, sobbing one minute and laughing the next. Laughing at herself crying.

Who was this woman, this aunt? The question struck at Jocelyn, slapped her into an awareness. How many times had she asked that as a response to a shock about her aunt? The funeral home. The first walk into Luna's. The art.

Now this.

The response struck back at her. *Yeah, and how many times have you flipped out only to discover you're an ass?*

Paula sat straight up, looking forward, her hands folded in her lap. *Such a lady* someone might have thought if the scene had been a snapshot instead of a conversation—said someone could not listen to the craziness and think *lady*. "We have trauma. It's encoded in our brain. A total bitch, especially if you're a child. It doesn't go away; it lingers like a cancer ready to metastasize. All it needs is a trigger." She gave a snort. "Like a fucking truck backfiring." Definitely not lady material.

Paula grabbed Jocelyn's hand and pulled it to her lap; she let it rest there, her own hand covering it. Jocelyn kept still and watched her aunt's face. Just then, Paula let go of the hand and laid back against the hardness of the chair seat. "Lord, I'm tired," she said. She bent over and hugged herself, rocked while she spoke. "If they could bottle this shit, it would knock out insomnia." She stopped rocking, held firm while she snorted out the sarcasm. "Of course, the warning label would be a real bitch. *Caution: PTSD may make you crazy.*"

"What can I do?" The words were a whisper, an invitation.

Paula rose from her slump and went back to sagging her back and head against the back of the chair. Jocelyn's breath kept its pace as the two women sat on two metal folding chairs in an industrial kitchen, the feet firm against the porcelain tile hard and cold below them, the steel cabinets equally hard and cold, sentinels on guard. Who were they, these two women, Jocelyn asked herself. A pair of crazies? That was obvious. Her mind searched her body through the heart, the gut, the fingers, all of her, the total of her that had been so locked all these years. Why, she wondered even as her mind searched? This isn't about you.

Are you so sure it's not about you? A clutch of fear—really, only the memory of that fear stoked her. The night with Alex in that bar, shadow man behind her, the desperation to escape and the roil of terror afterwards. *Aren't you the junior miss version of your aunt? Didn't you want to collapse on the street, sob and shake until the ground rose up and covered you? And stupid fool that you are, you didn't even know why.* She didn't have time to stab at an answer. Paula was ready to talk some more. Besides, answering that question would open a box that Pandora wouldn't even want.

"When I was a child, I learned a lot about closets." Paula's words held a grieving. "Closets did more than collect clothes; they collected nightmares."

Closets. Jocelyn reached back to the conversation they had once? Paula had made a crack about closets, how a child could be thrown into a clothes closet for a few hours. Jocelyn had thought it strange, never had thought Paula was talking about herself. The impact of that revelation, thrown out so blithely, clutched at her. A little girl in a closet, the dark reaching in, hour after hour, squeezing. Oh Paula, say it isn't so.

146

"Of course, I don't think it was ever for six hours. Never more than two or three. Mother's way of making me invisible. 'Sit in there for a while, you wretched child. Don't let me see you.'" She laughed, again a snort of sarcasm. "That's when having multiples helps. *Clinton* had to handle it. Poor kid. He really hates the dark."

Jocelyn focused on the plates and cups stacked across from them. All white. White is such a nice color, so pure.

"*Jen* doesn't like the dark either. Of course, her dark was with Grandpa." This time there was no laugh. Just a growl. Feral. "*Clinton* had it tough. But *Jen* . . ."

White dishes or not. Nothing very pure in this room right now.

Paula sat up, rolled her shoulders and cracked her neck before she said to Jocelyn, "How beautifully ironic, isn't it. I called you in to tell you I'm not a booze guzzler, and now I want a drink like it's some kind of holy water."

Jocelyn stood up, reached for her aunt, and pulled her up into a hug. She'd read somewhere that twenty seconds made a hug therapeutic. Good thing. Paula had sunk into her like a waif just rescued from the storm. Jocelyn wrapped her in security until Paula drew away. The aunt rubbed her eyes with both hands and blew out—what was it? Relief? Anxiety?

"Well, Jocelyn, I opened Pandora's box and let out the nasties. Let's go back and drug ourselves on sugar while we search inside the box for the hope."

Two boxes of Tasty Kremes and a plateful of cheese later, Jocelyn was well into a tutorial on the PTSD of abuse survivors. Yes, soldiers suffered from PTSD. During the Civil War, they called it "Soldier's Heart." All wars had their own particular name for the psychological echoes of biological trauma.

But soldiers weren't the only victims, even though Paula said, "Children enduring abuse *are* at war.

"The first time I started on a crying jag, I was in my early thirties. I thought, 'Why am I crying? What kind of an idiot cries like this?' I was in an art museum, thankfully by myself, when some kid—I turned around and looked at him smirking at me when the thing landed—tossed a milk carton and hit me in the head. No big deal. I stare down all sorts of goons like that kid. But he hit me from behind. The surprise. It's always the surprise that sets you off. So, not five minutes later, I was in the bathroom in the handicapped stall, crouched against the wall wailing like I had just learned my mother died." Paula frowned. "Wait a minute. Mother dying could never have reduced me to that sobbing mess."

Sarcasm in the face of crazy. Worked every time.

Something grabbed at Jocelyn. Forget the sarcasm. Listen. Paula didn't care when her mother died? Another woman had the same reaction as she had? She shoved it away. This was about Paula. Besides, given what she knew about her grandmother, the whole world should have rejoiced when that bitch bit the dust.

Paula's litany continued. "One time I fell apart while I was at a friend's house. I'm not really sure what the trigger was; it could have been a smell, maybe a tone of voice. Claire could really get a snot on, use her tone as a battering ram . . . "

Jocelyn shuddered. The memory of Frank, Evie's last and worst, laughing, "I can get you any time I want" had left a bruise on her soul that often still ached.

"Anyway, Claire sat me down after that sob fest, took my hand and asked 'Whatever is the matter?' I hemmed and hawed. Who really wants to talk about the bogeyman? She insisted. What the hell, I thought. People should know what it's like for some of the children in their quiet safe little homes. I let loose with some of the slighter stuff—beating me with a hairbrush until I was bloody seemed simple enough—and my good friend Claire looked like she had just sucked alum.

"See, Jocelyn, people don't want to hear about victims. Perpetrators? Sure. Everyone loves *Criminal Minds. Silence of the Lambs?* Clarice is the hero, Hannibal Lecter an obsession. But who cares about the Senator's daughter down there in the pit? She has no power. She has known the monster. Damaged goods, that girl. And in our world, that girl in the pit, the one who was snatched on her way to something, an ordinary event, that piece of detritus can be us. So squeal at the bad guy, especially if he is caught. And cheer on the hero. But leave that girl in the pit because it's a very scary place, one that could be yours.

"A milk carton from out of nowhere is bad. A *friend* who wants you to crawl back into a hole? That's much worse. Better to keep it all compartmentalized. That way you only have to feel bits at any one time instead of the gestalt of the hell that's your life.

"The trouble is that tidiness doesn't always work. Sometimes it all collapses together, each piece atop one another—when you sense attack—and the world crumbles."

Paula felt the relief of releasing those words, the sense of being in the world that came after catharsis—once the shit that hit the fan had dried at least. She felt it, that is, until a realization hit her. Jocelyn was still, bleakly still except for her two index fingers strained against her lips. Nothing moved. Not her shoulders, not her head, not even the fingers as they locked against her mouth.

"Aunt Paula, that's some heavy shit."

"The heavy shit," Paula replied, "is what made you succumb to childhood helplessness in the first place. You told me not long ago, you feared being a loon. The question isn't about you. You are the recipient of trauma, betrayal, whatever you want to call what's heaped upon you. It's those in your world who think their words and actions are acceptable who are looney."

Jocelyn's head nodded. She felt a strange numbing in her arms as she listened to her aunt and squeezed her own hands into fists to bring back the feeling.

The aunt stood up and offered her hand to Jocelyn. "Come now. Let's refill our cups and finish off these treats." Paula had dismissed the wraith of the past, at least for now. Right now, all Jocelyn knew was the stories of now. Imagine the stories certainly waiting to be told. For this moment, though, they were two woman, one young, one not so young, stomachs giddy on their way to more treats while the Chicago weather laughed at its citizens.

Still, Jocelyn wondered, why that moment? Sure, a truck had backfired, but that sound was as ordinary as the Chicago wind. What had Paula seen, heard, that thrust her into the need to engage in such a ritual of trauma? Would Jocelyn hear more of the stories? The questions surely had answers, but the strength of those questions began to fade as another sense rose within her, one that centered between her deadened arms, a dank chilling, its gauzy essence black and tangled. Paula wasn't the only one with a story. Jocelyn had stories within her, wrapped in darkness. How many nights had she stared through the dark while the darkness within her slithered up from her gut and took over a brain that surely remembered something—didn't all the shrinks say all your memories are somewhere? It was smoke and yet form, smelling of nasty. It wrapped within her, even settled in her nose, behind her eyes.

Paula had sobbed because she remembered. Jocelyn understood that. That was one thing. Sometimes Jocelyn wanted to sob because she couldn't remember

CHAPTER 30

From the journal of Paula Ross

*B*ack seats were places of terror. Frozen terror, the kind of terror that iced me in place. Helpless. At those times, my sister and I shared a rare connection. Our father had done it again. Sometimes he missed a turn, ran a light. One time he plowed into a garbage can left on the curb. This time was worse. This time a cop saw him. "Keep your mouths shut, girls. Not a word. Not one damn word." *We knew the drill. Practice makes perfect.*

I really thought that now he would get caught . The cop had to know. How stupid could one police officer be? Why couldn't he see what was right in front of him? The thought turned my throat to cement.

"Any trouble here? Girls?" *How could he not have noticed? We were boards as we whispered our no's? The front of the car was up on the curb, for God's sake. Our mother was in the front seat, a grimacing robot.*

"We're just on our way back from the Oak Park Beach. Tired, but happy. Sorry about that, officer."

The man was on the way back, all right. On the back end of another bender. We got to swim. He got to mix his slushies with booze. Good thing for him vodka didn't smell. Bad thing for us.

Once the officer pulled away, he didn't even bother looking at us. Just laughed as he backed onto the road. Another cop, another lie, another drunken trip home. Fun day at the beach? You bet.

The next day Mother was her usual self. "Wasn't that fun yesterday?" *Just like always, she didn't wait for an answer. Just clipped in that goofy tone,* "Eat your cereal."

I hate cereal.

CHAPTER 31

The next day, Wednesday, Jocelyn sat at the bar. Morning classes were over, Luna's had a mid-afternoon lull, and she was in a galaxy far, far away, taking full advantage, tugging at the opal pendant on her necklace, racing it back and forth across the chain, deep in thought.

"Earth to Ms. Quint. Come in." Cole's mocking voice brought her out of wherever she had been.

Good old Cole. Cole, the dutiful bartender. Cole, the shrink-to-be, the friend, Paula's truest friend, the woman had said more than once. Was he Cole the confidante? He knew about the alters; had to. Hadn't he said, "That's *Charlie's*" when she asked about the skull painting? Nobody named *Charlie* had waltzed in to Luna's and set up consignment, yet Cole let her name roll off his tongue like sugar.

Jocelyn leaned forward and put her elbows onto the bar. She had the necklace wrapped around her index finger, the chain taut.

"You're either going to choke yourself or break the necklace. Why not tell me what's up before there's disaster?" Cole's words were light, but his voice had that smooth deep tone that said, *Let's talk.*

Jocelyn unwrapped her finger and let the opal dangle, kept her thumb and index finger holding her chin.

"You know my Aunt Paula."

Cole let out a chuckle, the same one he always gave when he waited for more information from a tentative Jocelyn. "Yeah."

"But, do you *know* my aunt?"

"Define *know.*"

Jocelyn sat up and folded her hands behind her head, elbows out and arms tight against to head. "Aaagh. You freakin'-A know what I mean by *know*. Don't play games."

Cole crossed straight over to Jocelyn, leaned over and put his hands under her chin. "I play plenty of games, but never with my friends, at least not the kind of games I think you're implying." He placed his hands on the bar on each side of her. "And I sure as hell don't think I want to play any now."

Cole had just sworn. He never swore. Said it tarnished his image.

Jocelyn sat back, this time with arms folded against her chest.

"You know, that body image of yours right now suggests need for protection. There a reason for that?"

"Do I need a reason?"

"Look, you started this conversation."

Jocelyn breathed in, relaxed her shoulders but still kept her arms folded. "You know about *Charlie*, that she did the painting that sold last week."

Cole pursed his lips and gave the slightest nod.

"Do you know about the others?"

"By others, you mean . . . "

Jocelyn cocked her head and stared Cole down. "You know exactly what I mean." She spit out the words. "Do you know *Jen* and *Joey*; do you know *Mother* and *Chelsey* and . . . "

"Yes." He said the word as fact, not admission. "Paula has talked to me about her alters. I also know she's talked to you. And I need to tell you, straight out, that I have Paula's permission to talk to you about them. Otherwise, we would not be having this conversation."

"That's fair. I can respect that."

"So now that all the preliminaries are taken care of, what shall we talk about?" Cole was back leaning against the wall counter, outlined in the best of booze. Jocelyn wished she could start in and sample them one by one. That would make this whole conversation much easier.

"I get the whole alters thing, the splitting. It's just such a weird way to cope."

"You say it like it's a choice, like picking out your socks for the day or your vegetables at the grocery store."

"I get that. Paula's a victim. She had no choice. The worst maniac couldn't have devised a more screwed-up family. Nothing about life with that bunch was her fault. She knows that. I know that. But she had this

153

crying jag that scared the hell out of me." Jocelyn looked to Cole to check his response. He nodded his head. The guy really did know Paula.

"All that pain. How does she stand it?"

Cole let out a sigh. "That was the toughest part in some way. She had to face the pain, look the pain in the eye. No one validated her when she was a child. She didn't even have a glimmer of what every child needs to develop a healthy sense of self. She had to learn to validate herself. That woman deserves a medal for that. But then came the toughest part."

"Are you nuts? What's tougher than that?"

"She had to choose to heal. She had to choose to move on."

Cole stayed silent while Jocelyn took in what he had said. She made sense of it by hearkening back to her sophomore year in high school. Until Jocelyn met the guidance counselor and teacher who had saved her, so long ago back in tenth grade, she never knew that validation existed. She was more than a simple Goth chick; she was a mass of anger. Cold, steeled anger. It had wrapped itself within her like barbed wire, cutting at her, making her bleed even as she spit at the world. Letting them in was a choice. A painful one.

Jocelyn didn't have the capacity right then to even frame a question. "Tell me." It was all she could say.

"I think it was her husband Joe who saved her. The man adored Paula and she adored him, adored him so much that she trusted him, even let him be her whipping boy when things went south."

Jocelyn thought about her aunt when she talked about her husband. She didn't talk about him often, but when she did, she glowed.

"And things went south often?"

"Not so much. But when they did, Paula told me, he would cradle her while she shook and love her back to the now. That was easy. He also took her beatings when she raged, let her pummel him. Sometimes, he had to get rough. She'd feel dead inside, couldn't feel anything, sort of like a drug overdose. That's when it was scary."

Aunt Paula liked it rough. Hmmm. And old Joe gave it to her. Jocelyn shook her head. "I'm having a little trouble picturing that."

Liar, liar, pants on fire.

The Jocelyn talking with Cole was picturing just fine, picturing Doug, the lover who made her the most alive in bed when he held her hands

154

above her head by the wrists and growled words pretty little girls weren't supposed to want to hear. That's the way she liked her men.

Cole interrupted the thought. "I don't see Joe as the kind of husband who enjoyed that kind of therapy. Paula told me that when she could feel again after that kind of ritual, she had to hold him. Gotta respect the guy." Cole turned away, grabbed a towel and wiped at a spot that didn't exist.

The red door to Luna's shot open. "Where's my girl?"

Doug. Jocelyn startled at the intrusion, and then felt the heat stir in her, the same heat she felt every time she saw him, that feral kind of glee that he instilled in her. His arrival at this moment, however, felt disjointed—the same drawing to him for sure, but now a snit of anger at the interruption of a private discussion that tried to grab her attention. She swatted it away. Her man was here. The same man who had been the focus of her attention these past two weeks.

Doug walked over to her and kissed her neck. "I've got something in the car for you. A present I couldn't help but snatch up. We'll go to my place and unwrap it."

Jocelyn wanted to jump off the bar stool and run out the door with him, but an empty bar was still a bar that expected customers and employees who respected their shifts. She wrapped her arms around his middle. "I have three more hours. You can stay here and wait, talk to Cole and me until things start stirring, or you can pick me up after my shift."

Doug shot a look at Cole who was shooting back some guy communication thing at Doug—pretty ominous from his scowl—and planted a kiss on her head. "I'll see you in three, baby." After he had walked out the door, Jocelyn looked at Cole. The scowl was still there.

Before she had time to retort, a six-some walked in and the job was on.

CHAPTER 32

Jocelyn sat on the leather sofa in Doug's apartment, sliding her fingers across the gold foil of the box. She loved presents, was a total sucker for them. Probably because she hardly ever had one as a kid. Her thumb rubbed against the velvet texture of the red bow.

"A little early for Christmas there, Buddy."

Yeah, like anyone had to have a reason. This was a present—with a red velvet bow. A present from a hunky man, her man, one she hadn't even asked for.

Doug stood behind Jocelyn, slightly bent over, his fingers playing with the back of her neck. He had a thing about necks. A thing that made Jocelyn a happy girl. Little spasms of pleasure danced within her, some from the present in her hands, some from those wondrous fingers of his.

"I can't wait until you open it." His words were a purr. The guy was lionine in so many ways, the way he walked—more stalk than gait—the depth of his voice, the tawniness of his skin and hair. Her senses always sharpened when he was near; and when he put his hands on her, she realized how women could get hard as well as men, only in different places. And he had chosen her. The thought wrapped around her like an aura.

The ribbon slid off, the foil was cast aside, and Jocelyn opened the box, unfolded the tissue that hid her gift. Inside lay four long pieces of red cloth, rolled up, cloth the same red as the ribbon, but silk instead of velvet, strips no more than three inches wide, but several feet long. She unwrapped them tenderly, letting her fingers again rub against the red of rich material as she stretched them out. She knew exactly what they were for, and she rejoiced in the thought. Sex, for Jocelyn, was all about letting go in her orgasm. The more she came, the harder her body convulsed in pleasure, the more tension from places she could not reach flowed outward and left her. When she lay spent, she luxuriated in the lethargy, the gift of the "little death."

Doug chuckled at her lack of inertia. Said it made him proud. He licked her when she lay there and praised her, running his tongue over her back and neck, promising more.

She had never indulged in any kind of play—she was normally a sex just for the sake of sex kind of girl—so the thought of being tied up while Doug worked on her made her wet.

"There's more, baby."

Jocelyn startled. "Oh," and then laughed and looked up at him standing over her from the back. She gave him a lazy smile. "I was having too much fun with the ties to keep going." She widened her eyes and her voice teased, "What oh what will we ever do with these ties? They're too long to put in my hair."

Doug reached over the back of his sofa, took one, loosened it, and ran it up along Jocelyn's upper torso and face. "Not to worry. I know exactly what I'm going to do. And I know you're going to love it."

Jocelyn set the remaining ties aside and went back to her present. Inside the next layer of tissue lay an emerald green bra and panty set. At least that's what she thought it was when she held up the pieces. Both the bra and panties were no more than wisps of material. This was not lingerie to wear on a date. At least not on a date outside the bedroom. The bra was cut out where her nipples would be, and the panties had no crotch.

Perfect.

Doug came around the sofa and looked down at Jocelyn. His eyes had deepened color, and the smile he gave her was such an invitation. She snuck a glance at his body. Oh yes, he was hard already. Game on.

Jocelyn wrapped the red silk around her wrists and held the bra in one hand and the panties in another. Doug bent as if to lift her up to carry her into the bedroom. She nodded her head *no*, stood, placed the clothing in his left hand and grabbed the other. She would lead this parade.

Neither had to say a word.

The lights had not been dimmed. Doug said he wanted to watch her, catch every nuance. No talking, he had said. He made her promise. Only moans and murmurs of pleasure allowed tonight, he insisted. He would talk to her, but she was not to say one word.

No problem, she had thought as he tied her up. What would they talk about? This was all about pleasure.

The silk around her wrists felt cool as did the silk of the sheets. When she moved, the silk of bra and panties lightly chaffed at her, an erotic chaffing. Doug had kissed her into oblivion, her lips, and stomach. She almost came when he nipped and sucked at her nipples, but he stopped when he sensed her peaking. Then he would start up again.

Naughty little girls could die of pleasure, oh yes they could. Lucky naughty little girls.

Right now he was rubbing her with this feather thing across her stomach and nipples—she would never see dusting the same way again. Her breasts heaved, begging for more pressure, some delicious pain. He tasted her this time on her stomach and began going down. Oh my, he was driving her crazy. She wanted to scream.

"Please . . . "

He drew away and looked at her." What am I to do with a saucy girl who does not know how to obey?" Before she could say anything, assuming she was dumb enough to open her mouth, he reached into a drawer and pulled out two clips.

"These are to punish you for disobeying. I can't put you in locks, but these will do." He snapped the locks onto her nipples.

The initial sting brought her body up, spine bent. Damn him! But then a slow sensation fought the pain. Her nipples hardened even more and a warmth grew in her breasts to match the warmth growing elsewhere. She lay back, supine and looked at Doug, her eyes inviting more.

He nodded in understanding. "Apology accepted, Baby. Now where was I?" He climbed back onto the bed and moved lower, his hands unclipping the devices and tossing them aside right before his head disappeared between her legs. That was the only time she wished for free hands. She was so hot, she begged for those clips again.

She didn't need them. When she came, Jocelyn hoped that a scream would not count as a word. If so, she was a babbling idiot. Each scream, each thrash of her head, her body against the bed, sent Doug deeper and rougher with his mouth, his magic tongue. She could hear that sound of his, only now it was more of a growl. When she was done, he slammed into her and came, and then collapsed on her.

Doug sat up, leaning against the headboard, legs spread out to accommodate the warm form lying against him in his bed. The red ties were still wrapped around Jocelyn's wrists, ends streaming across her thighs onto Doug's legs. Her back was pressed into his chest. She moved her upper torso in little circles, intent on feeling his skin on her even more deeply. With each movement, the lace of the bits of green she still wore was a tactile reminder of their explosive sex. She felt a stirring skin and loin.

Doug tightened his grip on her. "So, you little nymph, you want more?" There was that growl of his underlying the question.

She closed her eyes. "I have to admit, parts of me could dance all night, as the saying goes, but school calls." She lay there seconds more while he finished some lovely nibbling on her neck, and then moved away and off of the bed, and collected her clothes.

Minutes later, she was at the door, dressed for travel back to her apartment, presents neatly tucked back in their boxes.

She looked up at Doug who leaned against the door frame. "If I had to take a final in what we just did, I could study for hours."

Doug gave her a kiss, no more than a peck on the top of her head, and ushered her into the hallway. "Not to worry, child, we have much time for more tutorial. Study hard, put on those green togs when you need a break, and luxuriate in what is to come."

In the elevator, Jocelyn wondered what he meant by tutorial. He certainly had taught her tonight. She tightened her legs together just thinking of the more to come?

CHAPTER 33

The next morning, Jocelyn met Alex in the campus Starbuck's. They had an hour to go over review material for the semester exam before class, and a couple of latte macchiatos to spur them on.

Alex was in a bit of a grumble.

"You look pretty beat. Late night with Mr. Hot Stuff?"

"How do you know I wasn't working?"

Alex bent over and reached toward a large sack he had brought in. "Because I stopped by Luna's looking for you. Psych Guy told me you had a date." He stood up, slapped a Barnes & Noble bag on the table with a solid thunk. "I wanted to give you this." He patted the present. "It's supposed to relieve stress."

Jocelyn opened the sack. Inside were three blank sketchbooks, a set of micro-point pens, and the most super of all super-sized cartons of colored pencils.

"I figured you could do that doodle-scribble stuff you like." He had lost his grumble and was back to good friend.

Jocelyn looked up at his face. He looked like a little kid—nothing new there—all pleased as punch with a present he had picked out himself.

"Zentangle." Her word came out as an offer of surprise much more than a statement.

"What?"

"The patterns. They're called zentangle."

"Yeah, that weird word."

Alex had a lacing of satisfaction in his voice. He loved to show off new knowledge, even if no one cared. It was kind of cute.

"I remember; that's what you were doing the day we met, right here," he said.

"I walked in—jeez, it was so hot that day—and there you were in the corner drawing out little lines in the air with your pen."

"Zentangle patterns. I like to make them up in my head and practice."

"You were pretty cute, kind of like a little kid making up the universe. Hot artist."

"Stumme." Jocelyn punched him in the arm. "You horn dog. You were already scoping the campus in August."

"Nah. I just wanted to get out of that heat. I thought my balls would melt." He wore his dork look but it spread into something more. "You were drawing zombies. Walkers! Then remember what you told me?"

Jocelyn shook her head.

"You said *Walking Dead* was the only true reality show on the air."

Jocelyn gave out a snicker. "Oh yeah, I remember. I must have been on a snort that day."

"Nah. I figured you were a girl I could learn to love." He ruffled her hair. She flipped his hand away. She hated having her hair played with and he knew it. "I thought you'd like to take a break and doodle—zentangle—when things get tough. You don't even have to come up with anything big. Just color away. Unless, of course, you want to draw. I mean, you can add some lines if you want."

The poor guy was tripping over himself with excitement. The thought made Jocelyn glow.

Alex grabbed at the sack and lifted it. "There's colored pencils, too, forty-eight of them. Cool colors. I checked."

Watching Alex at the table, his face lit with the pure pleasure of giving an unexpected gift, Jocelyn felt a sense of sweetness tug at her. Her Alex. Kick-ass student, zombie fiend, now child of innocence. The feeling seeped through her—such an unusual emotion in her life—and she thought of opening the box last night at Doug's apartment.

Imagine, two presents in two days from two different men, both unexpected, both . . . they couldn't be more different. And Jocelyn wasn't sure which one she favored more. Aunt Paula, you think you have multiples. Move over for your niece. She chuckled inside. At least I know who I am when I'm getting mine.

But, a voice inside her said, which present is more who you are?

For the life of her, she didn't know. And the fact she didn't know nagged at her.

Jocelyn took out two of the pads and the top box of pencils. She handed one to Alex and kept one for herself.

"Before we dig into study crap, let's draw." She gave Alex a playful slap on his shoulder. "You sure know how to make a girl happy. One, two, three, chug your drink and start swirling. Then you can doodle away."

"Zentangle." Alex said the word as if he had discovered it. Smart ass.

That night, Jocelyn couldn't sleep. Post-test anxiety, she told herself. Give in and let it ride. No need to get up early—she started with the thought, *early in the morning*—then realized the truth was, *in a few hours today*. So she gave in to insomnia and sat at her kitchen table, pencil in hand, scribbling on a legal pad.

Two words, over and over. *Doug* and *Alex*.

So much for post-test anxiety.

The letters for Doug's name were dark. One of the top *D*'s had a bra hanging from it, a lacy thing with strategic cutouts. From the *g* of another, this one toward the bottom, she'd hung the matching panties. She'd scrawled circles around his name, series of loops that ran around it, one of the circles ending in a question mark, another in a line of *m*'s. She breathed in deeply as she worked on this name, a sense of warmth between her legs.

When she drew *Alex*, she smiled as she worked, but this doodling was simple fun, she and her buddy at play. This one relaxed her. Above one *Alex*, she drew a jaunty clown hat; several of his names had the *e* turned into an eye, that flashing eyebrow of his forming an accent mark above the letter. He always lifted his right eyebrow when he wore his smartass.

The page kept filling, now the *l*'s of *Alex* candy canes and bubbles, the bottom tip of one *x* extending into a hand that rested across the last two letters, the finger tapped onto the *l*. *Doug* and *Alex*, they ran and they looped and they flowed down and then up again, often crisscrossing, but neither name ever parallel.

The *Doug*'s, she noticed were so stiff and dark, primal, scary.

Her mind nudged at her. *Can you say subliminal?*

"Shut up," she said out loud." He makes me happy."

They both make you happy. You're only defensive about one.

CHAPTER 34

No school until January. Tests were done, grades in. Paula had ordered Jocelyn to take a few days off to pamper herself.

And that was what she was doing. Pampering herself in Doug's bed. With Doug. She was lying on her stomach, naked, taking in the strength of Doug's hands as he massaged her neck and shoulders. As his hands pummeled at her, he teased, "Those must have been hellish tests. You just had one gong-worthy orgasm and your muscles are still tight." His thumb pressed right below her neck bone and held the pressure, then stopped again and again. Bliss. He lifted her hair with the other hand and nibbled away on her neck, that magnificent thumb working its magic—not to mention the nip of his teeth and the sweet flick of his tongue on her neck.

All Jocelyn could manage was a low growl during her exhale. She lay there taking in the softness of his sheets on her belly and breasts, on the side of her face.

A sudden slap on her behind brought her to attention. She shot up to her knees and glared at Doug, accusation in her eyes.

"That was just a love pat, sweet girl." Doug kissed the top of her head as if she were a pouty child, turned and swung his legs over the edge of the bed, grabbed her hand from behind and pulled. "C'mon. I have something to show you." He smiled. Jocelyn knew that face. That was Doug's naughty face. Goody. He must have something up his sleeve. Oh wait. He's naked. Just like me.

Wonder what it is.

He held a robe out to her. He had slipped his on already.

"I'll grab the wine and glasses. Meet me in the living room. Movie time."

"Movie time? Now?" Doug's movies were for warm-up's, not cool-down's.

"Just wait for me on the couch. You'll love this, Baby."

She hated it when he called her *Baby*. She shuffled obediently to the sofa.

What the . . . She couldn't complete the thought even though the next logical word in the sequence poured from her mouth on a daily basis. How can you say it when it's right there in front of you? She had been sitting back waiting for whatever movie Doug had decided on, but when it started, she bolted up and turned to stone.

There on the screen, in her—for all practical purposes—naked glory, was her face, herself in her green lace writhing in Doug's bed while he played with his feather teaser and she twisted her nipples.

Where did that come from?

Stupid question. She knew damn well where it came from—a camera Doug had installed in the ceiling—a secret camera with a damn good zoom-in lens judging by what she was witnessing. She watched the screen as her face contorted with pleasure; she listened as her mouth emitted moans interspersed with growls.

That puswad. Actors fucking was one thing. Filming her—when she had no idea, when the lust was pure, intimate—that was betrayal.

Jocelyn gripped her wine glass. It was the only move she could make.

Doug was leaning toward her. "What do you think?" That voice that so turned her on was now the hiss of a snake.

"I think . . ." Those were the only words that could make their way out.

"Baby, you are a natural."

Baby. There was that word again. Jocelyn felt a rock in her belly. Good thing. Maybe she wouldn't puke. Her fingers begged her to throw the wine into his face. She bade them to calm while she reached over and set down the glass, calmly turned to face this monster that had taped their private pleasure.

She managed a smile, the whole while wishing for a head full of snakes for hair so she could turn this asswipe to stone.

Doug's hands were on her shoulders. She felt them burn but kept control.

"I think, Doug . . . that you are one demented son-of-a-bitch who should have his dick shrivel and die for what you just did."

164

Doug took his hands away and ran them through his hair. He was laughing.

"Jocelyn, this is for our viewing. Trust me." He was moving in on her, inching forward, one hand extended to go . . . where? Jocelyn batted it away.

"Keep your hands to yourself, movie boy." Tears were stinging behind her eyes. She wanted to cut out her eyeballs. She would not cry. Her throat tightened and that rock in her belly grew.

"Nobody will see it. I promise." He stopped, dipped his head ever so slightly. "That is, unless you want them to." Smarmy.

Jocelyn's mind raced back to their downtown Christmas season tour night, the last part when they ran into that weird couple. The girl had looked her over, said she was photogenic. Doug had reassured her, said she lacked a filter. Filter was not the problem. That broad was wacko.

And so was the guy Jocelyn had been sleeping with, the Great Betrayer himself.

She had opened up to Doug that night. Told him about that stupid flocked Christmas tree, how it had been her last happy Christmas memory before a drunk took it away with all of her hope for Christmas. Doug had pulled her into him and kissed her head, all Mr. Empathy. Oh for that dumb tree now. She could pick it up and whack the bastard with it. Flock you, buster.

It might have been the tree. Simple thing. A symbol of what she never had. She had let those walls down and he had ground that trust beneath his feet.

With all the calmness she could muster, Jocelyn stood up, ripped off the robe and hurled it at him. It caught the wine glass, sent it flying, flinging Malbec all over Doug's area rug before it landed on the rug and rolled onto the wood floor.

Of course he reached out for the glass instead of facing her. Doug prized his possessions. And by all that was holy, she wasn't one of them. The robe landed on his upper torso and head. Good.

He cares more for that stupid rug than he does for me. Her cool resolve melted in the realization. A white fury replaced it. Buck naked, she stomped over to the DVD, pushed *open* and grabbed the disc. With a wrathful glee, she broke the disc in half before she tuned to him. "Damn straight no one will see it!"

Doug stood there, arms crossed, watching. He wore a smirk that said it all. *Have your tantrum, child. Then we can return to life as I want it.*

That hubris-ridden clot of crap. Jocelyn twisted around. She picked up the DVD, yanking the cord out of the wall, and then banged it down on the metal corner of a bookcase. The player was sturdier than the disc. The crash only dented it. She threw the player to the floor. Doug raised the corner of his mouth. Bet he'd do more than that if his floor was wood instead of concrete. She grabbed a cement bookend off the recipient of the DVD player and aimed it at the TV.

"That's enough."

Oh, Dougie, you can buy a new player, but that television is your baby. And here, I thought I was. The violence had cooled her anger to sarcasm. That didn't mean she wasn't pissed as hell.

Jocelyn righted her posture, carefully replaced the bookend, and looked at the man she had thought her savior.

"Damn straight, that's enough." Then she walked to the bedroom to get dressed. She didn't' allow so much as a wiggle of her bottom. If Doug wanted jiggle, he could put in a movie.

Oh wait, she laughed to herself. He doesn't have a DVD player.

By the time she was dressed and ready to flee, Doug had moved. He loomed in the doorway, arms raised, hands on the upper jamb, buck naked.

For about one second—she would never admit to more—she took in his form and felt that same warmth between her legs. This time, however, as it rose, that rock in her belly held tight against it. She looked at him, so still in the doorway, so freaking smug. She could play his game and stare him down.

When he spoke, his tone matched the arrogance of his stance. "You want me and I want you. We're adults. Adults get to do adult things. That means fucking our brains out if we want to, and watching images of said fucking when we take a break. Grow up Jocelyn. I'm not Mr. Nice Guy. I'm the guy you like to fuck. Often. And well."

Jocelyn lifted one side of her mouth in irony. "You've got one thing right, Dougie. You are a fucker."

When she reached the doorway, she moved him aside like an annoyance, walked through the loft and out the door.

The bastard never said a word.

"I should have fucked her senseless. I *did* fuck her senseless." The rejected man stood in front of the door to his apartment and beat against it with his right fist and a whole slew of words. His hand hurt. It always did when he took out his anger on the door. The sucker would swell and he'd want to beat the door again for that.

Jocelyn had walked out on him. On him! Left him with a hard-on. He had wooed that cunt, poured the love on the bitch, did things to her that she'd never dreamed of. Made her moan that feral shout of pleasure. Her whole body had moaned for him.

And she had fucking walked out. When she arrived for their date, from his fourteenth floor window he'd watched her walking toward the building, enter it. His dick had been hard by the time she'd turned toward the entryway. He'd heard the ding of the elevator—the tone was so freakin' loud in this place—and smiled at what the night would hold. The victory was in his hand.

That is if she hadn't stormed out.

He stomped off to the computer, grabbed a flash drive from the stand's drawer and shoved it in. Like I wouldn't have backup, little Honey Pot. There she was, her head back sinking into the pillow, throat tight, that white skin of hers. When she came—and came again and again, she made this noise like a feral animal claiming its territory and rejoicing. His hand moved up and down his dick as much in anger as lust.

She'd loved it. Wanted it—over and over.

And now she'd walked out on him? On him! Over this movie, the one that could have won the whole pot. His group had been on his ass. "Bring us some shots, dude. If she's that hot, share the love."

He'd share the love all right. He'd have her on her back in no time. She loved it.

Nobody walked out on him.

She'd know that soon enough.

When Jocelyn reached her apartment, she shambled up the stairs, body parts fundamentally rag doll flopping—they couldn't seem to remember how to work as a team—even as somehow she managed to unlock the door and walk in. She backed against the door, gave it a full push from her left side—as much of a push as that raggedy body would allow. But the bolt on the door? That she jammed into place, and when she bolted the lock, she leaned in and let her index finger rub the bolt back and forth in thanks. By the time she reached the bathroom, she was naked—purse, coat, clothes discarded along the way.

Damn, she was cold. When had she turned the heat down?

She stepped into the shower, pulled back the shower curtain, leaving it open in the back, just in case—of what she wasn't sure. She studied the cheap plastic of the wall of the shower, the shower head, and the knobs for hot and cold before she stepped in.

How do you turn it on? Oh my, she took a shower every day, and for the life of her, she had no idea how to make the shower run.

She raised her arms and leaned in against the shower wall, forearms supporting a body that had recovered enough to hold her upright, and then she ground her heels into the floor drain, felt the scrape of metal against the bottom of her feet.

Finally she managed to yank the water lever. The first blasts were cold, but she stood there taking their iciness until the water warmed. She stood there in that shower, letting the warm water course over her until again, it returned to cold. She never so much as flinched. An hour wasn't enough time to make her feel clean. She needed more like two days.

This was December, the surge of the Christmas season, peace on Earth and goodwill enough to rot her teeth.

She was 21 and a porn star. Wrap that up and stick it under the tree.

CHAPTER 35

The next morning was a Wednesday—no work until Saturday night. The gray of December hung outside, an unwanted visitor this close to Christmas. Chicago, as usual, shrugged at the unwanted sky and continued on. Jocelyn had slept in. If she could call it sleep. She spent the last moments before waking in that surreal place where consciousness picks up on dreams and lets them linger as the mind lopes into awareness. There in that dream setting, Evie sat at their old kitchen table, a half-empty vodka bottle on the table next to her, a fresh cigarette in her mouth. She wore a green lace dress and a red satin ribbon tied loosely around her throat. It wouldn't take Cole to explain the significance of that get up. Jocelyn's mother had one leg crossed over the other and was leaning forward as if looking into a camera. She inhaled one great draw, took the cigarette from her mouth and waved it in front of her like an accusatory finger.

"Well Lady Jane, not so high and mighty now, are we? Remember when you turned your nose up at me, ran to those teachers like they cared? Where are they now? Look around you. No one here but your momma.

"Baby, you're just like me. Might as well face it. The men. You need them. Need their bodies and their soft words. Doug, what a sweet piece. He was all for pleasing you, smiling and whispering, and knowing where to touch. And know what? You walked away." She waved that cigarette hand again. Evie was always one for emphasis. "No loss. There's always another Doug. They line up for ones like you and me. The point is to enjoy them before they leave."

Dream mother's face turned, her eyes, even in death, darkened with despair, the bags beneath them more sagging and pronounced. "Yes, Baby, they leave. You love them. You make them happy. Then they turn and leave."

Evie leaned forward, cigarette again a wand of accusation. "Get used to it, daughter. It's the way of life for us."

Then dream mother leaned back and laughed until the laughter turned to a croaking sound and she bent over, coughing, her cigarette ash spilling onto the floor.

Tick tock.

Jocelyn sat up in her bed and checked her surroundings. Dream Evie had vanished. Jocelyn was in her own apartment, alone, butt-naked in her bed. The purple pig lamp was on the nightstand next to her, poster Darryl Dixon, kick-ass zombie killer, complete with crossbow still up on her wall reminding her to be tough in the Apocalypse. She reached up with both hands to feel her hair. It was a mass of tangles. She had gone to bed last night after that shower, hair sopping wet, not even combed out, laid in her bed for who knew how long, shaking, her wet head soaking the pillow, her upper limbs trying to solidify her sense of self, hands rubbing against the cold flesh.

She heard her ring tone. Where was her phone? She slid out of bed and followed the sound. There it was, in her jacket pocket on the floor in the hallway where her clothes lay strewn.

Doug.

A normal woman would have blocked it. But not her. She did manage to let her finger hover in defiance, but she could not claim her power. Nope. She stood there and took it, croaked a "Hello?" on the seventh ring.

"Baby, we have to talk." She gripped the sides of the phone, wanted to heave the thing against the wall.

"There is nothing to talk about. Ever." She hit the off button. End of call, buster. Permanently. After she dropped the phone onto the pile of clothes, she walked back to the bedroom, dressed herself in sweats she had lying near the door. Might as well dress in dirty clothes. Dirty clothes for a dirty girl. She headed for the kitchen. Coffee would help, wouldn't it?

Sure, if you lace it with rat poison.

She was right about the coffee, hopefully not so right about the poison. She just needed a good self-thrashing. Time for inventory.

On the bad side, she had let herself be duped by a perv—on the good side, he was gorgeous. Score one for her; she had good taste in perverts.

She had made a movie, not made it so much as engaged in the process, but at least she hadn't willingly participated. Nope, she had been too freakin' stupid to even know what said pervert was doing. So bottom line there, she was too stupid to live.

But hey, that wasn't her whole life. If she based her judgment on observation of the last few years, she hadn't done all that bad. Yes, she hadn't cried over her dead mother; but given that particular dead mother, that wasn't so bad. She had made it on her own through high school, turned in her dog collar and black lipstick for study habits and earned a scholarship . She was an honor roll college student. She had a job, nepotism not withstanding, was hard-working and always on time, even worked overtime.

Duh. Of course you work overtime. It's the least you can do for the aunt who spoils you rotten.

Fine. She had a good sense of humor for those in step enough to appreciate it. Maybe she had a penchant for the bizarre, but Alex needed someone to love him and Cole needed a challenge. And her aunt—why Paula had the daughter she always wanted—assuming none of her alters were a daughter. Hell, she was practically a social worker.

If she wanted it, she had a possible future in cinema.

Holy velvet whips and chains.

Maybe she should get the rat poison.

Paula sounded surprised to hear from her. "Why aren't you lounging around watching television and eating crappy food?"

"Because, Auntie, I would rather lounge on a barstool at Luna's. Got time for lunch?"

"Of course, I do, Love. I'm the boss. Can you wait until 1:30? It's pretty busy right now, but the place should clear out by then."

"Great. See you then. Love you."

"Love you, too." Jocelyn heard the unasked question in her aunt's tone. Damn, that woman had radar. She looked upward and gave a call-out to Madam Karma. "Please, no questions." Madam Karma had nothing to say. Jocelyn was on her own.

The lunch, of course, was lovely. Paula went on about today's rush, asked a few questions about the slew of Jocelyn's tests, all the polite chit-chat that a doting aunt might muster. Jocelyn played with the chocolate croutons in her salad—heavenly invention, chocolate croutons—just what the doctor ordered when you were having a crisis. She was spearing at the last two at the bottom of her bowl when Paula put her hand on Jocelyn's left one and gave her *the look*, the one that teachers and caretakers have when they recognize the façade.

"What's wrong?" she asked. Nothing dramatic, just an invitation, perhaps a bit on the plaintive side but most certainly given in love.

"Wrong?" Jocelyn held her fork in the air. "What could be wrong, except that I'm down to my last two pieces. Yummy stuff." She speared a crouton, brought it to her mouth and popped it in. The act bought her a few seconds of respite.

Might as well try to fake out a lie detector. Jocelyn gave a sigh and took a sip of water. "You know, the after-tests adrenaline slump." She shrugged her shoulders for effect. "Oh, and Doug and I aren't seeing each other any more. Kind of a bummer right before Christmas." Kind of a bummer all right. Her stomach clenched. *Do not, I repeat, do not spill the beans to your aunt.*

"You seem pretty cavalier about this. I thought Doug rocked your clock." Paula had the head tilt down just right, a thin icing of disdain in her voice while she waited for an answer. No big surprise there. Doug was not her aunt's favorite guy even if she respected Jocelyn's decisions. Paula probably wanted to bend over and hug her in joyous celebration of the breakup, at least check in on Jocelyn's state of mind. No smart-ass put off here from Jocelyn. Paula wouldn't let this slide.

Right now Jocelyn hated Doug, hated the beast who had wooed and betrayed her. Words could not begin to describe the torment that still knotted itself in her gut and her chest. She should have put up her walls and given some glib comment. She tried to summon the defense mechanism, but those walls refused to even form, much less rise. Walls knew better. They didn't work any more with Paula. The two women had too much truth between them to bring them down. To do so was betrayal.

But no way in hell was she about to unleash what had happened. Paula doted on her niece. They were each other's sidekicks, just as much as

Jocelyn and Alex. Oh my, Alex. If he found out, he'd do something stupid. She could picture Alex and Paula storming off to Doug's place, calling him out. What would they do? Beat him up. Duel at twenty paces with Alex's rubber sword?

Jocelyn was sick, sick with guilt, sick with overcoming the urge to call out the bastard herself. The urge to cry gripped her throat, choked her, as much for the truth as for the pain. *You're such a weakling,* she chided. You know part of you still wants him, you fool. Where do you think that guilt is coming from?

She let the fork slide from her fingers, dropped her head into her hands, and shook. The tears came, shaming tears, a freakin' torrent of them. She shook even more. There were still customers in Luna's. What a fool she was, breaking down and embarrassing her aunt.

She felt warm hands on her shoulders, a soothing touch, and the warmth of her aunt's voice. "There, there. Go ahead and cry. I'm going to take you upstairs and fix you some peppermint tea. Then you're going to lie down, and if you want to talk about it, and only if, we'll have a talk. But first, tea."

Jocelyn tried to stop crying, but gave up and let the water works have its way, confident that fighting would make things worse. She was a loser, a dumb broad crying over some stupid man who had wanted to use her. The shame that washed over her was acidic. How many times had she been the one extending soothing arms to a crying woman too dumb to know she'd been used? Paula knew her for the loser she was, just like Jocelyn had known about her mother. That's why Jocelyn never cried.

Right. Never cried? She was sopping her shirt with tears and snot, panting—Jocelyn, the tough one, the one who tossed around scorn like feathers at a pillow fight.

She slept at Paula's apartment through supper, woke up to darkness. She used her arm to wipe across her face beneath her nose. Residual snot had caked there as a reminder of her meltdown, her very own personal scar. She reached across to the nightstand for a tissue, blew her nose and wiped. There. If only the rest of her agony could be vanquished so easily. She looked at the clock. 10:07. Much of Chicago was readying for bed. She had to pull herself out of one and head home.

The apartment was silent. Jocelyn put on her shoes laid out in perfect parallel. Ah. Something was organized. She stumbled into the kitchen, turned on the light. A note was on the counter.

Sweetie. Supper's in the frig. Just heat it up. I'll be up later after we close. I'm here for you if you need to talk. And even if you don't.

Love you.

Paula.

Talk. That was definitely not on the agenda. Jocelyn found her coat and purse, left the apartment and headed downstairs. She knew Paula and Cole saw her at least walking out the door.

Thank you, good friends for letting me go. She knew their love went with her. It had better. She needed that to survive.

After an endless drive home, alone inside her apartment, her phone rang again. Doug. She wanted to refuse the call, but by the time her brain acknowledged a decision, her mouth was saying "Hello."

"I just want another chance. Give me a chance to make it right." No "*we*" there. No, an "*I*". *Maybe he gets it. Maybe he's sorry.*

Maybe you need a shrink—possibly a padded cell. How stupid do you need to be?

"Give me a couple of days. I'll call you." Anger kicked in again as soon as she ended the call. *Give me a couple of centuries, sucker. You can die waiting for that phone call; be nothing more than a husk with a phone stuck in a boney hand.*

She yawned. The day had been rampage of emotion. She needed to sleep.

That night there were no dreams.

The next morning, she opened the door to go downstairs to check on her mail from the past two days. A manila envelope lay on the mat outside her apartment door, a straggly thing that once had said *Welcome* but now was so threadbare, only the final "e" showed. Jocelyn bent over to grasp the envelope and pulled it up to her, felt the lack of heft. No writing on the front. Hmmm.

When she was settled at the kitchen table, she opened up the envelope. Two long red ribbons and a note tumbled out. Her stomach gave a lurch. No one had to tell her who sent this. She opened the note.

Miss you. The handwriting was strong. Masculine. She folded the note, stood up and walked to the trash basket, tossed it in. Probably should recycle it, she thought. But then, it might taint whatever throw-aways the note would share in the bin.

She walked into the living room and pulled open the drape facing the street. Yep. There it was. A black Range Rover.

You arrogant prick. You think I'm going to run out and invite you in, throw myself at you. She let go of the drape like it had cooties, and then sat on the couch, legs drawn up, arms around her, and rocked. She wanted to talk to someone; call Alex, call Paula. Hell, get Cole out here to shrink her. It took her breath away, the way this guy had wooed her, knocked her senseless with joy, and then turned on her.

Deep within her, parts of her began to have conflicting awareness, step up from swirling anger and self-loathing. She was tired, yes, even grieving what might have been. But a kind of settling bore a new sense of calmness, one of body more than mind. No siren calling to grab the scissors and cut. She thought back to all the times she had sliced into her skin. Nights when she waited for Evie to come upstairs. Afternoons after another hopeless day at school. They had begged for the disembodied rush, the whoosh of the pressure leveling as blood flowed out with the pain and self-hate.

Nothing sang to her, begged her. That was victory.

But the sister of the siren that had stayed quiet whispered as well alongside that victory. *Why couldn't he have loved me? What was wrong with me that he couldn't love me?*

Was there a chance that he would love her after all?

The sound in her mind, hidden from her consciousness tolled for her. Tick Tock.

CHAPTER 36

From the journal of Paula Ross

I knew it. Knew that man was no good. I crept into my bedroom at 6:00, right before supper. Jocelyn was still there, asleep. She looked so sweet lying there. You had to look for the pain, the sound of her whimpering—my, what had he done to her to make her whimper—the tear stains on her face, the way she cradled that pillow as if to let go was to be lost forever.

I sit here remembering what a counselor told me—how could I forget. Her words are stamped on my memory. For a woman, denied intimacy as a child, and then offered it from an abuser, even under the worst of circumstances, that abusive connection that has formed is so painful to break.

Doug and Jocelyn, they had intimacy. I could see it. I shuddered and thought of my sister. How could I have been so stupid? No wonder she clung to him. He wooed her. Made her believe in what she had never dreamed she'd know. How could she, given the male role models of her childhood?

I thought Alex was enough, that their bond could save her. Alex—one tiny pebble in a deluge of vile stone. Sweet Alex. Not enough chaos in the lad to satisfy her need for abuse; he has just to spark the excitement. Another slap I should give myself. How many nights had I searched for the bad boys, the ones that could titillate? How many bars lured me with their neon promise of gratifying a need that sprang from the pain of a child? It was all a bad girl deserved. Joe healed me and let me forget.

I cannot forget again. I dare not for Jocelyn's sake.

She will wake. And she will hurt.

We will be there for her.

Will it be enough?

It is Christmas, the season of birth and hope for an end to suffering. Please dear Lord, guide us to be a blessing to a lost, pained child. Let me put on the face I must—never questioning but ready to answer questions, never hovering but always aware, accepting boundaries until she is ready.

Let me be strong.

CHAPTER 37

The drive gutted her. If anyone asked Jocelyn why she was doing such a hair-brained thing, she wouldn't have been able to come up with an answer, at least not a rational one. Every mile—hell, every stoplight—she railed at herself. *What are you doing? Are you crazy? Forty-five minutes of your life to circle a place you have no intention of visiting?* The answer was pretty obvious. *Yes.* She never wanted to see him again. She had to know what he was doing. Schizophrenia was her friend.

So drive she did. Up Cicero Avenue, catch the Stevenson, I-90, get off at Lake Street, then straight on to the apartment. She was some teeny-bopper copping a sight at a celebrity's digs. Only this celebrity was no idol. He was Doug, ex-lover, cinema director, slime bod, a compulsion of her sick mind.

Why couldn't she just scrub her brain, get rid of all that had been Doug?

Instead, she drove.

She circled the apartment building—what if he was looking out his window—could he see her? What if he decided to leave and there she was, sleuth wannabe driving by for a reason she couldn't herself fathom?

It had started to snow during the last ten minutes, that kind of Norman Rockwell snow, big flat flakes that promised snow men and snow-ball fights. Jocelyn pulled over onto a side street, parked and sat back to watch the snow fall. So pure, that snow. Wafting down like it had nothing better to do than cover a city landscape and call to children. That's the trouble with snow. It starts out pure and beautiful, turns to slush, filthy and obnoxious.

She beat her palms against the steering wheel. She still wanted the bastard. After all that using her. *He was the first guy to get past my walls. He had validated her, made her feel whole, loved.*

How sick was that? How desperate and humiliating.

She sat up. *That will be enough of crazy. Drive your sorry ass home before the roads are clogged with traffic and snow.* As if to mock her, the snow stopped. *Thanks a lot. I had a perfectly good reason to get out of here—beat the snow—and now it's gone.*

You have a perfectly good reason to get out of here, snow or no snow. Get home before you do something stupid.

Jocelyn opted for reason, put the car into drive and pulled away. Much better things to do in her life than hang out in this neighborhood mooning over a man who didn't deserve so much as a sliver of thought.

On the way home, she did what she always did—stuffed down her feelings and unformed questions, put on her big-girl panties, the ones made of cement, and made plans.

Tonight, Jocelyn had an errand to run. Errand wasn't the right word, and she knew it, but she couldn't understand, much less handle the feelings raging within her. All she knew was that she had to face the man who had deceived her. No more phone calls, no more notes, no more Doug—that was the plan. The man had broken her trust, left it in pieces as she fled from him. Staring him in the face would never rebuild any relationship with the bastard, but it could rebuild her trust in herself.

Even as her resolve gathered, the fight within her battled, echoes of the same fight she had wrestled with her entire life when the rug had been pulled from under her. Only this time it was about a man, not a mother.

He treated me like a princess. I felt so special. It couldn't be all fake.

Your judgment is off. That puts you in danger. You can't be in danger. You've been there too many times. Why do you think you need walls?

If I can trust him, I won't be in danger.

Are you that stupid? It is totally illogical to trust him.

But there's nobody out there who's better.

Oh really. Can you say Evie? Face the deceiver. Get your power back.

She had sent off a text message—*on my way*—to a number she thought she would never use again. After tonight, that would be the truth. Wouldn't it?

179

The trip this morning had proved that. She couldn't hide from him. No. She had to face him, alone, calm, in full control, detach him from her life. That had been her slow realization as she drove home from her surveillance. She had to trust in herself. That was the trust she needed.

She was smart enough, and honest enough to know that this would be on the top of a long list of journeys of pain. In her well-worn apartment, she sat there on the edge of the couch, ran her hand along the red ribbon. The material, so soft to her touch, held fast against the shaking of her hand. She took in that softness as an omen. She sat there for a few moments longer, taking in her breathing, a long, deep rhythm. This would be a battle, no doubt about it, but battle she must, for her own sake.

Forty minutes later, Jocelyn breathed in as she stepped off the elevator to face her dragon. Second door on the left. Fourteenth floor. Lake Street. She had stood here enough times before, but now the hall seemed so much narrower. A knot twisted in her stomach. Sitting there in her apartment, the idea had been a quest, she a hero. So easy as a plan in formulation.

Right now her feet begged her to turn and run. Who the hell had died and named her a hero? Didn't heroes sometimes die?

Don't kid yourself, she thought. *Heroes have to do something heroic to even make the battle. There's no way you'll die, but you might want to, especially if you cave.*

She pushed one foot forward, then the other. The walls of the hallway whispered his words. "You're so sexy. You know you want it. Your body tells me you want it. The camera will love you." They were Doug's words, but the voice of the wall was her mother's.

In the back of her mind, she heard the haunting directive of so many of her dreams playing a cadence against the whispering of the walls. *Don't put your efforts into foolishness. He'll use you and you will love it. Just like me. You're Momma's daughter. Tick tock. Move along now. Time's a wasting.*

Shut up, Mother. I may fall into acting like a fool on occasion, but I don't wear being a fool like stigmata.

But that was the fear. She had to not only face the man; she had to face how the man had made her—still made in her in parts she didn't want to acknowledge—want to submit.

He had played her like the men in her mother's life, nuzzling against her neck, his breath warm when he tried to justify what he had done. "When you're not with me, I can watch you wanting me."

Who was he kidding? Watching her all right. Him and eight thousand other guys. Lights, camera, action. Let the whore begin.

She grabbed at her purse and pulled it against her. The truth was a punch in the gut. And yet, she still walked on.

What did she have? Twenty more steps? Thirty? She'd knock. He'd meet her at the door. Probably bare chested and ready to roll. Him and his equipment. All of it.

That small part of her feeling that urge, the warmth in her gut, between her legs—she swatted it away before it could sting and take hold. She had work to do, and that remnant of her mother had no place on this mission.

And yet she was there. She knocked on the door. Once. Twice. She could hear him; hear the steps against the wood floor.

Her head was a band of steel, tightening, tightening. Shapes and color and movement swirled inside. She eyed the steel of the door. Was its shine laughing at her? Could she hold fast? At least not run like a baby? More steps from the inside. A banging. His voice. "Fuck." Something had fallen. What? Who cared?

"You know you want it." His steps tapped out the message. The ultimate in trite.

He opened the door. One day she would look back at this moment and bless it, see it for the miracle it was. For now, she was outside her body watching herself reach into her purse to pull out a sheet of paper, slap it against his chest while he watched her in utter smugness. She was pure reaction, her screaming from what little sense of self she had at that moment even as her words held contempt.

"Here's your note. Contrary to what you want to think, I not only do not miss you; I am sorry I ever laid my eyes on your cheap lying ass. Do not contact me. We are done."

Before he could even react, she hauled her purse onto her shoulder, turned around, and walked away. No stomping. No muttering. Just a solid walk along a hallway to an elevator that would whisk her away from this shit.

Evie, my ass.

When she reached the elevator, she pushed the button *down* twice, how many times. It couldn't open fast enough. A voice bellowed behind her. His voice. "Jocelyn? What the fuck. Baby, get back here!"

The elevator doors opened. Jocelyn fell into the opening, pushed the button for ground floor. When the doors closed, she allowed herself to breathe. She lay against the wall, the bar against her back to keep her from collapsing. At the ground floor, she dashed outside into the winter night.

The air outside slapped at Jocelyn. It had begun to snow again; more big wet flakes added to the white layer, snowfall that this evening would make a filter against the street lights and the white lights of the decorated trees along the way. Jocelyn pulled up the collar of her coat and plunged forward. She had to escape. Only darkness was behind her, not the darkness of a snow storm, but that blackness that had tried to seduce her into whatever kind of surrender—fear, or worse. If she hurried, she would make it. She became a rock, a piece of total solid stone, bound for her car. After a couple of blocks, she stopped and took in huge gulps of air. She was by the park, the same one she had parked near the first time she had visited Doug. Then, it had hardly caught her attention. She unlocked her car and climbed in, locked it again. She reached for the keys and started her car, ready to flee. Instead, she kept the car in park and turned on the radio. The station was playing *Little Drummer Boy.*

Shall I play for You, pa rum pum pum pum, on my drum. Innocent little kid wanting to make the baby Jesus happy. Nothing sweeter.

What would Doug have played on her today?

She sat in her car, didn't even turn on the heat, wrapped herself in the cold and the music as the snow fell, covering the windshield, the side windows, the back. She was wrapped in a cocoon of snow, the pure white stuff of Christmas blessings here on a day of . . . she wasn't sure what it was; she was incapable of seeing its worth.

She gripped the steering wheel. Inside her purse, her phone rang. She let it ring, each sound painful, enticing. If she answered, she would hear his order. Would she turn her car around and go back? And if she went back, what then? He would break her, gouge into her cavity until she was nothing.

"Throw me away like a piece of tissue, my ass, Mom." She shook as she said the words as much a prayer as a commitment. She grabbed her coat closer and ran out from her car, loped through that blanket of snow that insisted on covering Chicago. There was a fountain in the park, turned off for the winter months, two benches on either side. She stomped toward the fountain, and just short of it, laid down in the snow, spread out her arms and legs, and like a young child, made a snow angel. Each thrust of her arms was a celebration. This was a baptism, one of white and purity. As the snow fell on her, she opened her mouth and let the fat flakes melt on her tongue. The snow, so fresh and pure, soaked into her, melted the bad. She was without original sin, the sin of her mother. She was without sin, sin of her own making. She rejoiced in the moment as the snow cleansed her.

CHAPTER 38

Friday night, the last Friday before Christmas and Luna's was hopping. Outside, the wind was howling off the lake—no surprise there—every time customers opened the door, a swirl of wind and snow came with them. No one seemed to mind. Another excuse for a welcome, or another round.

From the bar on back, the place was Norman Rockwell drunk on Christmas party festivity. Brandy Alexanders, eggnog, rum concoctions that sang with festive cheer—arms raised in toasts or wrapped around friends, even if said friends had only just met, that was Luna's for this night. At the back tables, appetizers, cookies, even Paula's special Norwegian krumkake lay in all their glory. The questionable art that put Luna's on the map had been taken down for the season. Nothing but Santa's and elves against the walls, at least until the 28th. Two guitar players wandered the room strumming the same Christmas carols. A few customers sang—the help had to—while others listened or spread their own cheer. If she could have bottled it, Paula could have brought world peace or at least a respite from the whatevers that ailed the world.

Jocelyn couldn't help herself. The stress of last night had died with the cleansing in the snow. Christmas spirit was an added bonus. Sporting a felt pair of Reindeer antlers wrapped in tinsel and a beautiful copper bracelet Sonia had given her—Lord love the woman—she joined in with guests and helped in the addictive excitement.

Funny that Sonia wasn't at the party. Jocelyn had asked her aunt about her, but Paula had dismissed the question with a strange "Sonia doesn't do Christmas."

Absence wasn't all bad. Doug, arrogant bastard, was a ghost not even worthy of turning up in chains as Jacob Marley. Let the party carry on.

Around 11:30, after the third round of Jingle Bells, the door whirled open once again, complete with wind and snow. Doug stomped in. A very grim-faced Doug whose eyes bored through the crowd on an obvious mission. Jocelyn had her back to him, taking orders from a foursome at one of the mid-room tables. Paula and Cole were slamming out drinks behind the bar, and Alex was downing beer and trying to sing at the same time. A new waitress, hired on for the season, approached Doug. "Merry Christmas." She nodded toward the bartenders. "We have all sorts of specials tonight . . . "

"Grey Goose on the rocks." No spirit in his tone. Jacob Marley may not have turned up, but Scrooge had certainly entered with his own sense of humbug. Doug returned to scanning the room and then jerked around and strode to the bar while the waitress put in Doug's order with one of the three bartenders. Further down the bar, Cole was in the middle of one of his flirting routines when he stopped mid-flirt and stared at the newest customer. "What can I get you?"

Doug leaned in. "You can get me Jocelyn, tough guy. Now."

Cole gave a dismissive grin. "You can get her yourself. You're good at that. I just stick to 'what are you drinking?'"

The waitress picked that unfortunate moment to hand Doug his drink. "Grey Goose on the rocks, sir. That'll be . . . "

Doug grabbed the drink, tossed a ten-dollar bill at her tray, turned and walked away.

She turned to Cole. "That guy's got a Christmas tree up his butt. What an attitude."

Cole watched Doug as the man snaked his way through the crowd. "Attitude? You have no idea. Wonder what he's up to."

Fists clenched in concern in spite of the smile he kept on his face for the customers, Cole watched the answer to his question unfold before him. Doug had found Jocelyn near the back table munching on a cookie while she talked to one of her customers, her head bobbing, the tinseled reindeer antlers lurching dangerously. He itched to leave the bar and head out as back-up, but a "Not now. Let her take care of it" hissed from behind him, kept him in line. Paula was right. This was Jocelyn's battle, even if it was in their territory and the villain in question still wore a rigid body language that threatened. Cole stayed silent but checked for Alex. He was still hanging with the singing group wassailing away. A vast network of potential danger spread its strands invisible to the crowd, each strand pulsing in connectedness to the players in a dangerous game brewing within Luna's.

A drink order called his attention. He started grabbing bottles and glasses, but he kept one eye toward the back of the room. That sense of impending disaster still clear and building.

Doug made his move. He wedged himself between Jocelyn and the customer, sending the poor woman backward without so much as the meanest of apology. Cole could neither hear what Doug was saying nor read the guy's lips, but he knew it wasn't any message Jocelyn needed to hear. Jocelyn whipped around him and marched toward her customer who was busy mopping a spilled drink from the front of her Christmas sweater. Tacky sweater. Tackier assault.

"Now." Paula sent Cole a clear message with that one word. Doug dropped his bar towel and headed toward the end of the bar. Before he had time to make any headway toward the back, Jocelyn had soothed the splattered sweater lady, turned to Doug, poked him in the chest and sputtered, "What the hell do you think you're doing!" These words Cole could read, so fiercely Jocelyn's mouth had spit them out. *'Atta girl!* Cole stopped and watched. Jocelyn was holding her own just fine. Hopefully, the bar would do so as well.

Slowly the place quieted: guitar strumming, singing, and conversation had stopped, that is except for one couple near the front that kept laughing at some stupid joke. A guy standing in watch next to them nudged the joke teller with a "Shhh" and pointed toward the main event. Cole took that in, and then checked out Alex whose face and fists were as equally unbending as Cole's own.

Doug made his move. He grabbed Jocelyn by the left arm and yanked her forward. "Grab your coat. We're going." The man's face was flushed, totally at odds with the purpose of the evening. Cole braced his feet, ready for action. Out of the corner of his eye he watched Alex take a few steps slowly forward. Was he ready? Dumb question. Cole watched in wary anticipation as the scene continued to play out.

Perhaps Jocelyn understood all that was expanding. Perhaps she was too caught up in the explosion that was Doug to come up with any sensible reaction. She certainly didn't seem fearful—but then when had she ever? She looked like she wanted to throttle her abductor. Good sign. Jocelyn in throttle mode was a Jocelyn not to mess with, indeed.

By now, Doug had yanked Jocelyn near the entryway, not twenty feet from the bar. As the man she had just last night spurned—who would have thought she could ever loathe him more—increased the pressure on her arm, Jocelyn yanked her arm away and pushed at his chest with her right hand. Doug held his ground, but at least he stopped. The man was less a physical presence to Jocelyn than a menace that needed to be extinguished, except for his eyes; they sneered at her, dark slits in a grim face.

"Look, cunt." He reached out to grab her again. "I said, get your damn coat. Now."

Jocelyn felt the rage grow in her. She gathered the force in her arm and fisted her hand. Too late. All she could see was Doug's back. That and Alex's arm shoot forward, his fist connecting with Doug's jaw while he yelled, "You do not call my friend that name, you mindless piece of shit!" Holy cow! What was her Alex doing?

Doug caught himself as he started falling backwards toward the bar, resettled his body stance and pulled back to swing.

Alex stood ready to keep at it. He even smiled as he waited for a reaction. Too bad. Jocelyn grabbed a serving tray and smashed it over Doug's head. The tray careened to the side and Doug went stumbling to the floor, wound up on his knees, hands planted to keep from falling even more.

"My name is Jocelyn. Take that and make a movie of it."

Oh shit. Did I really just say that in front of everyone?

She didn't have time to worry about the answer. As she straightened, she looked up and scanned the bar. Some customers were agog, others snickering, most out right smiling. They were all looking at her. Sweater Lady started to clap. The applause was scattered at first, but spread quickly like gossip. Alex and Cole grabbed Doug by the armpits, hoisted him up and escorted him to the door. Several customers reached out to open the door, no doubt wanting to see what would transpire outside. Good thing the wind had died down. She was able to catch a few words of advice to the dickhead in the night air before the door shut on them. She smiled, confident; based on the little she heard, Doug wouldn't be coming around again.

One customer, the one standing beside Jocelyn, heard her say, "That's Ms. Cunt to you," and winked his approval. Luna's owner wove through the crowd and hugged her niece like she had just returned from the war.

What the heck, he thought. *Maybe the girl had.*

When Cole and Alex came back in, Cole had his hands in his pockets, Mr. Cool, while Alex shook his right fist up and down. Alex's grin, followed by a wince and another shaking, let Jocelyn know that, for him, the moment was a sweet mixture of pain and celebration. Jocelyn felt a mixture of pride and sisterly concern. The guy was a hero.

Cole, too, of course, but something about Cole exuded *take charge and kick butt where needed.* Alex was more the clown of Halloween, the green-haired victim of a meat cleaver—not the cape-wearing type at all.

What could she do with a friend like that? How could she not throw her arms around him and give him a wet kiss? Or at the very least let him wear her reindeer antlers? She looked around. Damage control had swept away any detritus from the melee. Guitar guys were back leading a group in *Up on the Housetop. Ho, ho, ho, who wouldn't go* all right. Jocelyn headed toward the two guys behind the bar and swept her arms around both of them and hugged tightly, reveling in the warmth, in the safe place that they bestowed to her. Dougie might show his sorry ass eventually, but as long as she had these two, and her aunt, she was safe.

She kissed each of them on the cheek, took off her felt antlers, and put them on Alex's head. He actually blushed—imagine that from her Alex. The room swam with conversation, singing, and laughter. Paula was at the back corner giving a surreptitious wave, her face iridescent with emotion. Cole turned to fill a drink order. That left the two buddies leaning into each other.

"Well, Ma'am. Me and my deputy run that desperado clear out of town. He won't come around pestering a lady like yourself no more." Bad grammar, and an even worse John Wayne voice, but the sentiment was the best Christmas present of her life.

How could anything go wrong with a friend like that?

CHAPTER 39

Saturday morning—such a flip from Friday night. No phone calls, no threatening cars outside her apartment. Even the weather was in a good mood—cold enough to crisp up a walk, but sunny enough to make said walk exhilarating.

That is, if you were into walking. Others had work to do.

Jocelyn sat in her kitchen, armed with fresh coffee and dressed in her *If Daryl Dies, We Riot* nightshirt. She had dragged it out of the laundry basket last night in honor of Alex; it seemed the least she could do. She was looking at the ribbons that Doug had sent her, long and red and sleek and lying in the middle of her table. She could throw them away, of course, but somehow a ceremony seemed in order. Burning them first crossed her mind, but that seemed so ordinary. What special ritual could best exorcise demon Doug from her life? What could honor the friends who had helped her?

A ray of sunlight cut through the top of her kitchen window. Sunlight was a miracle of sorts in this place. This ray cut down the middle of the ribbon, a spear of yellow that split each piece in two. She looked down at the pile, stood up and snatched scissors from a drawer. After running from Doug, she had felt relief about not cutting. Silver lining in an oh-so-sucky black cloud. Today was a new day. She'd cut all right. But not skin. She'd cut the ribbons. She'd slice these bitches to smithereens. She was seamstress Jocelyn remaking more than just a couple of red ribbons. Sometimes she'd cut thin strands. Other times, she'd take the edge and unravel. Before long she had a lovely pile. Why, she could use these to wrap Christmas presents for her aunt and the two guys in her life. Perhaps someday she'd even tell them where the decorations had come from. They would be so proud. The whole day while she gathered supplies to make Christmas presents and handled the more mundane chores of her life—the laundry, the cleaning, the scoffing whenever she thought of the giver of the ribbons, she'd pause in her kitchen in passing to celebrate last night, take in an energy from the pile of red that she controlled, whose future she would determine.

The next morning, the pile of red was still on the table. Christmas presents to make. What a great way to spend the day. She had fresh laundry put away, floors and porcelain sparkling, dust eliminated, even some Christmas lights hanging around the window she had found in a thrift store down the street along with an old wooden sled with—she could hardly believe she had succumbed—a ratty four-foot Christmas tree complete with ornaments on sale for $1.98. Now she could dig into the remainder of her tasks—home-made Christmas presents.

By late afternoon, the remnants of the ribbon lay piled on the sled, out of the way, since the kitchen table was a mass of art supplies—baked clay for Paula's art deco jewelry, a stack of Alex and Jocelyn zombie pictures to work into trading cards, and the best picture of Cole smoking a pipe ala' Freud, gel medium, window screen pieces, stamps, paints, pens, the leather cover of a DSM-5 psychiatric disorder book cover to frame Cole's picture superimposed onto one of Freud right down to identical pipes. The place was a mess all right—not her usual style, but messy with creativity—just the way she loved it.

The first time her phone rang, she was elbow deep in gel medium and paint, the second time she was varnishing the clay pieces to ready them for inking. Sorry folks. When she had time to check the voice message, the high of her projects took a hit.

Doug. Both times. He was sorry for last night. He missed her. They could work this out. Did this man not understand? How many times did he need to be humiliated before he gave up?

Look at you. No panic. No woe. Not a single emotion to stuff down. Way to go. She could make a present for good old Dougie, only if the ribbon were wire for a special yuletide garrote. But this was a thought, not an urge. She turned her phone off, put it down, flipped it the bird—only once, mind you—and went back to her fun. He had called her a "cunt." Big mistake "That's Ms. Cunt to you." The memory of the retort made her smile. And the guy was still calling. What a creep.

Then, another round of self-loathing started in, the thoughts gathering inside her head like an army of specters coming together in the haze of dawn, ready to ride rough-shod over the innocent. She leaned against the kitchen sink, head down. Yes, she had been the dumbest of the dumb. She still was, in that tiny place that grieved for what could have been. The man had seduced her so he could make porno films. What could be more pathetic? Any longing for the creep won the dumb award, hands down.

Almost as soon it had started, the slams at herself faded in light of a new celebration—the focus of all the nows to come—last night, she had heroes, friends who believed in her, stood up for her, loved her. At this moment, she began to understand the Jocelyn of last night, surrounded by chaos yet firm in protection and courage. She felt that in her arms as she shredded the ribbon, felt it for the first time, such a virgin to these feelings, to this unconditional love. Her high school teachers had helped her, loved her in their own way. But Paula, Cole, and Alex—that dork, that sweet, sweet, dork—had been more than mentors, more than allies. They were family. Family. What a new and strangely wonderful concept

Dashing through the snow . . . off-key Christmas songs filled the apartment as Jocelyn worked away, the busiest—and no doubt messiest—of elves.

By that evening, three Christmas presents lined up under Jocelyn's tree. The Magi couldn't have put more care into their own gifts, though Jocelyn's were precious for the love that had made them rather than some ancient market value. The wrappings were whimsical, white paper hand stamped, lacey tissue paper crushed and glued for texture. Two had lovely strands of red ribbon weaved through the tissue forms; the third had stiffened forms of red wisps looking like eyes with blood running down from them. A red tissue hat trimmed in white completed the image. Of course that one was for Alex. Nothing says Christmas like zombie Santa.

They were lovely, just sitting there like good little children waiting for a trip to a party.

Finally, before Jocelyn could hardly blink, it was Wednesday, December 23rd, the last night before much of the country started to gather near and far with family. Cole, Alex, Paula, and Jocelyn would meet for their special celebration before Cole took off for Dunkerton, Iowa, to meet with Heiples and Magees, and Alex took off to Lincoln for his clan gathering.

Christmas Eve and Christmas Day were reserved for family. What a concept. On those two days—foreign territory for a girl like Jocelyn who was an orphan long before she lost her mother—normal parents would grumble about packing up the car and facing traffic while their children readied themselves for "Are we there yet?" But it was all show. Cousins and Nanas and crazy uncles would hug and eat and tell stories; Christmas wrapping would pile up in whatever room the family tree might be; and eventually, through good will or good eggnog, families would love each other for at least one day.

On Christmas Eve and Christmas Day, Jocelyn and Paula would have the run of the Luna's building, which pretty much meant cozying up in Paula's apartment and pigging out on leftover Christmas goodies—provided Cole and Alex hadn't finished them off—and beginning seasonal traditions of their own.

Tonight, though, on the eve of Christmas Eve, the four would come together for their own private celebration. Paula, of course, had gone crazy with the decorations. Luminaries lined each side of the two stairways up to her apartment, their candle glow sending off what once might have terrified Jocelyn, but now warmed her as she climbed the stairs. Paula had already warned Jocelyn that the season meant decorating run amok. Christmas trees of all sizes were packed inside the apartment. The woman had firmly stated that the season demanded at least one Christmas tree per room.

Immediately inside, Jocelyn quickly learned that "at least" meant "as many as you could pack into a room." Two six-foot trees stood sentinel beside the fireplace, several short fat ones were clumped in threes wherever Paula could find room, and one huge eight-foot Douglas Fir stood in the corner holding reign over the living room. Paula's guest took in the beauty of the white lights of each of the trees, the glow of the candles and fire, and then she let out a yell as she looked at the Douglas Fir. "Bubble Lights! I love bubble lights!"

She almost dropped the red-ribboned presents as she tore toward the tree and stood there like a small child enraptured by Christmas magic.

As a matter of fact, she was that child. Never had she been in a home so beautifully trimmed. For a brief second, the flicker of watching lights with Doug flashed in her mind, but the bubbles—green and yellow and blue and red—snuffed out that flicker with ease. That moment claimed her as she knelt to place her presents under the tree, knees bent, hands out as she placed the presents gently upon the tree skirt. Her head was forward and up, taking in the lights, the sparkle of the ornaments, the ribbon twisted around, going up and up toward the angel at the top. Tears built within her, tears from her whole body, not just her eyes. Hands softly set on her shoulders, and a voice touched her ear. "Ever since I healed, I promised myself that Christmas would be a time of the exquisite to extinguish the ugly from my head. I pass this on to you, my dear."

Jocelyn felt the choking. Her throat and her chest took on the palpitations of a heart that was about to burst. She wiped at her face—no crying, not one tear; there had been too many of them shed lately—and reached around to Paula. "Thank you. Thank you. Thank you." It sounded like a gracious reply for the room. Both women knew it for so much more.

Paula kissed the side of her head and they both stood up. Paula said, "Take your coat and purse, and go back there with your suitcase before someone walks in and trips. Just set them in the spare bedroom. It's all set up for you."

As if on cue, the doorbell rang and two voices shouted out a deep, "Ho-ho-ho!" Both women laughed. Paula went to answer the door, and Jocelyn headed for the bedroom. When she came out, their male counterparts, Santa-hatted and arms full of presents and goodies were grinning like kids while Paula shouted from the kitchen, "Two rum and Cokes coming up. And Jocelyn, I have a new wine for you to try." The party was on.

This Christmas would be a blessing Jocelyn never could have believed she deserved, more of a fairy tale to those too gullible—or lucky—to live the reality of a season that promised but never delivered. During her childhood, Christmases loomed as a disaster: more cigarette smoke, more booze, more bodies crashing into walls as they stumbled through the hallway, each smell and sound obliterating any hope a child might have for celebration.

Images from the past zapped through her mind in a slide show too fast to even form a thought. Jocelyn hugged herself with the knowledge that the past was there—in the past. This Christmas let loose a small part of her that had held onto hope. The fiasco with Doug had certainly put a damper on the spirit Friday night, but at least he was gone, no doubt sliming his way to another hapless victim. Now she was with a family, blood related to only one, but family nonetheless. That and the bubble lights was enough by themselves to grant hope.

Of course, the four of them ate themselves into pure gluttony within an hour. Then the magic. Time for gifts. They all sat in a semi circle on the floor like little kids. Paula, Cole, and Alex hugged and swooned over each one of theirs—Cole had given Alex a Psych Guy Wannabe tee—Alex snapped it at Cole but then gave him a high-five. No one knew the significance of the red ribbon, but Paula noted the decorations as a triumph. Alex and Cole looked at her, dumbfounded. "A guy thing," Paula explained. When the three opened theirs from Jocelyn, the faces on the three sent a clear message that the handmade gifts were stellar.

Jocelyn was the last to open. Not a problem, she said to herself even as her fingers itched to start ripping. When Jocelyn opened Alex's present first, out spilled throw pillows and a beautiful sofa throw. Awesome. Cover up the ugly with a little beautiful. She hugged Alex, tears wetting her eyes while she rocked back and forth, arms firmly gripping him in thanks.

Cole's box was huge. She ripped into the box and pulled out a floor lamp. Pillows were cool. This was incredible, something new, something beautiful, something that left her speechless. Life in thrift store land had just morphed into actual cool furnishings. For her! The only problem was how to set these gorgeous presents in a room with a couch and chair that had been repaired with duct tape.

"Hey dude, this is mind-blowing. Thank you. It's so awesome! I mean, it's metal and it's not even chipped."

"What can I say? You light up my life." His smile let her know that he meant it. Still, everyone groaned on cue. That's what family did.

Jocelyn straightened up, raised her head in perfect sanctimony. "I want you to know that in honor of these luscious pieces of décor, I am going to redo the couch and chair in new duct tape. Can't have old tacky with these." She waved her arm at the presents. "This grouping demands new tacky."

Paula's present was last. It was a huge box, even bigger than Cole's, one to truly gush over. Not big enough for a refrigerator, but too big for a toaster. What was in between? Standing up, Jocelyn tore into it with glee, pulling out tissue like a kid looking for a pony. The tissue piled up as she yanked out layer after layer until, at the bottom of the box, she found an envelope taped to the bottom.

Okay, Auntie Paula. What's up? Inside, at the very bottom, was a picture taken at Furniture Gallerie. A picture of a taupe sofa and matching armchair. Holy new apartment!

She turned to Paula. Her mouth hung open until she could focus the words enough to utter them. "You bought me furniture? Furniture! I can't believe it!" Even as she said the words, she felt the strangest feeling—an excitement, a compulsion even, to actually make a home. The world had tilted on its axis and Jocelyn couldn't have been more satisfied. She drew in a breath and let the pleasure of the inhale warm her before she took one leap at the three gift-givers and plowed into them, arms flailing, mind trying to figure out how to hug them all at once. She settled down and started with Cole on the one end. "You are such a friend. I promise to listen to your advice and not give you shit in front of stupid girls."

Cole snorted. "Don't make promises you can't keep."

Jocelyn grinned. "You're right. Okay, I promise to go into the kitchen and mix you another drink."

Before she stood up, she turned to Alex and said, "You are the best buddy I've ever had." She shook her head and added, "Of course, you're the only buddy I've ever had—next to Cole, of course." Jocelyn was no dummy. In the middle of her vow, she had caught Cole's inadvertent scowl. "And when the Apocalypse comes . . . I promise to save your sorry ass."

Alex did his eyebrow lift. "I bow to your survival savvy. But if you truly feel that the decorating elves have visited, thank the lady next to me. She took us shopping. She let us pick out whatever we wanted—as long as it was on her list." Jocelyn groaned and turned around to grab a pillow, but then just hugged him again.

Next was Paula. Jocelyn wrapped her arms around her and hugged tightly. "You are the best aunt ever! I thought the purple pig and the clown were a big deal, but this—this is too much!"

Paula unwound the hug and gave Jocelyn a kiss on her forehead, then took Jocelyn's hands into her own. "Think of it as a Christmas bonus. Cole prefers cash over furniture, but I wanted to do something special for you. If you don't like it, we can return everything and let you pick out what you want."

"No way! It's all just perfect." She was beaming. "The only problem is that the walls are so scarred, my place will be the decorating equivalent of *A Tale of Two Cities*, the best and worst of times."

Alex chimed in. "Hey, no problem. Part of my present is free painting service. We can knock out a couple of rooms in no time. I come complete with frog tape."

Jocelyn couldn't help herself. "Frog tape is for not smearing. In your case, it's toad tape."

Alex grabbed a pillow and swung it at her. In seconds, they were down on their knees, fake-slapping at each other. As Alex loomed above her, Jocelyn froze. Her arms were suddenly petrified, nothing but bone heavy and stiff. And they ached. She thought she would retch right there, right in front of the people who meant the world to her.

"Give up, huh." Alex saw the moment as a sign of surrender. Good. It must have only lasted a few seconds. Otherwise he would have been all over her with questions.

"Uncle it is." Jocelyn jumped up and headed for the bathroom. "Have to pee." She had to leave, yes. But not for the reason she gave. She had to calm down, collect herself, and figure out what had just happened. This was the best night of her life. She wasn't going to let some weird freak-out ruin it. She tightened into control, turned to Alex as she left. "Go ahead and gloat. Retribution will reign when I'm done, Stumme."

In her aunt's bathroom, she sat on the edge of the bathtub, leaned forward and shook her arms into life. Whatever kind of attack this had been, it had lasted only seconds, yet it had the run of her body, Halloween all over again. Her head cleared and her arms became hers again. She stood up, went to the sink and threw water on her face. Good thing the mascara was waterproof. As soon as she left the bathroom, she hollered out through the hallway and into the living room. "Stumme, get ready. Your ass is mine."

Her head tightened, right above her eyes. What was the deal, she wondered, with a stupid pillow fight?

CHAPTER 40

The next morning the two women faced the chaos of the party remains. They had managed to put the food away before they went to bed, but dirty dishes and scads of wrappings loomed.

In the kitchen, Jocelyn shuffled to the counter, slippers slapping the floor. She hollered out, "I'll make the coffee." Her head managed a weak *good idea*—perhaps one, no, two too many drinks last night—hot, black coffee sounded like an excellent way to begin the morning.

"Oh my goodness, yes. Tell the coffee maker to work double time." Evidently, Paula's intake last night had matched Jocelyn's. "Can't imagine why I'm so creaky this morning. Must be the eggs in the eggnog."

"Of course it's the eggs. All that protein. Has nothing to do with the rum, not to mention that we didn't make it to bed until three o'clock." The teasing in Jocelyn's voice mixed well with her own sense of after-party remorse. At least that's what her body said. Three hours of sleep did not make for a productive morning. Her mind was another matter entirely, still elated from the wonders of last night. She would have kept them all together until the last candle burned down. Even after Cole and Alex left and Paula was asleep, Jocelyn sneaked out to the living room, turned on the Christmas tree and wrapped herself in the throw Alex had given her while she watched the bubble lights work their magic. She woke at dawn, still wrapped in the throw, her head on one of the orange pillows, rose from the floor, still wrapped, unplugged the tree and went to bed. Instead of sugarplums dancing in her head, the three most special people in her world—the three she could call family—had laughed and played. So this morning, she said to herself, let the wear and tear of last night have its way. So what? Coffee and the promise of a nap—a long nap—would take care of any problem.

"Where's the throw Alex gave you? All the presents are stacked, but I don't see it." Paula was standing at the edge of kitchen, trash sack in hand. When Jocelyn turned around to answer, her face had a sheepish look and she shrugged her shoulders. "I slept with it last night. I guess I couldn't let the party end."

"Excellent idea. It spent some quality time in my apartment before it moves on to yours."

Even as the coffee maker sputtered its announcement that coffee was ready, Jocelyn stepped away from it to hug her aunt, the sack of wrappings crushed in the embrace. "I don't think I've ever had such a special time in my life." Her throat tightened as she whispered the words.

Paula stepped back and put one arm on her niece's shoulder. "Sweetie, that's the best news I've had in a long time." Eyes tearing up, she dropped the sack and pulled Jocelyn into a hug. "And I'm here to tell you there will be many more to come."

Jocelyn sniffled once before she broke the embrace. "So, Auntie, let's clean up this place, pull out the cookies, pour the coffee, and veg out on corny Christmas movies.

Paula noted, "Perfect." In less than an hour, they were settled, Jocelyn on the sofa, Paula in the large chair at a ninety-degree angle, goodies in hand, watching Jimmy Stewart learn the meaning of Christmas. Then came *Silent Night Romance*. Midway through, Jocelyn—once again wrapped in the throw that now had become her security blanket—plumped a pillow on the end of the sofa, and before anyone could say, "Oh, they'll live happily ever after now that they've saved the Christmas tree ranch and each other," Jocelyn was sound asleep. Paula sat back in her chair, ready for more romance—she was such a sucker for these holiday movies—and munched goodies while she watched. So caught up in the sugar all around, she didn't notice Jocelyn's furtive sleep noises.

"No! I won't. You can't make me." Jocelyn shot up and looked around, her eyes both startled and wary. She shook her hands, quick, sharp movements. "What?"

Paula started, "Camera?" She was silent as she studied Jocelyn, her brows knit together. Then she questioned "What happened?" Even as she spoke, Paula shot over and grabbed Jocelyn's hands, held them steady.

"You're having a nightmare. Relax. Breathe." As Jocelyn obeyed, Paula continued, "That's it. Take in the breath. Hold it. Right. Now exhale. Good."

"It was so awful. He had a camera. He was leering. They all were." Jocelyn continued her breathing; this time her inhales were gasps.

"Camera? Whose camera? Who's 'he'?"

The music from the television started coming at them faster. Action was speeding up. Music always let the audience know when to pay attention and have expectations. Jocelyn took in the sound, let it mix with the blurred images left over from the dream, the quivering that raced through her body in an endless arc of panic. How could she even begin to tell Paula the truth about Doug, about herself? The whole mess made her sick. She couldn't begin to imagine what Paula would think.

"Perhaps it's time you unburdened yourself. Had Paula said that or was Jocelyn struggling with herself?

She turned to Paula. Her aunt's face held probing, that was for sure, but in the Christmas Eve morning light, it also held a softness and a yearning. Paula stroked Jocelyn's hand. "Nightmares are messages to us that have to be neutralized in the light of day. But in order to let them go, they must be pried apart."

The television announcer sang out, *A Jingle Bell Christmas* is up next. No one would be dashing through the snow right now. They had a Grinch to uncover and bury.

Paula tilted her head and leaned forward. "Don't you think it's time to unload what's hurting you? I've seen the hurt, you know, when you think I'm not looking."

Jocelyn felt a renewed sense of terror. The choices she had made. The dupe she had been. Hadn't they flown away like a bird released? Why were the remnants of those choices here, circling her like a buzzard waiting for supper to die? How could she spill the slime that had been her relationship with Doug here in this place of love?

Silly girl, where better to spill?

"I was dreaming of Doug? Don't worry. It was definitely a nightmare."

"Yes. And . . . ?"

"I told you we broke up. That's not quite the whole story."

Paula kept quiet.

Jocelyn kept her head bent, wringing her fingers like Lady Macbeth spent on washing away the blood.

"I thought it was a big romance. That I was special. He made me feel so damn special."

"I saw that. Your face and voice told me that so many days when you came in to work. So you were special." Paula kept stroking Jocelyn's hands. They were cold.

Jocelyn let a grim smile take hold. She was looking away at the tree, as if she saw some kind of truth in the lights she so loved. "Every time I looked at him, I said to myself, *What is this gorgeous guy doing with me? I wanted to scoop him up and run through Chicago shouting, 'Me! He wants me!'*"

"So far, his only flaw is that he has good taste."

The snort sent Jocelyn's head upward. Her shoulders shook with ironic laughter. "Oh, he has good taste all right. Most pimps do."

Paula's face went white. She dropped her hands from Jocelyn's. "What? He wanted you to be a prostitute! I'll kill him myself. Give me his address. I'll wait a few days, take Cole along for backup. But by all that's holy, I'll do the killing."

Jocelyn turned to her aunt. This time, Paula's hands were the ones being held, pinned down in supplication.

"No, he wasn't a pimp that way. He's much more upscale and into technology." She took a deep breath before she said the words. She had to. "He wanted me to make porno films."

There. It was out. She had said it. She stole a glance at the ceiling. It hadn't fallen in. Paula, however, looked pretty caved. Not to mention white and deeply breathing.

"Please, Aunt Paula, I'll tell you about it, but let me do it in my own way. No comments until I'm done. Deal?"

"Deal." The word came out soft, but Paula's teeth were gritted.

She lay back against the pillows of the sofa, closed her eyes while she spoke. "He wooed me. I mean he *wooed* me. That first night he brought a picnic after my shift. That's what started it. I was shit-faced star struck. Star struck as in finely stupid." Opening her eyes, she leaned forward. "Remember how you and Cole teased me about a suitor? I mean, the guy was that good. All 'golly' and joking and schmoozing; I should have known."

"How? How would you have known?" Paula's cheeks had two red splotches. Keeping quiet was not on her agenda. "Maybe, just maybe he's had a lot of practice. Men like him are rodents, sniffing out what they want, scurrying back and forth to touch and turn everything they touch to slime." Her voice carried a bitterness borne from experience. As soon as the words left her mouth, she clenched her lips together, teeth digging into the upper one.

Jocelyn was in her own world, though, the world of her pain. She failed to notice her aunt's agitation. Her story would unfold, memory by memory, even if those memories now had a bite to them. "He took me to dinner. Remember the night at the Pump Room? That was just the beginning. He knew all the stops to pull. I was such a sap."

Paula extricated her hands and folded her arms. "That's enough. I know I promised to be quiet, but you blaming yourself is beyond ridiculous. You were the victim." She almost spat the words out as she repeated, "The victim!"

"I don't know all that went between you two. Obviously you were intimate. A man like that knows how to slide women into his bed like clean sheets." She stopped. "Sorry for that. There was nothing clean about him."

"Oh we were intimate. Explosively so." She stopped and held up her hand. "Sorry back to you. You may not want the details."

"Honey, I don't want the details, not because of a sleeze factor, but because this is the exact same story of women, one told over and over. Has been for centuries. All I want to know is what I can do to help you put this away—no, you can't put it away any more than you could put away your need to breathe. You need to look this *thing* in the eye and see it for what it is—seduction and betrayal. He groomed you, child. You never had a chance. If you can't grasp that for what it's worth, you'll live it over and over, reinforce it until it is your life."

"But I should have seen it. I watched men work my mother my whole childhood. And still I danced the dance. How laughable is that?"

Paula shook her head and put one hand on Jocelyn's shoulder. "I look at you and I see the whole mixture—pain, confusion, self-loathing—such a toxic mix. Do you really think watching my sister would teach you anything positive? She modeled the worst of the worst. Having Evelyn Quint

201

as a role model for dealing with men would be like having one of those zombies you love watching so much model compassion."

Jocelyn shook her head as Paula spoke and suddenly dropped it onto her knees. Arms folded over her head. Paula had to drop down to listen to what she said, so quiet was her voice. "The worst of the worst has nothing to do with my mother. It's me, the darkness of me." How could she tell her aunt about the longing, that she hated herself for that pathetic part of her that missed the man the rest of her despised? He had groomed her all right, used her neediness—the wanting that she hated about herself—broken her own like a rag doll plucked piece by piece until she was nothing more than a heap of string.

And yet she missed him.

Paula leaned forward, taking Jocelyn into her arms, the words coming out just inches from the girl's ear. "Let me guess. You're not so sure about what you've done. You're proud that you left. Wonderful. But you have to fight the want to go back. Maybe it'll be better this time."

Jocelyn scrunched herself into an even tighter ball. How did her aunt know her shame? Was it so obvious? Her shoulders shook with the knowledge. And within her, the images of last night played on her again, not images of Doug. Her whole life was colliding within her, Doug in the nightmare, somewhere else—old memories for sure, swift images of the walls in her bedroom, always the wall by her bed—fuchsia rose wallpaper, green peeling paint, more than the room in only one apartment—for sure, always the muscle memory of the coarseness of her blanket. She'd dragged that stupid blanket from place to place until it fell apart. Forget exorcising Doug. How about trying to stay sane? Merry freaking Christmas.

She managed to stand up, whispering as she walked away. "I can't do this. I need a nap. We can talk later."

Paula watched as Jocelyn walked away. *I hope we can talk later. Lord knows that we need to.* She turned off the television and went to find her journal—this time to read instead of write. Surely answers, or the start of answers, were in there.

CHAPTER 41

Christmas Eve for Jocelyn, at least the afternoon and evening, turned out to be a blank for Jocelyn. The hours blurred by.

She slept—a lot—played at watching a couple of movies, but mostly slept. She and Paula spoke a few words, but nothing more meaningful than "Where's the mayonnaise?"

On Christmas Day, Paula was up first. When Jocelyn came into the kitchen in the sweats she had worn to bed, her aunt had the kitchen table set, snowmen plates and cups, blue linen napkins held by snowflake napkin rings. A flying pig piece of pottery held a white candle. She plopped down on a chair and took in the scene, Christmas decorations for sure—what a flying pig had to do with Christmas she wasn't sure—her aunt busy making blueberry pancakes and brewing tea.

"Good morning, Dear," Paula chirped. "Hope you slept well."

"Marvelously so." Jocelyn could play.

"Thought we'd have a special treat this morning. Blueberry pancakes are my favorite breakfast. Just the right amount of sweetness."

"Of course."

"And we needed a new look on the table now that the remnants of your party are gone. What do you think?"

What do I think, Aunt Paula. I think you're up to something, but have at it. Strange. No walls were going up. Of course not. All of her wanted to see what Paula had in mind. "I especially like the Christmas pig. Interesting concept. Angel pig."

Paula wiped her hands on a tea towel and turned around to face her niece.

"Nope, no angel pig. Angels are angels." She took a few steps toward Jocelyn, her face bemused.

This ought to be good, thought Jocelyn.

"This pig with wings has a special message for you." She couldn't have been cheerier had she been Mrs. Kringle herself. That is before she put her hands on her hips. "I am here for you. I will only desert you when pigs fly. So take that candle and put it somewhere . . . appropriate. Perhaps on your dresser so that you can think about what I just said before you go to sleep."

Jocelyn stood up, walked the rest of the way to her aunt and hugged her. "Point taken."

Paula returned the hug, gave Jocelyn an extra squeeze for good measure, and then let her go. "Good. You fix the tea. I'll finish the pancakes. Oh, and the syrup is in the refrigerator somewhere in the back." She let out a snort of sorts and said, "I need to make pancakes more often" before she returned to the stove and began dropping the berries onto the pancake bubbling up on the griddle.

Christmas Day turned out to be an onslaught of more movies rather than more distress. The two talked about going out for Chinese—the only restaurants open—but decided that leftovers were easier, less need to brave the cold just to be the only pathetic customers there.

Then it was time to move back into reality. December 26th. Back to work. For the entire mid-holiday week, Jocelyn would stay at Paula's and work shifts daily, at least until after New Year's to let some of the help have time off. For those on shift, and for the regulars who stopped in despite Chicago's homage to Arctic temperatures, she knew she had to brace herself for the inevitable, "How was your Christmas?" No problem. She would smile and say, "It was Christmas. Merry." That certainly beat the truth, "Gee, I had a great time Christmas Eve with my aunt. I walked around comatose and she watched trying to hide her concern behind a brittle smile."

Cole would know better—he always did, that psych head—but she could count on him to keep his distance, at least as far as her mental state was concerned. The night of the Doug fiasco, Cole had pulled her aside and given her an uncle-like kiss on the top of her head. "You're brave. You're strong. We're here." Then he spent the rest of the night multitasking, naughty bartender flirting his way through the remaining hours, naughty spy every time she caught him watching her. If she didn't have to face him, she wouldn't have to look at his discerning eyes. Later, they could talk. Maybe.

The morning bustle to set up was hectic. Funny how closing down for more than one day sent them all scurrying—more to dust and rearrange, more to chop in the kitchen, sale prices to post, and for this day a kind of sadness. In two days all the seasonal fun would be put in storage. Sure, the hundreds of lights in the ceiling would stay up, there would be hats and horns come New Year's Eve, but the place wasn't the same without the wonderland of Luna Land at Christmas.

They were about to face lunchtime the day after Christmas. Christmas sales were a mania in Logan Square just like the rest of America. Bundled Chicagoans lugged the unwanted back for exchanges. Women lined up for half-price decorations from the boutiques; at 10:30, Jocelyn saw three women clogging the sidewalk, loaded down with artificial trees completely decorated. The madness had begun. She was half way though scoffing about *adding more crap to your house that you don't need* when she thought about the bubble lights on Paula's tree and mentally slapped herself.

Christmas wasn't a season. It was an obsession.

And now, that obsession was for everyone, even her. Buck up, buttercup and face the mistletoe.

The days passed and the tips at Luna's flowed. Her level of cash approached sanity. Life should have been good. The thing was, Jocelyn was tired; no, she was bone weary exhausted by the end of the week. Part of it was the work. Hauling down twelve tons of roping—had to be at least twelve tons—was bad enough, not to mention that she was working every day, ten-hour shifts. But part of it was something more. She knew both Cole and her aunt were watching her, secretly, of course—and she longed for nothing more than to sit at a table and spill to the people whom she had called family just days before. But she didn't have the words, even for herself. Good thing Alex wasn't back yet. She didn't need him as a complication.

The thing was, she kept having more flicks, always about life with her mother when she was young. They kept zapping at her brain out of nowhere. Take a minute out to catch a breath? Zap. *You are at Luna's working; you are at Luna's working.* The mantra could head them off, sometimes. But the bitches sneaked up on her, demanded, sent her into confusion.

She never saw herself in these. She just knew she was no more than eight or nine, maybe younger. The same stirring, sights, touching sensations, that dumb blanket again. In the flick, the blanket was rough to the touch. The thing was, that blanket had been the only soft thing she owned. That's why she loved it. Why was it so coarse in her memory? Why did the sensation make her stomach lurch?

Occasionally, she could zoom in on a distinct memory; that is, if she had flicked about it enough. Sparks of images started to come together. Marvin. One of the *boyfriends* Jocelyn actually liked, a thug of a guy with beefy hands and a beefier laugh. He was a paid "enforcer" that should have scared her. He played *Chutes and Ladders* with her and always let her win. When she thought about him, the blur subsided, along with the panic. Marvin. Nice guy. For a thug. For a thug that liked her mother.

But others choked her. One customer put out a cigarette by crushing the butt on the floor of Luna's. Tacky? For sure. Cole took care of perpetrator, but as Jocelyn watched, she felt a sense of rage growing inside her. The emotion rocked her, tasted vile. Her mind lingered on that butt stubbed out so cavalierly. In her mind, a dark form loomed over her. No way could she identify it other than to know it was a man. She rocked on her heels as she smelled cigarette smoke—no one was smoking in Luna's but here she was, nauseated by the phantom smell—she was dizzy with the smell.

Time turned, one day after another. School started up again. She and Alex painted the living room and kitchen. "No, we can't zentangle zombies next to the television." Funny guy. Work was demanding, but the three people she loved most were there for the simple price of a few sore muscles and aching feet.

Yet, as one day curved into the next, the single common denominator in her world was the spinning of her mind. Out of nowhere, she would lose focus. The sound of a glass breaking. Metallica from the 70's. It didn't matter where she was—a trigger and then the flicks played with her. Her life had finally turned around. She was dancing on the edge of safety, for crying out loud. Why did she feel about to be engulfed in lunacy?

Why did she go home every night and sleep with the light on?

Her friends noticed. She knew that. How could they not when she jumped at noises or shuddered at a smell? "I'm fine," she would say.

Sometimes she would start the conversation. "I truly have been struggling with the Doug fiasco, but I want you to know that I'm fine."

She could have an "I'm fine" button made to wear every day. Then she could look at herself in the mirror and try to convince herself that was true.

Yes, she wore the "I'm fine" mask with precision. But for the life of her, she could not begin to grasp what wasn't fine.

CHAPTER 42

The phone rang. Jocelyn grabbed for her cell phone on her dresser. 9:00, the clock read. "This is Furniture Gallerie. We have a delivery scheduled for you today. Will 2:00 work?"

Her initial *what the hell?* was replaced by "Absolutely. 2:00 is perfect." She had been awakened by a lover, this messenger, kissed with the news of a wonderful day. After she disconnected and set the phone back, she lay back in bed, hugged herself, and called her aunt.

By noon, Jocelyn and Paula had vacuumed and washed linoleum floors and battered walls that Jocelyn and Alex hadn't painted. Those walls still looked battered; the floors weren't much better, but they were a clean battered. And the freshly painted ones were ready to welcome more new. The old couch and chair had been carted away in Paula's SUV to the same thrift store where Paula had bought them—nothing like recycling to put a kick in your step. Let someone else mess with the duct tape and sags, the stuffing that kept on giving—mostly onto the floor. Back in the apartment, Cole's lamp held court in the corner looking out into empty space and waiting for company. At 2:30, the delivery guys showed up and had the new sofa and chair in place along with a coffee table and area rug. Jocelyn had protested; Paula shushed her with a promise to knock off more presents at least until her birthday in February. "Think of it as an early birthday gift," she said. "Besides, this was a place for furniture orphans. I'm just trying to make the apartment a little happier."

"Well," said Jocelyn, "the way the tips have been coming and you've been feeding me so I don't have to buy groceries, my apartment will be on the decorators' tour before you know it."

Paula lowered her head and pursed her lips. "Let's just go for nice place to visit instead of a furniture orphanage."

Jocelyn laughed at her. "Never took you for a snob." But even as she uttered the words, she sat back against the pillows on the sofa, put her feet up on the coffee table, and sighed. "Wheels on a coffee table. Love the rustic look—just have to keep Alex from trying to ride the thing."

"Don't worry. The wheels are in the center on each side. He'll slide onto his butt before he gets any momentum."

The picture of a prone Alex made Jocelyn snicker. This was a fun day, a day of grace and happiness. And yet, as she sat back to take it all in, her arms ached and a sense of hollowness filled her. Jocelyn was still exhausted, had been for what seemed like forever. Work at Luna's had lightened up. Her new classes this semester were only slightly past the syllabus stage. No reason for her being so tired.

"I could sit here, the queen of cool all day long, eyes closed, and just smell the new."

"You probably should." Paula's words were edged with censure.

Jocelyn's state, evidently, was no secret. "For the past weeks, the bags under your eyes have been carrying luggage. You're pale and edgy. You can tell me what's wrong or I can take you to the doctor. And don't give me that 'I'm an adult' baloney. Adults take care of themselves." Paula was on a roll. "Talk to me or I take the wheels off the table and spill tomato soup all over the rug."

Head resting against the back of the sofa, Jocelyn pulled a pillow against her face, forearms resting on the orange cover. A strained silence hovered in the room before she yanked the pillow away and sat up. She couldn't look at her aunt, only the wall across the room. "You're right. I feel like the truck that ran over me had a good time and decided to do it again." That admission, an act of bravery in itself, didn't cover all that was wrong. It was just the tip of the iceberg, one that ran through her. This morning Jocelyn had looked in the mirror, seen a withered scarecrow with mottled skin and skewed limbs. She was tired, for sure, but she knew she didn't look that bad, that the flickers and the lack of sleep had not only worn her out, but distorted her perception of herself.

She had fought the flickers these many weeks—been terrified yet curious as they started to morph into more solid images that seemed familiar and yet untrue to the sense of what seemed to be the past she knew. She had held it all in, tied it into another knot that she stored. She didn't dare speak of it. Paula would have come unglued, and the new-found sense of peace these weeks had brought in the world outside Jocelyn's exhausted mind were too precious to upset.

But trudging through, day after day, of wild uncharted memories and nights of waking up sweating shook her. At night, while she sat in her bed dripping like it was the middle of summer, she felt this alarm that something was driving her from deep within. She didn't know what, but she did sense that she was heading for a cliff somewhere, and falling off would shatter her. If she looked haggard, it wasn't nearly as bad as she felt.

Jocelyn leaned forward, shoulders hunched and hands on her knees. "Okay, you've got me. I need to talk to someone, and I can't think of anyone better than you."

Paula's face registered a higher level of concern. "It's not about that Doug guy, is it? He's not back in the picture?" She shook her head. "You keep telling me everything's good . . ."

"No. No, nothing like that. He's gone."

Jocelyn popped up and headed into the kitchen. "Let me get a couple of sodas and we'll talk. Want ice?"

"No. I want you back in here sharing with me. We don't need drinks; we need words. I may not be a cowgirl, but I know bullshit when I hear it."

Funny. *Please Lord, let me get through this.* She tossed up the prayer not sure what *this* was going to be. Something was working her. She could feel the tangle. She also knew that she needed to talk. *I'm fine* was turning into I'm *about to lose my mind.* The steps to the fridge for that soda were far too few.

With a sigh, Jocelyn returned to the sofa; Paula stayed seated on the chair—shades of Christmas Eve morning. Paula's face was calm and inviting, either by her own command or a hope for the conversation.

Jocelyn started in. "Part of what's bothering me is that I'm happier than I've ever been. I'm more than half way through college, stellar student that I am. I have a job that keeps me eating, and an aunt that keeps me spoiled. I have a family. I should feel fucking exquisite."

"That well may be. Keep going. So the problem is . . . "

"I want to cry with joy, to leap around and savor the way my life has tilted in the best of directions." She stopped. What were the words? How could she explain the craziness going on inside her, the foreign dance that controlled mind and body?

Paula kept silent. She might as well have been a monk waiting in his cave for a pilgrim to ask the secret of life. Was Paula nurturing acceptance or did the woman have a sense of where this might go? She had been through her own hells; many parts of her had taken the trip.

Jocelyn took a swallow of the soda she had brought for herself. "Start me out?"

Paula stayed in her monk persona. "What do you mean?"

"I just told you that life is one great big happy dance."

"And yet you look torn apart."

"You told me how when trauma hit you as a child, you'd split. That an alter would take the trauma. So when that happens—when *Jen* or *Chloe* or *Joey* take that on, does Paula remember it?"

"No. They have to tell me about it. They help me picture it, work through it until I have a sense of the trauma. A lot of the time, the realization will begin with some symbol, that is until I can handle the knowing. It's much easier seeing a witch than my mother or fire rather than . . . well, whatever the fire would represent." Paula's eyebrows furrowed and her lips pulled together. "Sweetie, what are you trying to tell me? Are you worried that you're dissociating?"

Jocelyn felt a sense of panic rise inside her. "No!" She calmed herself—as much as she could, given the morass inside her. "No. This is all me. One single Jocelyn. One tired fucked-up single Jocelyn." A cement block was pushing on the top of her stomach. Nausea rose in her throat. She was opening and closing her fists; the one nail she had left from incessant gnawing dug into her palm.

Paula came over to the sofa, sat next to Jocelyn and leaned forward.

Jocelyn lunged back, away from her. "Please. No hugs. If someone touches me right now, I'll fall apart for sure."

Paula scooted away to the edge of the sofa. "No problem. But, niece, you have to talk to me. You watched me when I fell apart. You listened to me explain my dissociation. You trust me. Trust me enough to talk. What's going on?"

Jocelyn bent over, hugging her arms, hands against the sides of her under the armpits, cocooning her middle. She had closed her eyes. She could only whisper. "They're in my mind. These images—no, not images, pieces of images. They come out of nowhere, when I least expect them, and take over. I can see them, feel them swirling." She pulled her arms apart, began to hit her thighs with her fists, eyes still closed. She could talk to her aunt, but not look at her. "They drive me crazy, and the craziest part is—I don't know why, why I have them or why they make me crazy, and that's so . . . so . . . crazy!"

She opened her eyes and stood up and strode around the apartment—out of the living room into the kitchen, into the hallway, her bedroom, back out into the living room again before she sat down, this time on the floor inches in front of the new chair, just a few feet from her aunt, legs crossed like a yoga student ready to begin. She pulled her head and shoulders forward and took in the release of the tiny pops in her back as cartilage loosened. Her toes played with the softness of the area rug—life was so good without shoes. She crossed her forearms and relaxed them against her thighs, bowed her head, kept silent. How could she not? She was clueless as to where to begin. Eyes closed again, she refused to watch the chaos. So much easier to talk when you're blind.

"Good. How do you feel?" Her aunt's voice was warm, distant. Sitting there on the floor, Jocelyn could picture Paula on the sofa, her face masked in a concern that Jocelyn couldn't bear to watch. The thought of hurting her aunt brought such shame. She simply listened.

"I don't mean *feel* as in your mood. I mean *feel* as in 'What is your body physically feeling?'" The question was strange, the tone of Paula's voice gently commanding.

Jocelyn's outside body was numb, had been for as long as she could remember. All the action went on inside. The rest of her didn't have room to feel. "I don't feel anything. I can't—at least in my limbs and torso. Am I supposed to?"

Paula's voice turned soft, broken. "Yes, darling, you are."

Way to go, Quint, way to hurt your aunt with your stupid pity party.

Before her critic could shame her more, Jocelyn's aunt spoke again, voice restored to stability. "It's time to face some truths. Open your eyes and look at me. I don't bite."

212

Jocelyn obeyed, sat up and looked at Paula, a red stain of blushing on both cheeks coloring an otherwise pale face.

Paula said, "Never mind chastising yourself. I'm a big girl." Smiled as she said it, a loving smile, welcoming and motherly—at least it seemed so to a girl who had never seen such a smile before she met her aunt. She paused. "And I've been where you are, shut down and numb. That's the thing with hiding. It's a two-sided sword. Sure, it protects. But spend enough time doing it and you lose the ability to feel."

"Hiding? I don't hide anything from you. I just don't talk about everything."

"Jocelyn, I mean hiding within yourself. Building walls for self-protection."

Walls! How did she know about the walls?

Paula chuckled. "You should see your face. Yes, I know about walls. How else could I hide all those urchins living inside me? They'd scamper around inside, and outside I'd be so collected." The laughter faded as she inhaled. "Sometimes I built walls. Sometimes I'd fill my throat with cement."

Jocelyn knew she could talk about her walls. She had to. Not just because she could, but because she knew that it was time. Inside her, she could feel a beating, a ticking of time as it marched onward. Tick Tock. Her dream mantra. Her mother! She relaxed the panic. Not a molecule of her mother was present here. Whatever the clock sound represented, it had nothing to do with Evie. She felt the relief wash through her.

So what was with the clock? Jocelyn grabbed a pillow and bent over, cradling herself.

"Whatever makes you build those walls is knotted deep within. Our emotions are tangled with our bodies. We can't help ourselves when we seek to protect. It's survival."

Her aunt spoke truth. Every time she brought down those walls, it was a primitive reaction. Sometimes they surge upward and she had to run through tunnels to find the safe place; mostly they lowered downward, set themselves with a firm clunk—what it took to make sure the *me* was safe.

"So how do I undo the walls? Or the need to build them."

Paula had moved beside Jocelyn, a few feet from her. She didn't touch her. She just spoke—like a shrink, or maybe a mother. "You trust and you talk." She took in several breaths and exhaled slowly. "And you breathe."

"I am breathing. Even when I don't want to."

Paula voice was gentle, but still a command. "Not regular every day breathing. Controlled breathing. It's the difference between walking around in a daze, and walking, observing with focus."

Walking around in a daze? That called for more energy than she had to spare.

"Jocelyn, I want you to stretch out your legs and lean back against the sofa."

Jocelyn obeyed, eyes still shut. Blinded, she could move through the instructions.

"That's good," her aunt continued. "Here. Let me put a pillow between you and the furniture."

Jocelyn felt the cush of material relaxing the nape of her head, her neck, and her shoulders. Aahh.

"Good, let's start. Breath in, filling your lungs with air. Let them fill. Give the inhale a count of four, hold the breath, and exhale for six counts. Force that air out."

Jocelyn did as her aunt said—took in breaths—one, two, three, four, held for one count, and exhaled for six. After two times, she felt her shoulders drop, her legs fall outward; she came to an awareness of the reward of structured breathing. How calming. "This is awesome. "I'll be Jell-O before you know it."

"Good. Just keep the breathing pattern, four in, one hold, six out. When you're ready, you can start talking to me. Forget the count, but keep breathing."

While she exhaled, Jocelyn's mind became aware of something—she couldn't call them memories, not even images, and more sensations that would have form but couldn't quite come together. She knew that in her mind's eye, it was night. She was in bed. Just a kid.

"I slept with a baseball bat from the time I was twelve." It was important to start there, why she couldn't say, but she knew to begin with the bat.

"I remember you telling me." Paula's words floated toward her. Jocelyn felt like they had been spoken in a different universe even though she could hear them distinctly. She resumed the breathing ritual, eyes still closed.

The bat. What about the bat? She felt the hardness of it in the darkness that was her room. Was it raining outside? Cold? She didn't know. All she knew was that her bed was warm and the hardness of the bat made her feel safe.

Then the bat was gone, and yes, it was raining, hard. The flare of the storm lashed against her bedroom window. She drew deep under her covers and kept her eyes shut. Footsteps sounded against the linoleum out in the hall, coming closer, coming into her bedroom. A sudden whoosh. Someone was sitting on her bed.

Her body tightened—at least her stomach area and upper things. That sense of a someone.

This wasn't the first time child Jocelyn had felt the settling of a body onto her bed. Her mind searched through sensory memory for more information. Sometimes it wasn't raining. But she knew about the steps and that crawly feeling that would come when the form sat down. She tried to recall the feel of her blanket. Yes, it *was* soft, not like in the flicks that had hounded her. But another sensation stole the softness. A hand, a big one, brushed across the blanket covering her; it started at the top by her shoulders—Jocelyn felt her own adult shoulders tense in muscle memory— and then made its way down her arm, her leg, come back and rest on her bottom, a circular stroking immeasurably soft but so disquieting.

Jocelyn moved her head back and forth. Her mind moaned. Did she make the sound? There, on the floor, the woman Jocelyn, with her own Jocelyn child within, sat up and opened her eyes, began to rock, just simple rocking, as the sensations of memories uncalled for clouded in her mind. Her toes dug into the rug, not as happy as they were only moments before. She reached behind for the pillow, grabbed it to her chest.

Something was coming to her. She didn't want to know it. She beat it back with her mind as she rocked there and felt her life swirl.

That hand. It slipped under her blanket. She could feel the calluses even through her pajamas. Momma didn't have calluses on her hands. This wasn't her momma.

She beat one hand against the pillow, striking again and again.

"That son-of-a-bitch. He was feeling me up." Her words held wrath enough, but a new realization deepened her tone into a growl. "Oh sweet Lord in heaven. Not he." The rocking kept a cadence with the push of discovery. "Them!"

215

She bent over. This time she beat her hands against the softness of the rug beneath her until her palms turned red. She never felt the sting.

"No wonder I slept with a bat. I thought it would protect me against something that might happen." She began her rocking again. Her beating palms had become fists. The rage of her tone shifted. Now she was rolled into a fetal ball, keening like a wounded rabbit in the throes of death, her arms over her head to protect her from the world that had come crashing down.

Paula's words sounded like an echo, distant yet loud, metallic. "Let it out. That's what you need now. Just let it out." Then the words came closer; she felt them as they sang to her, a song so close as they brushed into her ear. Arms embraced her as she lay there curled into a ball; one hand smoothed her hair, brushed a kiss on her forehead. A mother's kiss. Of course, she needed a mother's touch, a mother's kiss. The filth, the coarseness of this revelation fell onto her like slime. She had been assaulted, molested. Why did Jocelyn have to wait so long for the love of a mother, and why did that love have to come from the sister instead of the woman herself?

A meanness filled her, the kind of mean she had covered herself with as an older child, a teen, even later. The men—they were detestable—that was a given. But her mother, the one who let them, or didn't know because she was in the kitchen passed out—and even as that thought flitted into existence another replaced it—of course she knew. That woman was not worth the oxygen she had breathed all those years. "Of course I didn't cry for that woman at her funeral. Why would I cry over someone so contemptible?" The words spilled out, the burden, the pain she had bottled within the walls she had constructed to protect herself. The anger.

Jocelyn laid her head in Paula's lap, felt the smoothness of the hand stroking her head as the words kept their tumbling. "My mother cried and cried for all the men who used her and tossed her aside. 'Why won't they love me?' she'd wail. And the whole time I watched her sink even lower, all I wanted was a mother who would love me, who would accept my love.

"She let them use me. Let them put their hands on me, their hard, weathered hands, scratching and hot." Jocelyn cried, just a few tears at first—she could still speak. "Why couldn't she love me?" spilled out over and over, like a mantra. Then she was sobbing, gagging, blinded by the

216

wash of pain and tears and snot, casting her grief outward as it spun into the air of the apartment.

For a time—she could not ever begin to know how long—she lay awash in the past as it pounded onto her, thrust out from somewhere so deep she could never have imagined its existence. When she was done, she collapsed into sleep, hard sleep, dreamless sleep, sleep of the dead.

She woke up the next morning in her bed—if anyone could call her state *waking up*. She could not remember moving from the living room to the bedroom. Had her aunt moved her? No way could Paula have carried her. Her body was a rag, her mind not much better. Her insides had been stripped; even her bones were hollow. Lying there, on her side, knees up, she let the pall of morning cover her. Perhaps she was a corpse.

The toilet flushed. That sound sent her rooting feeling down through her legs, out through her arms. Anything physical. She needed to contact reality. Someone was in the apartment. Her aunt, of course. No way would she have gone home after the meltdown.

Sure enough, Paula stood in the doorway, still dressed in yesterday's clothes.

"Good morning. I'd ask 'How do you feel?' but my guess is that you have no idea, other than a sense of being battered."

Jocelyn swung her legs over the side of the bed and sat there, head down, fingers kneading her head.

Had anyone else witnessed whatever last night had been, Jocelyn would have been horrified. Instead, the sight of her aunt was a comfort. That, by itself, was a win.

"Remember, at the cemetery, when you said I wasn't a loon? Want to take that back now?" Despite the unleashing and recovery—or perhaps because of it—Jocelyn was embarrassed.

Paula did not move. "I think that you are a brave woman, a very brave one at that."

"Oh, I'm brave all right. So brave I want to crawl back into bed and never come out."

Paula walked forward toward Jocelyn, bent down and kissed the top of her head, moved away only a few inches. "I know better. I know you, honey. You're me."

She stood up, walked to the door and turned around. "Up and at 'em, niece. Brush out that mop of hair, wash your face, and come into the kitchen. I'll get the coffee going. We have a lot to talk about."

Jocelyn's body struggled with the orders. Walking while hollowed out is no mean feat. But despite the exhaustion, she felt an inner quiet, even strength that had not been there before.

"We have a lot to talk about," her aunt had said. Somehow, that seemed like a gift.

CHAPTER 43

From Paula Ross—paper found at niece's apartment,
to be added to journal later

O*h what have we wrought? If that's not Shakespeare, it should be. Jocelyn has remembered. I have been working for this moment, praying for this moment, promising the alters that the moment would come—but that's another story.*

I held Jocelyn while she keened; the keening could have been my own—my muscle memory holds the story of when I lay in Joe's arms. Such a sisterhood I have with my niece, one not just of blood, but one of that which could not be named but must be named. Survivor.

It's not the same, of course. Mine meant all of us holding Charlie, letting her recognize, come to terms—if such a thing is possible—with a grandfather who molested her starting at five, raped her in his garage when she was ten. "Let me show you how much Grandpa loves his little girl." No wonder Charlie wants to be a boy. No wonder she impales grownups on barbed wire in her art.

Some of the alters try to tell me that Jocelyn is lucky. Fingers only scorch. They don't go deep and they don't tear. They don't make you writhe in pain as the old man's stick tears you apart. There's no blood. I say, "No matter." Horror is as horror does.

I said that we would talk.
Guide me, Lord. Help me know what to say.
Help me to know what to say to myselves.

CHAPTER 44

Jocelyn lay on her sofa, grasping onto the softness of the throw Alex had given her on Christmas Eve. She had bundled it up and now held it like a child's beloved toy. "I thought the swagger would protect me. That and the walls." As Jocelyn ushered the words from the narrow halls that lived in her chest, her heart, her mind, those parts constricted in a ritual of birth. "Sure, I let my guard down if Evie seemed to want a daughter. Occasionally, she could bring me out and display me to her *friends* . . ." She stopped as she said "friends" as if she might choke on the word. ". . . at least when I was young and cute. She might even have loved me—once, assuming that she could love—especially when I filled some sick need to fill whatever was empty in her. Tough to figure out when so much time is compressed in a place I can't touch—or couldn't until last night." Jocelyn paused as the touch of those words sifted through her, made her want to synthesize them with what she knew of herself.

"School was easy—at least the work. Fractions? No problem. Hell, I was one. Nothing whole number about this kid. Young child me stood on the sidelines, alone in a herd of youngsters that jostled and ran and hollered and teased. I needed so much, found nothing, tumbling along the hallways of school, the playground, aching for some fool to reach out and pick me up. I learned to be stone, feel nothing, that is except for a freefalling anger that rumbled around inside—once in a while burst through.

"Amazing what a stone can do if it practices."

"What about the teachers—what were their names?" Paula's voice was more of an invitation to continue than one of inquiry.

"Amber and Marti. Amber was my English teacher. She found out that I could write." Jocelyn laughed. "That is, when I wasn't ripping the paper with my pen." She rubbed the edge of the throw against her arm. "Marti was—is—the guidance counselor. They were the first saviors." Her face softened as she spoke of them. "But still, after I graduated, I went on with my life and they went on with theirs.

"Amber's married to a guy who came to our school to be a resident writer for a few weeks. They live in Wyoming. I get a Christmas card every year. Marti calls once in a while to check in. I tell her how I'm fine. Maybe she believes me."

"You haven't seen her since graduation?"

"Nope. Didn't even tell her Evie had died. Guess she never saw it in the paper. Why would she?"

"Don't you wish you had?"

Jocelyn sat up, still hugging the throw. She wrapped her arms around it, sat cross-legged on the sofa, bringing the throw to her face to take in the softness. She shook her head with the confidence of someone who knows she's right. "Nope. See, if I would have been able to rely on Marti, I wouldn't have had to learn to rely on you."

Paula couldn't help it. The tears welled in her eyes. She well knew her voice would shake even as she held herself back from drawing Jocelyn into her arms. But she stayed detached—at least physically. She had to. This was too important a time to turn into a sentimental crushing of hugs. They had work to do, sense to make of the revelation of last night.

"Jocelyn, I love you for those words. And more important, I love you for you. You have had such a huge secret to carry. Worse, you didn't know it even existed. You plodded through life while that millstone around your neck weighed you down.

"How do you feel?"

Jocelyn drew her head back, lifted her eyes upward. "Lighter."

"Of course. You shed a tonnage."

Jocelyn ran two fingers between her brows. "Not just lighter. Less hollow. I mean, I'm exhausted, wrung." She ran the same hand from elbow to shoulder. "I have this tingling in my arms , not nuisance tingling, just a feathery feeling—as if my arms want to tell me that they're there. It's like I'm accepting what I didn't even know I was rejecting."

She sat forward, excitement growing—as if she were just discovering some truth. She was. "And it's so weird. I want to sleep. At the same time, I want to run out into the street and scream, 'Hey world, listen up. Sit down while I tell you my story. I was molested. Yep, sucks to be me.'"

221

"That could be liberating." Paula was ever the master of understatement.

"Liberating? It is freaking mind-blowing. I mean, I was shambling through life days ago saying 'I'm fine' and now I want to run to Millennium Park and put my story up on Crown Fountain, let the ice skaters read it while they glide back and forth in their winter innocence."

"I hate to tell you this—I mean, telling you that you are normal might seem insulting . . . "

Jocelyn snickered. "You know me so well."

"What you're experiencing is normal. Your memories stirred in you, demanded to be heard, rose within you as those misty, disjointed flicks."

Jocelyn was nodding her head. Her eyes told her aunt to go on.

"That whole 'I'm fine' was you in denial. You had to take the edge off the trauma of remembering."

"And now?"

"Now you can accept what you know to be true. Knowing is one thing. Processing quite another."

Processing. The word seemed liberating.

"Figuring this all out is a piece of cake compared to what I really have to come up with."

Paula eyed her, questioning. "And that is?"

"What do we tell Alex and Cole?"

"Sweetie, you just told me you wanted to tell the world your story."

"The world isn't Cole and Alex. The world doesn't care. The world would listen, nod its head and move on." Jocelyn slid down the sofa and covered herself with the throw."

"Don't go hiding on me now. The four of us are family. As family, we will come together. Your days as a stone, my dear, are over."

"That's what I'm afraid of."

Paula reached forward, put her hand on Jocelyn's. "You were strong enough to remember. That was the hard part. Now be strong enough to reach out."

Reach out. The thought terrified her.

CHAPTER 45

The morning teased Chicago. One of those January mornings when the temperature climbed above freezing, and drips from the eaves seemed like harbingers of a spring long due, yet far into the future.

Of course, Paula took this as an omen. "See? Even the weather is hopeful. We'll fill the boys with pancakes and good news about your breakthrough."

Good news? Right, Jocelyn thought. Cole will understand, of course. He's Mr. Psych Guy. Hell, he'll probably interview me for a paper. But Alex? He'll run. Fast. One thing to know your friend has issues; another to meet the nightmare head on. She tried to numb the rock settling inside her chest.

Good luck with that.

The doorbell rang. Functioning alert. Jocelyn opened the door to the two guests standing on the shabby hallway mat, each holding a bottle of Febreze. Rasping in his best Igor, Alex announced, "We're here for the ritual."

Cole piped up. "Don't worry. We won't destroy the new furniture smell. Just one quick poof and the furniture is sanctified." He stuck his left hand into his coat pocket, searched for something, and then pulled it out and snapped his fingers. "Dang. I forgot the ashes."

All night, Jocelyn had wandered in the darkened apartment. The reds and blues and greens of the neon signs blurred through her curtains while she wrestled with what she had discovered, unnerved by the impact of her discovery. Now here were these two goofballs standing in her doorway. The web of concern lowered its hold on her mind, the rock in her chest loosened its grip, and she smiled. How could she not?

"I usually tell peddlers to head off, but you two are especially compelling." She pointed to one of the plastic bottles. "And you've obviously cleaned up your act. Come on in. I may even feed you."

Cole turned to Alex. "The lady says she'll feed us. There is hope for the infidel, yet. Come. We must proceed with the blessing."

Not to be outdone, Alex snapped back. "Blessing? I thought we were here for an exorcism."

Jocelyn started to close the door in their faces. "Have a nice day. Come back when you're sane."

Alex eased in first, a couple of feet past the threshold, Cole close behind. "C'mon Joce. It's a beautiful moment, and we're hungry." Cole hollered over his shoulder, "Hey Paula, tell me we're having blueberry pancakes."

Her voice came through loud and clear from in the living room. "Absolutely. Hurry up and get in here to help. Have you picked the berries yet?"

Jocelyn muttered, "Everyone's a comedian" while she stood aside to let in the guests. "Hang your coats on the back of the door and grab some coffee."

Will we be laughing an hour from now? Hardly.

The blessing was first on the agenda. Of course, all guests made a great deal of the addition the Christmas presents made to the ambiance of Jocelyn's apartment. Amazing how taking out the duct tape worked wonders. Paula beamed at the laughter and exclamations of décor perfection. Alex pointed out that the painting job must have been done by professionals right before he and Cole started a Febreze war with each other. Paula clenched the forearms of the two, hollering, "Enough!"

She pointed them toward the new additions and said, "We honor you today, oh visions of comfort. May you provide light and color, comfort and peace." She turned toward Alex, then looked back. "And may you be ever warded against the evil droppings of pizza, drinks, doughnuts, or whatever dregs and effluvia may seek to tarnish your beauty." She nodded once, twice, and said, "Gentlemen, you may commence. " In perfect unison, Alex shot a mist at the chair and coffee table; Cole covered the sofa area.

224

Jocelyn stood in the doorway between kitchen and living room, arms folded. She smiled at the antics even while her inside grew tight once again

A reckoning was coming. Soon. Paula promised her the guys would understand if she shared last night with them. "The sooner, the better," she had insisted. That meant today.

Sharing what had unseated her last night—was such a thing possible?

Before she could react to her question, Alex had his arm around her shoulders, moving her forward toward the kitchen table. Wasn't he just doing the misting thing?

Great. Now you're losing time. Proof positive you're nuts.

"Take a seat," he said. "We can make breakfast and you can relax and enjoy." She sat down next to him, her mind whirling while Paula chimed in, "Right. If 'making breakfast' includes munching on doughnuts, you're a real help."

Alex had the class to blush. He couldn't say much, sitting next to Jocelyn, his mouth full, a blob of custard on his outer lip.

When had he grabbed the doughnut?

Paula spouted instructions. "Cole, you can get the batter and blueberries out of the fridge. Alex, if you can tear yourself away from the goodies, you can pour some juice. I'll heat the griddle." Her voice relaxed. "Jocelyn, you sit there and enjoy. This kitchen was built for one. We're maxed out as it is." Cole had his job done before Alex could mumble agreement.

So as the team took care of business, Jocelyn sat at the table, back against the wall, thankful for the reprieve. The three people in the world who meant the most to her were bunched together in her tiny kitchen, jostling one another, at least two of them oblivious to her life reduced right now to a single terror of sharing a journey that had only begun last night. She felt herself rising above her as her body sat there, rigid, and watched the parade before her.

"I think Jocelyn needs a cup of coffee. We were up late last night talking."

She pointed to Cole. "Take over here while I get her a cup." The switch passed easily. Paula leaned over as she poured and whispered in Jocelyn's ear. "You're brave and we love you. Deep breath."

Easy for you to say. You're not the one coming apart.

The meal ended with sighs and thank you's. When Cole started to stand to take his plate to the sink, Paula waved a hand at him and said, "Don't worry about that. We have plenty of time for clean up. Just sit back and finish off the coffee pot."

Finish off. Ominous words. As in finish me off. Jocelyn armed herself for battle, brought her safety walls fully up and formidable, her sense of self hovering over the scene taking in all the expressions. Even as Paula spoke, Jocelyn could feel her aunt's hand patting her thigh. She took in a deep breath, held it, exhaled for a slow count. Cole was watching her. Alex was turned around looking at the littered counter—no doubt searching for more sugar.

Jocelyn picked up her spoon and clanked her coffee cup. "I have an announcement to make." Alex turned around, sang out "Dut-ta-dah-dah." Cole and Paula sat back in their chairs, observing.

"First, I want to thank you for the tremendous support on this auspicious day."

Alex started a "Hear. Hear," but let it fall flat. Did he sense something? He was no fool even if he acted like one.

These are people who love you. These are people you can trust. Jocelyn made it a mantra as she searched for the words. Both hands gripped her coffee cup. *Please Lord, don't let it shatter. Please Lord, don't let* me *shatter.*

Jocelyn's voice came out in a monotone, like a little kid explaining why she had done something naughty, part explanation, part plea. While she spoke, her right palm rubbed the rim of the cup while her left hand clenched the cup. Her eyes fixed on a spot in the middle of the table. "When I invited you all over, I had planned to make this all about fun. Something happened last night to change that. Paula was here to help me . . ." Her voice caught and she gave a little shudder. She looked up. All three friends were quiet, watching her. Paula was nodding her head.

"I'm okay. Really. But we think . . . I think . . . I need to share last night with you, Cole and Alex." She looked up at the two guys and gave them a smile—more a tight smirk than a smile—and then brought her focus back to the safety of the table. By now she had her napkin in her lap and was twisting it.

"Ever since my mother died, I've been having these dreams—really weird ones—probably as weird as some of Charlie's art." She gave a scoffing

226

sound and looked around. No one was laughing.

"Anyway, lately, while I'm awake, I've been seeing pictures in my head—just quick flicks of things, evidently from my childhood . . ."

Cole's eyes deepened. He leaned forward just a nudge. Alex was stone still. She scoffed again, looked up and brought up one side of lips into a smile. "I mean, one minute I'm delivering a couple of beers and the next, I'm seeing peeling wall paper in my bedroom from one of those crappy apartments we lived in. That was weird in itself. But the thing is, I've been so damn tired all the time, and these flicks pissed me off."

She turned to Paula, nodded once. Paula nodded back, her warm eyes promising Jocelyn that she could do this. "Paula and I talked about it." Her voice dropped as she looked at Cole. "I guess I could have talked to you, but you were tending bar and couldn't play Psych Guy . . ."

He smiled. "No problem. Paula's way smarter than me—and better looking." He paused. "Keep going. You're doing fine."

Jocelyn sat up in her chair and put her hands on the table with a slap. "Well guys, seems I remembered all sorts of things—in this great big swoosh that explained why I slept with that baseball bat all those years. Kind of helps explain why I'm not too fond of Evie."

Cole and Paula were steady. Alex's face had paled and he was thumbing his fingers.

I haven't had time to take all this in, myself. How am I going to unload this, especially on Alex? Jocelyn felt Paula squeeze her hand. The woman was psychic.

"Essentially, I was kind of a party favor for some of Evie's boyfriends, at least after the drunk fest was over. That's something I couldn't remember . . ."

"What the fuck!" Alex's voice split the tension mounting in the kitchen. He stood up, grabbed his coat off the hook and stormed out. The door crashed against the wall.

The three of them sat stunned until Jocelyn broke the silence. "I guess he's not going to help with the dishes."

Cole looked down at the table, his head shaking back and forth for thoughts only known to him. Paula took Jocelyn in her arms. "He'll be back. Give him some time."

Jocelyn could only think, "Will he?"

227

CHAPTER 46

Alex strode along the sidewalk outside of Jocelyn's apartment, hands slammed into his jacket pockets, his breath heaving. He had to calm himself, get control, and get back in there. But he couldn't. Not yet. He wanted to grab the next stranger he saw—at least any nameless guy over forty—pummel him until his own knuckles bled out the rage that coursed through him.

He turned into the outer alcove of an appliance store and sat down, leaning against the door. George's Best Deals, the sign said. Who the hell was George? Was he some slobbering pervert that hurt little girls? Alex put his head down, elbows on his knees. Strangers walking by might think he was a kid sobering up or maybe some poor slob newly homeless. Who cared?

He was a schmuck who just learned that his best friend, the girl he loved in ways he had never let himself count, had needed him and he was too stupid to have helped.

Water plopped from above George's and hit a puddle on the sidewalk, each hit echoing disdain. Even Mother Nature knew he was a loser. The signs had been there. Pushing away last fall after Evie died. The freaking out on Halloween. Going after a tool like Doug. How stupid was he? His mind traced back to the first time he had seen Joce sitting in the corner of Starbuck's jabbing at air. One girl against the world. He had immediately liked her—figured she was feisty. At least he got that right.

You must be fifty shades of stupid, pal. He raised his head and beat his thighs with his fists. Go ahead and hurt yourself, asshole. That's nothing compared to the hurt Jocelyn has felt. All the crap he gave Joce about her aunt—was she strong enough to handle a woman with alters, all those statements slapped him in the face. He had to go back inside, come up with an expression that didn't look like he was shocked or pissed or whatever he was. He had to come up with the right words.

He stood up and walked a few steps forward into the sunlight. A drip of water hit him on top of his head. He looked upward but didn't move. "Yeah, I know. Too stupid to be walking by myself."

Once he was inside the apartment, he stopped two feet into the kitchen. Cole and Paula were sitting at the table, quietly talking. They both looked up at him.

"Where is she?"

Cole pointed just as Paula said, "In the bedroom." She sniffled. "She's waiting for you."

Cole was more direct. "Don't fuck it up, buddy."

She was sitting on the edge of her bed leafing through a magazine Alex knew she wasn't reading. She looked like hell, breakable, like her skin was parchment and if he grabbed her, it would crack and splinter. Scars stood out on her arms, old ones. He had always wanted to ask about them, but couldn't. Now he didn't need to ask.

"Joce?"

"Stumme." Her voice betrayed nothing. She set the magazine aside, placed each hand on the side of the bed next to her thighs. Alex walked over as if he were stepping on glass and kneeled in front of her. He put his head in her lap, left his arms at his side. He didn't deserve to touch her, at least with his arms.

"I didn't know. I should have known. I didn't know." His voice held his grief.

Jocelyn stroked his head. "Alex, *I* didn't know. How could you?"

Alex raised his head, watched her, his face white. What could a man do at a time like this? He sat behind her, wrapped his arms around her and rocked with her rhythm in absolute silence, the warmth of his body a blanket for the weeping child. When she had cried herself dry and lay down, consumed by the keening, he covered her with a blanket and stepped out of the room.

How could he fix this? He clenched his fists, walked to the kitchen, grabbed his coat, and walked out the door.

Jocelyn's childhood had been like one of those kid's puzzles where elephants hid in trees and grasshoppers grew out of the fireman's helmet.

What's wrong with this picture? They knew the answers, but he was damned if he knew how to budge that elephant from the tree.

CHAPTER 47

From the journal of Paula Ross.

*H*ere I sit in my apartment, the place of my refuge, processing what has happened. This is a history that must be logged. I need to record to understand. She needs me to record—her words, her actions—in order to recover.

We've pulled the Band-Aid off, Jocelyn and I. Too bad it's made the victim hemorrhage instead of scar. Of course, that does not surprise me. I have bled as well. What is crucial is where we go from here. Where Jocelyn chooses to go.

Saturday night, the night she remembered, her anger spilled in waves as she stormed back and forth in the living room. "Petulant!" The word came out as a growl. "My mother called me petulant. Poor little girl all moody and pouting, hiding in the corner. Hell yes, I was petulant. Some dirtball rams his hand up your crotch when you're five, you'd be petulant, too!" By now, her voice was a feral scream.

I had to sit there, calm, in the shade of her unleashing. I watched her, the glint in her eyes as she searched the room. She grabbed her purse and sat down on the floor, pulled everything out of it and heaved the contents around the room—keys, pens, wallet, wadded Kleenex, bits of detritus I couldn't recognize—weapons of her mass destruction.

Poor child. I remember my own pain so well those times I exploded. Wave your arms and lash out. Stomp your feet and grind them into the floor. Howl at the moon in your visceral rage, anything to release the storm within. I watched her, bent over, beating her fists at her head, snarling.

Then she lifted her head. I watched her watching me. When she spoke, the words shot out. "So what do you think, Aunt Paula? Do I get to paint a picture now? Can I join the fucked up artist club?"

My own pain, the pain of not being able to hold her, to not be able to make this all better. Me, the therapist. What a laugh.

"You're angry. Of course you're angry," I told her. "And you need to feel the anger intimately, turn the anger into, if not a friend, at least an ally. If you let the anger own you, it will eat you up.

"Now you know why I paint. I direct that anger onto the canvas and let it fill the space. If you want to paint, fine. Paint. Draw. Take up archery. It all comes down to you being in charge."

We talked and cried and talked some more.

And then, bless her, my bright, beautiful niece announced, "I think I need to do some cleaning before I find my muse. *She got up onto her knees, picked up the chaos she had made, and proceeded to clean her purse. Useable items ever so neatly repackaged. Garbage collected in her hands. When she walked toward the kitchen to throw away the refuse, Jocelyn the cynic was back.*

"We have a lot to do to get ready for tomorrow. Can't have the place a mess. Even if the hostess is a mess herself."

So like her. Internalize. The walls were up.

Tread carefully, child. Take it in, but not all of it in. You are beginning to know the story of you a long time ago. *What is the story of you still to be told has not yet been written.*

Take those walls down. Slowly as you must. But take them down. If they fall on their own, they will crush you.

I could only shake my head and say a prayer.

I think it was Alex who turned the corner for her. I don't know what went on in her room on Sunday. Both of them walked out, faces blotched, his eyes reddened, hers hollow. We cleaned up the kitchen while Jocelyn watched television—Sunday morning Reality Parade—as if she gives a flying fig about Chicago housing. When the boys left, she was sound asleep on the sofa.

Fool that I am, I dropped a cup, shattering it. She sprang up, Medusa-haired, eyes darting. "No!" *she screamed.*

Then I could hold her. I had to. We talked. That is, once I comforted her, assuring her safety, no monsters in the fog.

"I hate the sound of crashing. It makes my stomach curl into knots."

"Tell me about the crashing."

Her words explained the trigger. "Glasses on the floor. Bodies against the walls. Laughter with the crashes."

She shuddered in the memory, fighting it. "Tell me about the crashes, sweetheart."

"He crashes down by my bed. His knees thud on the floor. He calls me 'Baby.'"

She beat against me with her fists. I grabbed them, soothed them with my hands. "Shhh. You're safe."

"I hate it when he calls me 'Baby.'"

I held her and let her cry out her pain.

Later, we sat at the table with me, paper and pen in hand, doodling. "Maybe I will do that painting." For her, that was a joke. She had come far.

As she sketched circle and boxes, question marks—nothing of any form and yet saying so much, I watched her pull up fragments, and then calm herself as she examined them in perspective. Here was this woman—child really— who had every reason to be writhing in her new-found knowledge, drawing and talking calmly.

"The truth is so cold. I thought it would be hot. It's not. It creeps in like cold metal. How strange. Tick Tock. Evie said that in my dreams. At least I thought it was Evie." She wrote the words down and circled them. "It wasn't my mother. It was me."

She kept her focus on that page, circling the words over and over until she had framed them. She smiled. "I knew it was time to remember. And that's okay."

She put down the pen and hugged me. Hugged me! "How else can I stand up straight in this world and belong if I don't know the truth? Face it? I really will *be fine."*

I patted her, this niece I love. If only I could show her that the road back on her journey has only begun.

But the truth, it is a good beginning.

CHAPTER 48

"I don't understand. I know what happened. I faced it. It's over."
Jocelyn was sitting at the bar at Luna's on Tuesday morning, her posture upright, arms folded, back military straight, ready for the face-off. "I mean, how *healed* do I have to be?" Good Lord, what do they want me to do—wear a tee-shirt that advertises *I was molested*.

Cole answered her. "The fact that you say 'healed' like it's a joke instead of a goal pretty much answers your question."

And thank you, Mr. Psych Guy. Want to open my head and paw around?

"Cole's right." Paula shot him a look. "Even if he's a bit abrupt. You have managed to come out of this ordeal like a trooper. You deserve to be proud."

Jocelyn looked at Cole, her nose raised just a bit, her mouth a smirk. *Take that*, it said. *I don't need no stinkin' tee-shirt.*

"But . . . " Paula continued, "and this is a very important *but;* there is a big difference between surviving and thriving. We are proud that you have survived. Remembering without total collapse is a battle well won." Jocelyn had lost her smirk. She knew Paula, owed so much to the woman, trusted her, and looked to her as mentor. If there were a fairy-mother in this story, Paula was it. Still, Jocelyn remembered. She cried. She was done. Wasn't she?

"You have ripped off the scab on a terrible wound, made that wound bleed and staunched the flow." Paula's words were filled with pride.

"That's what I'm trying to tell you. I won." Jocelyn's words tried for finality. "I'm sitting here, whole." She dipped her head forward and patted the top of her head. "Look inside. Not a wall in place. I am a freakin' open book."

Paula laughed and placed her hands on each side of Jocelyn's face, gave the top of her head a kiss, and pulled it up to look her straight in the eye. "Yes, you won. But the war, my dear, is hardly over."

As Jocelyn backed away a few inches, her eyes fixed on that face, so much like her own. She thought back to the first time she had seen her aunt, that day at the visitation. Paula's face had been so familiar on such an unexpected stranger. Only months ago, Jocelyn had first seen that face. And yet, the two of them, aunt and niece, had lived a lifetime in their days together.

Paula said that Jocelyn was only beginning to come to terms with her past life. How could that be? She didn't need to have every minute detail. She knew the truth. She understood—no—she forgave herself, even dismissed the notion for why she hadn't cried for her mother. The woman deserved no tears. What better sentencing for neglect than a daughter who shed no tears at her funeral?

The past was that, the past. This was now. She laughed at herself for her "first day of the rest of your life" thinking. How corny.

Jocelyn knew that Cole and Paula were wrong. She was healed. She was whole. No more barriers. No more solitude. *Thriving*, her aunt had said. Isn't that what she could look forward to; was even beginning to do right now? How could she not thrive with the family she had now?

She bent forward, kissed her aunt's cheek, turned to Cole for a high five.

"Hey, it's Tuesday. No work and plenty of goodies in the kitchen." As she hopped off the bar stool and headed back toward the kitchen, she celebrated her freedom. No limits for this chick. Her hip swayed and she stepped into a dance step to notes only in her own mind. Chocolate in the kitchen. Tragedy faced and exquisite times ahead. What more could a girl want?

Jocelyn woke up at 2:00 am, shaking. In her dream, she had been sitting on the floor of the last apartment she had shared with her mother. Evie was drinking and chanting, "This little piggy went to market . . . " Jocelyn was in her nightgown on the floor, legs akimbo, right hand holding a knife. "On every one of her mother's "This little piggy," Jocelyn sliced along her thighs; at the end of the cut, she dug a little deeper with the tip and then flipped the tip upward. Evie clapped. "That's a good girl."

Out of the haze in the dream scene, a train whistle blew and a porter appeared out of nowhere. He carried a large suitcase, scarred and decrepit, set it down next to her. "I say, miss, can you put down your knife for just a moment, please? You've forgotten your baggage."

Evie turned surly. "Thank the man, daughter. You are such a careless child, forgetting all that you own. You'd forget your own head if I didn't thump you once in a while. You'll need to take that baggage with you on your trip. Now where were we? Oh yes, and this little piggy was a bad little piggy. Tell me, Jocelyn, are you a bad little piggy?"

Jocelyn threw back the covers and sped out of bed. Her heart was palpitating, her chest covered in sweat. She trounced out of her room, flipped on the hallway light, and stalked back and forth, fists clenching and unclenching like a prisoner pacing in her cell, confined to a small space but adamant to walk out her angst.

"You will not rule me. You will not rule me." The words became a litany as she stomped her way through the small hours of the night until, exhausted, she collapsed onto her sofa, arms tight around her knees, and stared into the night. Only when the first light of morning—that world of grayness that says the sun is coming eventually—slowly curled its way from underneath the darkness, only then did she snatch some sleep.

CHAPTER 49

The next two days dragged along, classes and work both juggernauts for a working student robbed of rest. She didn't dream, at least not really. Pieces of dreams floated in her head, flakes of images from her childhood that she knew—at least now—falling through her unconsciousness looking for a framework but finding none. Jocelyn tossed throughout the night, never waking, but never finding quiet sleep.

Tonight her shift was over at 9:00. She'd be back in her apartment before 11:00 easily, have some time to read a couple of chapters for her morning class before she fell into bed once again.

And then what? More memory fragments? More textures of what was utterly devoid of context? She slipped into Luna's kitchen, unloaded the hodgepodge from her tray, and sneaked into a corner. Crouching down flat-footed like a frog, she grabbed onto the now empty tray and held it against her chest like a shield. One of the guys prepping stole a glance at her, then turned his head and went back to chopping veggies. The din of kitchen work made her pull into herself even more.

Five minutes. Just give me five minutes to take a break. The tiled floor was hard under her feet, but the two walls held her back as she leaned into where they joined. Even in the racket of the kitchen, she felt herself drifting off.

If I can close my eyes for a second—just a second, I'll be fine.

"You know, I've fired people for less."

Jocelyn started, then fell onto her butt, tray still shielding her. Paula stood above her, hands on her hips, a scowl on her face.

"You got me." Jocelyn struggled to her feet, rubbing her backside. "But before you can my sorry ass, at least let me sit down for a few minutes."

"Of course you can sit down. What do you think I am?" Paula's words came out in a snit. "All my workers take breaks. That means you, too."

The boss was on a roll. No teacher had ever reprimanded her mischief-maker student more solidly than Paula did now. She had all but spit the words out.

Jocelyn tried a little humor to calm the moment. "You know, Aunt Paula, you would have made a hell of a nun. All you need is a wooden ruler for my knuckles."

The joke fell flat. If Paula had pursed her mouth any tighter, she would have eaten her lips. "I'll give you knuckles all right." She pointed to her left. "My office. Now."

Paula sat in her office chair, rocking and silent. Jocelyn sat across from her desk, taking in the objects—piles of papers, a calculator big enough to be called *Vintage,* lap top, hand-crafted cups holding office desk paraphernalia. Her eyes focused on one in particular, a broken glass mosaic in swirls and circles embedded in gesso.

"Sonia made that for me. I like it." Her voice was still a snap. "Look at me."

"I'm sorry I took an extra break. It's not that we're so busy right now; we won't be for another hour or so." Even as she sounded explanation into her voice, Jocelyn couldn't grasp how she should react. What expression should she have in her tone for this situation?

Paula waved her hand in dismissal. "I don't care about a break. If we've eased up and you need to sit down, do it. But don't go hiding in the kitchen corner." She slapped the desk. "And don't go hiding from me."

Jocelyn sunk back into her chair while Paula leaned forward. "We have been through trauma together this past weekend that most people cannot begin to imagine. Have you any idea what it's like to watch you—knowing what I know—see you withering and drawn and not be able to fathom where you're at right now?"

She wasn't being fired? Relief rushed through her right before a sense of guilt took over. She saw Paula in her mind last weekend, walking her through her breakdown, picking through its craziness and comforting her only when it was safe to do so, not for Paula, but for Jocelyn.

Instead of trusting her with the aftermath of these past days, she had slipped into her old pattern of hiding. What was she thinking? Hadn't Paula earned her trust?

"I watch you dragging, bags under your eyes—again—like you had after that Doug creature. Do you think I don't know what you're feeling? What you're fearing? Do you not know how the same hollowness, the same madness filled me? My Lord, if it weren't for Joe, sometimes . . ."

By now the two women were both crying.

"Jocelyn!" Paula slapped the desk again, this time with both hands even as the tears choked her. The room snapped with the sound of the slap. "I would have killed myself! I longed for death and needed its relief. I watched you leave last night, wondered if you'd crash—suicide by car is so inviting to those in pain. If I lost you . . ."

Jocelyn raised her head and hollered through her own tears, "I'd never kill myself, never, never, never!" Her eyes blurred. She could barely speak. "I'm so sorry I scared you. I didn't know. I didn't think . . ."

"Of course you didn't know. How could you? That's what normal families do. You've never known caring, never known consistent love from family. You've never had a decent normal relationship with someone of your own blood. Of course you didn't know."

Words of guilt trickled through Jocelyn. *You've been saying "I didn't know" a lot lately.*

Paula stood up and came around her desk, knelt down in front of Jocelyn and put her hands on her thighs and looked upward. "I told you the goal is not surviving; it's thriving." She shook her head. "Sweetie, you're barely surviving."

Jocelyn thrust her head back, closed her eyes. She thrust them open. Damn flashbacks assaulted her even in her aunt's office. She glanced over her aunt's head and stared at the desk. Cool pen in the mosaic cup. It had tiny springs on the end encased in plastic. Springs. Itty bitty ones. Imagine that.

She could talk to Paula. Really. She just had to make up her mind to do it. She took a deep breath but still kept her eyes on those springs.

"Of course I'm tired. I can't sleep . . . or when I do catch a break, I dream. That's the worst. What does it matter? This truth I'm so fortunate to now know, it's all I can think about. I haven't even talked to Alex since Sunday. He opened his heart to me, and I can't talk to him."

Paula stood up and sat on the edge of the desk. "Look at me."

Jocelyn obeyed, reluctantly. Watching springs had no repercussions.

"Remember me, Charlie's host?" Jocelyn shuddered at the thought but kept her mind open. She had to. "We've ripped off the Band-Aid here. And the blood is covering everything."

Paula stopped, clasped her hands, rocked as she sat on the desk. "After I met Charlie, every child I saw was a victim of sexual abuse. Who had clutched that little one and made her scream within? Who had penetrated him and made him scream aloud? I stumbled about, not eating, my whole body feeling like road kill."

Jocelyn listened and watched in horror. Yes, she was exhausted. Yes, she was troubled. But seeing abuse all around her? Then she thought of a little girl walking with some man she had seen on her way to work, how she'd gripped the steering wheel and shuddered at the thought of what that man could do to innocence.

"There's no going back, niece. No going back, not even forward. Just through."

Two days ago Jocelyn had laughed at Paula and Cole for berating her. She had dealt with it. Now forty-eight hours had slapped her in the face. *Through* made her shake.

CHAPTER 50

W hen all was said, Jocelyn went back to work, a robot. Paula told her, "You can take more than a break upstairs. Elsa begged for a double shift even though I didn't need her, and I gave it to her. Go. Rest."

As if. Resting wasn't an option, not after the gut wrenching of their conversation. Jocelyn steeled herself, put aside her—I am-here-but-if-you-knew-what's-been happening-you'd-run-for-cover persona and went back to work. Luckily, the place was busy. She might look like hell; she'd cleaned up as much as possible, rubbed some concealer under her eyes, but she knew the term *rode hard*, to coin a phrase, still showed. So she worked up a happy mood, let out her usual sarcasm with the regulars, and gathered in hefty tips

Before she left for home, Cole and Paula pulled her aside. Cole did the talking while Paula nodded in emphasis. "Tonight's been hard on you, and we know it's too late in the evening to accomplish anything. But we . . . " Cole hugged Paula as he continued, " . . . we want you to do something as soon as you're able. You may even have to do it tonight if you want to get any sleep."

Jocelyn looked at the two of them, hesitation creeping over her face. What did they want? A blood sacrifice? She could always grab a chicken on the way home, but did mojo work on frozen chicken?

Paula grabbed Jocelyn's hands. "We want you to write a letter to your mother. Tell her what you've discovered, how you feel, what you want her to know."

Jocelyn tried to break away, step back. Paula held firm. "Darling, you must confront your abusers. You don't know the men—except for that last one, that Frank person who's been in jail, but you haven't heard from him. So the men are out." Contempt smeared Paula's face. "And yes, your mother is dead." Paula grabbed Jocelyn's fingers, the rabid contempt replaced by a gentle pleading. "Write to her. As many pages as you need. Write from your heart, from your pain. Let that sister of mine know what she has done to you."

Jocelyn stood there, nodded her head *yes* in promise, even as her body shook in alarm. The collar of her coat scratched against her neck. She felt hot standing there with the two. "I will." The words came out in a whisper. She turned and made way for the door, one step in front of the other, and was able to turn the handle on the door and make it out into the night. Her aunt's voice trailed behind her. "Call me when you get home."

Traffic chaos echoed from the main avenue two blocks over. She had a long ride home.

She'd make it. She knew she would. She had studying to do and a letter to write, an army of words, some to make her wise, others to use as weapons against a woman who would no longer claim her.

"Love you, too." Jocelyn hung up the phone, changed her clothes, and spread out her studying materials on the kitchen table. Time to be a student, craziness or not. Finally, shortly after midnight, she looked at her closed textbook. Funny how an agenda could kick you in the face. She had read the chapters, outlined key ideas in the margins, annotated the heck out of the thing. She didn't have a clue what she had read. She was a junior in college, knew all the ropes, had the chance at one hell of an internship next year right here in Chicago; all the steps of a good little student lay behind her in a row—and she might as well be in some foreign country wondering how to even say *hello*.

She lay her head down onto the closed book, as if osmosis would give her a jump start, and closed her eyes. This was ridiculous. She'd never have a moment's peace; probably flunk out of school if she didn't get a handle on her warped psyche. She rose, crossed the kitchen and rummaged through the junk drawer for pen and paper.

How dense she had been, thinking she could study first and then write. Evie was hovering over her in a vaporous pall. Nothing could come in while her mother took up all the room in Jocelyn's mind. She'd write a letter to her mother all right—now. Hopefully it wouldn't catch fire and burn.

She could write, set it aside, and then maybe she could finally get some sleep, study tomorrow early.

So it began.

Dear Mother—

The pen almost rippled across the paper spelling out the two words; by the time she was scrolling the "*r*", *she was drawing a forked tail on the end of the last letter. Dear* and *Mother.* Both words were a joke. Evie had been neither dear nor a mother. Never mind, she scolded herself. Get on with it.

She scratched out the design, replaced it with a finger stemming out of the end of the last letter. *I'm flipping her the bird,* she chortled. The thought settled her. She could touch the old Jocelyn, the smart ass, the one who wasn't out of control even as she stretched to understand her now by speaking of the before.

The conversation was within her. She only had to begin.

Not sure how to start. Forget the finger. Drawing is for fun. This is for serious. Letters usually began with some sort of connection, a sense of purpose.

"*Get back to me as to what level in hell you're inhabiting. Must be a pretty deep one.*" She pictured her mother tied up in a river of vodka, her tongue swollen with thirst, her eyes ravaged with desire for the liquid. Boyfriends danced around her, lapping up the booze and cackling, "None for you, old lady. None for you."

No, that's mean, and I want to save mean for later when I can't help myself. She stayed her hand from writing the description.

How about a confession?

I actually felt guilty about not crying at your funeral. Can you believe that? Poor stupid Jocelyn standing at that casket looking down at you, dry-eyed and guilty. I had the tissue ready, wanted to squeeze at least a couple of tears out, but nope. Zero. Nada. Dry as a bone. Such an unfeeling daughter. How could you have birthed such a child?

Hey—now I know why. Funny how the mind works. I mean, I could remember you drunk and stupid, occasionally sober and stupid, certainly needy, whatever your condition. That deserved at least a sniffle of sympathy. But it's what I couldn't remember—could not fucking fathom in fact—a

243

woman who could turn her daughter, her small child, over to men to be used as a handy wipe for their pervert gratification. It's one thing to reject your kid. Parents do that all the time. I learned to deal with your rejection. But this. Lady, you were one selfish bitch.

I remember you hounding me about sleeping with a bat. Why did I need a bat? Like you didn't know. But that was always your way. "I didn't forget your conference. They never sent home a slip." "Maybe Louie touched your butt. I don't remember. But then, you have such an imagination." "So, we got drunk and he puked outside your room. He made me drink too much. Just clean it up."

I discovered the most wondrous coping mechanism. I learned to cut. Loved it. Started out sticking safety pins in my fingers when I was little. I'd sneak them out of the sewing kit you never used. The pain took away some of the pressure. Later, I notched it up. Knives were so much better, actually downright lovely, sharply pointed and lovingly steeled. They would do. Really, I wanted to shove my fist through a window clear up to my armpits, but I settled for slits in the late night. You never even asked me why I wore long sleeves even in the summer. But then, that would have been too motherly for a woman such as yourself.

Funny, we do have one thing in common. We're both sluts. My sexual roamings are better now that I have a sense of family—like you'd even know what that is—but for years now, every time I felt out of sorts, like something was pushing up from inside me, I'd go out and get laid. Was good at it. I could turn a guy inside out and then walk away as if I had simply shaken his hand. Of course, I never fell in love. I couldn't. I grew up seeing your desperation, how you'd do anything to keep a man—and don't I know now how far that "anything" went—and I'd run. Now, I know I have to figure this all out some more. See, feelings are a shut-down no-no and I have to know why. The irony is, all this time I thought my problem was I was becoming you. Nope. My problem is ridding myself of you.

Your sister—you know, the one you never told me about—she's pretty much saved me. I live on Aunt Paula's hope, that and the hope of my friends Alex and Cole. You'd hate those guys. They like me, think I'm important, worth their time. And Paula. What a saint. The anti-Evie. She tells me you two never got along. I think I know why.

Anyway, Mommie, just want you to know that I curse you. I waited years *to see if you'd ever love me. Now I know better. You couldn't love anyone but yourself.*

Have fun in hell. You deserve it.

Jocelyn.

She put the pen down. Had she said enough? Probably not. No matter. Jocelyn stretched out the tightness in her upper shoulders and neck, stood up and headed for bed.

1:00. She turned out the bedroom light, pushed her arms up over her head and stretched out some more, turned over and fell asleep. When the alarm went off at 8:00, she slammed off the buzzer and sat up. A good night's sleep. Damn. Who would have thought?

CHAPTER 51

That good night's rest put all sorts of things in perspective. The girl in the mirror this morning had some color in her face. No dark smears under her eyes. No more saggy jaw. She might have as yet miles to go, and her woods may still be dark and deep as the poet said, but she had put in enough steps to at least not be stupid with fatigue.

Robert Frost had her nailed for sure. Miles. More dark woods. But writing had released so many of the phantom limbs Jocelyn had hauled around for so long. She itched to fill in Paula and Cole about last night. Paula for sure. The poor woman had no doubt worn out some of the wood in the floors of her apartment pacing. Jocelyn would call her before she left for class; Paula could fill in Cole.

Alex. She needed to check in with Alex. All this week, they had texted daily.

He'd write, "How are things?" She'd text back, "Hanging in there. Catch you later."

A week ago, they had held each other, he begging for understanding, she reassuring him, each of them a wretch undone by a dark truth. And now they were reduced to messages too mundane to say anything. Yes, she needed to reach out to Alex.

She grabbed her phone, brought up *messaging*, and punched in "Starbucks. 4:30?"

She called her aunt, ate breakfast, brushed her teeth, and looked over the notes she had taken hours earlier. Pretty good start to the day.

And then came the afternoon. She finished up with classes, checked in with her advisor, and put Paula and Cole to rest with a quick phone call and promise to stop in. By 4:00, Jocelyn sat herself down at Starbucks. By 4:25, she was still there, gnawing at her thumbnail, feeling the unwieldy lurch of the time gap tumbling in her body. Five minutes—if he was on time—and the security blanket of texting would be over. When had she started worrying about what to say to Alex?

When he had a meltdown in your lap, lady.

She glanced around. Starbucks was full. Big surprise on a Friday night. That made it a safe Friday night. Too many customers scurrying around with their own agenda to worry about a college girl in the front corner by the window letting her coffee go cold and her treat uneaten.

She had her head down, caught in a moment of reflection on something—she forgot what as soon as she sensed him. He had slid into the booth across from her.

"Hey," Alex said.

"Hey, back at you."

Such a change in the universe around her, within her. He was her Alex. He was here. Just his presence was comforting. She took it in like a gift. Was this a permanence in her impermanent life? Could she truly, truly count on that presence? He'd always been there for her before, but this—this sewage she called her life—but could he continue to handle it?

He's here, dumbass.

She watched him sitting there, his face so openly hopeful, scared, doubtful all at once; she clutched to the hope in her chest, that tiny bud that was now replacing all the worry she had let into the booth with her. Here she was, Jocelyn, sitting across from her best friend, the only guy her age she could call friend since Cole was older and others guys came and went without a thought—too self-absorbed, too swaggering, too clinging to their techie toys. Alex had proved himself so many times, and being here, he proved himself once again.

That hope inside her warmed at the possibilities. In the deepest recesses of her, worry still snipped—*don't forget, for you, hope is such a fickle wench, turning on you without a moment's notice.* She walled it away. She was with Alex.

"Thanks for coming," she said.

"You knew I would. Didn't you?"

Jocelyn cracked a half-smile. "I'm not much of an expert on knowing much of anything right now—at least about other people."

"I get that." He sighed. "That's why I'm so pissed at myself."

Jocelyn leaned in, that smirk gone, eyes widening by the declaration. "Why in the hell would you be angry with yourself? You didn't do anything."

Alex ran a hand through his hair. "That's the point. I didn't do anything." He looked up. "I mean it. You shared with me. You've been sharing with me all along—at least once you let me know your mom had died, but this—this crap was so from your gut. That means you trusted me."

His voice cracked. "I was such a dick. And when you said, 'I didn't even know'—when you swept away my shame and my ignorance with those four words, my heart sank with this heavy sort of joy. I didn't deserve those words, but you gave them anyway. I didn't know what to say. I still don't."

All the worrying about him, and now she had stepped into the story of a humbled Alex. The man vexed her—in a loving sort of way.

"Stumme, you blockhead. I could never have come this far without you." She stood up. "And I don't have any intention of keeping on this path I've carved out alone. Think about it." She pressed her index finger against the booth table. "I'm going to get you some coffee—hot coffee so I can use yours to warm up mine—and if you're lucky, a cookie. Then we're going to hug and make up." She grabbed her purse and walked away.

So Alex watched her standing in line, one heel tapping out whatever emotions were riding her at this moment; he calmed the quivering inside himself, thanked the universe for the grace he had just been given, and waited for that cookie.

While Alex and Jocelyn noshed on sugar and reconnection, Paula shared a wine with Sonia at Luna's. Her crafting friend had come to visit Paula, her bags of goodies in hand. Or at least two bags. Pretty scanty haul, but no surprise, Paula thought, what with the holidays and all. And yet, odd. Sonia always came in on Saturday morning. Why the rush for a Friday night?

Oh well. None of her business. Besides, Jocelyn and Alex were stopping in after a movie. If Paula needed to fret, she could always fret about her niece. Or perhaps not. Jocelyn's phone call had been beyond expectation. A sense of tenderness swelled in her belly at the progress Jocelyn was making, pushing against the worry that lay there daily, but the warmth was too new to set aside months of worry.

Enough. Sonia was here. The two of them would sit in a booth and have a drink; Paula would select the beautiful. Put away something special for herself. Wait for her niece. Not a bad night—except for the fretting about Jocelyn. But that would take care of itself in a few hours after—what had Jocelyn said they were seeing? *Zombie Love*. Things couldn't be too bad if they chose to immerse themselves in gore, especially gore with a love interest.

So Paula set aside the concern, clicked wine glasses with her old friend and said, "Now my lovely Sonia, what do we have here?"

CHAPTER 52

From the journal of Paula Ross

*S*onia Cooper stopped by last night. Said she needed to get out, wanted to show me her latest collection. Can I believe her? The waxy grayness in her face. Those blotches. A few new wrinkles in what—six weeks?

Who am I to comment on wrinkles? They're part of nature, part of the journey. War wounds of a sort. But what war would be carving at her now?

Sonia and I share a fear of the dark. And we share its cause. We laughed about it in group. What do you say to a kid who's afraid of the dark? "Come out of the closet. It's dark in there."

But I carry that fear in the lowest bowels of my gut. The fear is etched on me like primitive cave paintings, unseen and lying dormant for so long.

Imagine, a grown woman needing night lights.

In the closet, a child learns fear. Perhaps I spilled my milk. Perhaps I looked at Mother wrong. Who knew? I always suspected she tossed me in there just so she didn't have to look at me.

Couldn't she have sent me outside to play? No. That would have meant pleasure.

The first thing to do is check out the territory. Acclimate yourself. The lightbulb in the wall socket. You dare not turn it on. She'll see the light, and sitting on that floor with fresh welts on your bottom only adds to the misery. But study it before she shuts the door. Imagine that it can turn on if only you could make Mother happy.

The coats hanging above you. Soon, in the dark, you'll feel them reaching down to grab them. That will be your imagination. Coats cannot be monsters. Only people are monsters. In the dark, in your mind's eye, picture those coats hanging there waiting for someone who needs them.

Take it all in. Memorize it. See it in your mind while you huddle for hours alone with the coats and the dust bunnies.

The door shuts. Strange just how dark a closet can be. No light sneaking in. Mother even added rubber stripping to the bottom of the door. Can't give a naughty child the hope of light coming through.

The minutes go by. Or are they hours? You trace the key hole of the lock with your fingers; they are a connection to the light, your only one. Eventually you chew on your nails. Mother lets enough time go by between punishments. Is this on purpose so she can chastise a child with gnawed stubs? Soon you'll taste blood. Or if that doesn't work, you can always bite your tongue. The blood lets you know you're alive. Are you sure you want to be?

The music for Mother's first soap opera of the day breaks the silence. Noon time. Your stomach growls. Pavlov's dog. A learned response practiced over and over.

No lunch for you. But now you have a sound from your body and the memory of that taste of blood.

Time crawls on. You begin to cry. You don't want to. Crying is for babies and you're what—five, seven? Too old to cry. You cry, bent over like a rag doll, until the hiccups mix with your sobs. Your stomach hurts. Your back hurts and your shoulders. You are a mass of sobbing pain huddled there in the dark. And then, the biggest humiliation. You wet your pants. Right there on Granma's rag rug. You had followed the pattern of the weaving with your fingers while you sat there. Now the stink of your urine mixes with the smell of old wool.

Stupid, stupid girl. How could you have been so stupid?

A key clicks in the lock and the door opens. You squint against the light, sitting there in your shame, look up at the giant staring down, her face stern and disproving.

"What am I going to do with a child who has no control?" She spits it out as she shakes her head. "You know what this means."

And you do.

Yes, Sonia and I know of dark places. Seeing her reminds me that we are both survivors. Seeing her makes my body numb even as I celebrate surviving.

I should be writing about Jocelyn and her progress. Alex and Jocelyn were all laughter and moaning last night. Much must be well. But even as I celebrated the children's gaiety, something about Sonia had grabbed at me, pulled me back to what we share.

I'll give her a call. It's the least I can do for an old friend.

251

CHAPTER 53

O utside, mid-morning sleet suddenly pummeled the windows. When had that started? Jocelyn had stayed overnight at Paula's apartment. Last night, a couple too many "Zombie Love" cocktails, created especially in honor of the evening's movie, had sent her upstairs singing and bashing into the walls as she pulled herself upward.

Nothing like acting out a scene from your childhood to make the night.

But that was last night. The gods had, no doubt, sent the banging rain to punish her for her indulgence as soon as she woke up, but a few Tylenol and some black coffee cleared her head.

Take that, mischief-making gods. I am safe and secure and ready to talk.

By 11:00 inside Paula's apartment, the two bodies in the living room sat across from each other on the sofa, a rite of healing flowing between them.

Jocelyn shook her head, voice hoarse with emotion. "Last night was great between Alex and me, as if we were on vacation from all the crap that's been happening; we put it away and just had fun. I mean, it was pretty tense at Starbuck's for a while, but then bang, I was done with lashing out and falling apart. I had my Alex back. We were good."

Paula took a sip of coffee before she talked. "I'm so happy for you, sweetheart." Her face did not match her words. What's up with Paula? No mind. Humor her.

"It's like you always tell me—be present in my life." Jocelyn chuckled. "Look at me, taking advice. That's a step in itself." She reached over and took a croissant from the plate on the coffee table and took a big bite. It was a reward for having conquered the monster within. Flaky crust. Sugar. Self-satisfaction. What a trio.

"Do you think you're ready for therapy?"

Therapy? What therapy? Jocelyn jolted. She'd remembered the exploitation, confronted it, written the letter, made up with Alex. What was left? Her inner child gave a bit of a cough. Funny how now that adult Jocelyn had taken down her walls—a least with Paula—she heard from that munchkin daily, not like one of Paula's alters, just a part of her that had been ignored for too long and needed attention. Adult Jocelyn ignored that part of her. Paula had just pulled the rug and Jocelyn had enough to send her sprawling.

"I don't get it," Jocelyn cried. "Therapy is for clients who don't understand their issues. I understand mine just fine."

Paula looked at her, mouth set, and shook her head.

"I'm fine. Really. You and Cole and Alex have been so supportive. I've kicked down my walls, vented, did all the things shrinks want you to pay for. I mean, I get healing and a family. What more could a girl need?"

"Forgiveness."

Jocelyn felt a flash of insurrection against her aunt. All the warm fuzzies from their previous moments died in the air. "Are you out of your mind? I have to forgive them—those thugs who stole my life?"

"No, dear. You have to learn to forgive yourself." Paula's face, so immediately guarded for the seconds before, now opened up.

In her mind, Jocelyn circled back over all that she and her aunt had said about the storm of betrayal that had been her mother. And those men. She was supposed to let them off the hook for what they had done? She looked at her aunt's face, so calm and detached right now. She wanted to slap it.

"Me? Are you nuts? I'm the victim!" She bolted up. Hands on her hips, she screamed at her aunt, "Hell will freeze over with those assholes in it before I engage in anything that remotely resembles forgiveness!" She walked toward the nearest wall, slapped it so hard the two pictures hanging there came unbalanced. How appropriate.

Yet, in her anger, Jocelyn felt a twitch of shame, as if her abused self were looking at the outer Jocelyn with deep remorse, blushing. How many times had she come back home after a night of trolling and drawn into a fetal position, assured once again that she was nothing but worthless?

How many times had she sliced her skin so the blood could sluice down her shameful thighs?

Jocelyn leaned against the apartment wall, shaken.

Paula stood and came over to her, took Jocelyn's hands, now limp.

Paula squeezed those hands. "You're partly right. You have come an amazingly long way. And we're all glad to have helped. Look at you—you've done the work and you should be proud. The first part is the worst—when you slice open the numbness and see the infection, slice it open and let the pus ooze out. And you've conquered that."

Jocelyn's eyes were closed, but she nodded. Her mind could only focus on the word "therapy." She'd have to sit in someone's office, spill out her guts, her secrets to someone who would take notes and ask "And how do you feel about . . . whatever?"

The phone rang. Jocelyn started. Paula uttered a word she hardly ever used. Neither moved. After six rings, the apartment was once again silent.

Paula led Jocelyn back to the sofa. When they sat down, the aunt once again took her niece's hands.

"I wish I could help you through this. I know what you're facing; as much, I know I can't lead you through the work you must do. I'm too emotionally invested. Neither can Cole. You need a professional."

Jocelyn closed her eyes again. The stinging behind them insisted. She squeezed them and again shook her head, this time the movement no more than a weak back and forth whisper of a nod.

Paula's voice took on a teacher tone. "Open those eyes right now young lady and look at me."

Jocelyn 's throat constricted as a sense of clarity arose in her. *The woman loves you. The woman loves you. Listen to her.* She obeyed the command and even managed a wisp of a smile.

"The hurt. It's in your cells. You can't change biology, sweetheart. But anger is different. You can let the anger go. You've got it sewn up in a bag like a snarling cat. You're going to have to let the cat out of the bag, sweetie —and believe me, the old adage is truer than you can now understand."

"It will take years," Paula insisted. "Not all at once. You'll be doing your 'going through' perfectly well, and then the healing slips a notch. But the next time is not as foreboding—more of a tune-up. That's the thing with 'through.'"

Jocelyn was gapping with shock. "I could never have done this without you—you and Cole. You've guided me. What can a professional do that you can't?" It wasn't a question; it was a protest.

"Be professional."

"C'mon." Jocelyn didn't know if she was chastising or begging. Maybe a bit of both.

"You're scared. I was scared, too. You've not only been abused; you're the child of an alcoholic. That means chaos. You remember the chaos of your life. You fight it. And that's uncomfortable. So you bring chaos into your healing life just to feel the comfort."

"That's nuts."

"My point exactly." Paula sighed. "Honey, I would love to be your counselor. I've watched the signs of your collapse and first steps. They're my signs, too."

Jocelyn looked at her aunt, her eyes blurred, yet thankful. She had no words.

Paula kept on. "But just because we share some of the same abuse doesn't mean that I can counsel you. I will be here while you heal, but I can't guide you through your pain. It just won't work."

Paula pulled Jocelyn up, led her to her coat and purse, picked them up and looked at her niece. "Go home. Think about it. Do some writing. Amazing how writing can offer clarity and a healing of itself. Trust me. I know. Sleep on this. Sleep on it for more than twenty-four hours. When you're ready to talk some more, I'm here."

Jocelyn slowly put on her coat and put her purse strap over her shoulder, then stood there, her own zombie in non-action.

Paula hugged her. "You know I'm here no matter what. I love you. And loving you means telling the truth, no matter how it hurts. You've had too many broken promises and lies. I will never do that to you."

She gave her niece a kiss on the forehead and turned her around. "Go home. Do your work." With a pat on Jocelyn's rear end, she said, "There. I'm your therapist of the moment. And I bet you feel dismayed."

Jocelyn left the apartment, stumbled down the stairs, and left Luna's. She wasn't sure how she felt. No matter the options, comfortable of mind was not an option. She knew her aunt was right. She just didn't know how to process that truth of it.

Paula lay on her sofa inside the apartment. She checked her fingernails. Better get a manicure. Two nails were chipped, and a cuticle had torn. She looked at the window. The sleet had stopped. That was good. She'd make an appointment for her nails on Monday.

Wonder who had called her earlier? She'd have to check on that as well.

Jocelyn had left. Her niece was, no doubt, sitting in her apartment, cursing her life. For Paula, there, alone in her apartment, the whole of these last few hours came down to nails and phone calls. Nothing else she could do. Tears that had insisted their way upward into her consciousness finally took over and she cried. For a long time. Then she rolled over on her side, covered herself with the throw from the back of the sofa and fell asleep. Thankfully, no dreams interrupted her rest.

She woke up groggy and looked at her watch. 4:30. Goodness. No wonder her body was numb. In the kitchen, she checked her phone messages. Only one—from Sonia. A clutch of apprehension momentarily held her hand away from the phone, but she managed to push *play*. The same apprehension stayed but moved above her, hovering, like a ghost from a past long ago and suddenly remembered.

"Paula." Right away she heard the desolation in Sonia's voice. She had been there, in that dark place, herself too many times. "I need to talk to you. Can you give me a call? Right away?"

There was a pause in the message, laced with what sounded like a choked-off sob.

"And Paula, dear friend, I want to thank you for the friend you have been." Another pause. "You've always done the best you could."

Oh dear Lord, no. This wasn't a thank you; it was a goodbye and it terrified her. She rushed out, grabbed her coat and purse, checked twice for keys, and hurried herself down the stairs and toward the front door of Luna's.

Cole's voice called out from behind the bar, "Hey, boss lady . . . "

"Not now!" Paula waved his call away with a slap of her hand as she yanked open the door and ran out into what was left of the Chicago daylight.

For the first four stoplights, Paula told herself that she was overreacting, that Sonia sometimes was down—just like all abuse survivors—and needed to talk out her angst. But as she sped toward the Avondale neighborhood, her hands gripped the steering wheel and she felt the pressure building right above her eyes. They had cried, these two women, held each other when the remembering leaped onto their backs out of nowhere and threatened to choke. They had laughed, a healing laughter impossible for those outside their story to understand, an indulgence in intimacy between sisters of a sort. And good heavens, they had talked themselves hoarse during those times when they just needed to unload.

Three years ago, Sonia had given Paula a necklace with tiny puzzle pieces on it. "I'm a puzzle that has been scattered all over the floor. People look at me with misgiving. They want to help, but nobody can ever do the straight-edged border pieces. You help put me back together."

Where the hell had she put that necklace?

When she turned the corner onto Talman Avenue, she almost ran her car into the curb. An ambulance was sitting in front of Sonia's house, lights still blaring red and blue. She looked out at the scene and felt her world crash. Two EMTs were carrying a stretcher down the front stairs toward the vehicle.

"Sonia!" Paula cried. "Sonia." Her grip tightened on the steering wheel and then she clambered out of the car and raced toward the back of the ambulance.

"Ma'am, I'm going to have to ask you to move your car." She was halfway to seeing what terrified her, and some young kid in uniform was pointing at her and talking about her car.

"That's my friend! I came to see my friend! She called me. I have to talk to her." As she ran forward, Paula shrieked to an uncaring sky and then fell to her knees, sobbing into her hands in front of the EMT who had ordered her to make way.

She felt a hand on her shoulder. He was squatting down, his face so near hers, his voice suddenly gentle. "I'm sorry, ma'am. We were too late."

"We." The man had said, "We." What did he know? Her nails scraped at her face. Wasn't that what people did in this kind of situation?

Inflict pain in such a time of pain?

Paula turned her head. The two men she had seen on the front steps had put the stretcher into the ambulance, and now stood, each one in front of a metal door as if a royal guard. Sonia's body lay inside an impersonal body bag. The EMT nearby helped Paula stand up. She edged her way toward the open metal doors of the vehicle, held her hand toward that long stretch of plastic on the stretcher. She neared it, made it almost there—no more than a foot separated her from her friend—and she stopped.

She turned to one of the men. "How?"

"A knife. Her wrists. Vertical cuts. She meant it."

He may have been ready to give condolences. Who cared? Paula turned from the death scene and went to her car. She had failed her friend. She was supposed to offer Sonia consolation. How far was that from condolence?

When she opened the door to Luna's and stepped inside, she did not want sappy hellos. She did not want questions. She did not want anything but release from the despair of the moment.

Alex and Jocelyn were both there; she could make out the form of their bodies. Had Cole called them? All three were looking at her.

"I'm going to my room. Please give me space."

The words hovered behind her, leaving the three gaping. Jocelyn started to follow, but Cole held her back. "Not now."

From the journal of Paula Ross
(written during her seclusion)

I just hung up from my latest check-in with Deb. The control is coming, such a far cry from when I called several days ago.

She wanted me to come in, but—once she established I wouldn't follow Sonia—she understood I couldn't face their eyes downstairs ladened with concern, the assault of questions that would be sure to follow.

Solitude. Comfort. Which do I need more? The need changes at any given moment.

Deb and I made a deal. I would take my meds, eat and sleep to care for my body, check in with her and do the assignments she gave me until I could venture downstairs.

I'm grounding myself, but still the gaps in time terrify me. Deb promises that one of the parts checks in, sometimes for comfort, other times to vent the rage, the fear, the shame that swirl in my head. Only the throbbing in my head lets me know of the dissociation that rules my life right now.

Thank God someone—I'm betting it's Cole—leaves food, wonderful comfort food outside my door. I could no more cook right now than fly. And yet, I promised to eat.

"It was her choice, Paula, not yours." Deb's words. I say them like a mantra. I did not earn this guilt—nothing but old behavior patterns of toxic shame shoved onto me from abusers fleeing their own responsibilities.

Funny how those old patterns are so hard to break.

But break them, I shall.

"Fine. She said she needed space. It's been days." Jocelyn was pacing back and forth in front of the bar, off duty but nowhere near allowing herself to be far away. "I read the note on her door, too. She's lost a friend. She needs us."

"Look," Cole said. "She's eating, even left a thank you for the food we leave her. She needs her space. She has work to do, and we need to respect that. I've checked in on her both days, knocked on the door several times and asked, 'Ready yet?' She answers, 'Not yet.' That and the empty dishes are good enough for me."

"Well, it's not good enough for me." Jocelyn stopped her pacing, faced Cole. "This is so freaking scary." She stood there, rocking back from toes to heels, head down, fists clenching and unclenching.

She blew out a snort, looked up, defiant. "Okay, you guys are so all about therapy, how therapy has led my aunt to such health. Why, I need to get therapy just like Paula did. Only a professional can do the job." She put her hands on her hips and spit out the words. "If therapy is so all-fire great, how come my aunt's up in her room, and we're down here?"

A quiet voice slipped over Jocelyn's back, a familiar one, a much-loved one.

"Because I can come down."

Jocelyn turned around and hugged her aunt, started shaking whether from fear or relief or both, she wasn't sure. Nor did she care. Her aunt was back.

CHAPTER 54

The four of them stood at the grave site. Evelyn Quint. The great common denominator.

As they formed their semi-circle around the winter-filled dead place—orphaned Christmas decorations faded and flapping in the wind on other graves near them, Jocelyn thought of the past days while Paula had worked out her grief and guilt. Jocelyn, Alex, and Cole had been there, listening and soothing—mostly listening.

Such a sense of weightiness had pulled on Jocelyn as she took up the rite of caring for her aunt during those days. But Paula had healed. Jocelyn thought back to what Paula had said, about going through that tunnel of healing, how every now and then she would need a tune-up, but enduring would become easier. But she must take the first step. And she must do it alone.

And here Jocelyn was, along with her family. She had Cole, her big Psyche Guy brother—he had gently guided her, pulling back as much as moving her forward. She had Alex, her safe place—he had held her while she keened, stuffing herself into a wet shudder uncontrolled and horrified, and he had stayed. What the two of them were now, she knew. What they might become was merely a promise. She had Paula—her aunt had followed the yellow brick road and found her own way back, wizard or no. Paula had recognized the problem—Jocelyn had sewn her hurt up tight but the hurt wanted out, pushed to see the light of day. Looking down at the brown grass of her mother's grave, she thought of Paula's wise adage, "If you don't take care of the baggage, it will take care of you."

What baggage had her mother had?

Who cared?

Soon, Cole and Paula would climb into one car to return to Luna's and wait. She and Alex would climb into another and head off to Dr. Eggers' office. Alex would stay in the car while Jocelyn made her first steps in therapy. She pictured herself in a chair. She'd face away, look at the wall. So much shame. No sense in even saying, "It's not your fault." Shame is shame.

But she'd talk. A stitch in that knot of hurt would pop. Then another. Eventually the seam that bound what she needed to face would open up, the contents of her agony edge itself out into recognition, and she could begin the process of dealing. It was enough, for now.

Ever the mother hen, Paula had already given Jocelyn a brown sack— Oreos and a bottle of soda. "You'll be exhausted when you're done and need a snack." She teased, "Alex can have one cookie, but only one." The sack, precisely pleated at the top, waited in the car.

They joined hands. Paula began. "May Jocelyn dwell in the house of healing. May Jocelyn heal herself." They held tight as they all repeated the phrase together, a litany of prayer. As Jocelyn sank into the breath and the words, she let the mindfulness of the moment take hold; the muscle memory of her mother so often drunk in their kitchen began to move, not the memory so much as the feelings associated with the memory. They moved from her gut, from her shoulders, moved with the exhale of her breath.

So that's how salvation feels.

When they were finished and had released their hands, Jocelyn bent over and picked up a tall jar filled with the scraps of the letter she had written to Evie. Even shredded, the words held a bitter power. She pulled a long candle lighter from her pocket and reached in to light the paper. The flames jumped inside the jar and ate at the paper. Jocelyn watched the scraps shrink as the fire consumed her words. She turned the jar onto its side and let the black-edged scraps, now mostly ash, fly out. The four watched as the wind caught them, spun them in a vortex above the center of Evie's grave, and took them skyward and out of their sight. They watched them soar and rejoiced in the moment.

The ritual completed, Jocelyn gave each of the three family members a hug, and in two's they left, Paula and Cole to wait, she and Alex to drive to her appointment. In the car, Alex gave Jocelyn a friendly poke in the shoulder. She, in turn, slapped him lightly along side the head. Then Alex turned on the ignition, put the car into drive, and off they went, into Jocelyn's future.

ABOUT THE AUTHOR

Barbara Harken was raised in Chicago and moved to Iowa at the age of sixteen. She teaches writing at Wartburg College in Waverly, Iowa and, in her spare time, dabbles in art. Barbara and her husband, Bob, have two adult sons, two grandchildren, and two patient daughters-in-law. This is her third novel.

OTHER NOVELS BY BARBARA HARKEN

The 86th Degree

"A Story of Abuse, Rejection, and Healing.

"Harken introduces the reader to the foundational issues of child abuse, verbal and physical, and the paradigm shift in philosophical, psychological, and legal implications being faced in our society today. Conflict, resolution, and more conflict keep the reader glued to the pages of this important novel which creates a social awareness and critique of the problems of abusive relationships and the importance of the availability of emotional caregivers." ~ Richard Blake

Degree of Guilt

A mystery novel about a woman defending her grandfather's name who must brave insults, pranks, and assaults on her life to find the truth and ensure justice—with the help of a ghost whit his own agenda.

"I loved it! Mystery, romance, honest sentiment all with a touch of Stephen King." ~ Leta Magee

"Couldn't put it down." ~ Janice Olejnik

"Unraveling a Mystery in the Northwoods." ~ Richard Hansen

"A guilty pleasure." ~ Janet Withers